55

"**Rumiko Takahashi** doesn't miss a single farcical opportunity as every volume is crammed with raging hormones, romantic entanglements, gender-swapping, and martial-art silliness. Boy changes to girl, man to panda, girl to cat -- and everybody's kung fu fighting."

Anodyne Magazine

"If you've never watched any of the videos, or read the comic books they are based on, you're missing out on some of the funniest, wackiest, and most character-driven cartoons around."

Tony Isabella, comics critic

"**Ranma 1/2** is a must for anyone who likes a wicked sense of humor."

Gamers' Republic

OTHER TITLES BY RUMIKO TAKAHASHI

RANMA 1/2
MAISON IKKOKU
LUM*URUSEI YATSURA
INU-YASHA
RUMIC WORLD TRILOGY
RUMIC THEATER
ONE-POUND GOSPEL
MERMAID SAGA

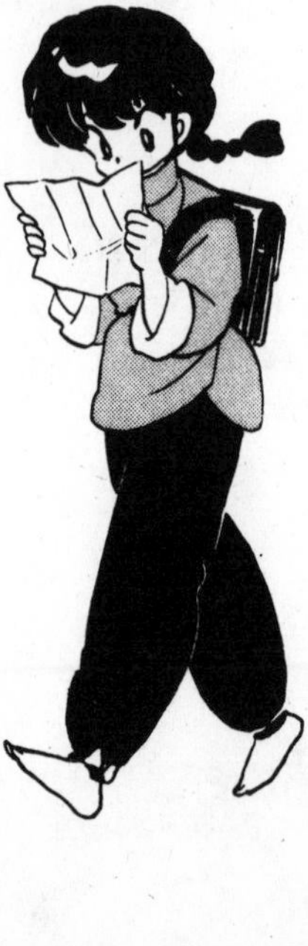

VIZ GRAPHIC NOVEL
RANMA 1/2™

14

This volume contains
RANMA 1/2 PART SEVEN #9 (second half) through
#14 in their entirety.

Story & Art by Rumiko Takahashi

English Adaptation by Gerard Jones & Toshifumi Yoshida

*

Touch-Up Art & Lettering/Wayne Truman
Cover Design/Hidemi Sahara
Graphics & Layout/Yuki Shimotoku
Assistant Editor/Bill Flanagan
Editor/Trish Ledoux

*

Senior Marketing Manager/Dallas Middaugh
Senior Sales Manager/Ann Ivan
Editor-in-Chief/Hyoe Narita
Publisher/Seiji Horibuchi

*

First published by Shogakukan, Inc. in Japan

*

Printed in Canada

*

Published by Viz Communications, Inc.
P.O. Box 77010
San Francisco, CA 94107

*

10 9 8 7 6 5 4 3
First Printing, September 1999
Third Printing, October 2000

VIZ GRAPHIC NOVEL

RANMA 1/2 ™

STORY & ART BY
RUMIKO TAKAHASHI

CONTENTS

PART 1

TARGET: PIGTAIL

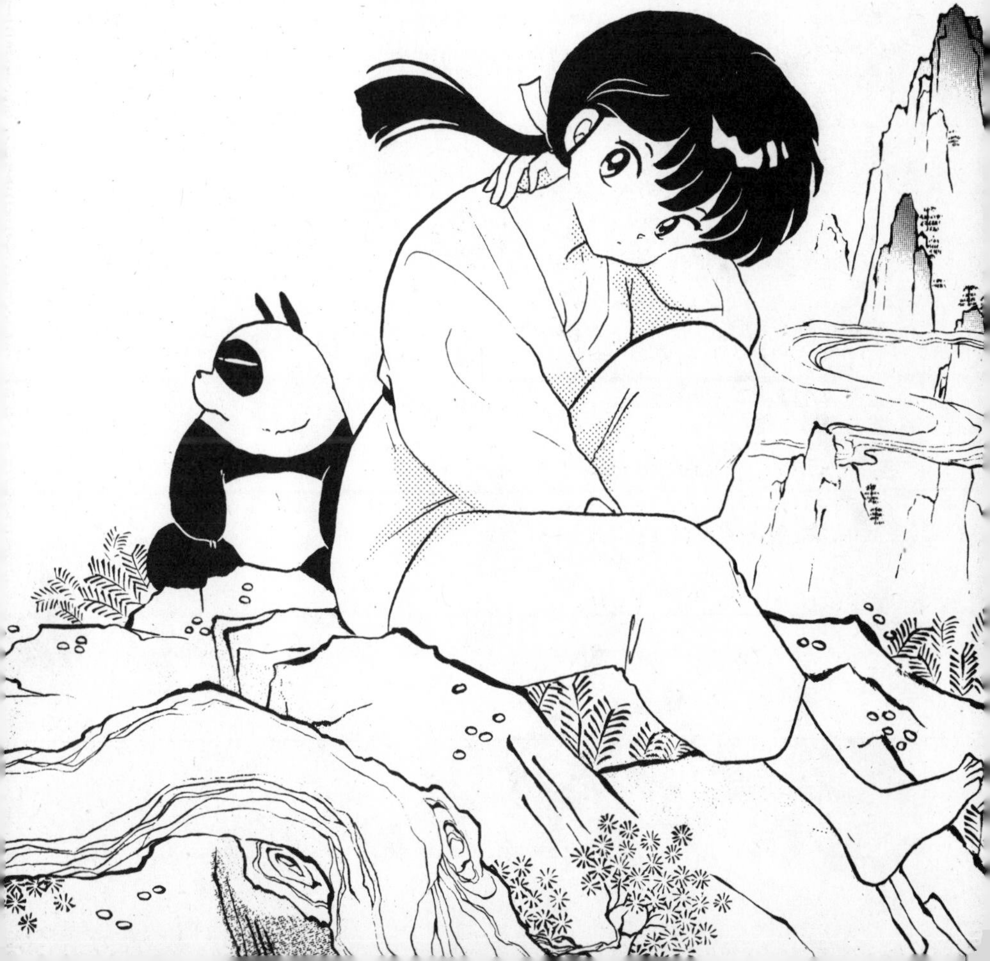

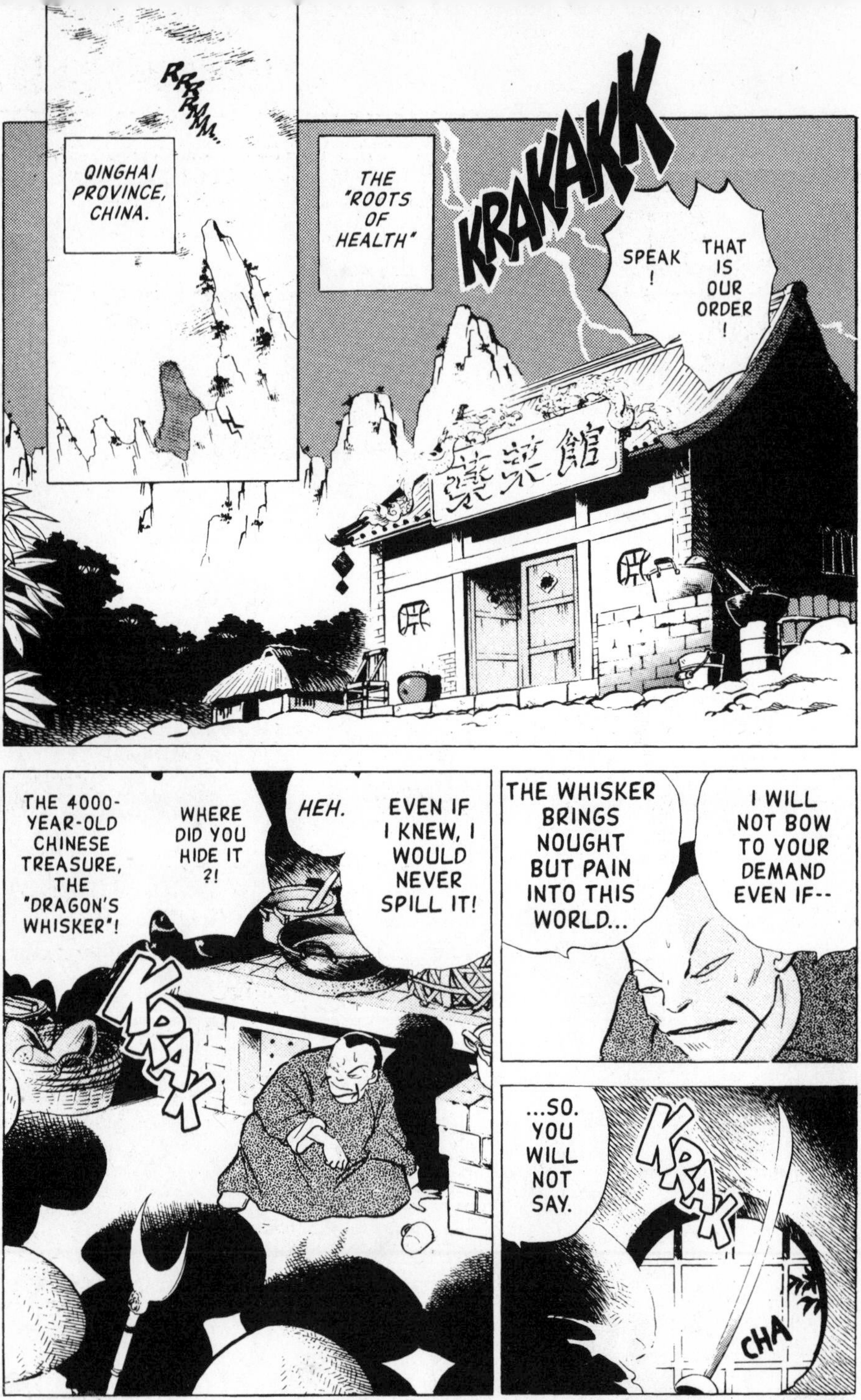
RRRRMMM...
QINGHAI PROVINCE, CHINA.
THE "ROOTS OF HEALTH"
KRAKAKK
SPEAK!
THAT IS OUR ORDER!
THE 4000-YEAR-OLD CHINESE TREASURE, THE "DRAGON'S WHISKER"!
WHERE DID YOU HIDE IT?!
HEH.
EVEN IF I KNEW, I WOULD NEVER SPILL IT!
KRAK
THE WHISKER BRINGS NOUGHT BUT PAIN INTO THIS WORLD...
I WILL NOT BOW TO YOUR DEMAND EVEN IF--
...SO. YOU WILL NOT SAY.
KRAK
CHA

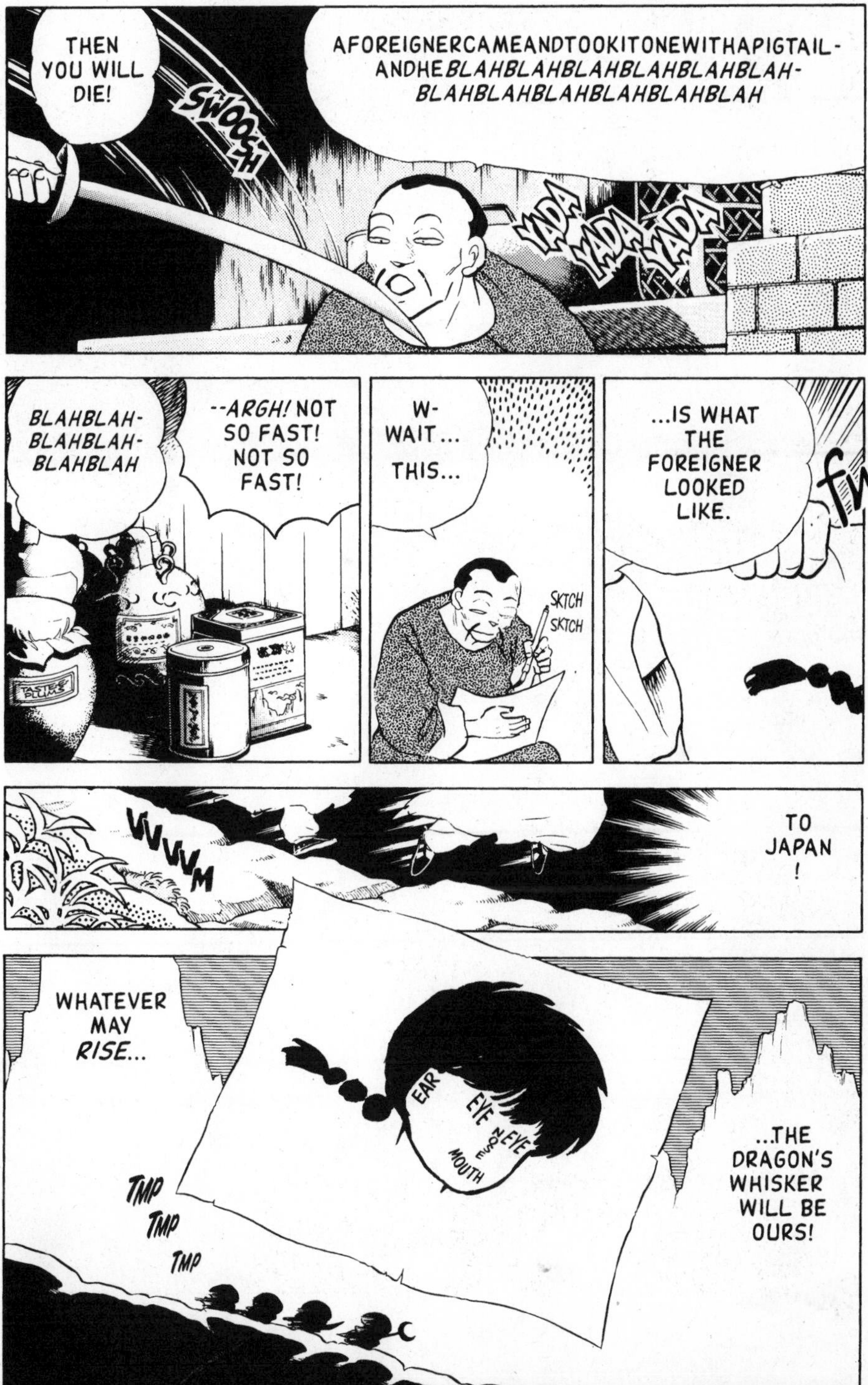
THEN YOU WILL DIE!
SWOOSH
AFOREIGNERCAMEANDTOOKITONEWITHAPIGTAIL-ANDHEBLAHBLAHBLAHBLAHBLAHBLAH-BLAHBLAHBLAHBLAHBLAHBLAH
YADA YADA YADA
BLAHBLAH-BLAHBLAH-BLAHBLAH
--ARGH! NOT SO FAST! NOT SO FAST!
W-WAIT... THIS...
SKTCH SKTCH
...IS WHAT THE FOREIGNER LOOKED LIKE.
fwa
VVVVVM
TO JAPAN!
WHATEVER MAY RISE...
EAR
EYE
NOSE
EYE
MOUTH
TMP TMP TMP
...THE DRAGON'S WHISKER WILL BE OURS!

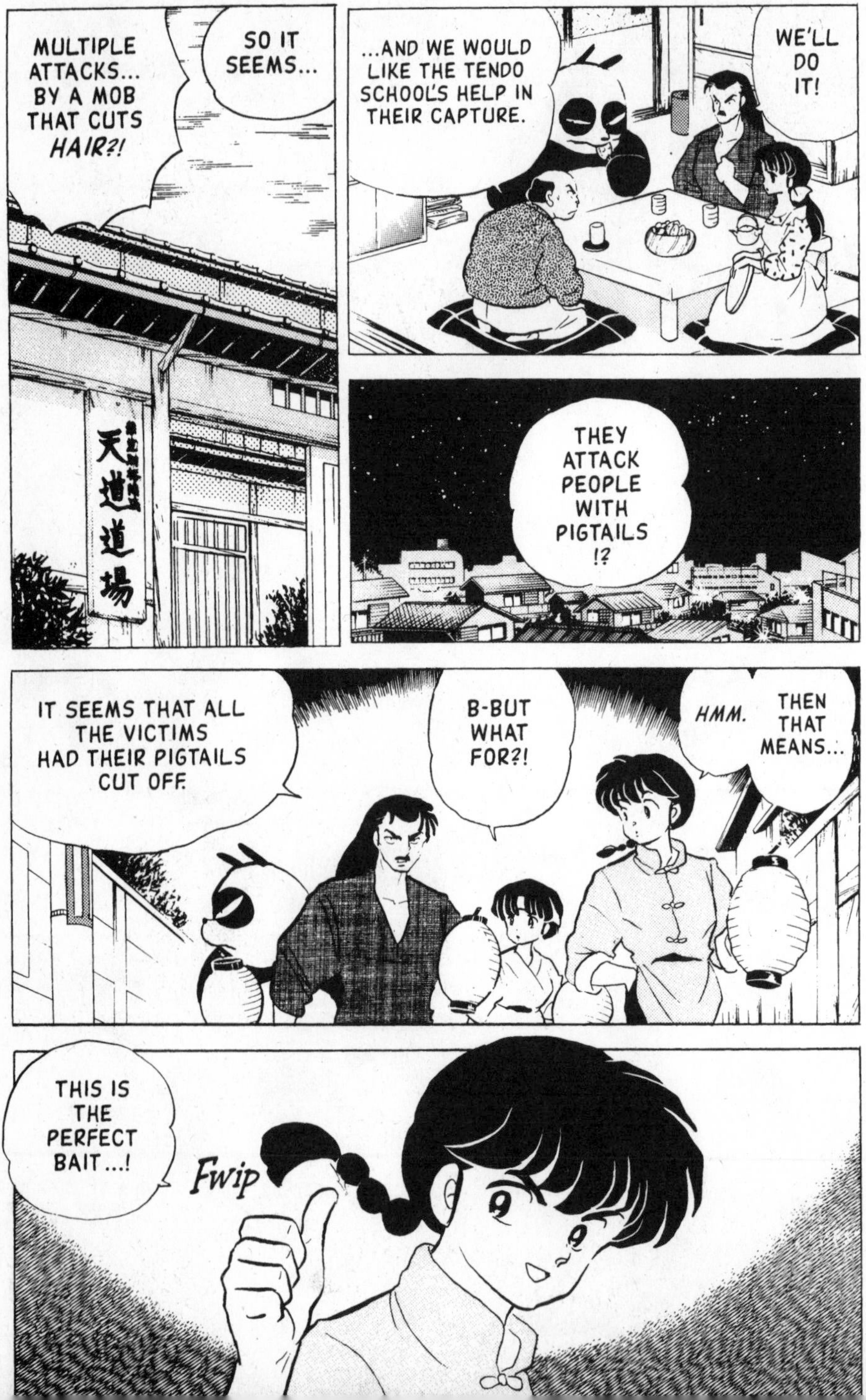
MULTIPLE ATTACKS... BY A MOB THAT CUTS *HAIR?!*
SO IT SEEMS...
天道道場
...AND WE WOULD LIKE THE TENDO SCHOOL'S HELP IN THEIR CAPTURE.
WE'LL DO IT!
THEY ATTACK PEOPLE WITH PIGTAILS !?
IT SEEMS THAT ALL THE VICTIMS HAD THEIR PIGTAILS CUT OFF.
B-BUT WHAT FOR?!
HMM.
THEN THAT MEANS...
THIS IS THE PERFECT BAIT...!
Fwip

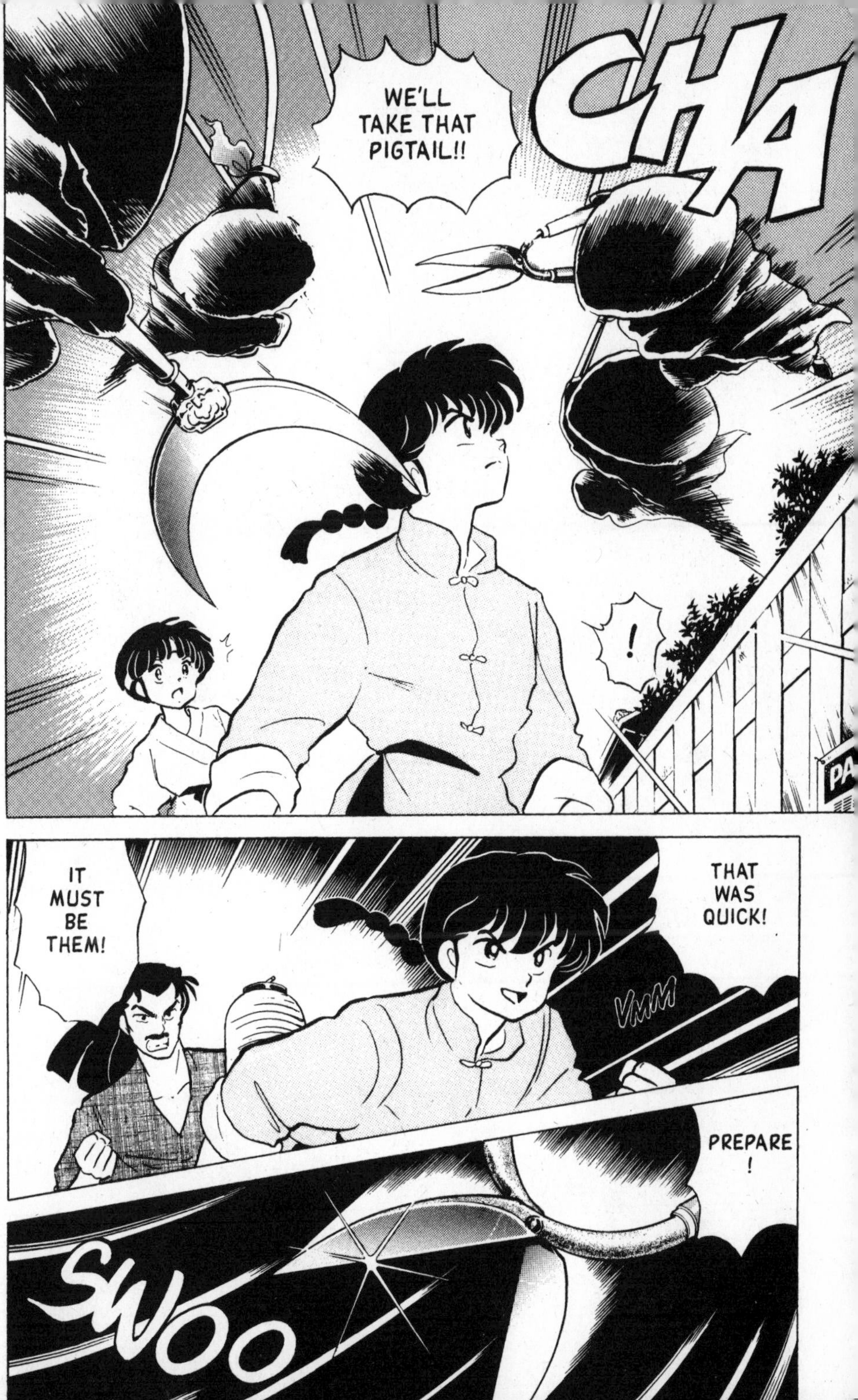
WE'LL TAKE THAT PIGTAIL!!
CHA
!
PA
IT MUST BE THEM!
THAT WAS QUICK!
VMM
PREPARE !
SWOO

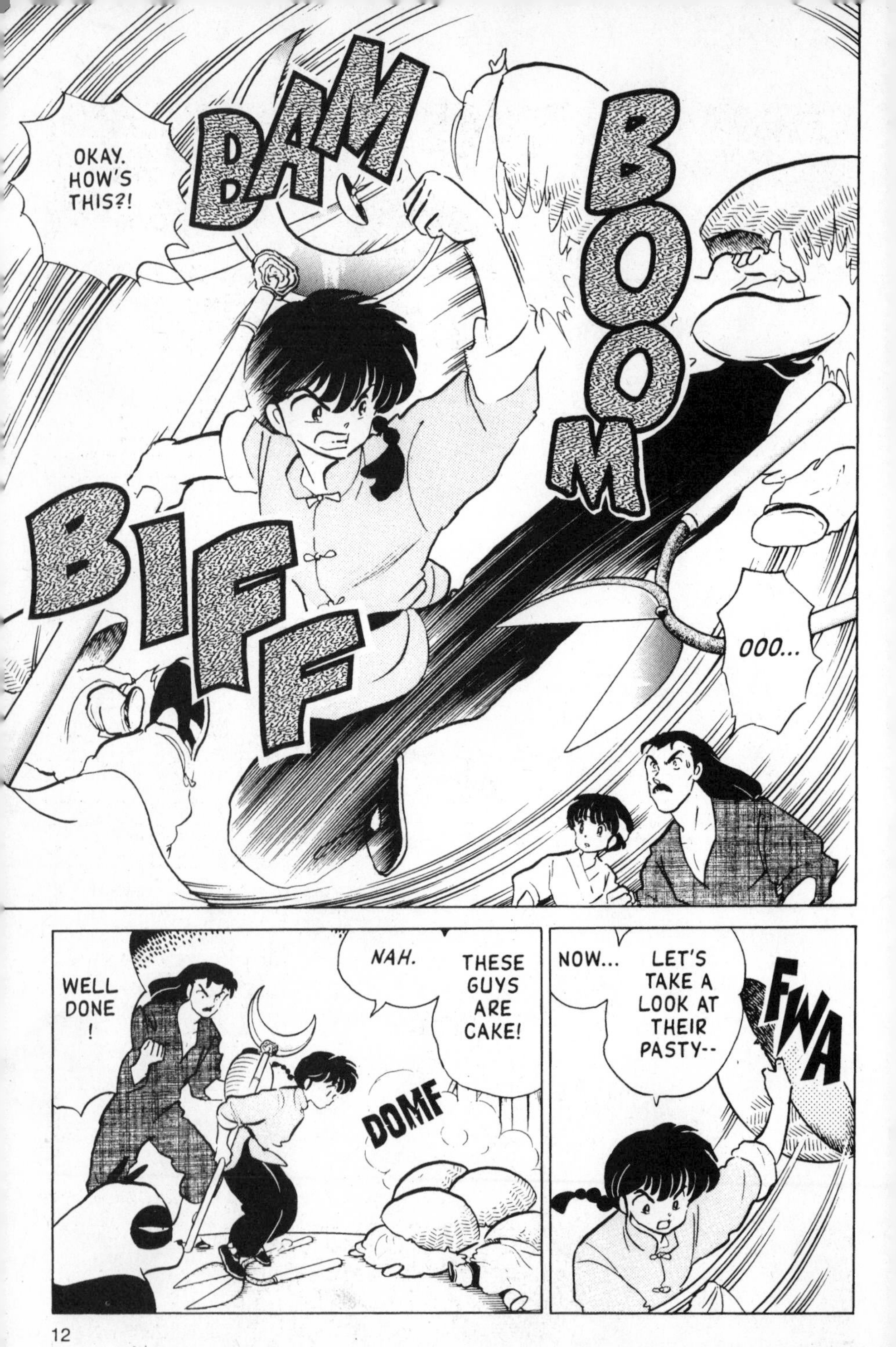
OKAY. HOW'S THIS?!
BAM
BOOM
BIFF
OOO...
WELL DONE !
NAH.
THESE GUYS ARE CAKE!
DOMF
NOW...
LET'S TAKE A LOOK AT THEIR PASTY--
FWA

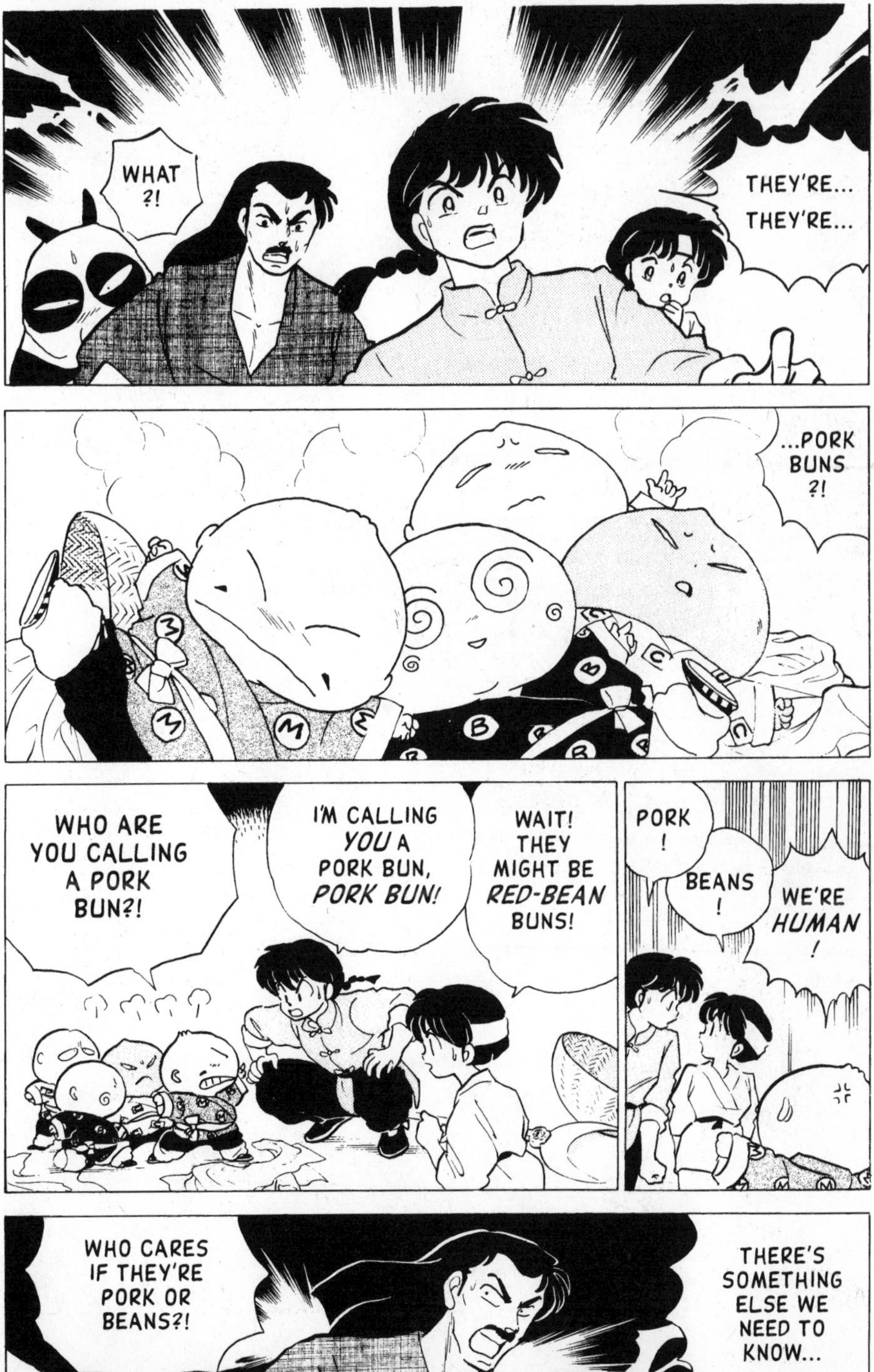
WHAT ?!
THEY'RE... THEY'RE...
...PORK BUNS ?!
WHO ARE YOU CALLING A PORK BUN?!
I'M CALLING *YOU* A PORK BUN, *PORK BUN!*
WAIT! THEY MIGHT BE *RED-BEAN* BUNS!
PORK !
BEANS !
WE'RE *HUMAN* !
WHO CARES IF THEY'RE PORK OR BEANS?!
THERE'S SOMETHING ELSE WE NEED TO KNOW...

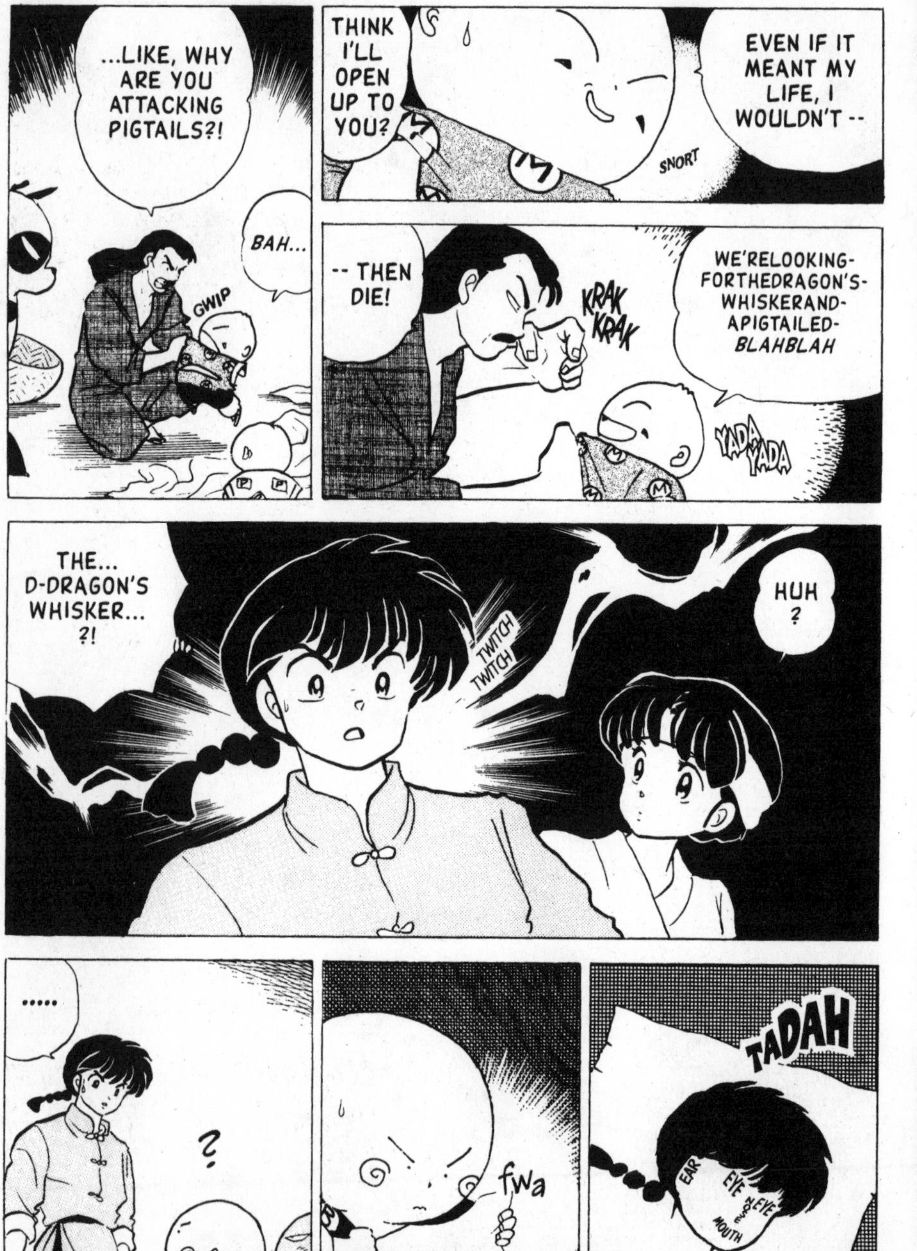
...LIKE, WHY ARE YOU ATTACKING PIGTAILS?!
BAH...
GWIP
THINK I'LL OPEN UP TO YOU?
EVEN IF IT MEANT MY LIFE, I WOULDN'T --
SNORT
-- THEN DIE!
KRAK KRAK
WE'RELOOKING-FORTHEDRAGON'S-WHISKERAND-APIGTAILED-*BLAHBLAH*
YADA YADA
THE... D-DRAGON'S WHISKER... ?!
TWITCH TWITCH
HUH ?
......
?
fwa
TADAH
EAR
EYE
NOSE
EYE
MOUTH

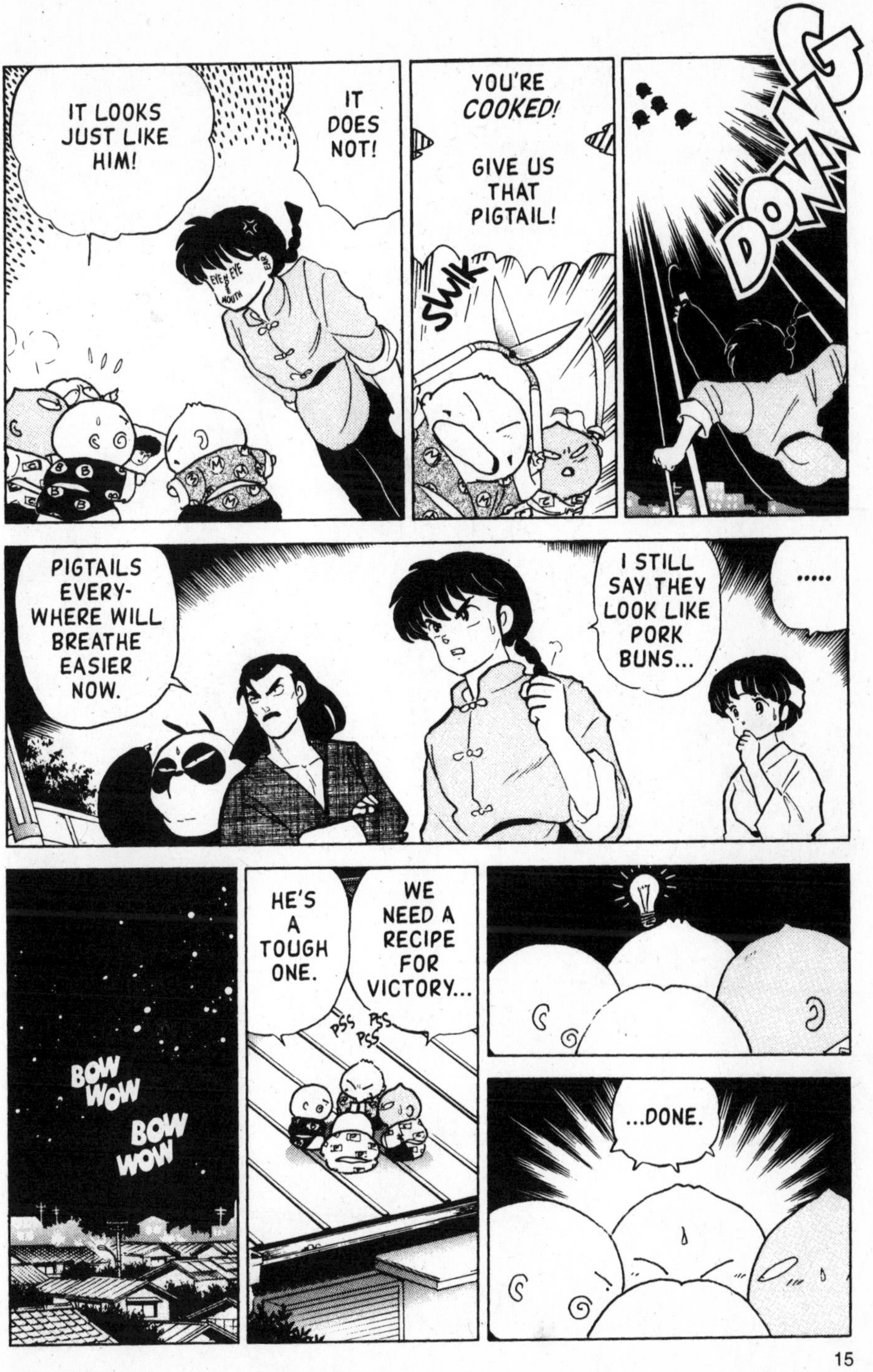
IT LOOKS JUST LIKE HIM!
IT DOES NOT!
EYE
EYE
MOUTH
EAR
YOU'RE COOKED!
GIVE US THAT PIGTAIL!
SWIK
DOWNG
PIGTAILS EVERY-WHERE WILL BREATHE EASIER NOW.
I STILL SAY THEY LOOK LIKE PORK BUNS...
.....
BOW WOW
BOW WOW
HE'S A TOUGH ONE.
WE NEED A RECIPE FOR VICTORY...
PSS PSS PSS
...DONE.

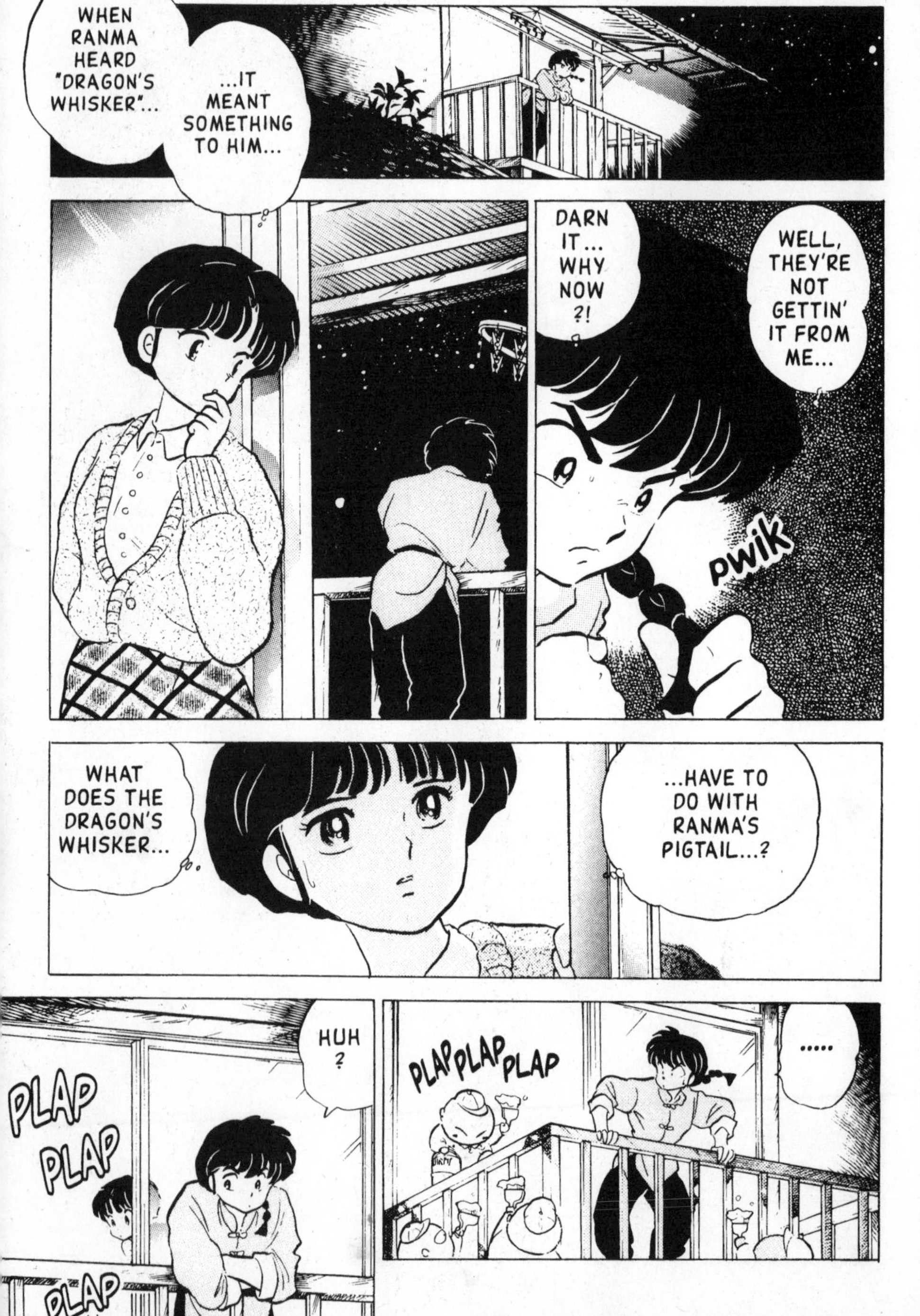
WHEN RANMA HEARD "DRAGON'S WHISKER"...
...IT MEANT SOMETHING TO HIM...
DARN IT... WHY NOW ?!
WELL, THEY'RE NOT GETTIN' IT FROM ME...
PWIK
WHAT DOES THE DRAGON'S WHISKER...
...HAVE TO DO WITH RANMA'S PIGTAIL...?
PLAP
PLAP
PLAP
HUH ?
PLAP PLAP PLAP
.....

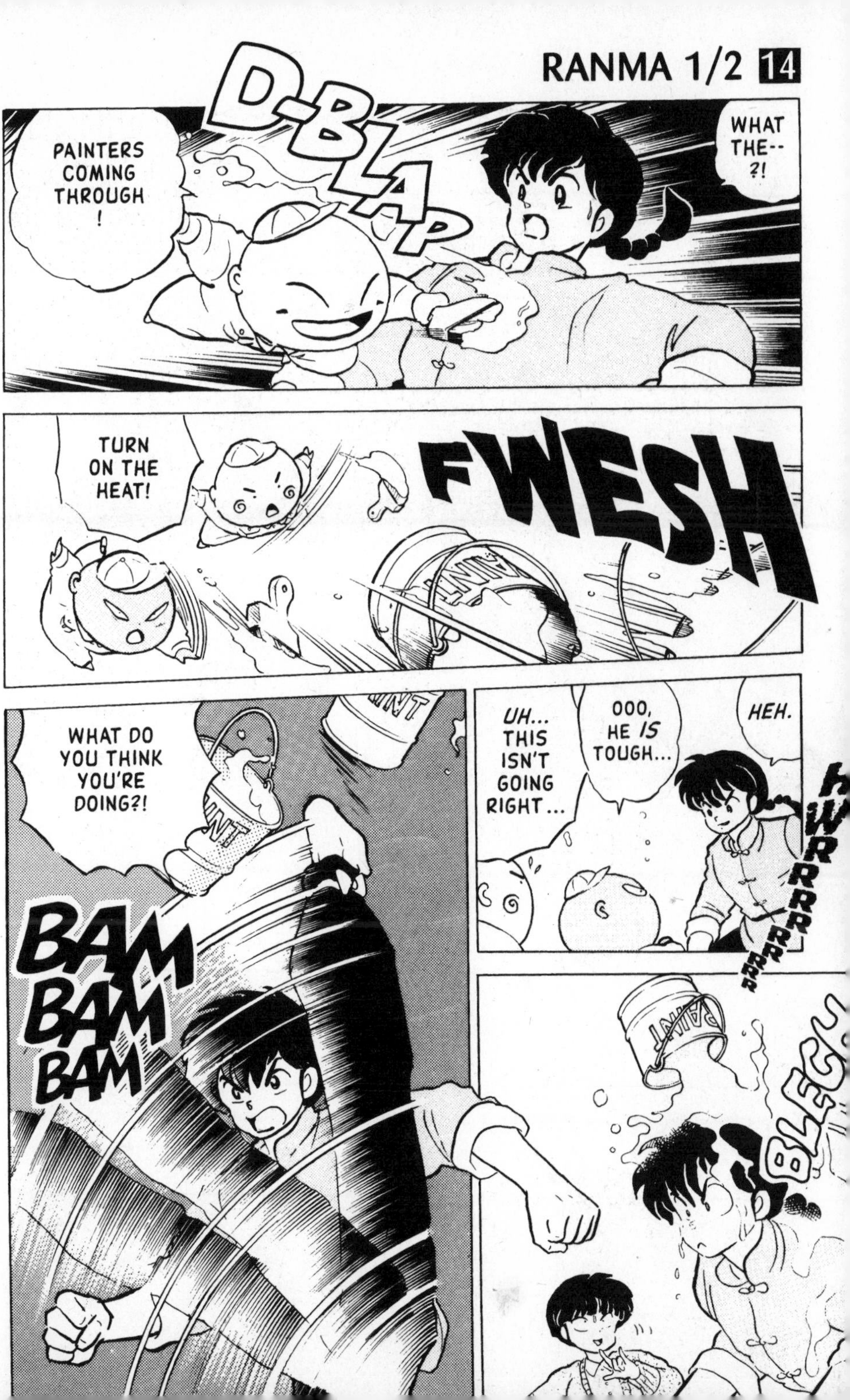
PAINTERS COMING THROUGH !
D-BLAP
WHAT THE-- ?!
TURN ON THE HEAT!
FWESH
PAINT
WHAT DO YOU THINK YOU'RE DOING?!
BAM BAM BAM
UH... THIS ISN'T GOING RIGHT...
OOO, HE *IS* TOUGH...
HEH.
HWRRRRRRR
PAINT
BLECCH

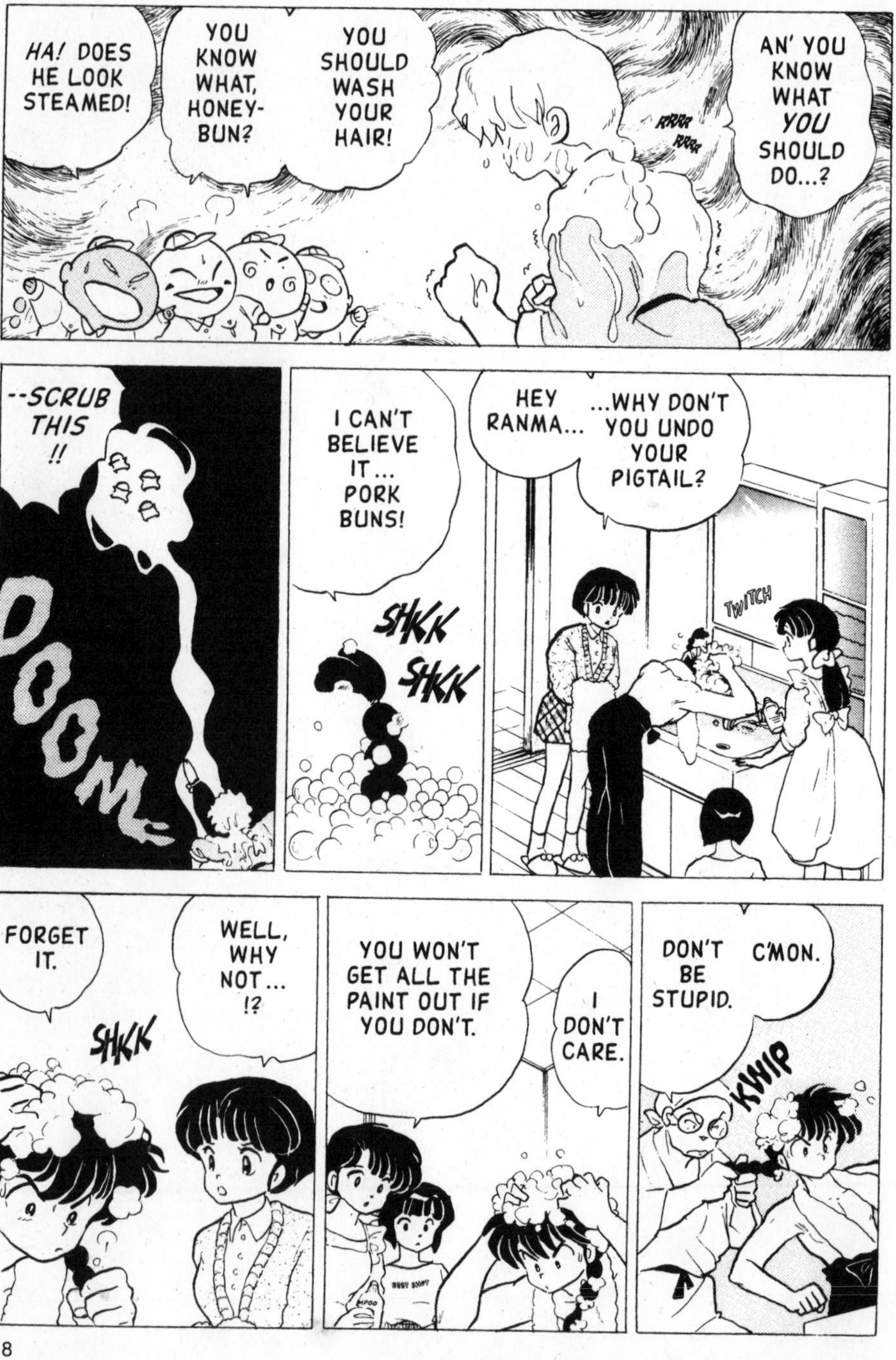
HA! DOES HE LOOK STEAMED!
YOU KNOW WHAT, HONEY-BUN?
YOU SHOULD WASH YOUR HAIR!
RRRR RRRR
AN' YOU KNOW WHAT *YOU* SHOULD DO...?
--SCRUB THIS!!
DOOM
I CAN'T BELIEVE IT... PORK BUNS!
SHKK
SHKK
HEY RANMA...
...WHY DON'T YOU UNDO YOUR PIGTAIL?
TWITCH
FORGET IT.
WELL, WHY NOT...!?
SHKK
YOU WON'T GET ALL THE PAINT OUT IF YOU DON'T.
I DON'T CARE.
DON'T BE STUPID.
C'MON.
KWIP

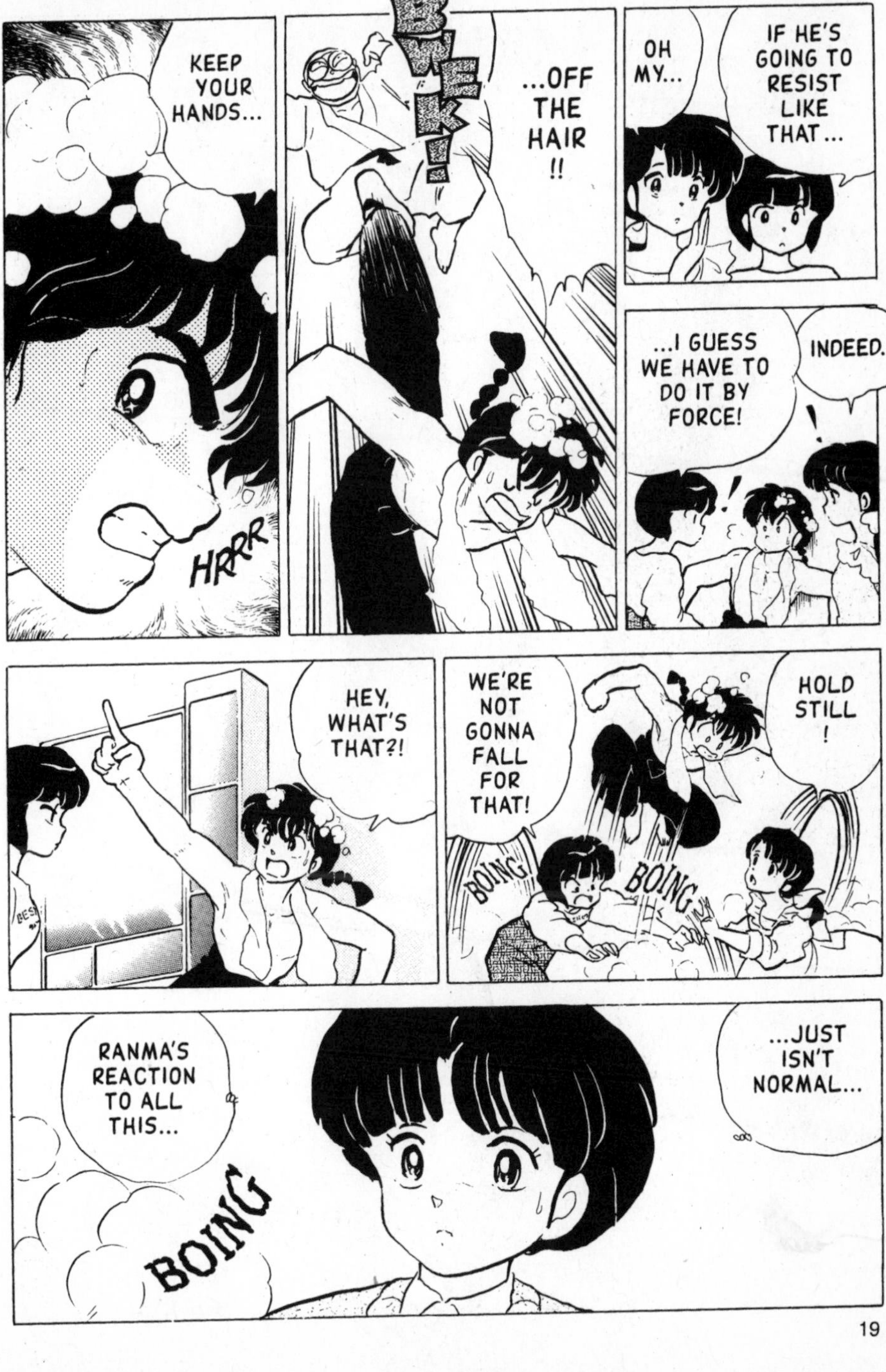
KEEP YOUR HANDS...
HRRR
BWEK!!
...OFF THE HAIR !!
OH MY...
IF HE'S GOING TO RESIST LIKE THAT...
...I GUESS WE HAVE TO DO IT BY FORCE!
INDEED...
HEY, WHAT'S THAT?!
WE'RE NOT GONNA FALL FOR THAT!
BOING
BOING
HOLD STILL !
RANMA'S REACTION TO ALL THIS...
BOING
BOING
...JUST ISN'T NORMAL...

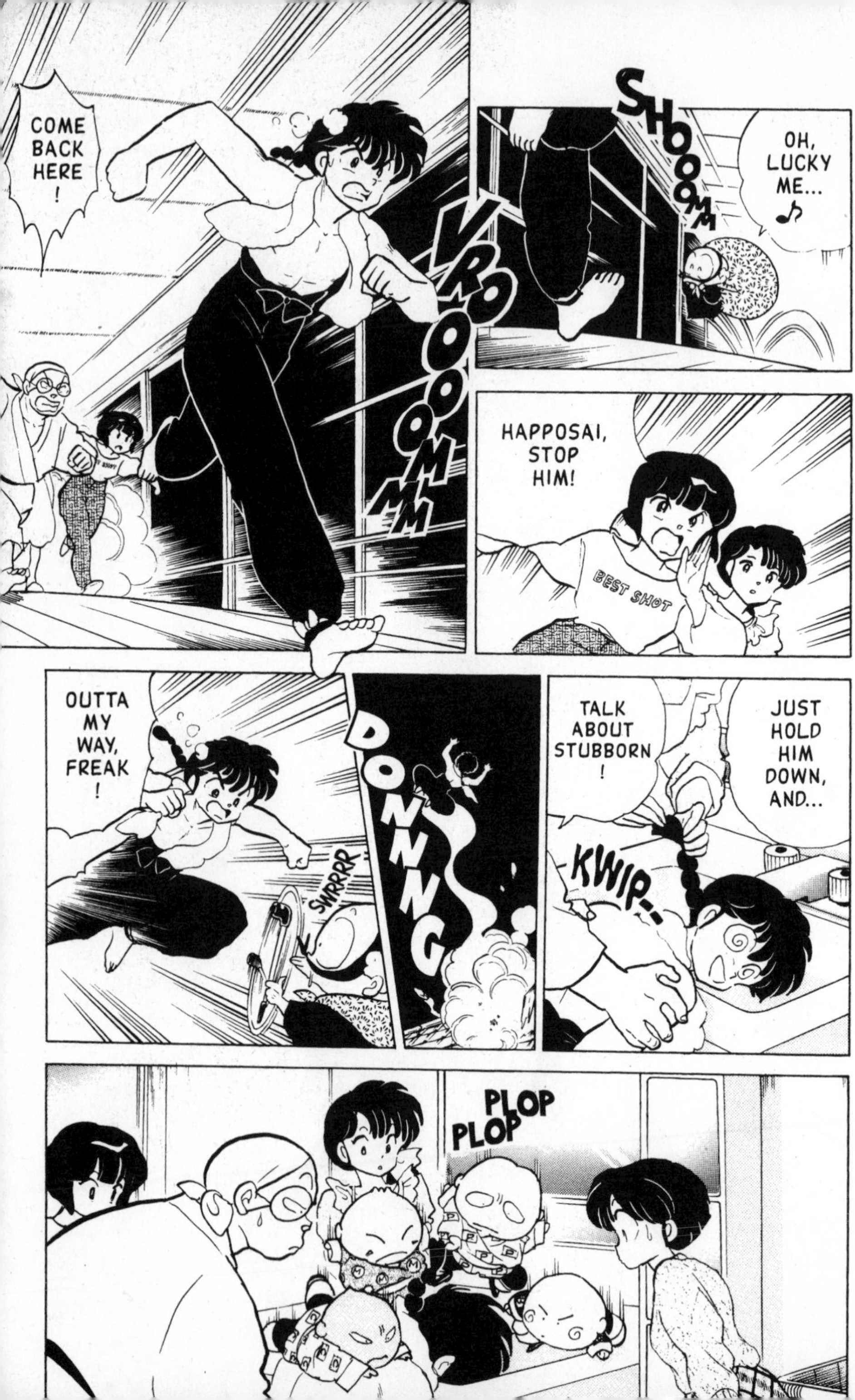
COME BACK HERE!
VROOOOOOMMMM
SHOOOMM
OH, LUCKY ME... ♪
HAPPOSAI, STOP HIM!
BEST SHOT
OUTTA MY WAY, FREAK!
SWRRRR
DONNNG
TALK ABOUT STUBBORN!
JUST HOLD HIM DOWN, AND...
KWIP..
PLOP PLOP

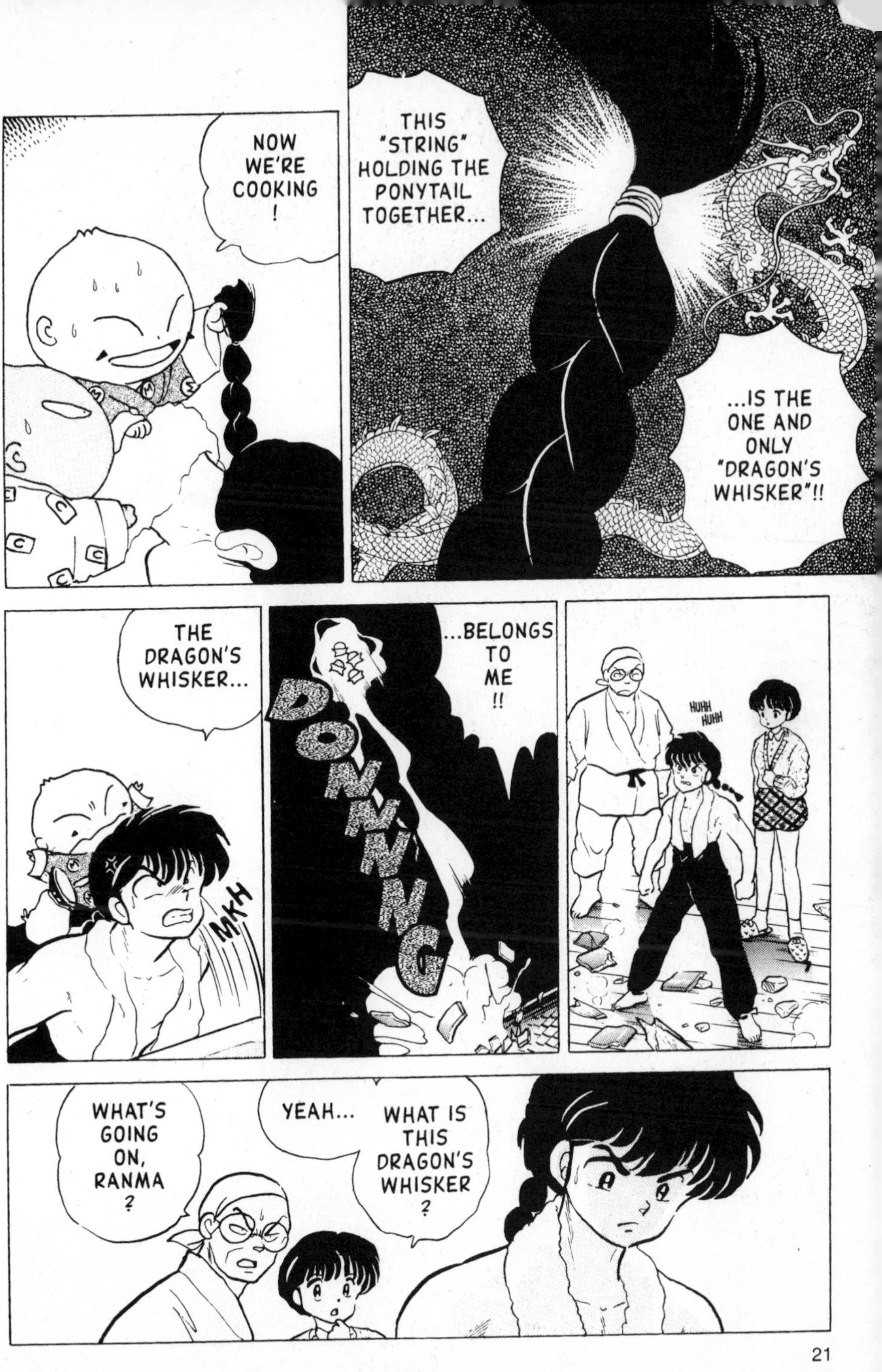
NOW WE'RE COOKING !
THIS "STRING" HOLDING THE PONYTAIL TOGETHER...
...IS THE ONE AND ONLY "DRAGON'S WHISKER"!!
THE DRAGON'S WHISKER...
MKH
...BELONGS TO ME !!
DONNNG
HUHH HUHH
WHAT'S GOING ON, RANMA ?
YEAH... WHAT IS THIS DRAGON'S WHISKER ?

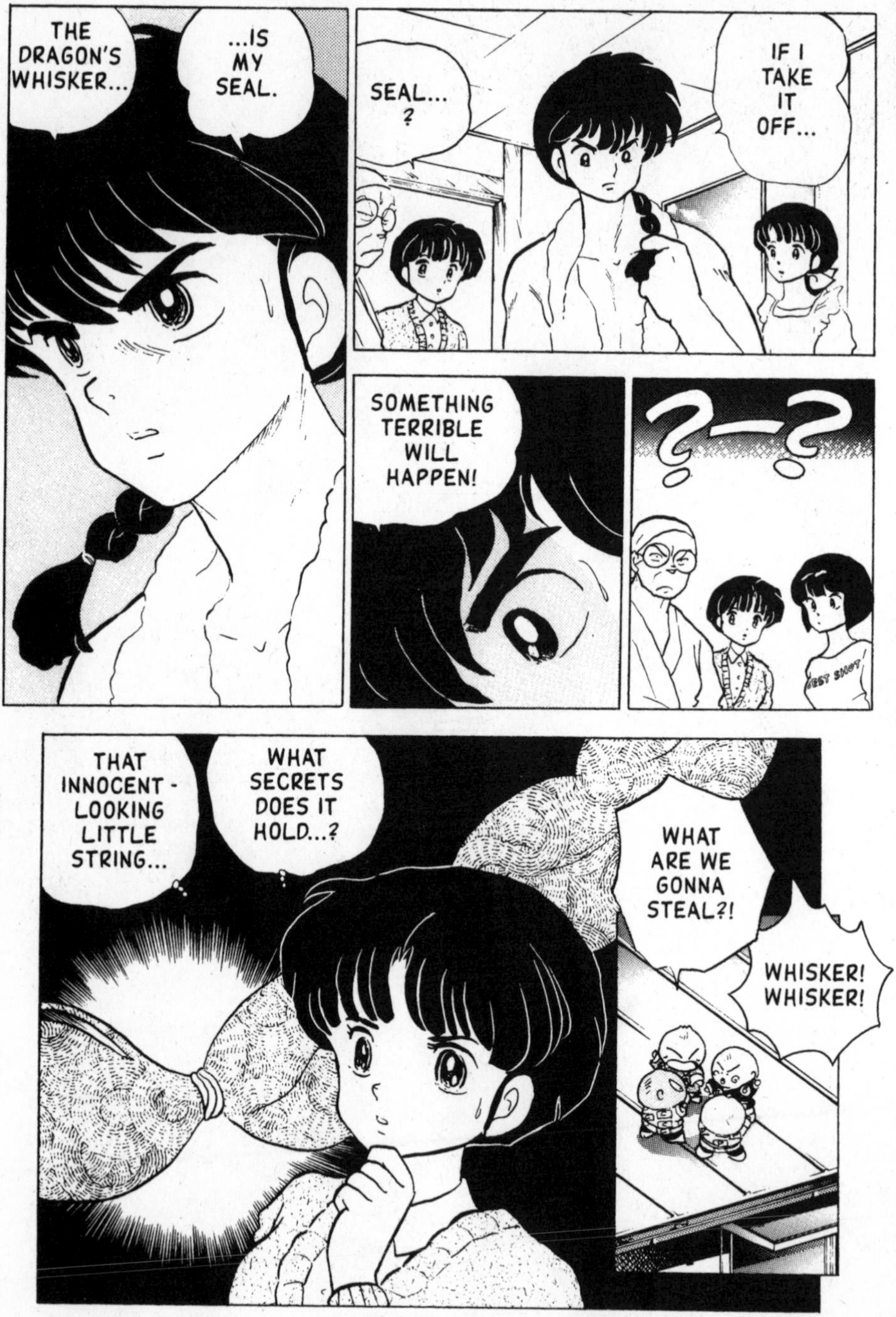
THE DRAGON'S WHISKER...
...IS MY SEAL.
SEAL... ?
IF I TAKE IT OFF...
SOMETHING TERRIBLE WILL HAPPEN!
?—?
THAT INNOCENT-LOOKING LITTLE STRING...
WHAT SECRETS DOES IT HOLD...?
WHAT ARE WE GONNA STEAL?!
WHISKER! WHISKER!

PART 2
LET YOUR HAIR DOWN

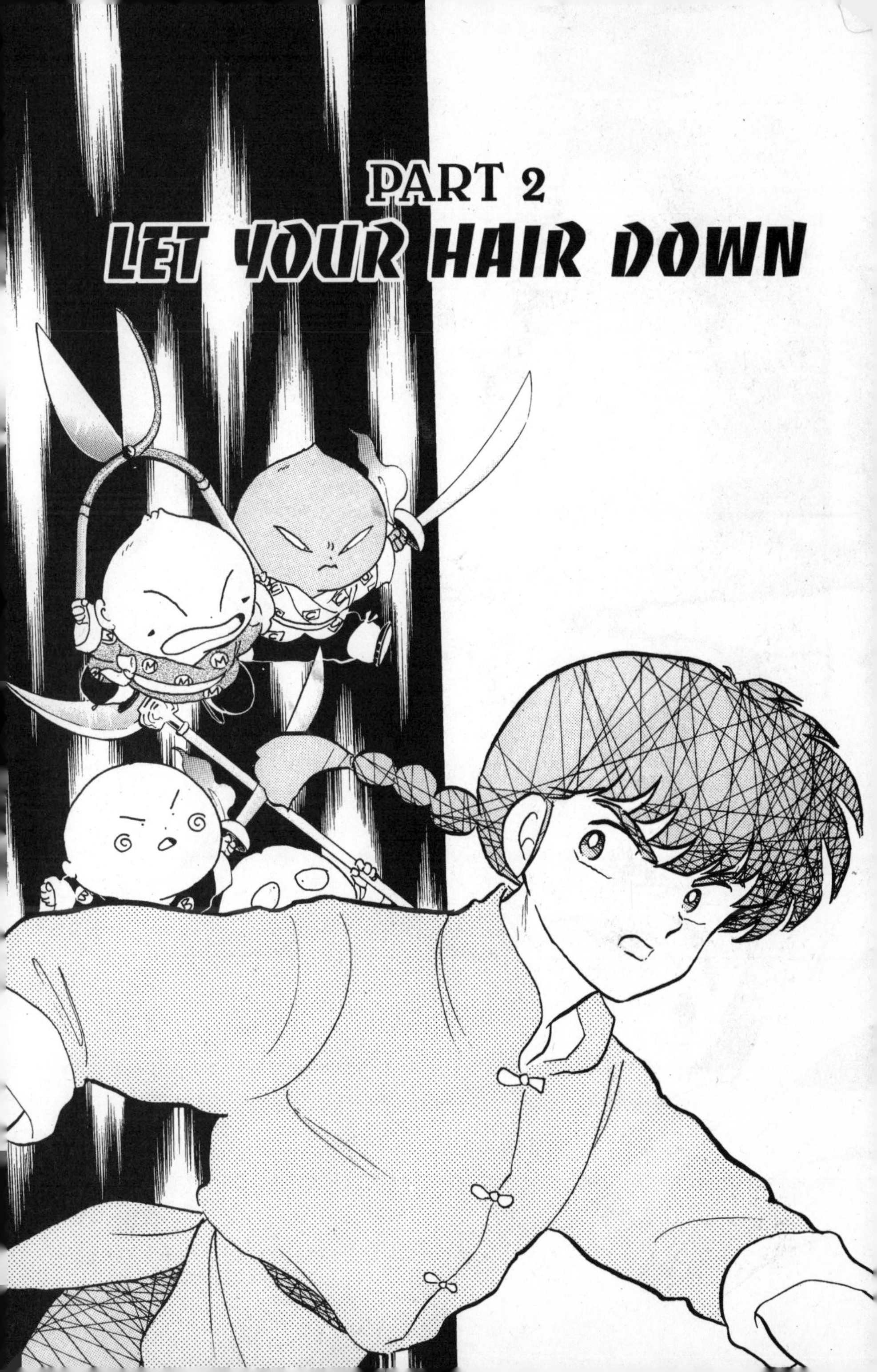

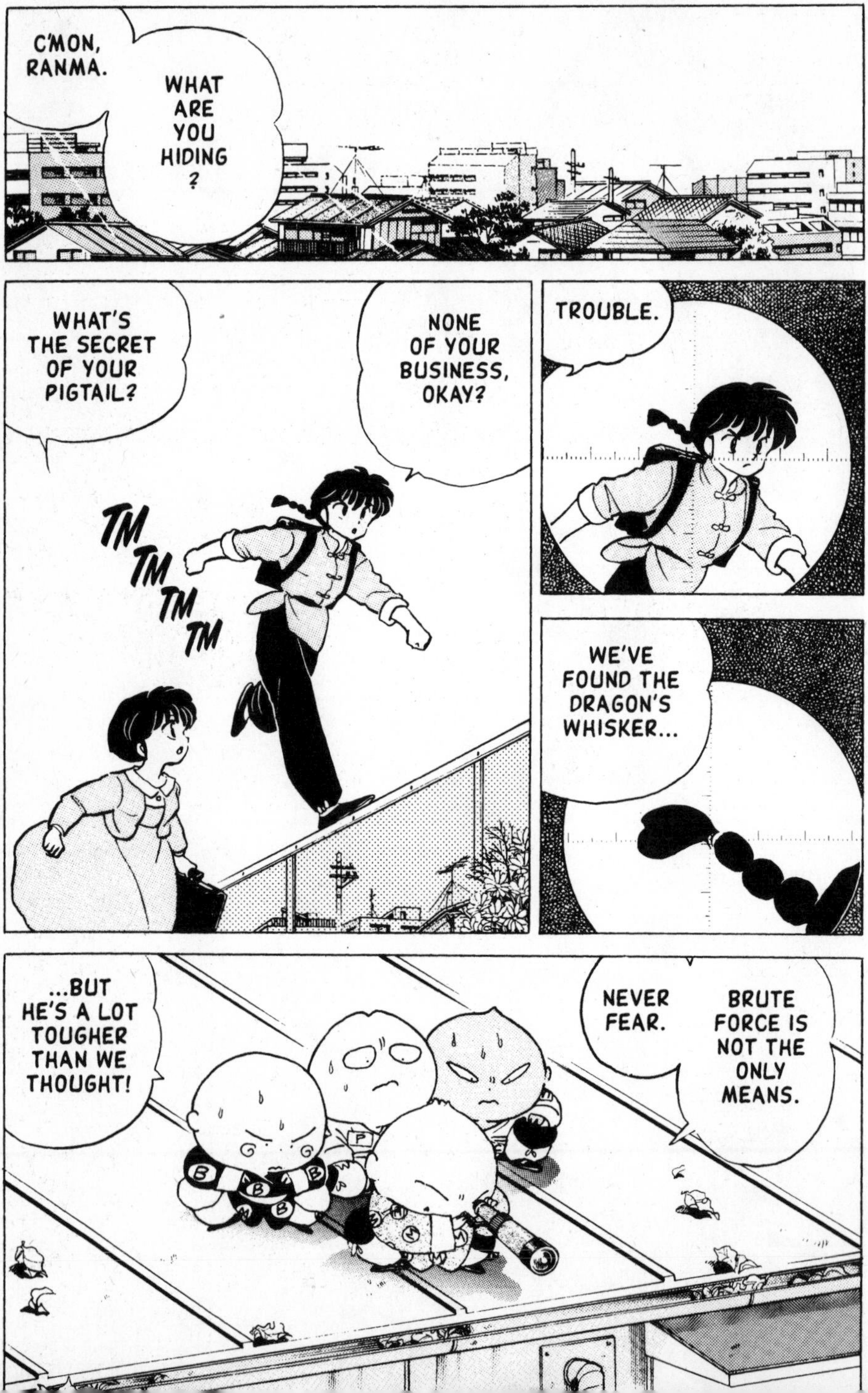
C'MON, RANMA.
WHAT ARE YOU HIDING ?
WHAT'S THE SECRET OF YOUR PIGTAIL?
NONE OF YOUR BUSINESS, OKAY?
TM TM TM TM
TROUBLE.
WE'VE FOUND THE DRAGON'S WHISKER...
...BUT HE'S A LOT TOUGHER THAN WE THOUGHT!
NEVER FEAR.
BRUTE FORCE IS NOT THE ONLY MEANS.

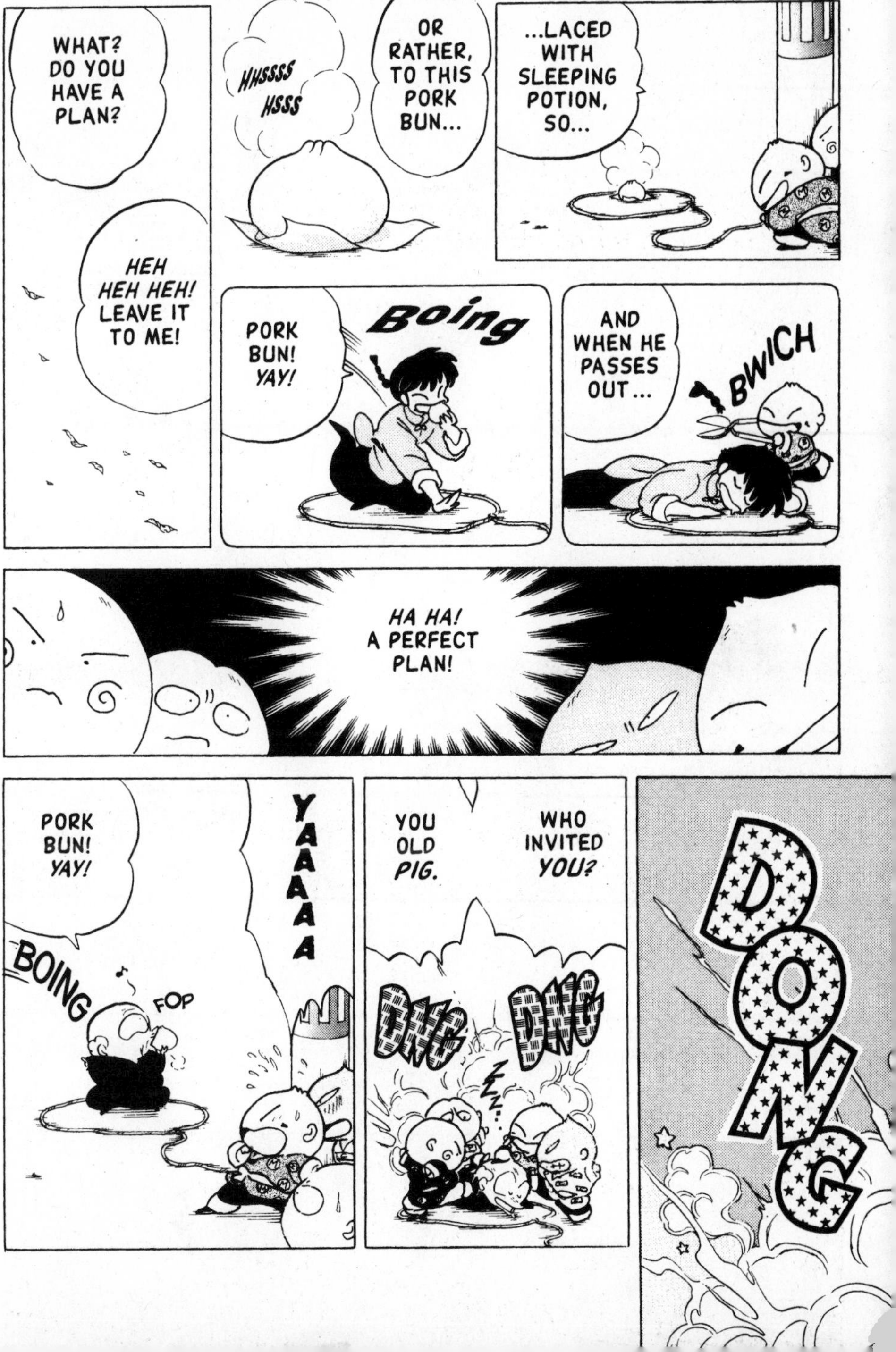
WHAT? DO YOU HAVE A PLAN?
HEH HEH HEH! LEAVE IT TO ME!
HHSSSS HSSS
OR RATHER, TO THIS PORK BUN...
...LACED WITH SLEEPING POTION, SO...
PORK BUN! YAY!
Boing
AND WHEN HE PASSES OUT...
BWICH
HA HA! A PERFECT PLAN!
PORK BUN! YAY!
BOING
FOP
YAAAAA
YOU OLD PIG.
WHO INVITED YOU?
DNG DNG
ZZZ...
DONG

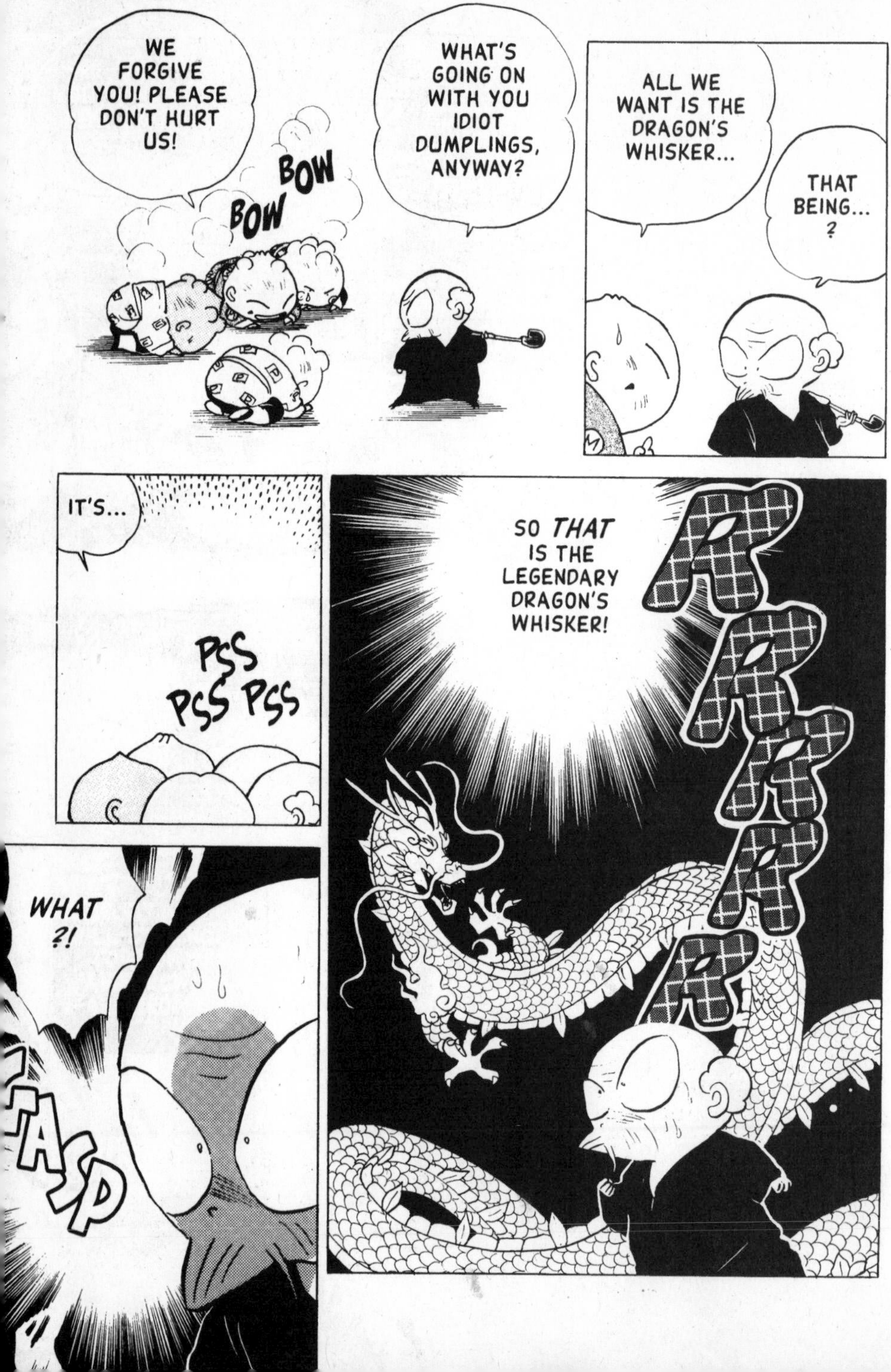
WE FORGIVE YOU! PLEASE DON'T HURT US!
BOW BOW
WHAT'S GOING ON WITH YOU IDIOT DUMPLINGS, ANYWAY?
ALL WE WANT IS THE DRAGON'S WHISKER...
THAT BEING... ?
IT'S...
PSS PSS PSS
WHAT ?!
SO *THAT* IS THE LEGENDARY DRAGON'S WHISKER!

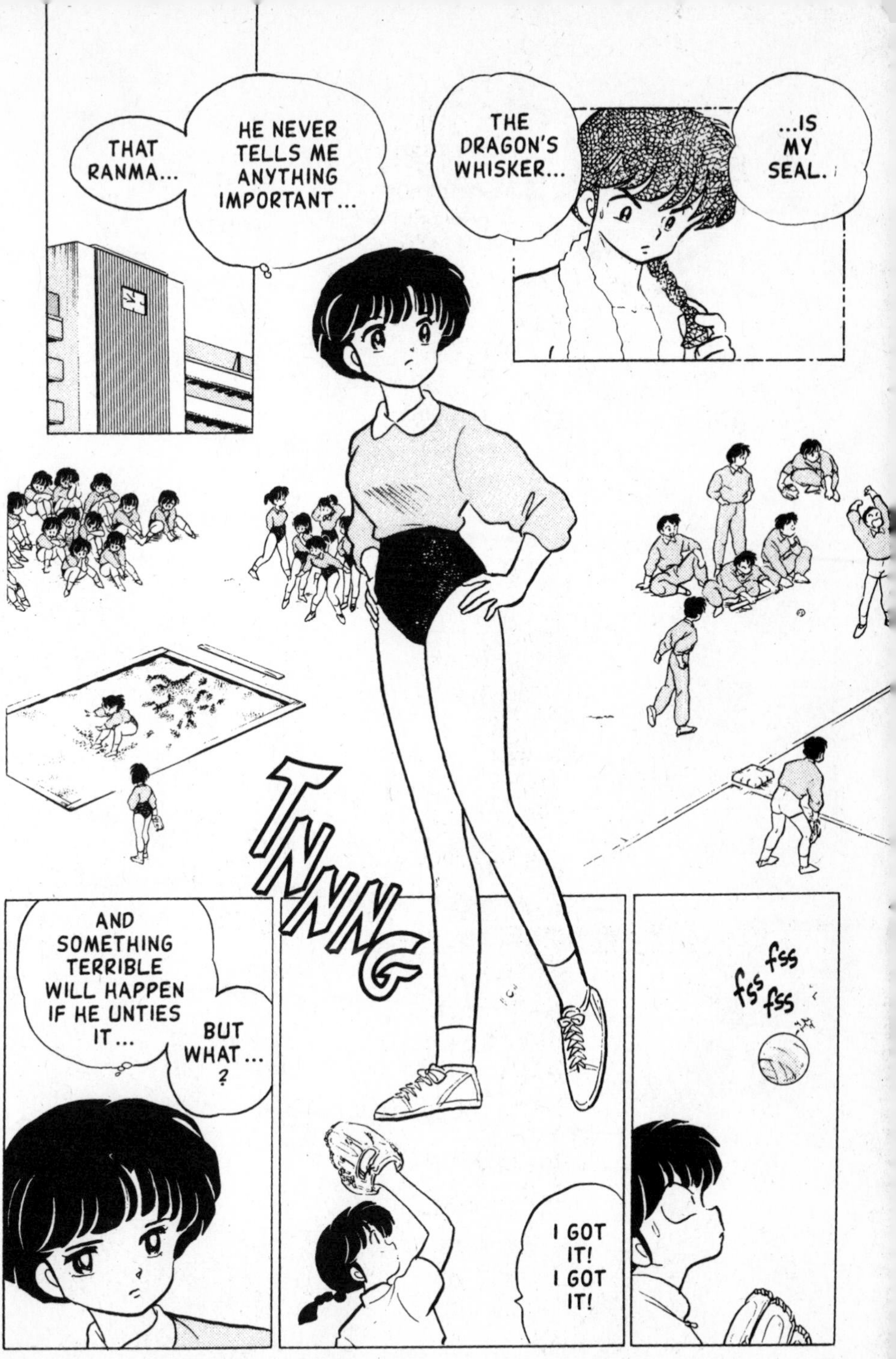

THAT RANMA...
HE NEVER TELLS ME ANYTHING IMPORTANT...
THE DRAGON'S WHISKER...
...IS MY SEAL.
TNNNG
AND SOMETHING TERRIBLE WILL HAPPEN IF HE UNTIES IT...
BUT WHAT...?
I GOT IT! I GOT IT!
fss fss fss fss

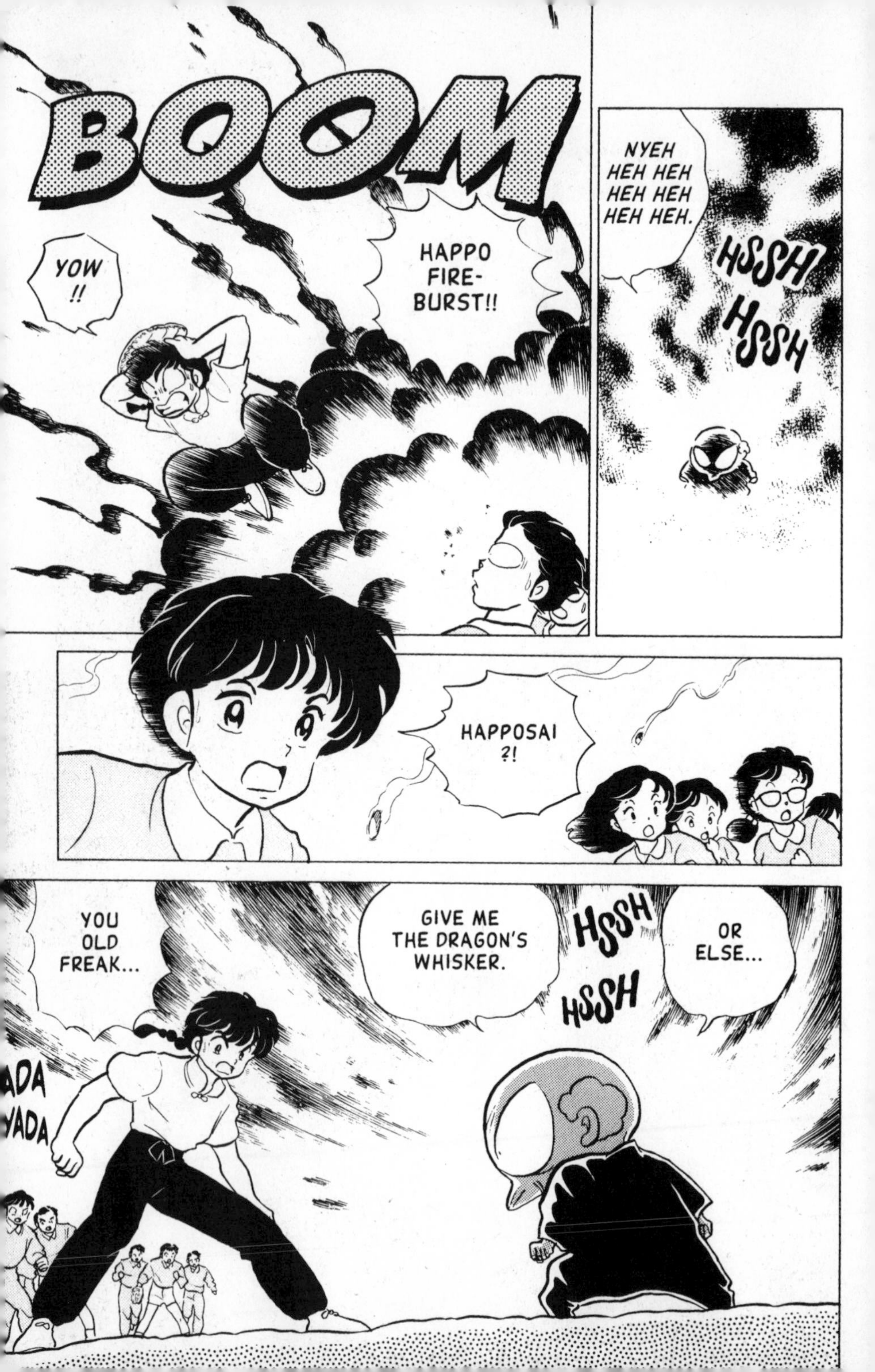
BOOM
YOW !!
HAPPO FIRE-BURST!!
NYEH HEH HEH HEH HEH HEH HEH.
HSSH
HSSH
HAPPOSAI ?!
YOU OLD FREAK...
GIVE ME THE DRAGON'S WHISKER.
HSSH
HSSH
OR ELSE...

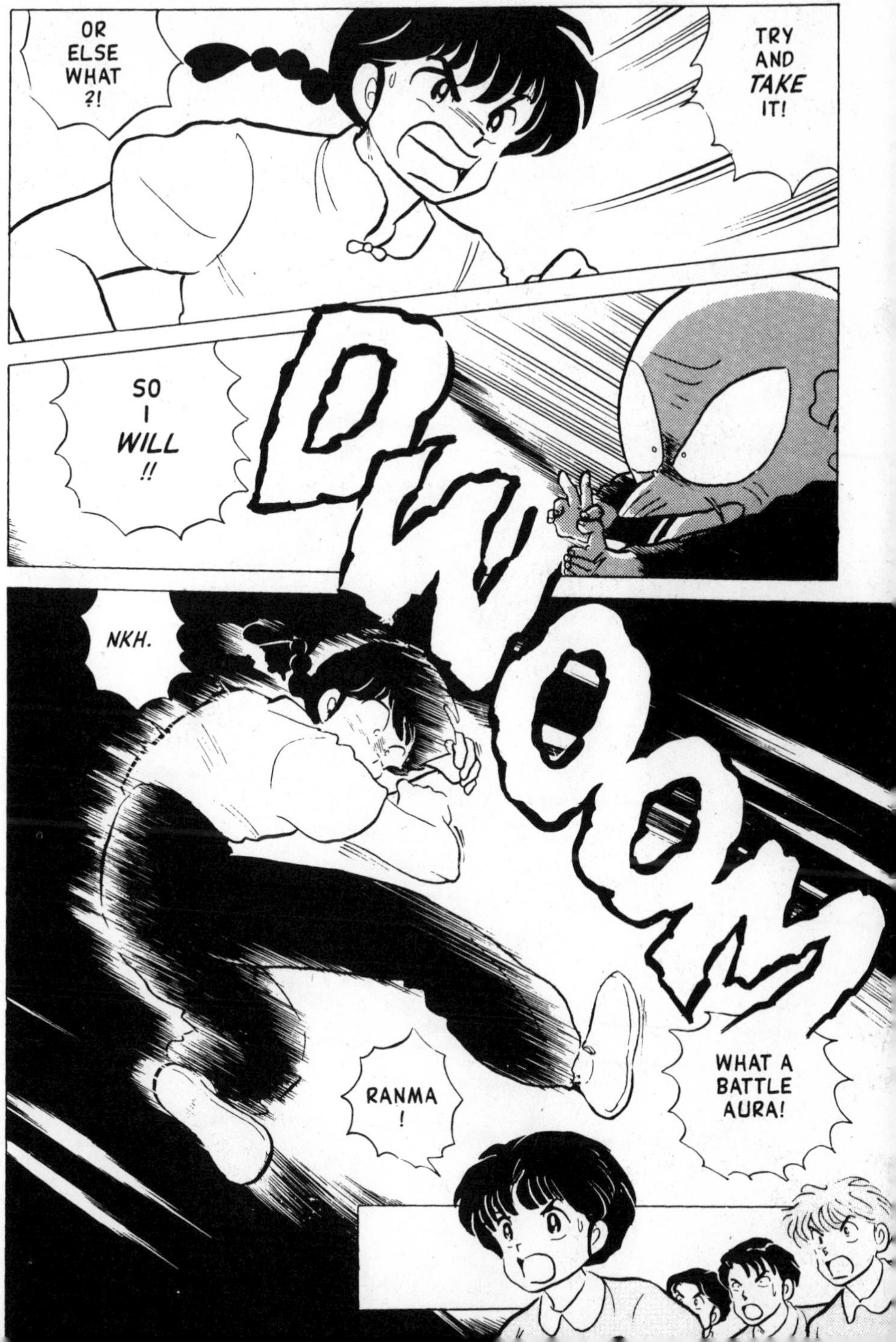
OR ELSE WHAT ?!
TRY AND *TAKE* IT!
SO I *WILL* !!
DWOOM
NKH.
RANMA !
WHAT A BATTLE AURA!

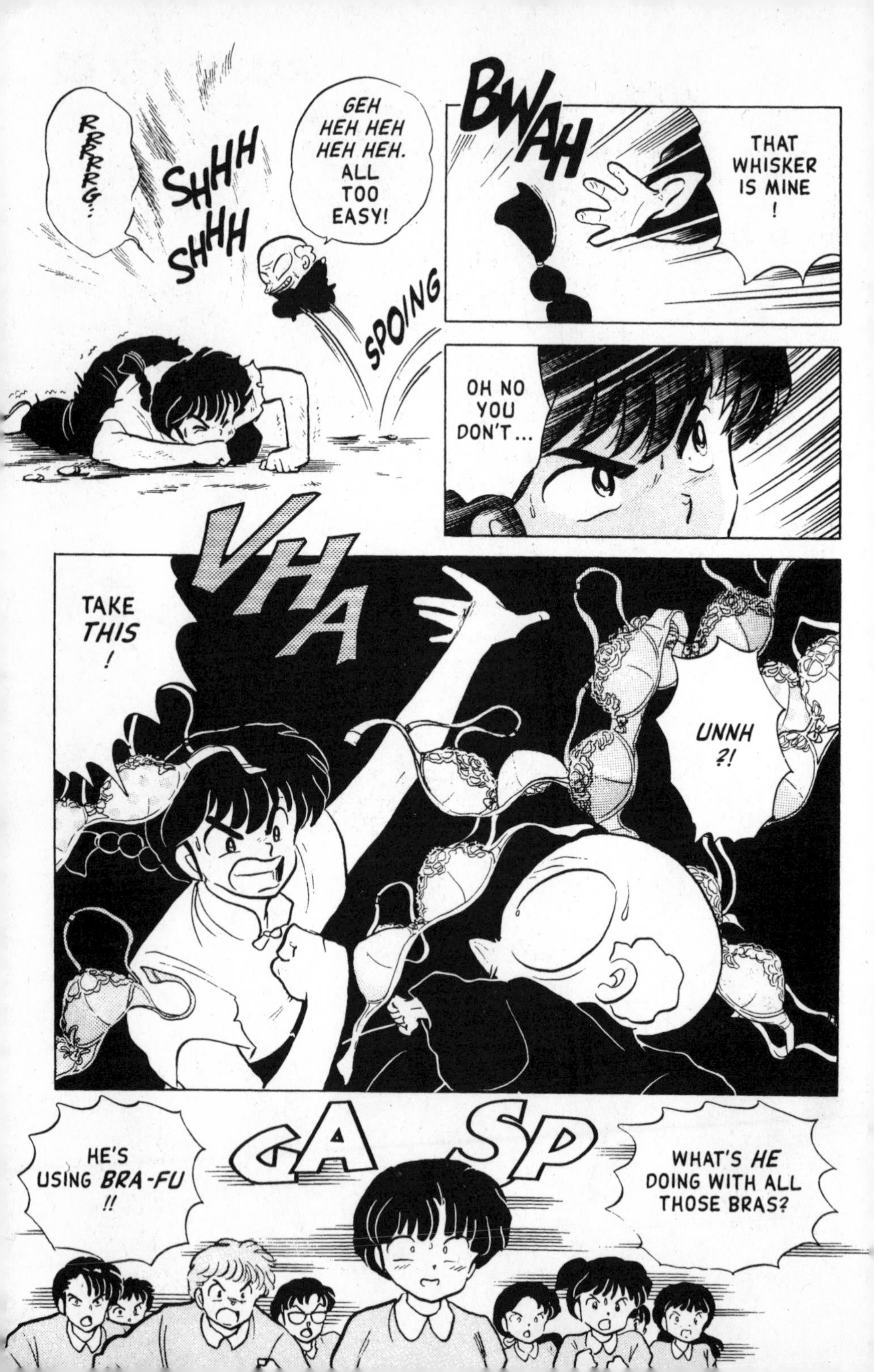
RRRRRG...
SHHH SHHH
GEH HEH HEH HEH HEH. ALL TOO EASY!
SPOING
BWAH
THAT WHISKER IS MINE!
OH NO YOU DON'T...
VHA
TAKE *THIS*!
UNNH ?!
HE'S USING *BRA-FU*!!
GASP
WHAT'S *HE* DOING WITH ALL THOSE BRAS?

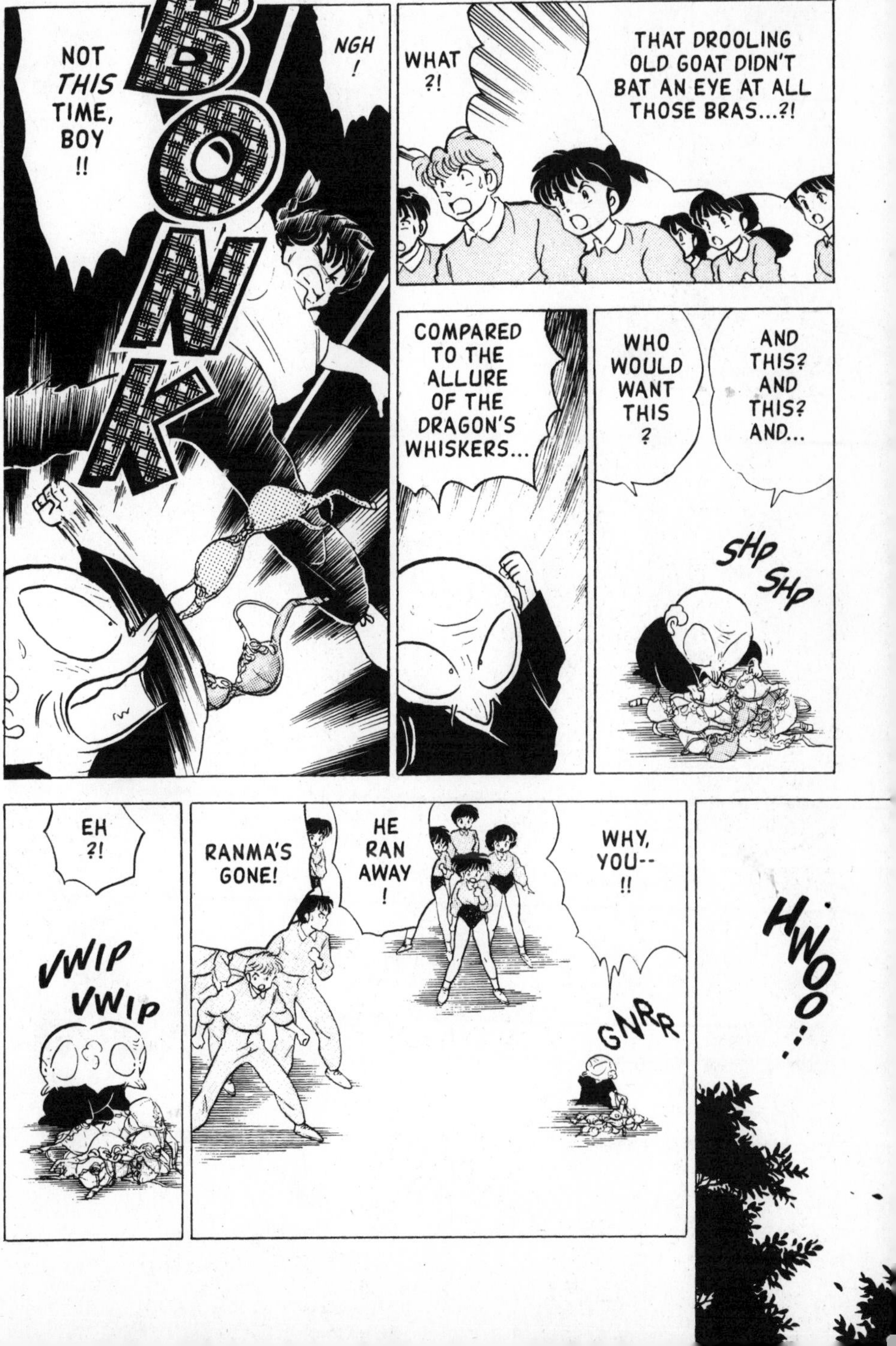
NOT THIS TIME, BOY !!
NGH !
BONK
WHAT ?!
THAT DROOLING OLD GOAT DIDN'T BAT AN EYE AT ALL THOSE BRAS...?!
COMPARED TO THE ALLURE OF THE DRAGON'S WHISKERS...
WHO WOULD WANT THIS ?
AND THIS? AND THIS? AND...
SHP SHP
EH ?!
VWIP VWIP
RANMA'S GONE!
HE RAN AWAY !
WHY, YOU-- !!
GNRR
HWOO...

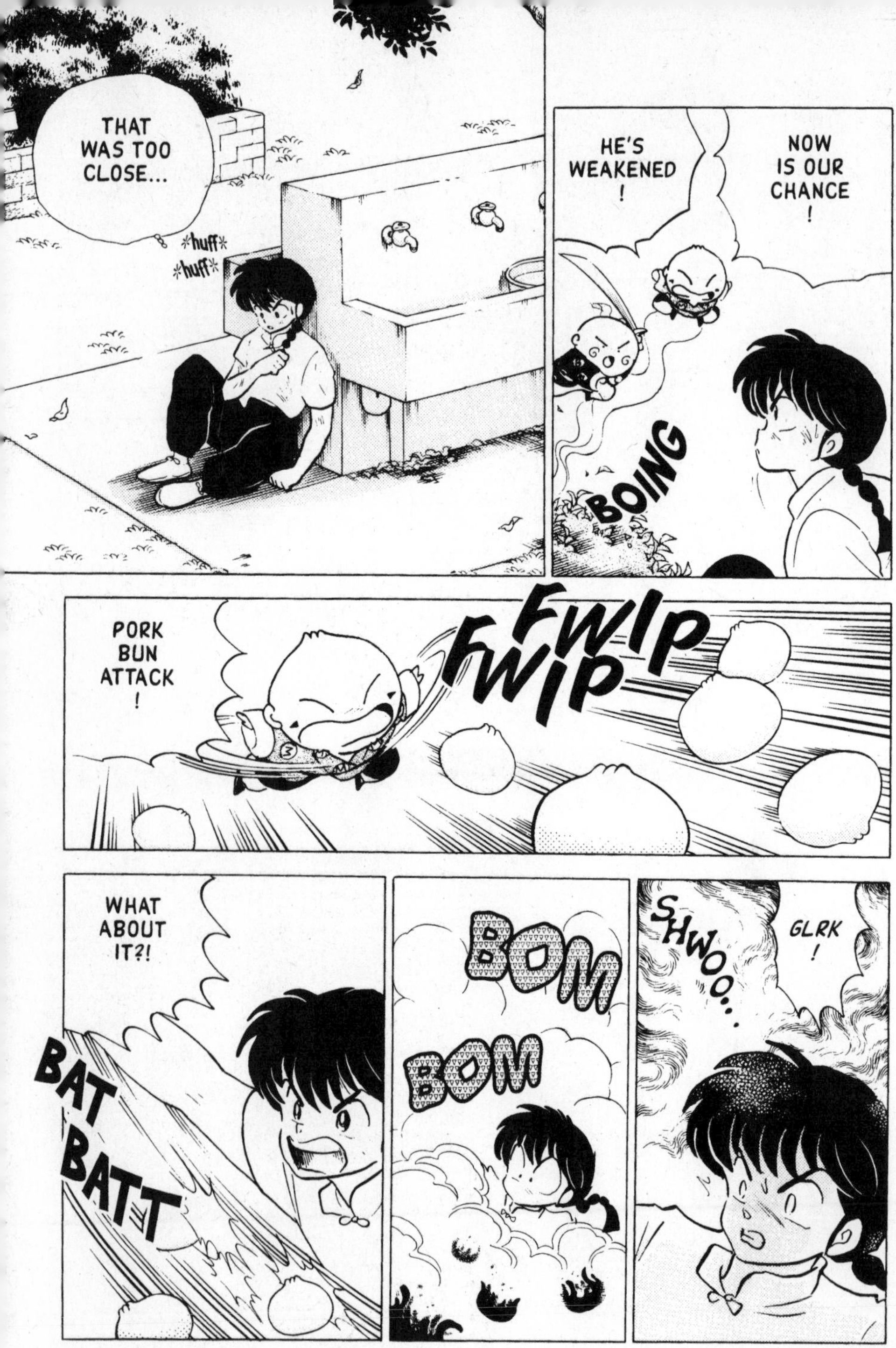
THAT WAS TOO CLOSE...
huff *huff*
HE'S WEAKENED !
NOW IS OUR CHANCE !
BOING
PORK BUN ATTACK !
FWIP FWIP
WHAT ABOUT IT?!
BAT BATT
BOM BOM
SHWOO...
GLRK !

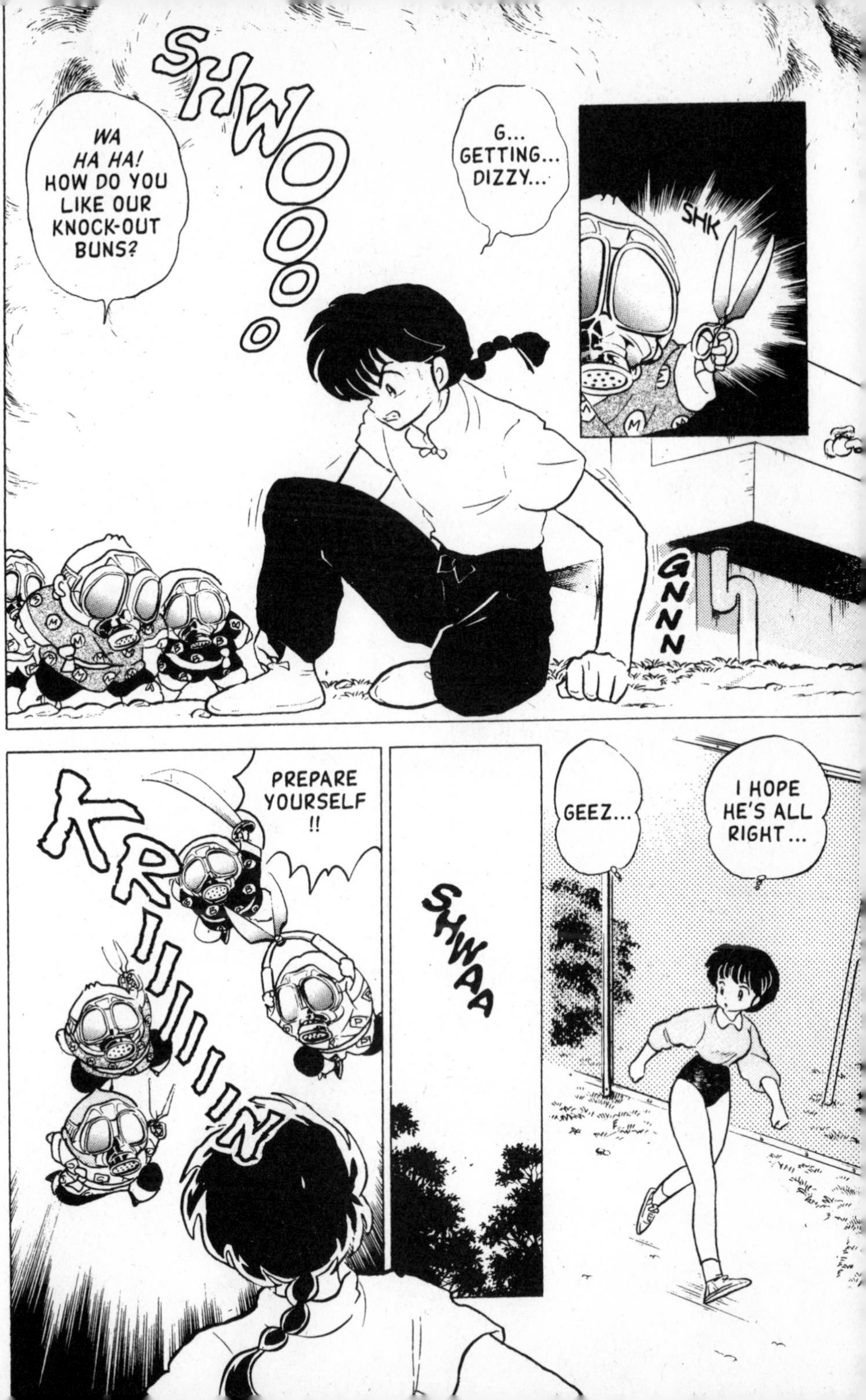
WA HA HA! HOW DO YOU LIKE OUR KNOCK-OUT BUNS?
SHWOOOOO
G... GETTING... DIZZY...
SHK
GNNN
KRIIIIIN
PREPARE YOURSELF !!
SHWAA
GEEZ...
I HOPE HE'S ALL RIGHT...

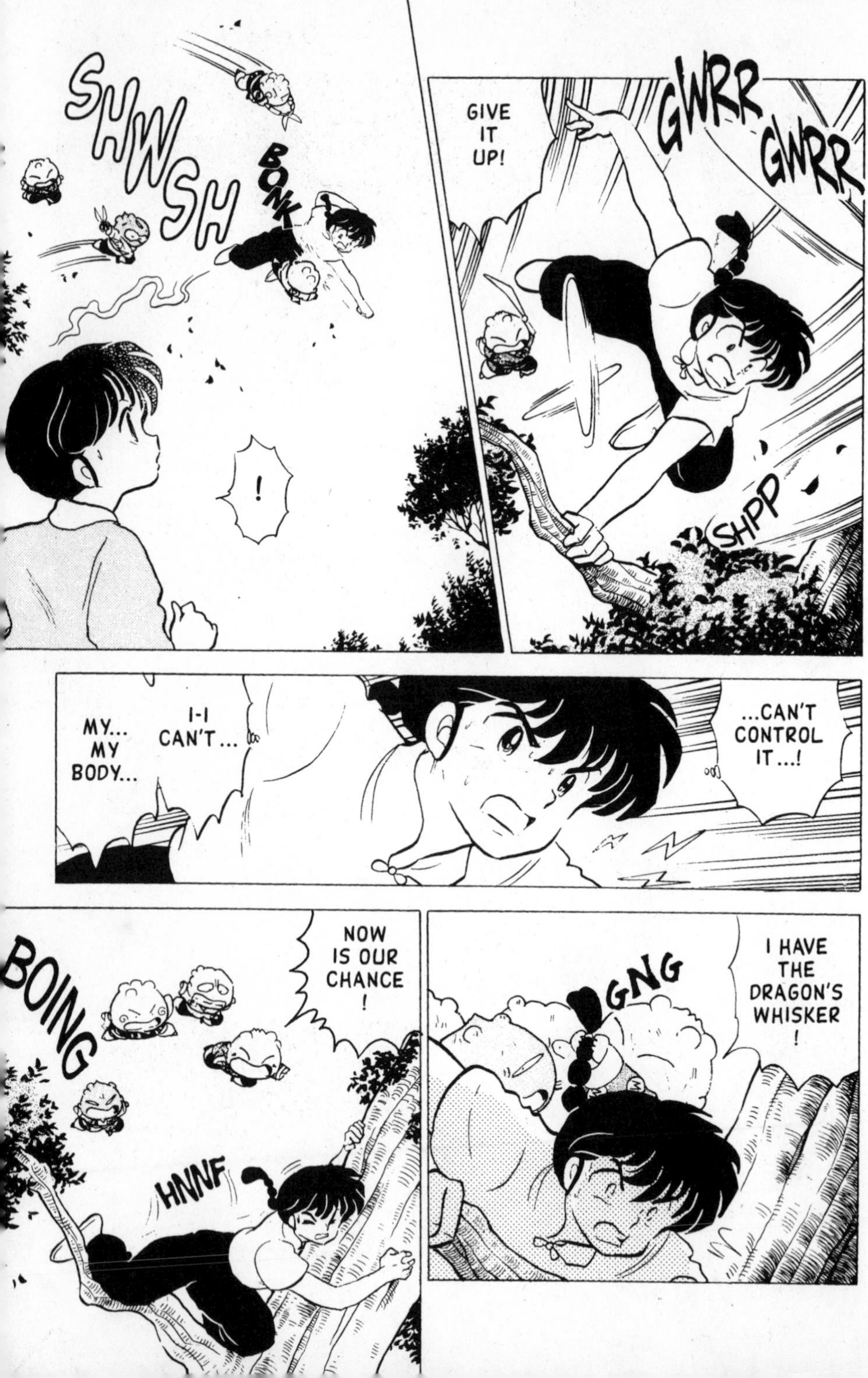
SHWSH
BONK
!
GIVE IT UP!
GWRR GWRR
SHPP
MY... MY BODY...
I-I CAN'T...
...CAN'T CONTROL IT...!
BOING
NOW IS OUR CHANCE!
HNNF
GNG
I HAVE THE DRAGON'S WHISKER!

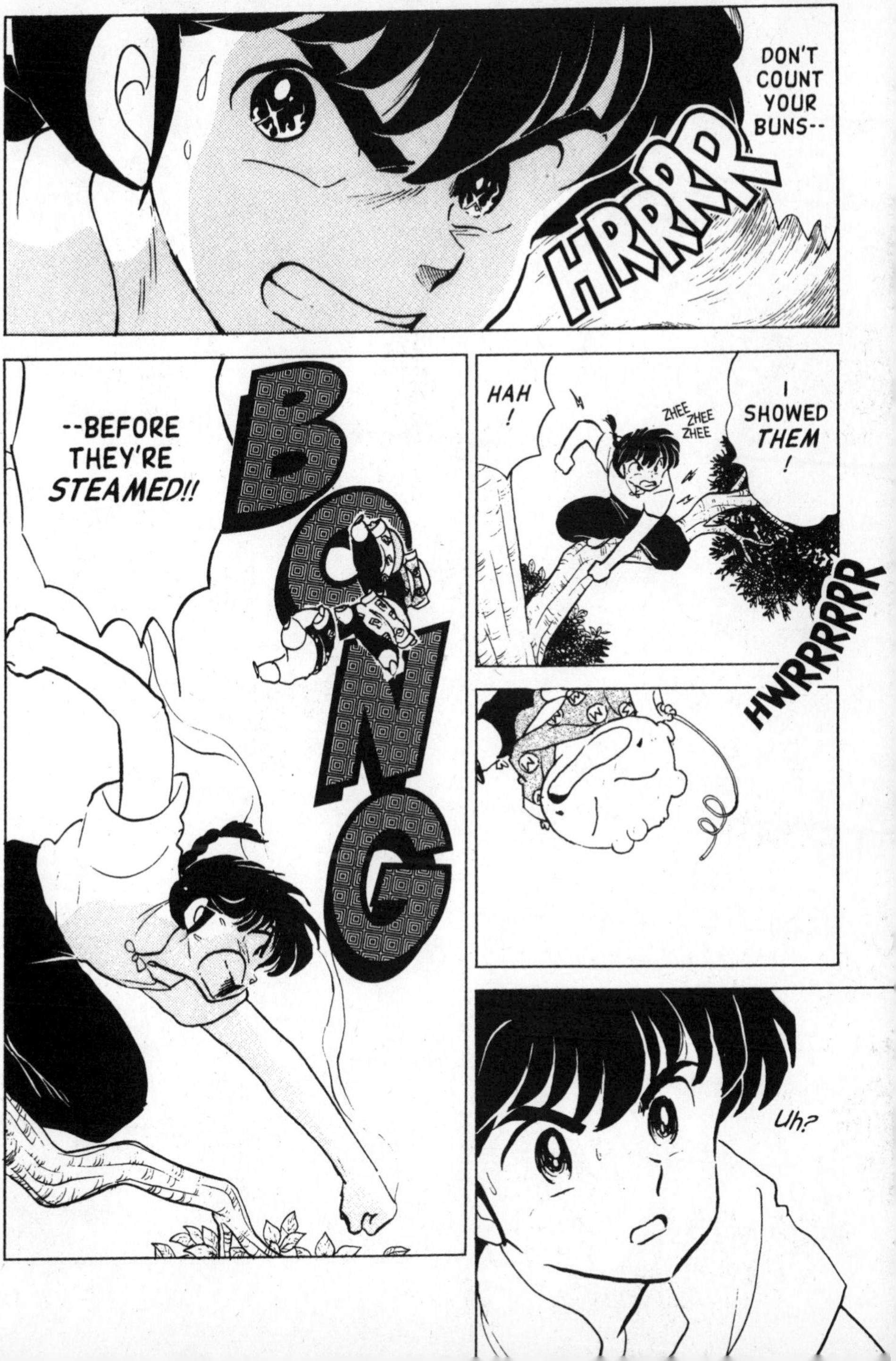
DON'T COUNT YOUR BUNS--
HRRRR
--BEFORE THEY'RE *STEAMED!!*
BOING
HAH!
ZHEE ZHEE ZHEE
I SHOWED *THEM*!
HWRRRRRR
Uh?

FSS SHHH...

YOW !

WE GOT THE DRAGON'S WHISK--

HRRRRR

RANMA !

GAH !

AKANE !

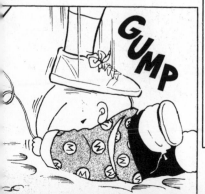

GUMP

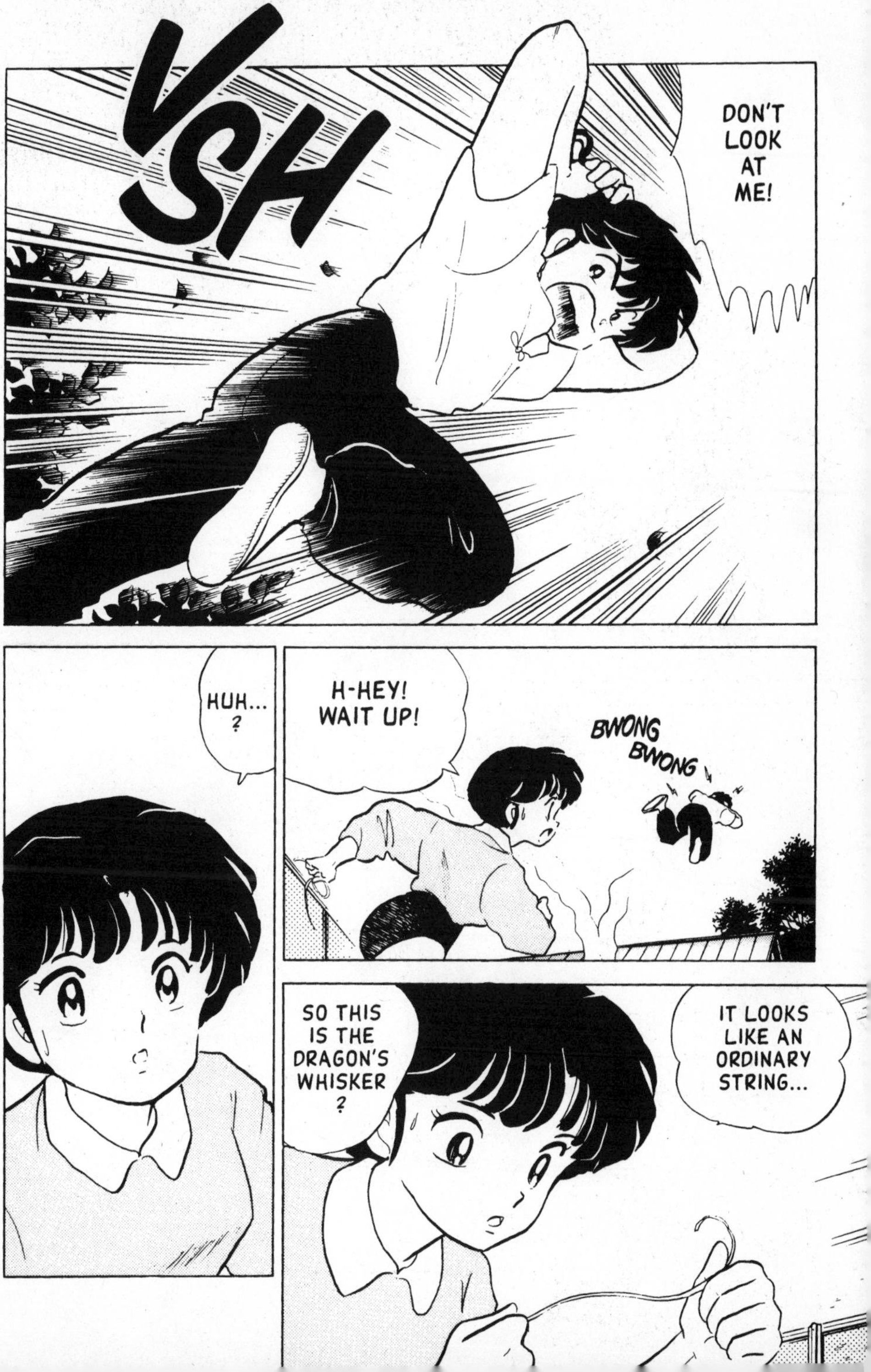
VSH
DON'T LOOK AT ME!
HUH...?
H-HEY! WAIT UP!
BWONG BWONG
SO THIS IS THE DRAGON'S WHISKER?
IT LOOKS LIKE AN ORDINARY STRING...

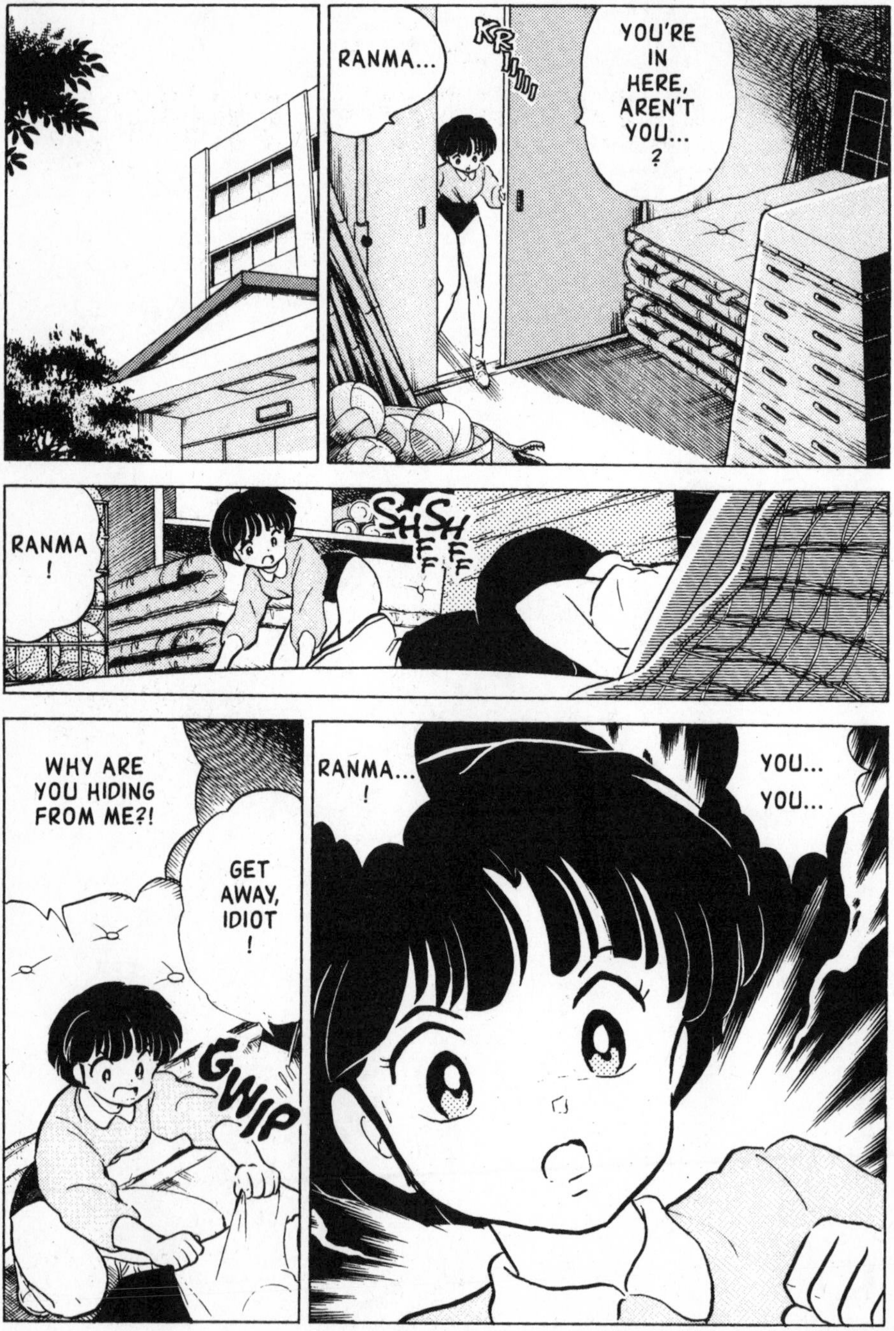
RANMA...
KRIIIII
YOU'RE IN HERE, AREN'T YOU...?
RANMA!
SHFF SHFF
WHY ARE YOU HIDING FROM ME?!
GET AWAY, IDIOT!
GWIP
RANMA...!
YOU... YOU...

PART 3
THE WHISKER'S SECRET

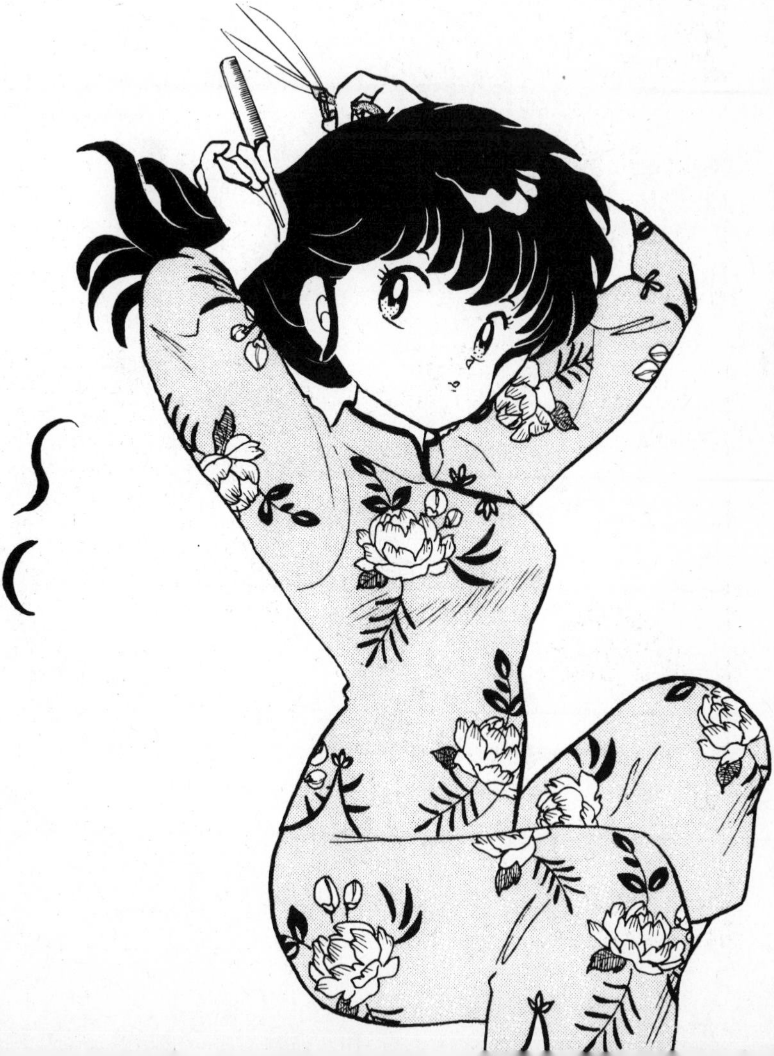

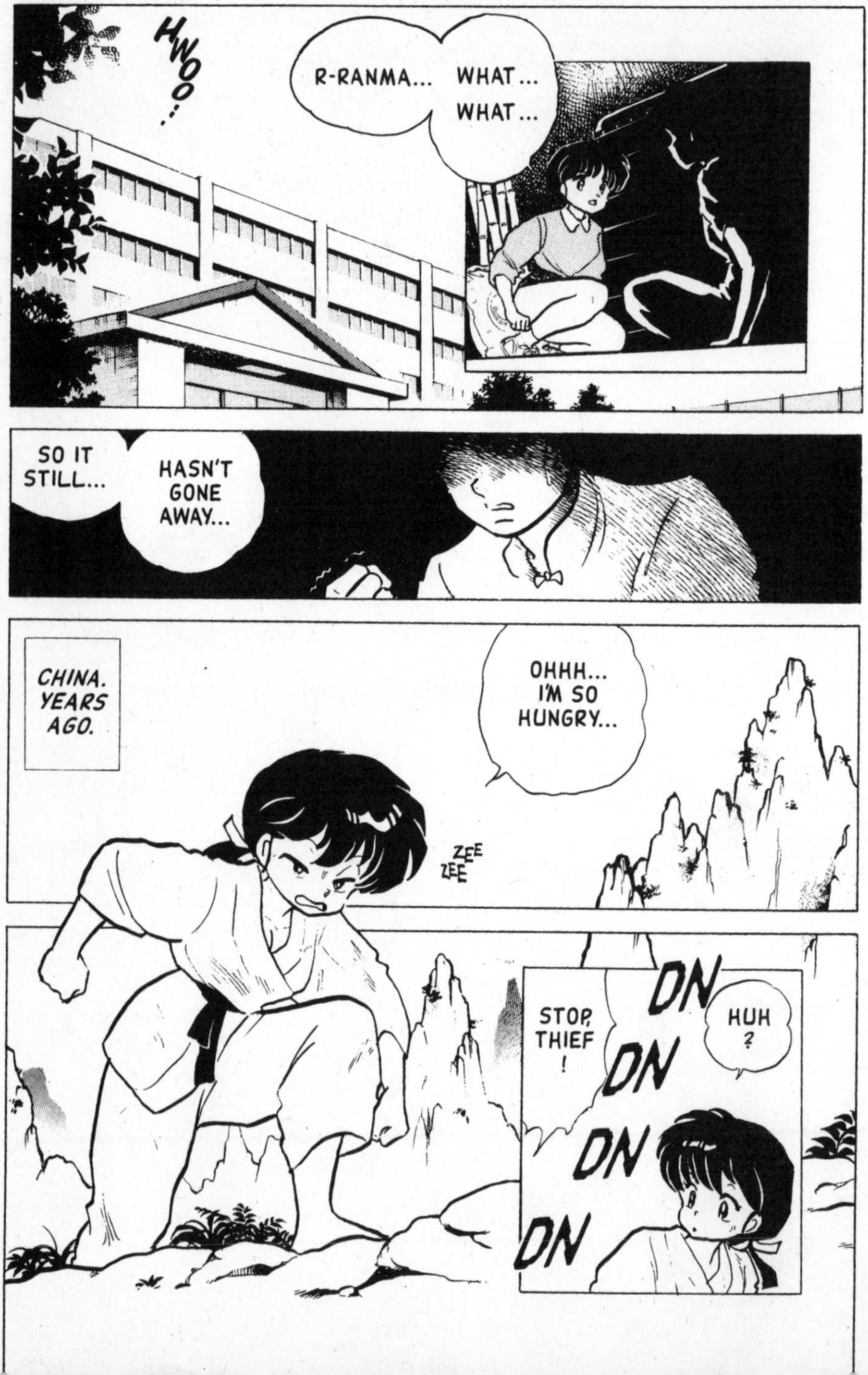
HWOO...
R-RANMA... WHAT... WHAT...
SO IT STILL...
HASN'T GONE AWAY...
CHINA. YEARS AGO.
OHHH... I'M SO HUNGRY...
ZEE ZEE
STOP, THIEF!
DN DN DN DN
HUH?

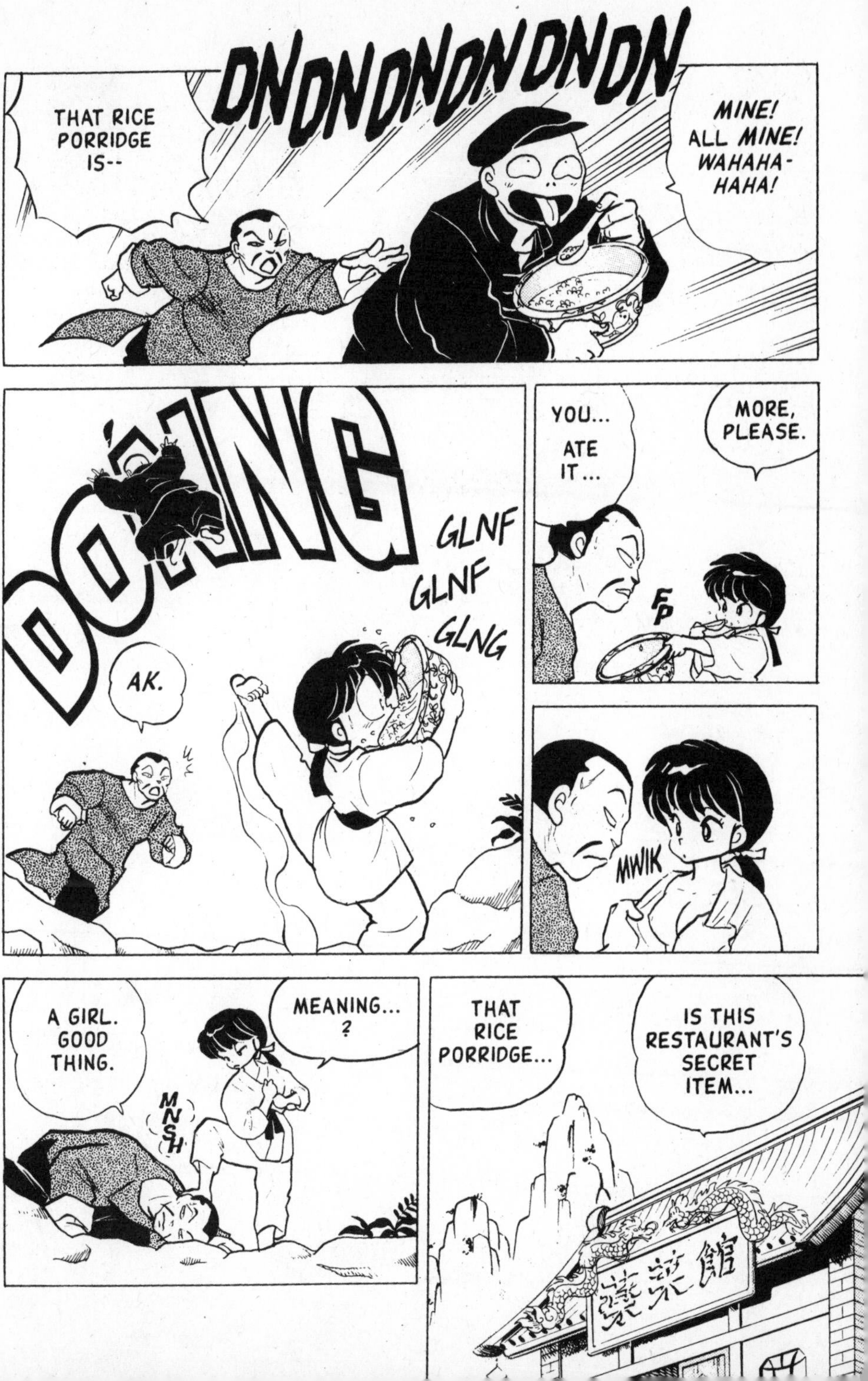

DNDNDNDNDNDN
THAT RICE PORRIDGE IS--
MINE! ALL MINE! WAHAHA-HAHA!
DOING
GLNF
GLNF
GLNG
AK.
YOU... ATE IT...
MORE, PLEASE.
FP
MWIK
A GIRL. GOOD THING.
MEANING... ?
MNSH
THAT RICE PORRIDGE...
IS THIS RESTAURANT'S SECRET ITEM...

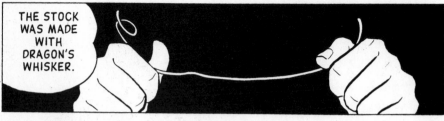

THE STOCK WAS MADE WITH DRAGON'S WHISKER.

DRAGON'S WHISKER?

A POWERFUL INGREDIENT FOR MEDICINAL COOKING.

IT HAS NO EFFECT ON WOMEN...

BUT SHOULD A *MAN* EAT IT...

WELL. IT FULFILLS A CERTAIN AMBITION.

MANY A BLOODY BATTLE HAS BEEN FOUGHT OVER THAT PORRIDGE.

IT'S TRULY LUCKY...

...THAT YOU'RE FE--

PLASH

42

WAHA-HAHAHA! SO YOU'RE A MAN!

HEY!

IS THIS WHAT YOU MEAN BY "AMBITION"?!

UNTIL THE EFFECTS OF IT RUNS OUT...

YOU CAN USE THIS AS A SEAL.

AND SO THE RESTAURANT'S COOK ALLOWED ME...

...TO BRING THE WHISKER WITH ME.

IF THAT'S THE WHISKER'S POWER...

...NO WONDER MEN FIGHT OVER IT.

YOU WANT TO KNOW THE SECRET OF THE DRAGON'S WHISKER?

CAT CAFE

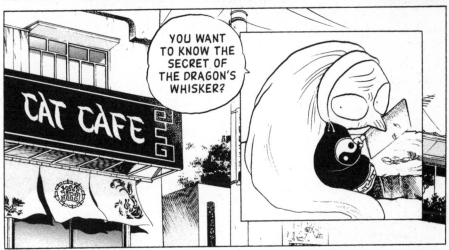

YES.

I THOUGHT IF ANYONE WOULD KNOW, IT WOULD BE A 3000-YEAR-OLD CHINESE GHOUL.

WHO ARE YOU CALLING A 3000-YEAR-OLD CHINESE GHOUL?!

SLURP

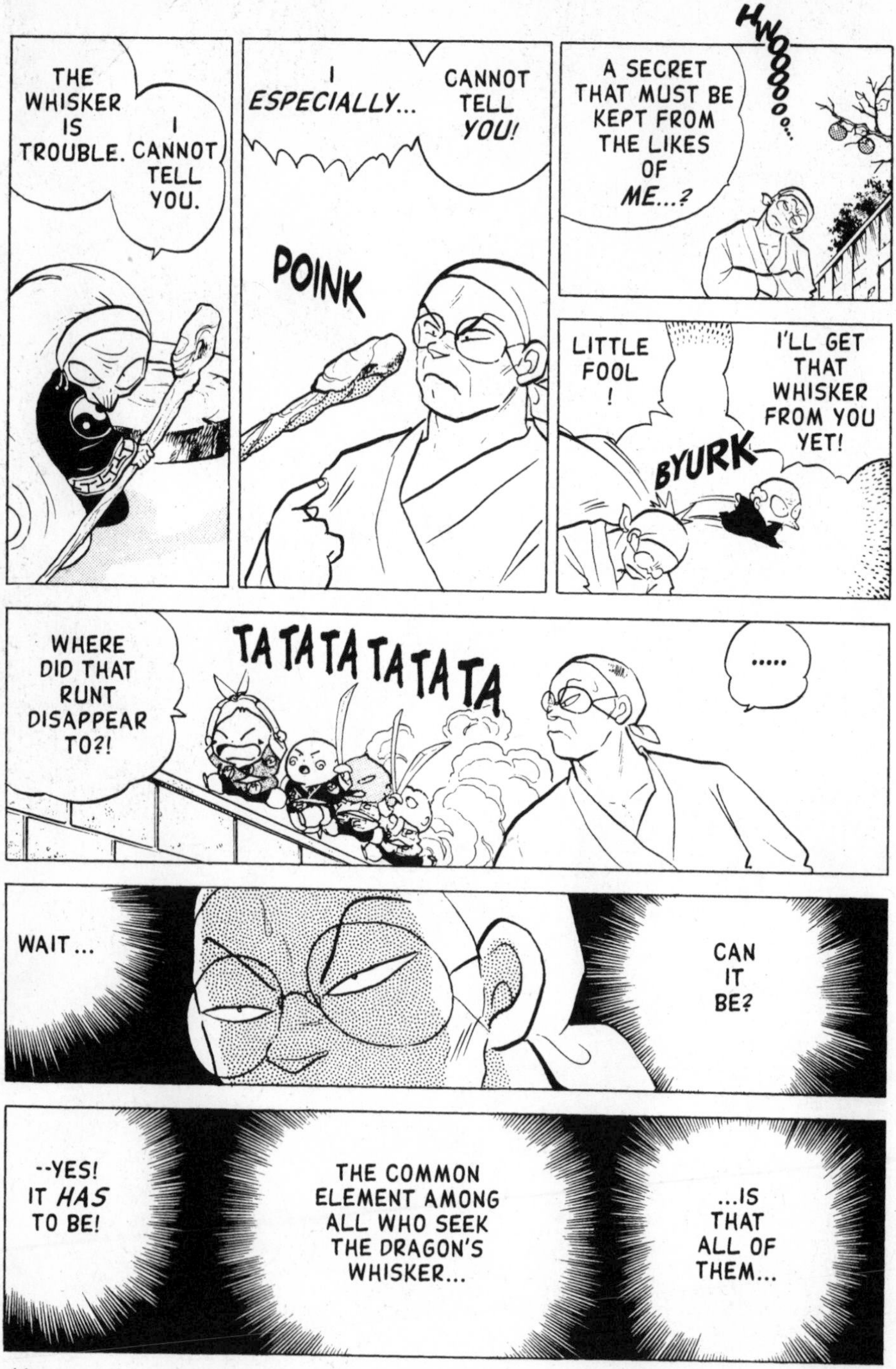
THE WHISKER IS TROUBLE.
I CANNOT TELL YOU.
I *ESPECIALLY*...
CANNOT TELL *YOU!*
POINK
HWOOOOOO...
A SECRET THAT MUST BE KEPT FROM THE LIKES OF *ME*...?
LITTLE FOOL!
I'LL GET THAT WHISKER FROM YOU YET!
BYURK
WHERE DID THAT RUNT DISAPPEAR TO?!
TATATATATATA
.....
WAIT...
CAN IT BE?
--YES! IT *HAS* TO BE!
THE COMMON ELEMENT AMONG ALL WHO SEEK THE DRAGON'S WHISKER...
...IS THAT ALL OF THEM...

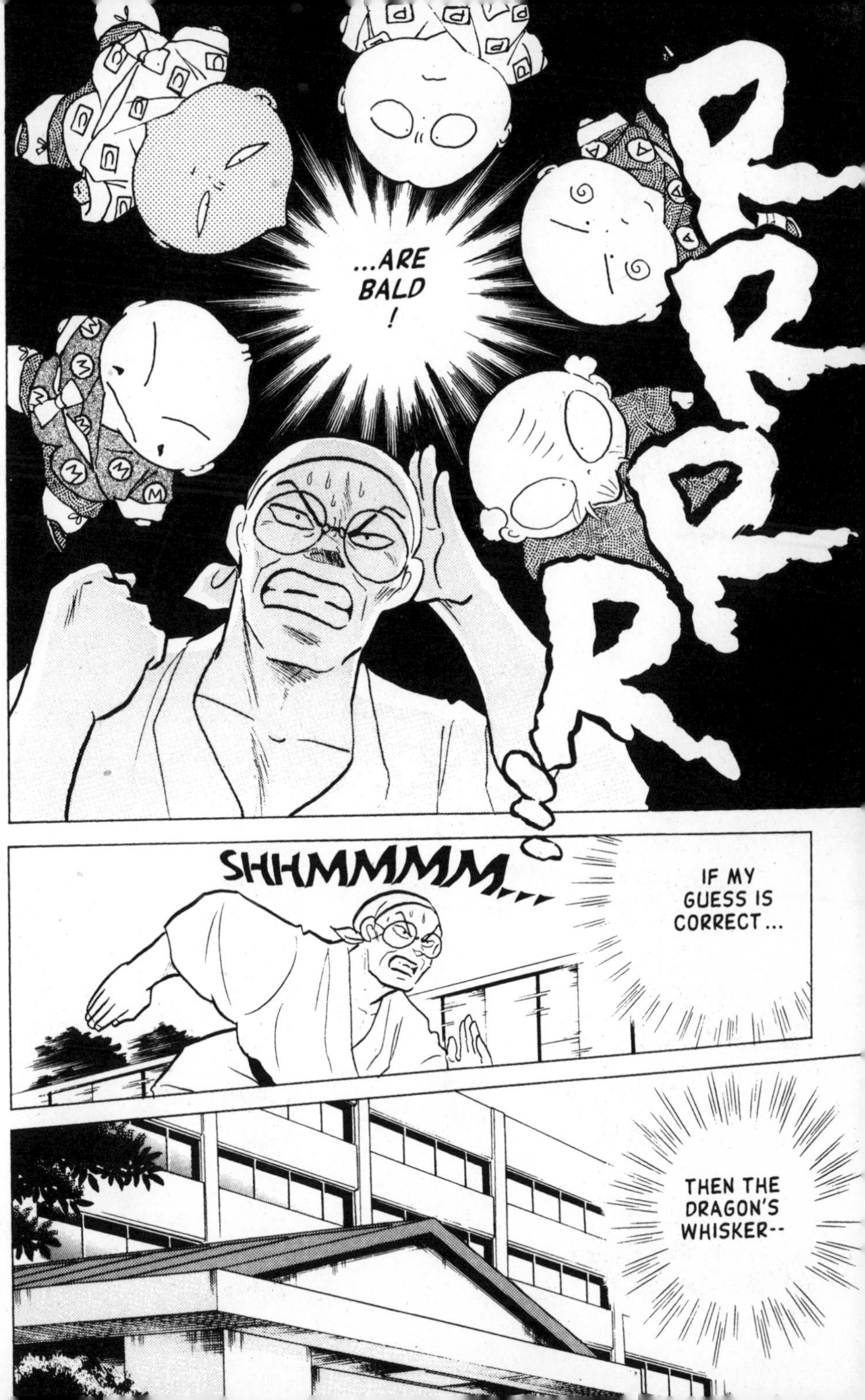
...ARE BALD!
RRRR
SHHMMMMM...
IF MY GUESS IS CORRECT...
THEN THE DRAGON'S WHISKER--

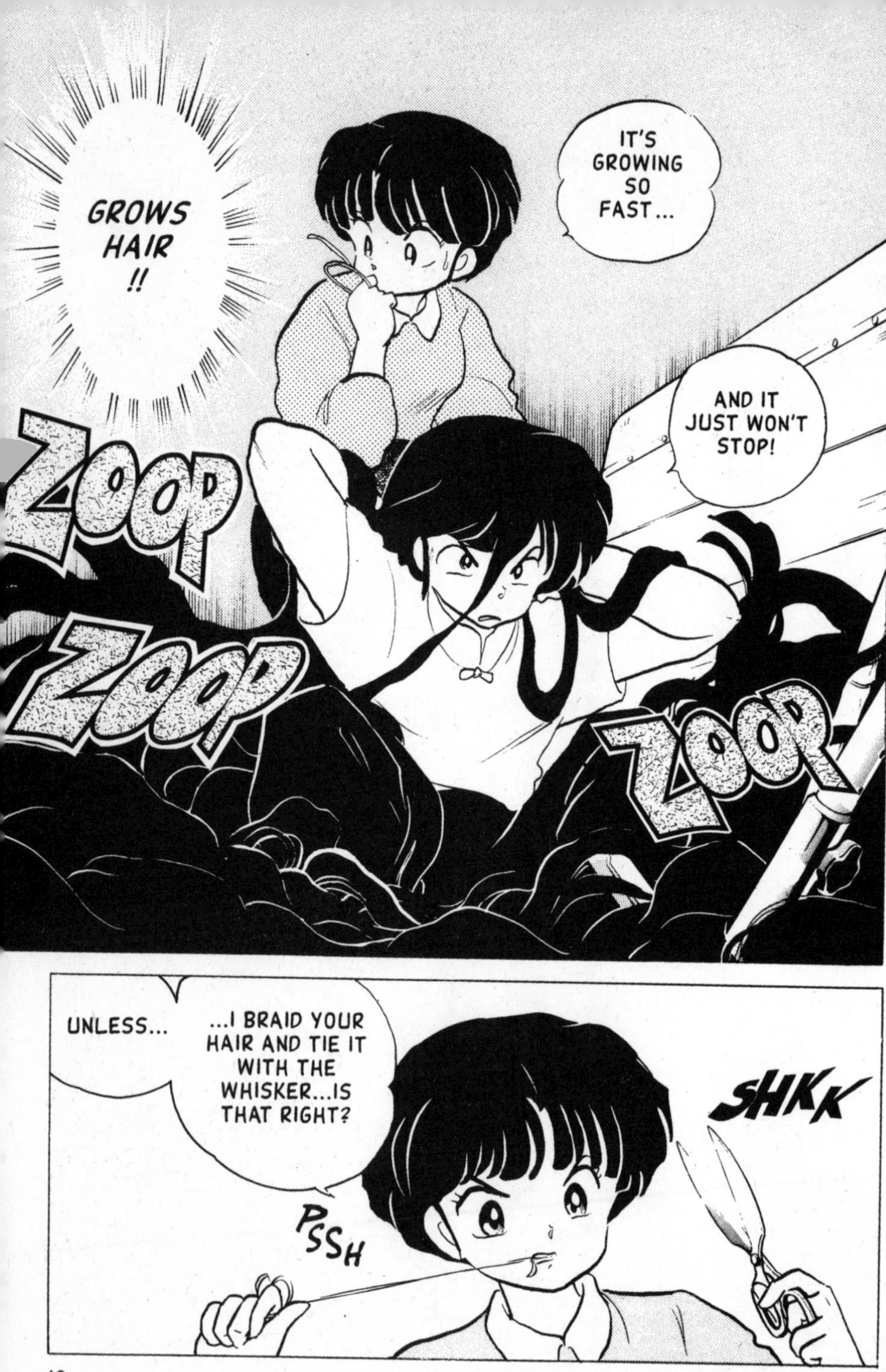
GROWS HAIR !!
IT'S GROWING SO FAST...
ZOOP
AND IT JUST WON'T STOP!
ZOOP
ZOOP
UNLESS...
...I BRAID YOUR HAIR AND TIE IT WITH THE WHISKER...IS THAT RIGHT?
SHKK
PSSH

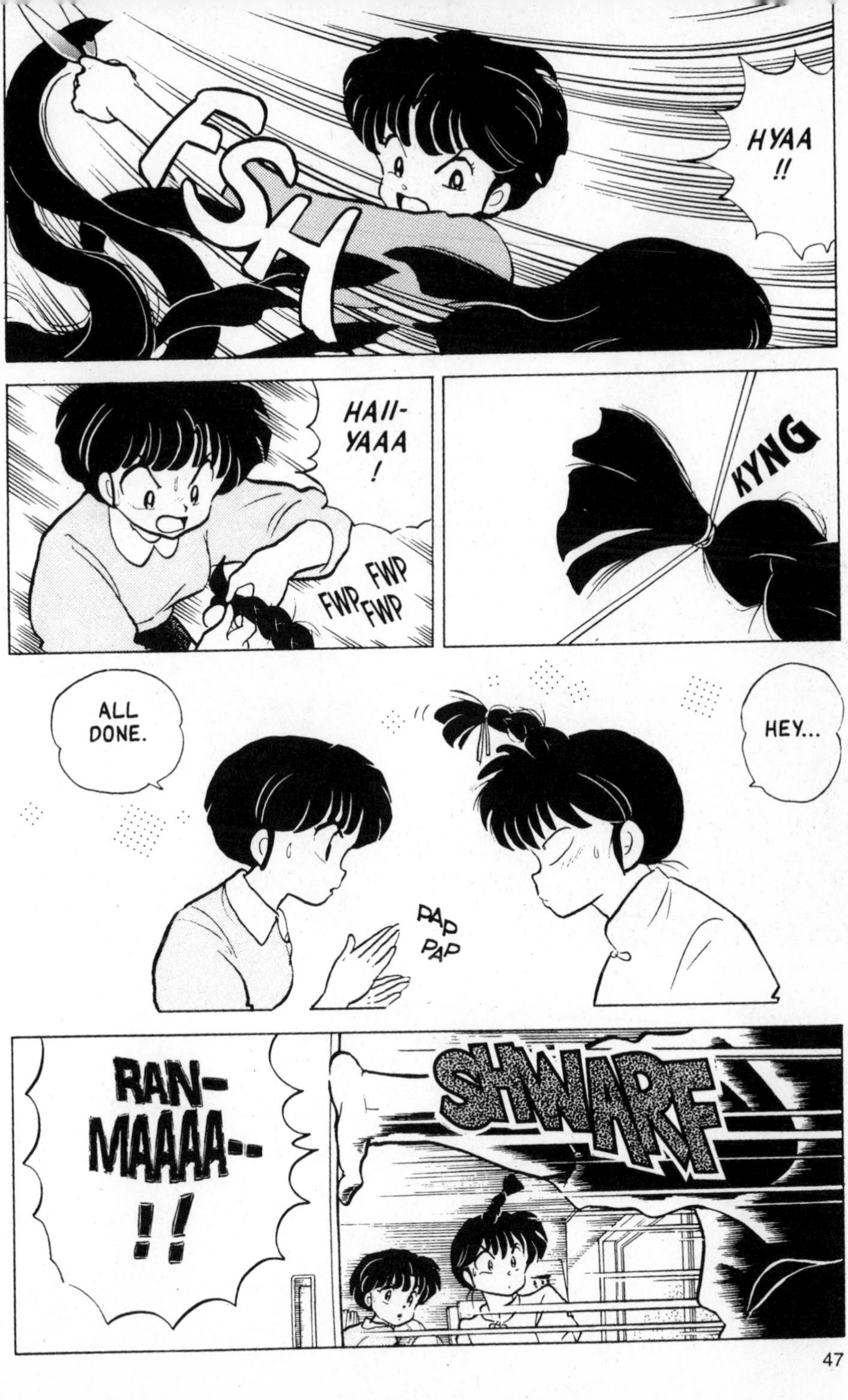
FSH
HYAA !!
HAII-YAAA !
FWP FWP FWP
KYNG
ALL DONE.
HEY...
PAP PAP
RAN-MAAAA-- !!
SHWARF

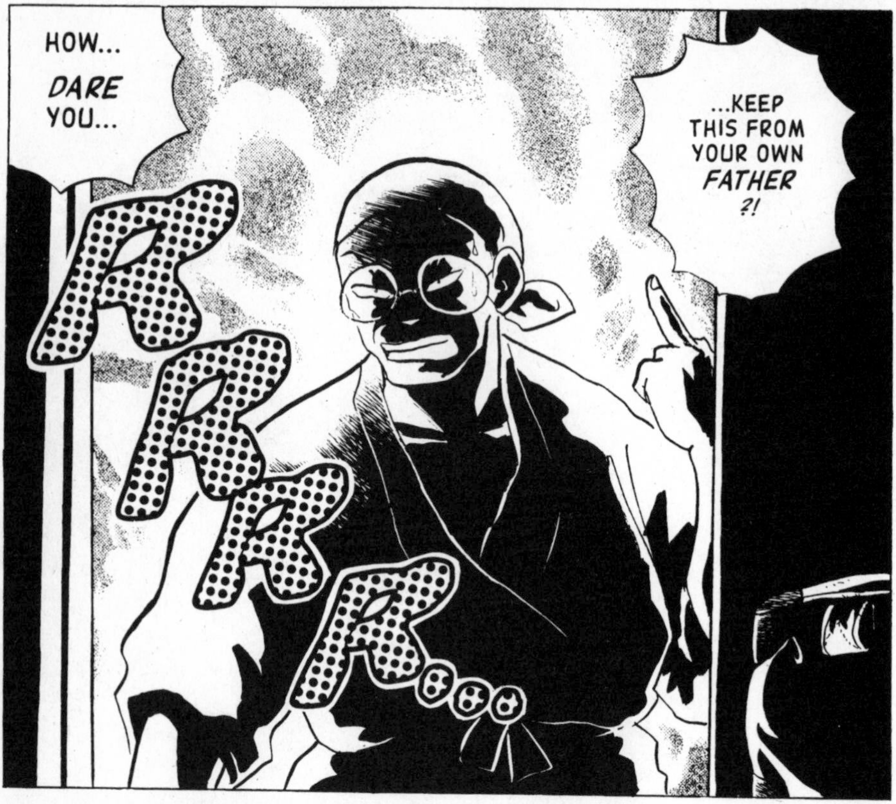
...KEEP THIS FROM YOUR OWN FATHER ?!
HOW... DARE YOU...
RRRR...
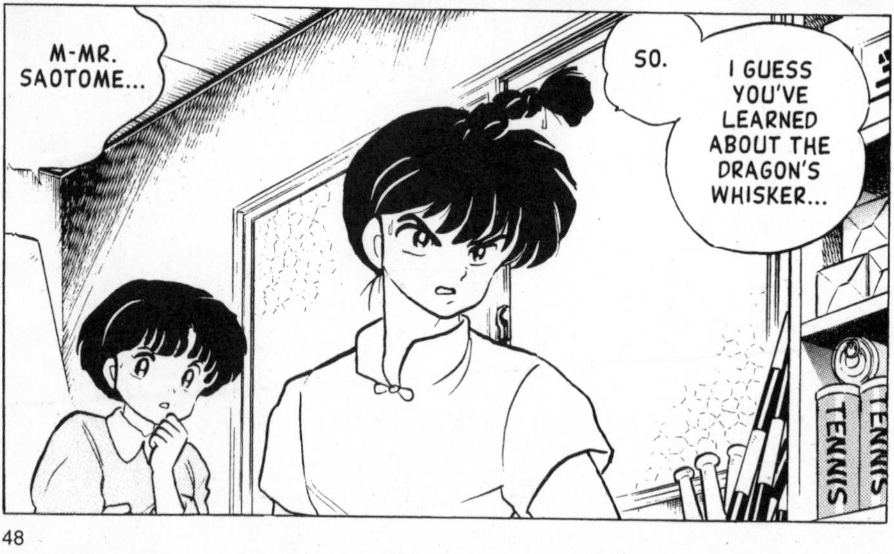
SO.
I GUESS YOU'VE LEARNED ABOUT THE DRAGON'S WHISKER...
M-MR. SAOTOME...
TENNIS
TENNIS

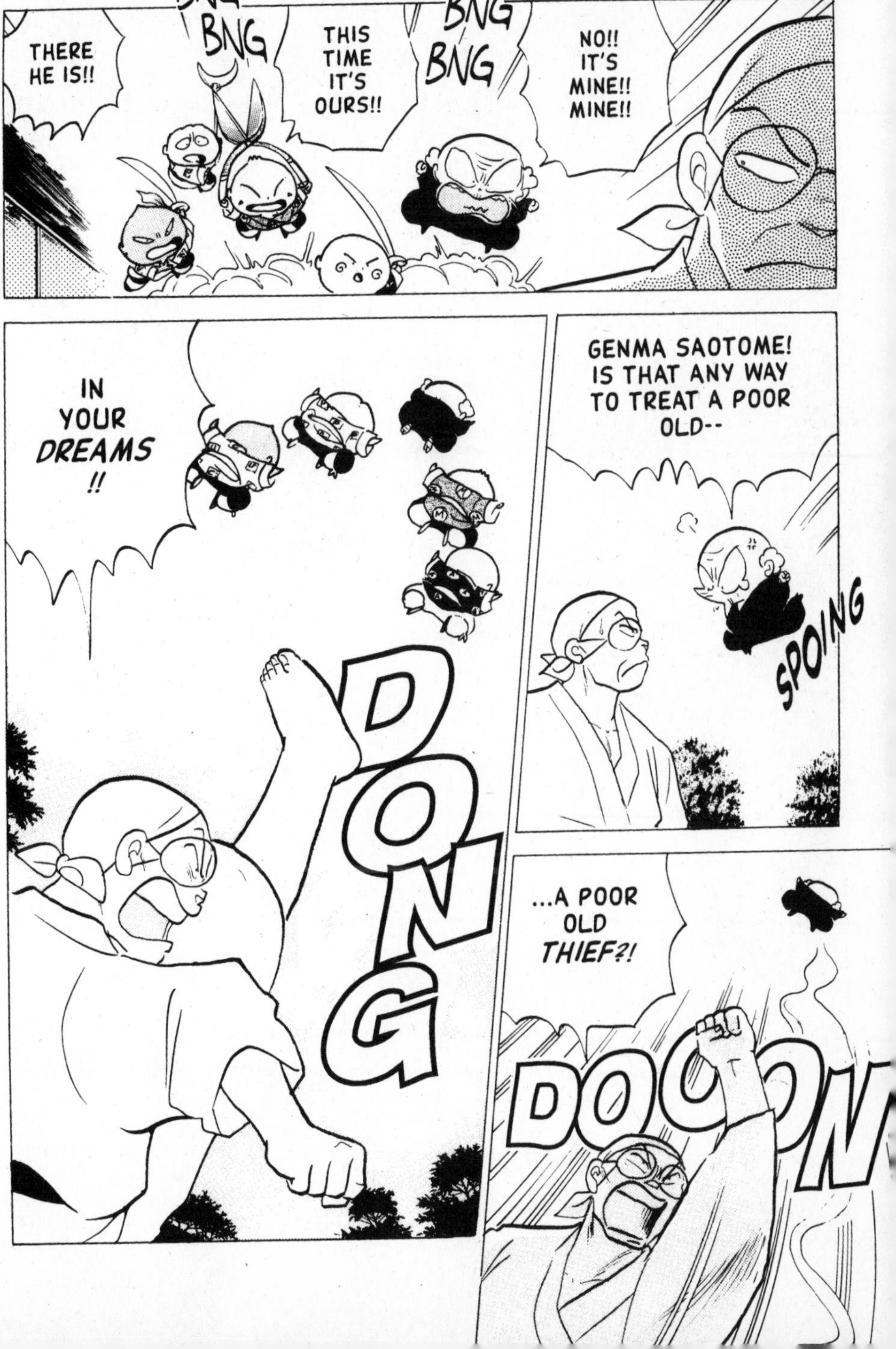
THERE HE IS!!
BNG BNG
THIS TIME IT'S OURS!!
BNG BNG
NO!! IT'S MINE!! MINE!!
IN YOUR *DREAMS* !!
DONG
GENMA SAOTOME! IS THAT ANY WAY TO TREAT A POOR OLD--
SPOING
...A POOR OLD *THIEF*?!
DOOOM

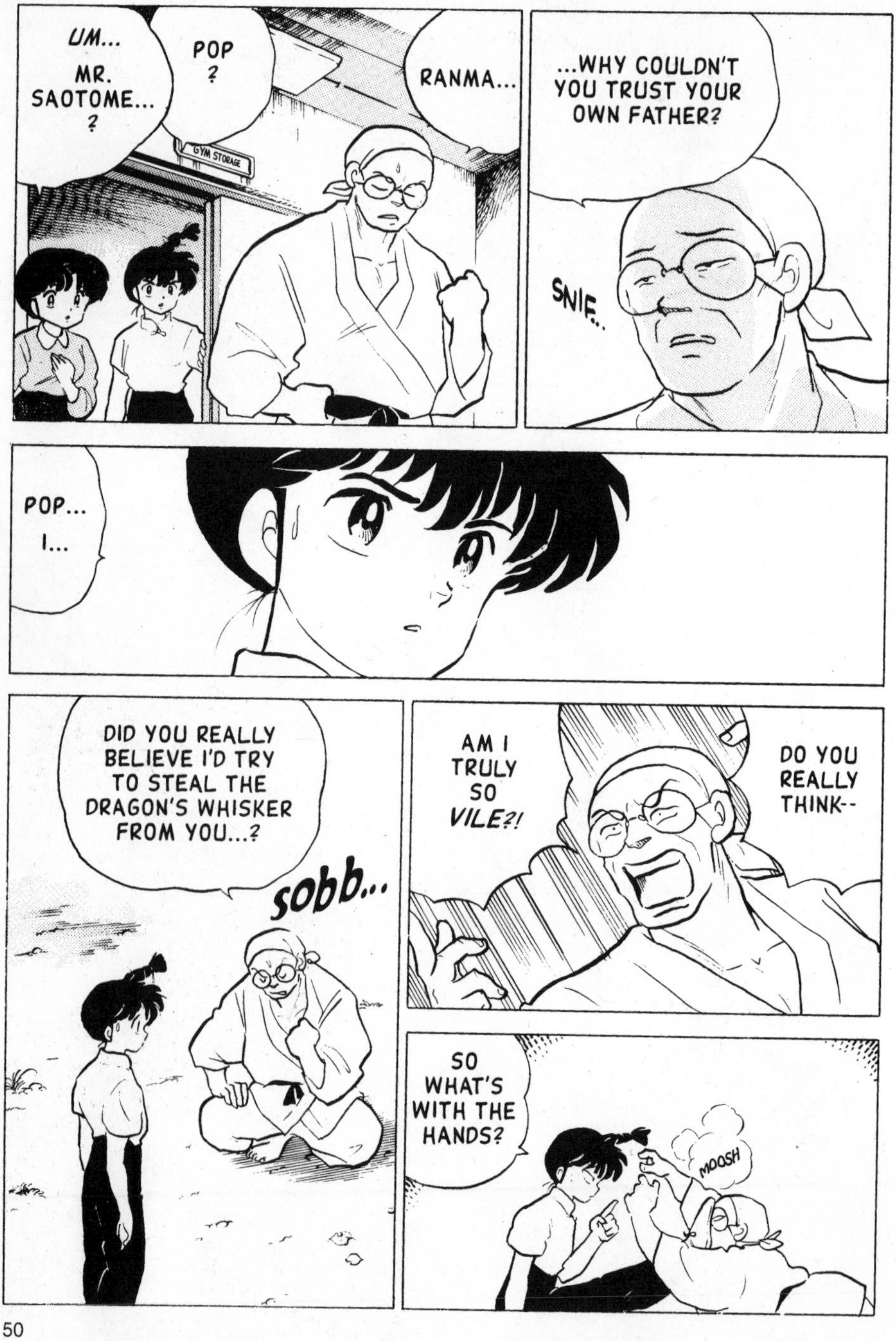
UM... MR. SAOTOME... ?
POP ?
GYM STORAGE
RANMA...
...WHY COULDN'T YOU TRUST YOUR OWN FATHER?
SNIF..
POP... I...
DID YOU REALLY BELIEVE I'D TRY TO STEAL THE DRAGON'S WHISKER FROM YOU...?
sobb...
AM I TRULY SO VILE?!
DO YOU REALLY THINK--
SO WHAT'S WITH THE HANDS?
MOOSH

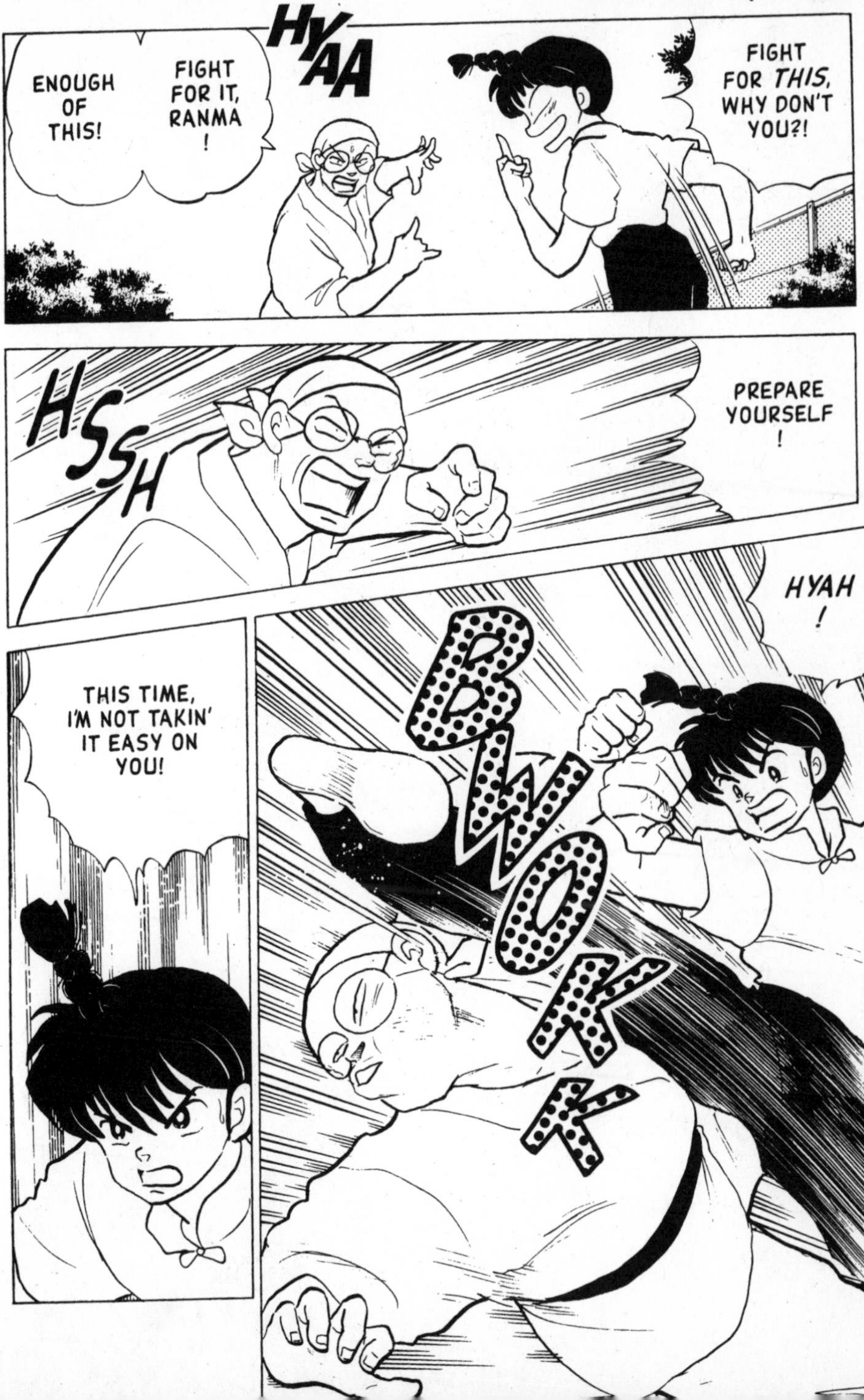
ENOUGH OF THIS!
FIGHT FOR IT, RANMA!
HYAA
FIGHT FOR THIS, WHY DON'T YOU?!
HSSH
PREPARE YOURSELF!
THIS TIME, I'M NOT TAKIN' IT EASY ON YOU!
BWOKK
HYAH!

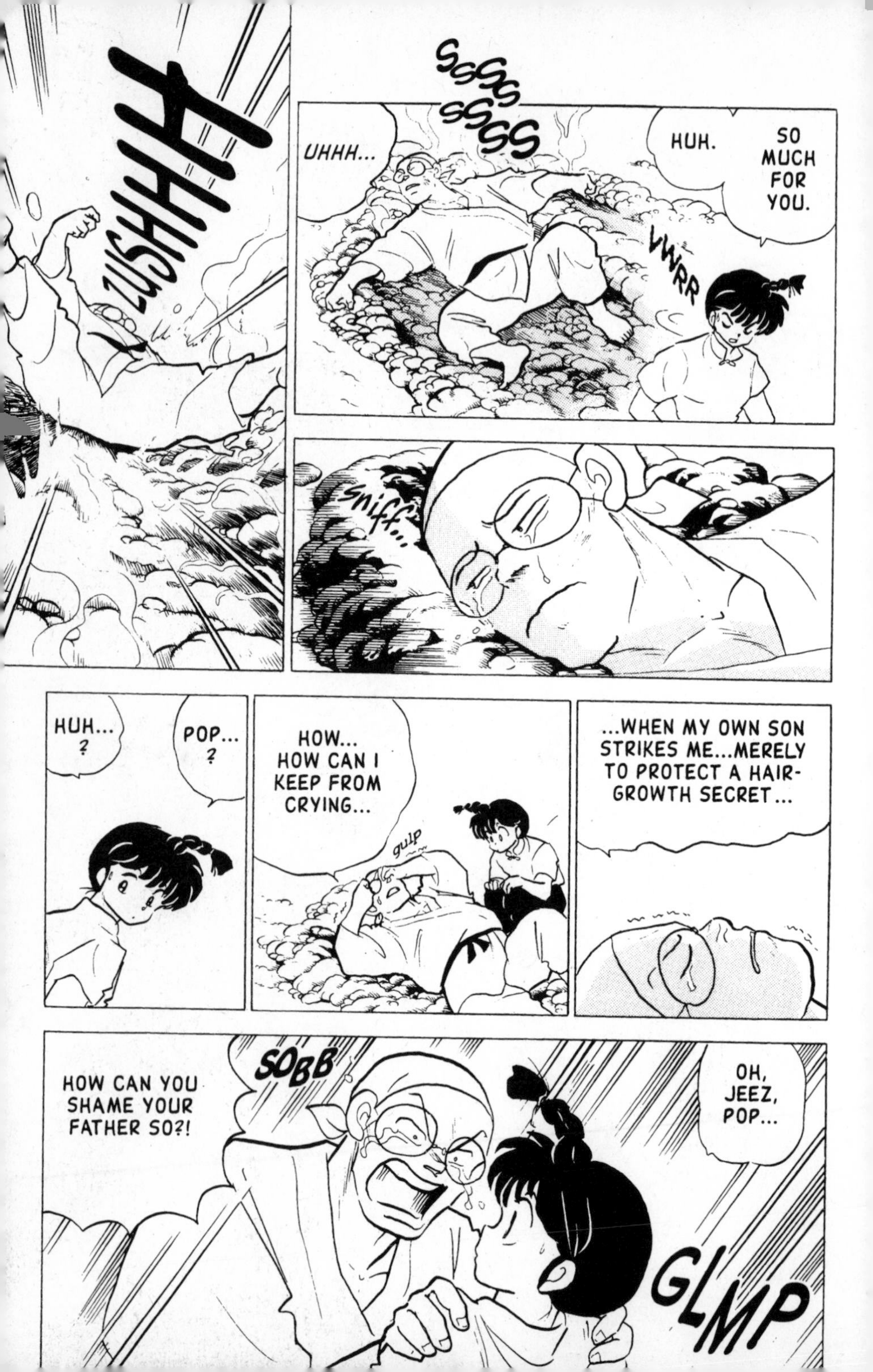
ZUSHHH
SSSSS SSSSS
UHHH...
HUH.
SO MUCH FOR YOU.
VWRR
sniff...
HUH...?
POP...?
HOW... HOW CAN I KEEP FROM CRYING...
gulp
...WHEN MY OWN SON STRIKES ME...MERELY TO PROTECT A HAIR-GROWTH SECRET...
HOW CAN YOU SHAME YOUR FATHER SO?!
SOBB
OH, JEEZ, POP...
GLMP

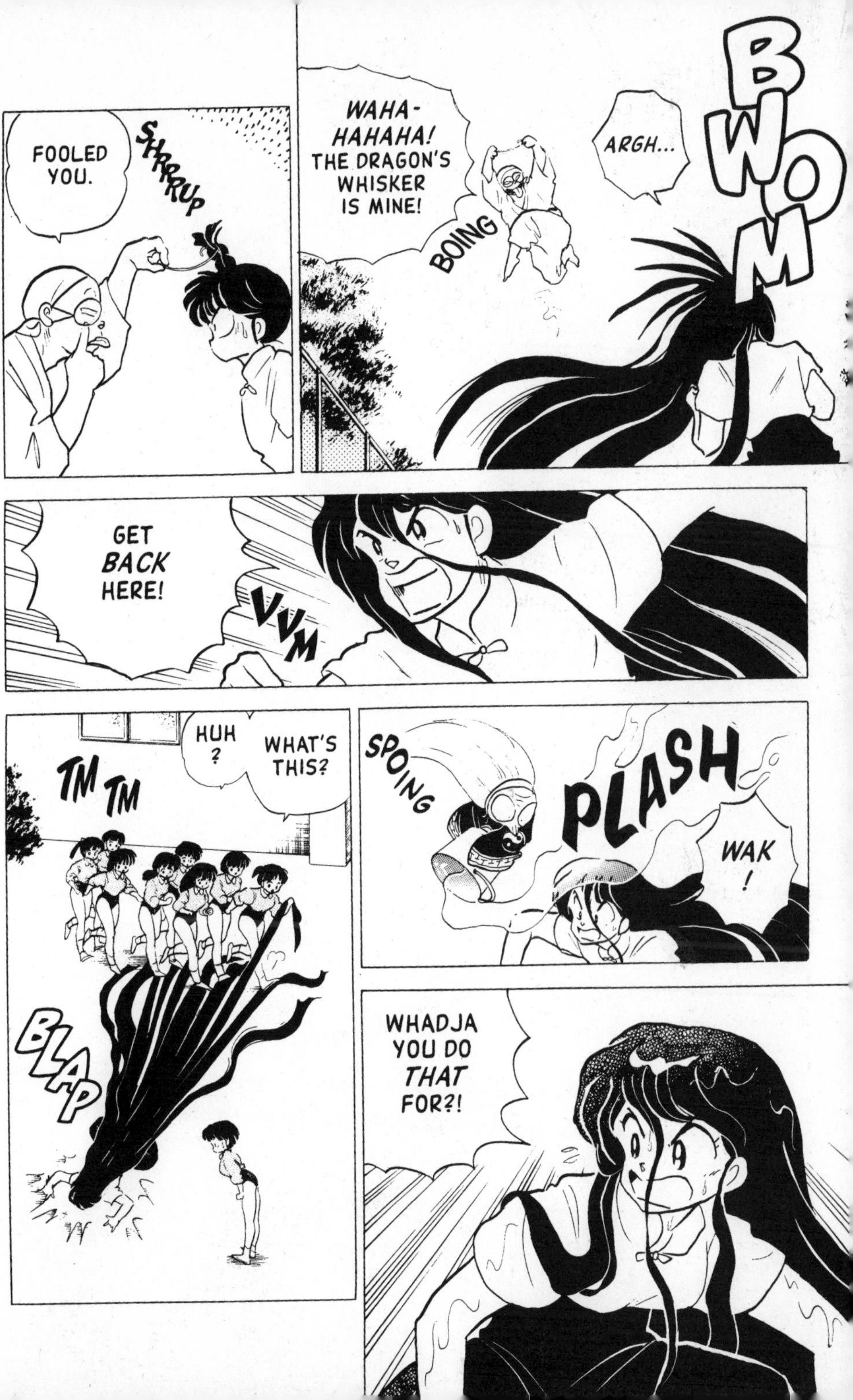
FOOLED YOU.
SHRRRUP
WAHA-HAHAHA! THE DRAGON'S WHISKER IS MINE!
BOING
ARGH...
BWOMM
GET BACK HERE!
VVM
HUH?
WHAT'S THIS?
TM TM
BLAP
SPOING
PLASH
WAK!
WHADJA YOU DO THAT FOR?!

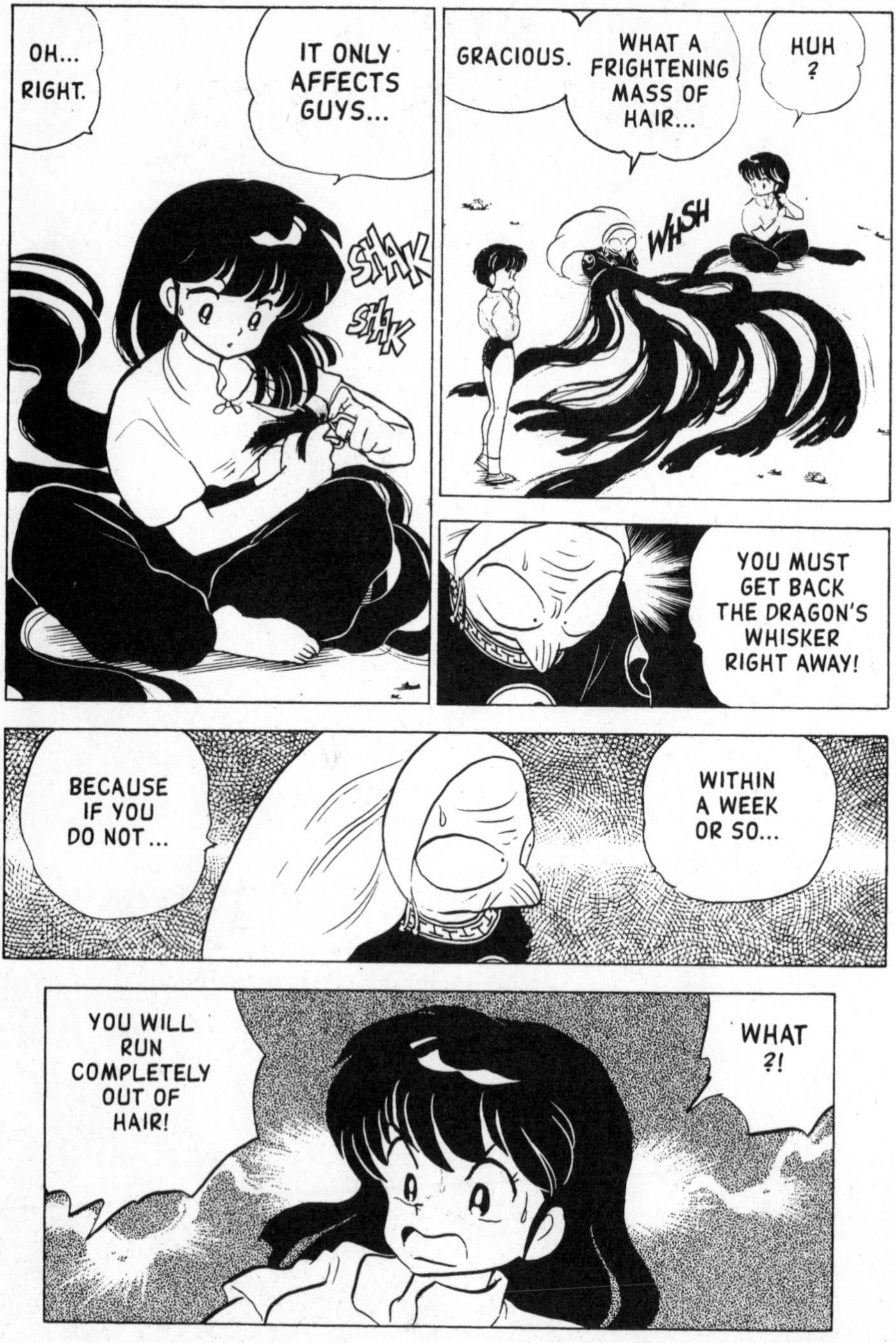
OH... RIGHT.
IT ONLY AFFECTS GUYS...
SHAK
SHAK
GRACIOUS.
WHAT A FRIGHTENING MASS OF HAIR...
HUH ?
WHSH
YOU MUST GET BACK THE DRAGON'S WHISKER RIGHT AWAY!
BECAUSE IF YOU DO NOT...
WITHIN A WEEK OR SO...
YOU WILL RUN COMPLETELY OUT OF HAIR!
WHAT ?!

PART 4
HAIR RAISING

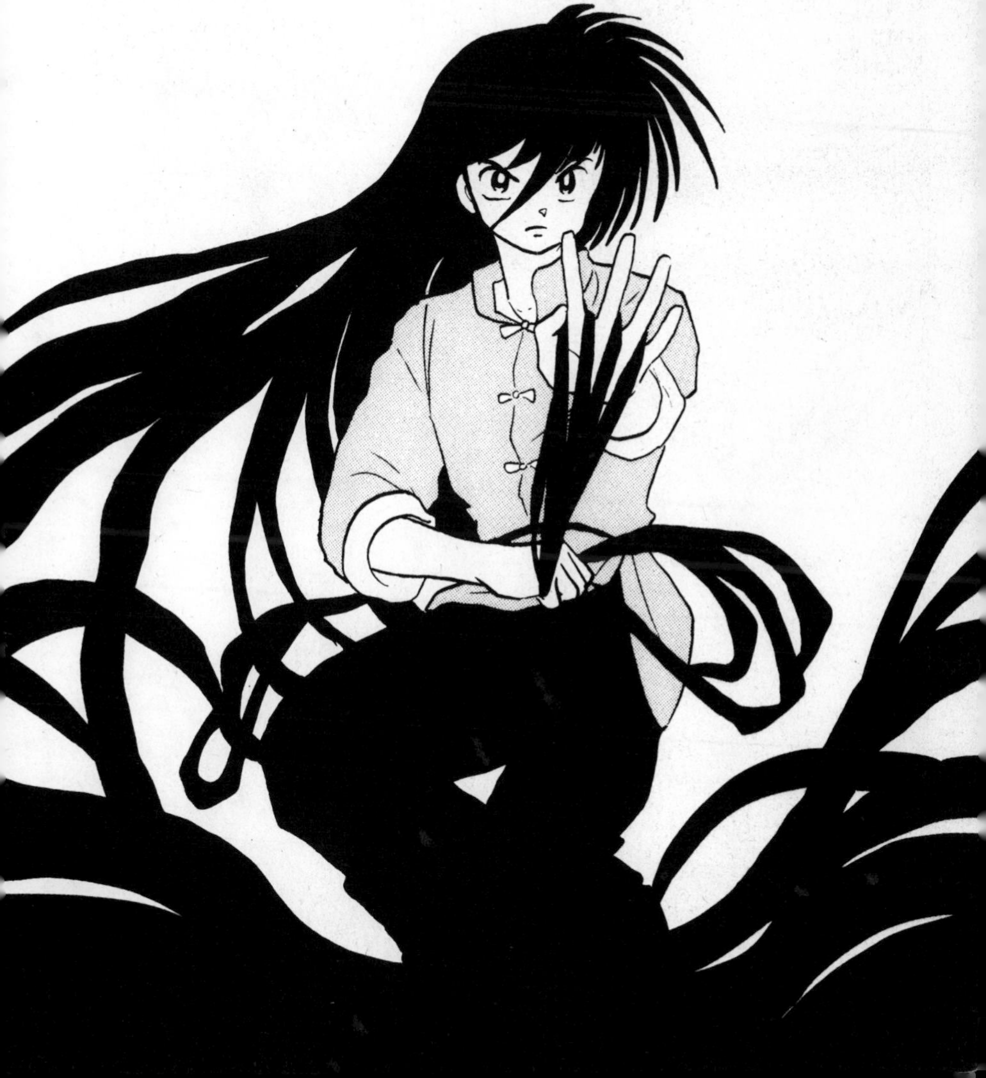

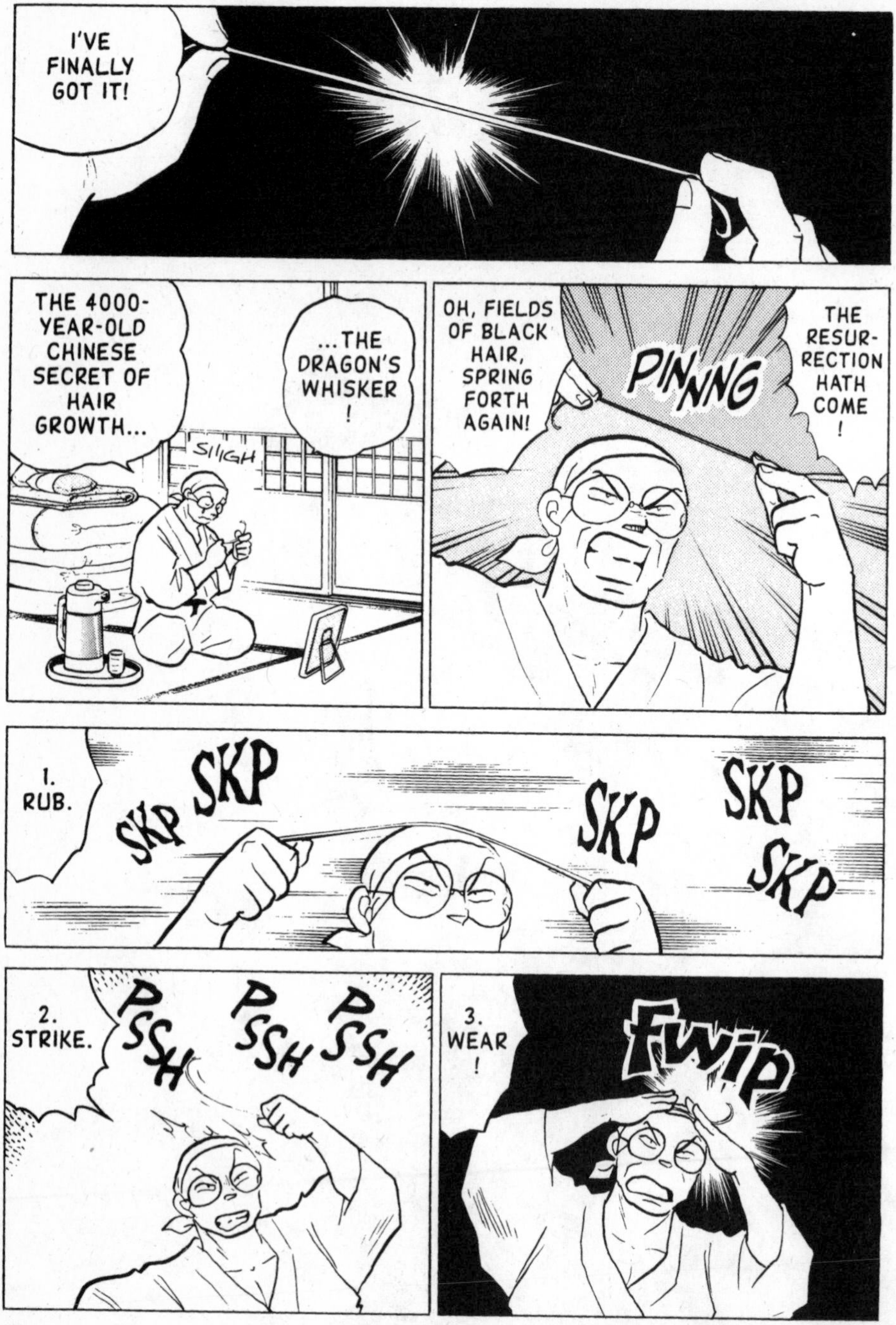
I'VE FINALLY GOT IT!
THE 4000-YEAR-OLD CHINESE SECRET OF HAIR GROWTH...
SIIIGH
...THE DRAGON'S WHISKER!
OH, FIELDS OF BLACK HAIR, SPRING FORTH AGAIN!
PINNNG
THE RESURRECTION HATH COME!
1. RUB.
SKP SKP
SKP SKP
SKP SKP
2. STRIKE.
PSSH PSSH PSSH
3. WEAR!
fwip

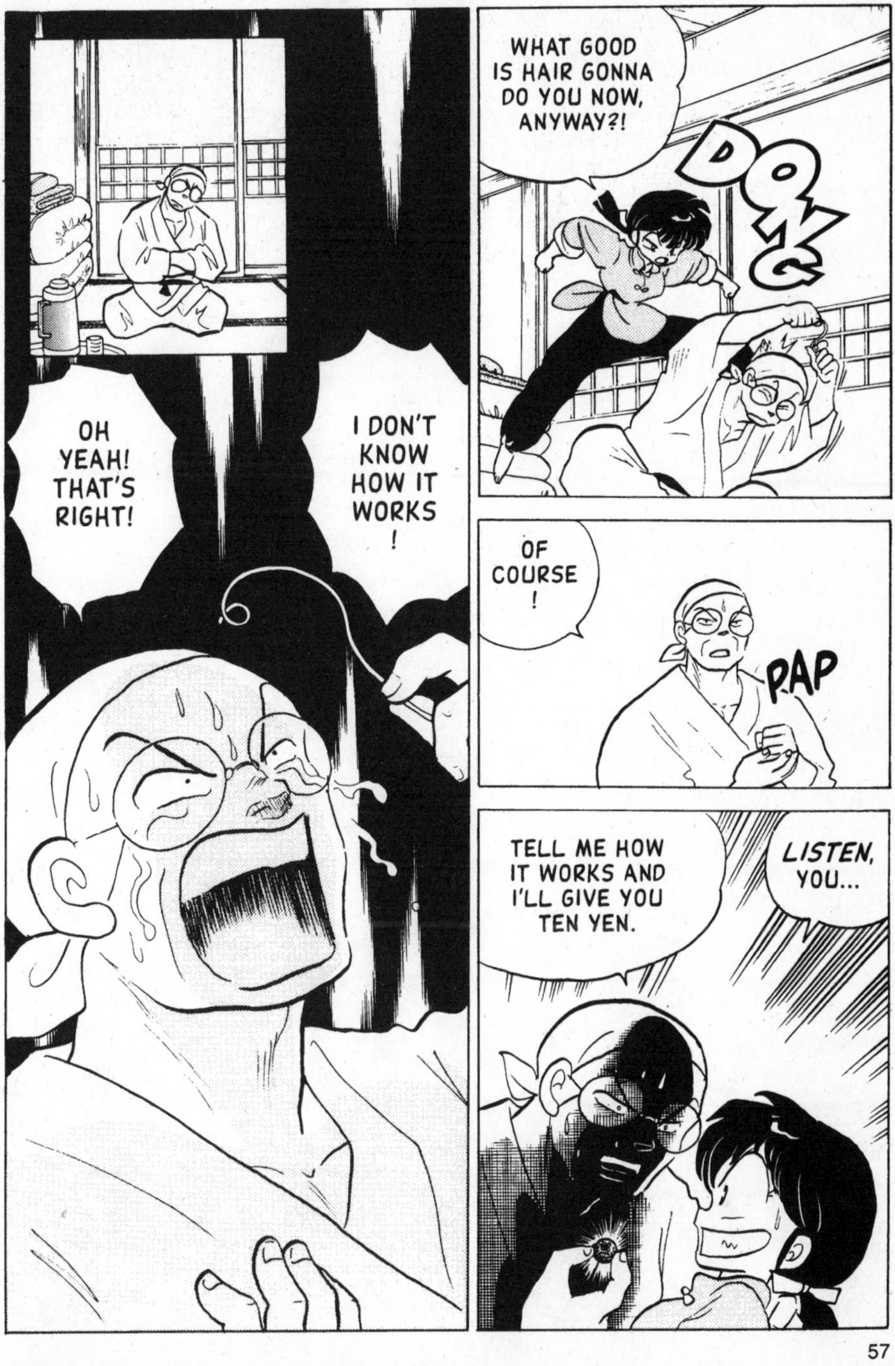
OH YEAH! THAT'S RIGHT!
I DON'T KNOW HOW IT WORKS!
WHAT GOOD IS HAIR GONNA DO YOU NOW, ANYWAY?!
DONG
OF COURSE!
PAP
TELL ME HOW IT WORKS AND I'LL GIVE YOU TEN YEN.
LISTEN, YOU...

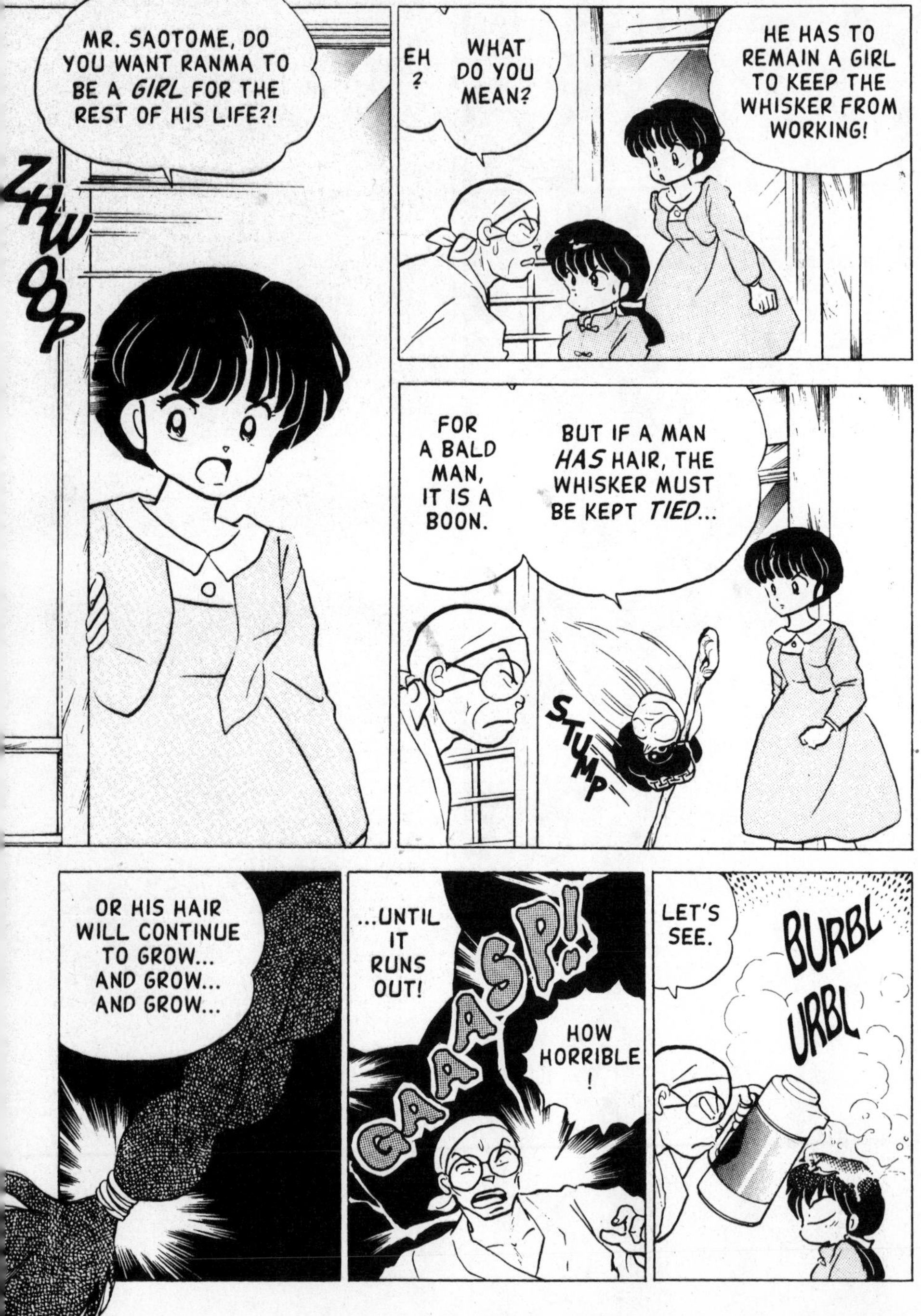
MR. SAOTOME, DO YOU WANT RANMA TO BE A *GIRL* FOR THE REST OF HIS LIFE?!
ZHWOOP
EH?
WHAT DO YOU MEAN?
HE HAS TO REMAIN A GIRL TO KEEP THE WHISKER FROM WORKING!
FOR A BALD MAN, IT IS A BOON.
BUT IF A MAN *HAS* HAIR, THE WHISKER MUST BE KEPT *TIED*...
STUMP
OR HIS HAIR WILL CONTINUE TO GROW... AND GROW... AND GROW...
...UNTIL IT RUNS OUT!
GAAASP!
HOW HORRIBLE!
LET'S SEE.
BURBL
URBL

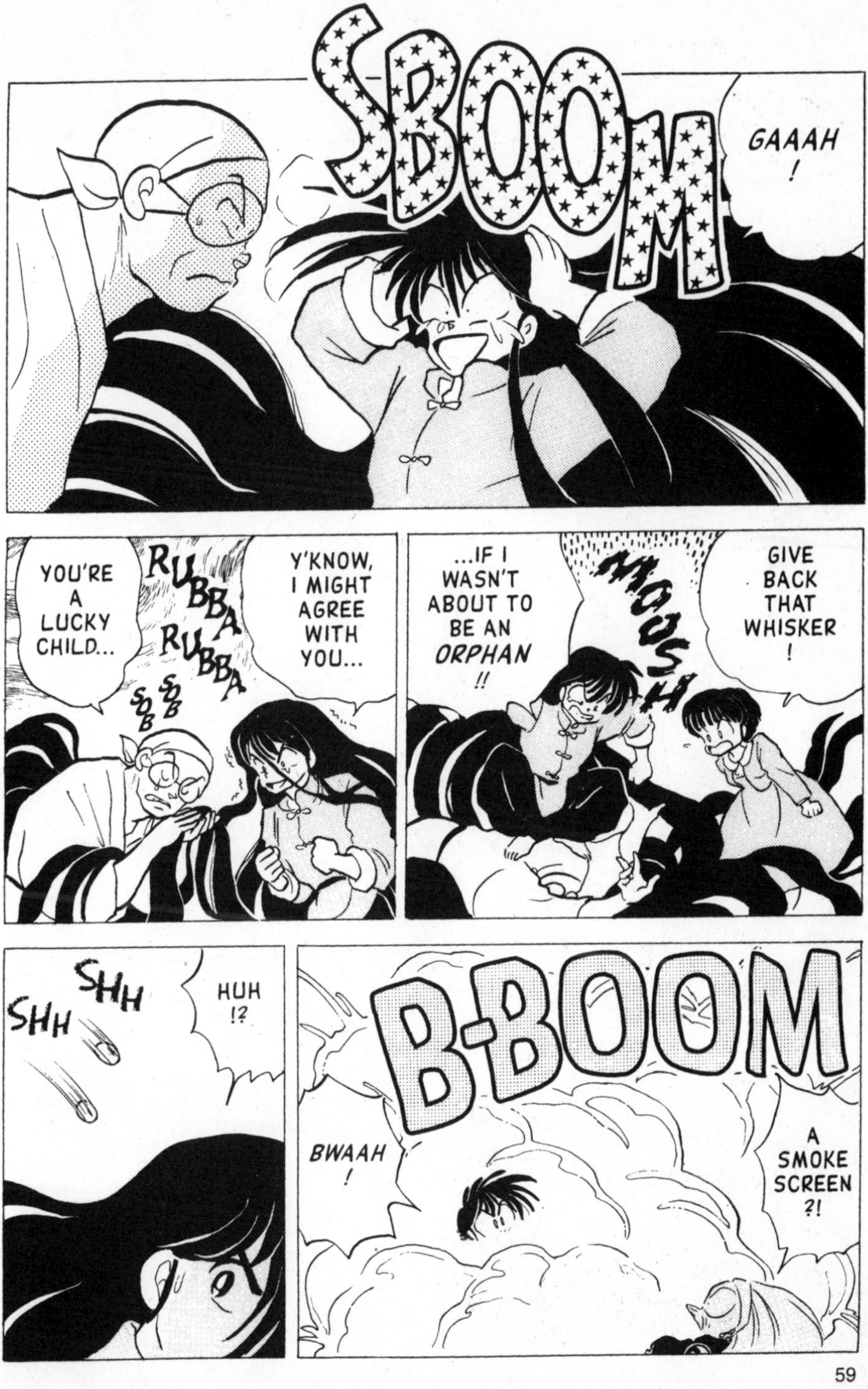
SBOOM
GAAAH!
YOU'RE A LUCKY CHILD...
RUBBA RUBBA
SOB SOB
Y'KNOW, I MIGHT AGREE WITH YOU...
...IF I WASN'T ABOUT TO BE AN *ORPHAN*!!
MOOSH
GIVE BACK THAT WHISKER!
SHH
SHH
HUH!?
B-BOOM
BWAAH!
A SMOKE SCREEN?!

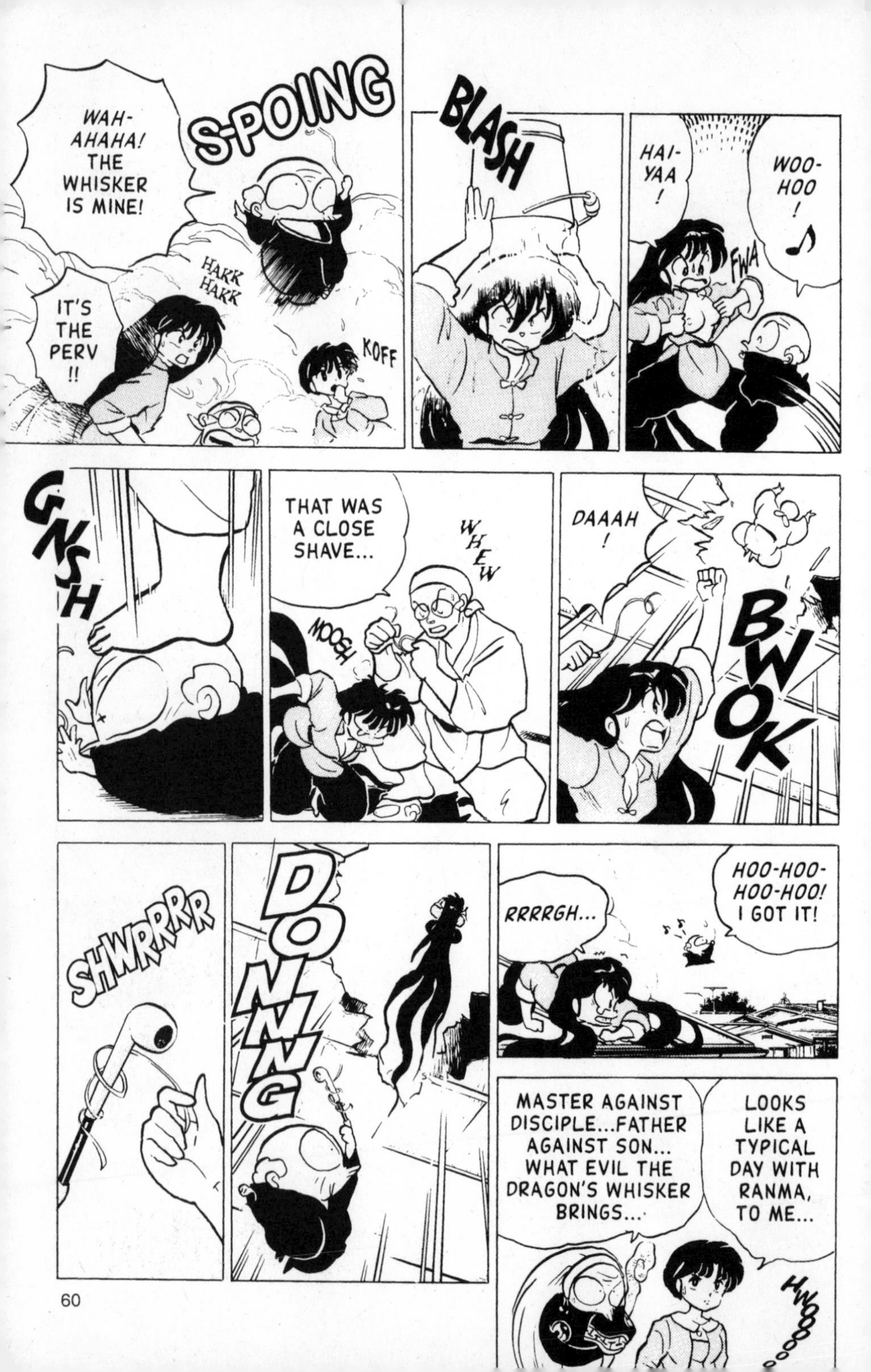
WAH-AHAHA! THE WHISKER IS MINE!
S-POING
HAKK HAKK
IT'S THE PERV !!
KOFF
BLASH
HAI-YAA !
WOO-HOO ! ♪
FWA
GNSH
THAT WAS A CLOSE SHAVE...
WHEW
HOOSH
DAAAH !
BWOK
SHWRRRR
DONNNG
RRRRGH...
HOO-HOO-HOO-HOO! I GOT IT!
MASTER AGAINST DISCIPLE...FATHER AGAINST SON... WHAT EVIL THE DRAGON'S WHISKER BRINGS...
LOOKS LIKE A TYPICAL DAY WITH RANMA, TO ME...
HWOOOOO

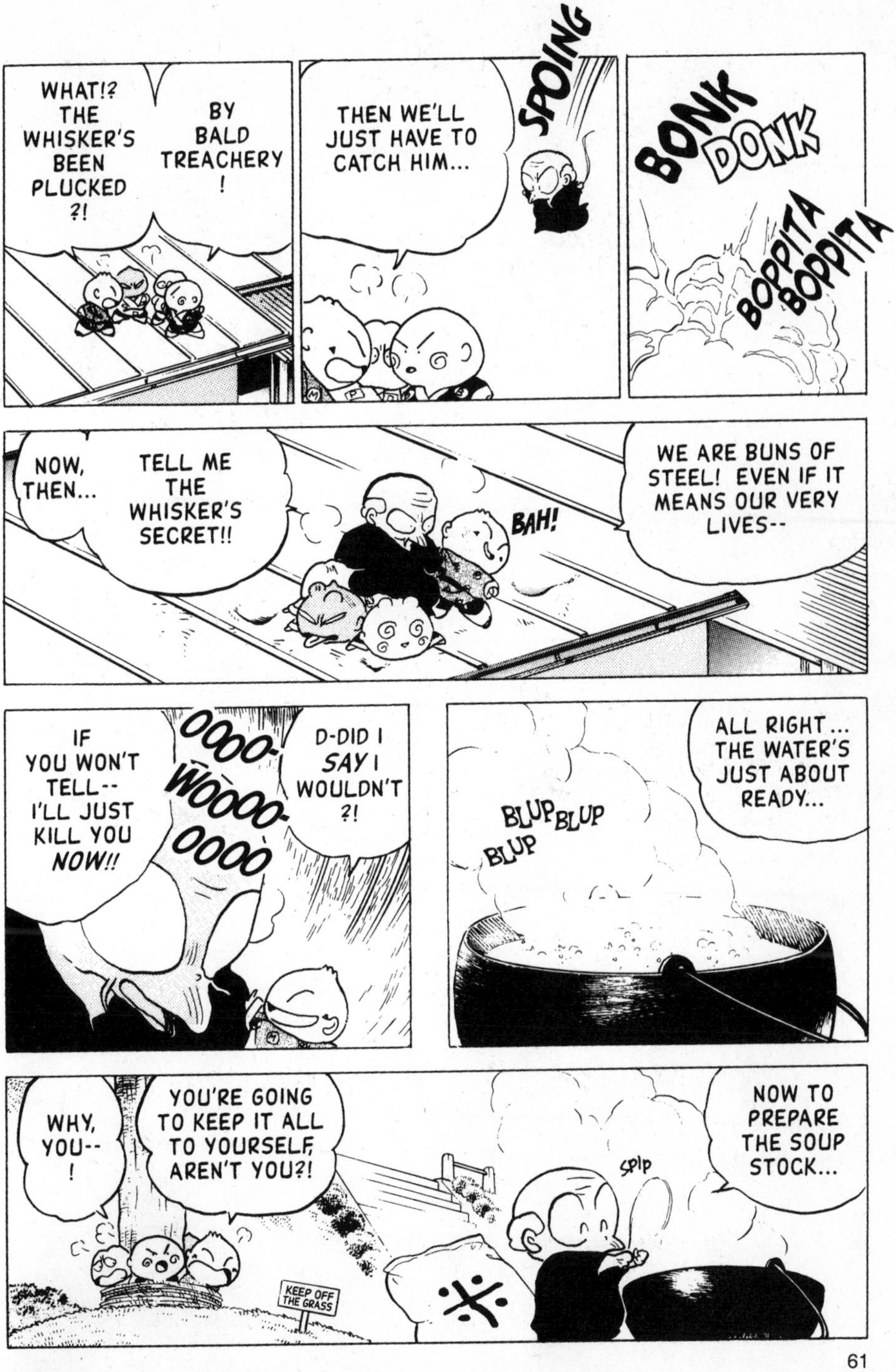
WHAT!? THE WHISKER'S BEEN PLUCKED ?!
BY BALD TREACHERY !
THEN WE'LL JUST HAVE TO CATCH HIM...
SPOING
BONK
DONK
BOPPITA BOPPITA
NOW, THEN...
TELL ME THE WHISKER'S SECRET!!
BAH!
WE ARE BUNS OF STEEL! EVEN IF IT MEANS OUR VERY LIVES--
IF YOU WON'T TELL-- I'LL JUST KILL YOU NOW!!
OOOO-WOOOO-OOOO
D-DID I SAY I WOULDN'T ?!
BLUP BLUP
BLUP
ALL RIGHT... THE WATER'S JUST ABOUT READY...
WHY, YOU-- !
YOU'RE GOING TO KEEP IT ALL TO YOURSELF, AREN'T YOU?!
KEEP OFF THE GRASS
SPIP
NOW TO PREPARE THE SOUP STOCK...

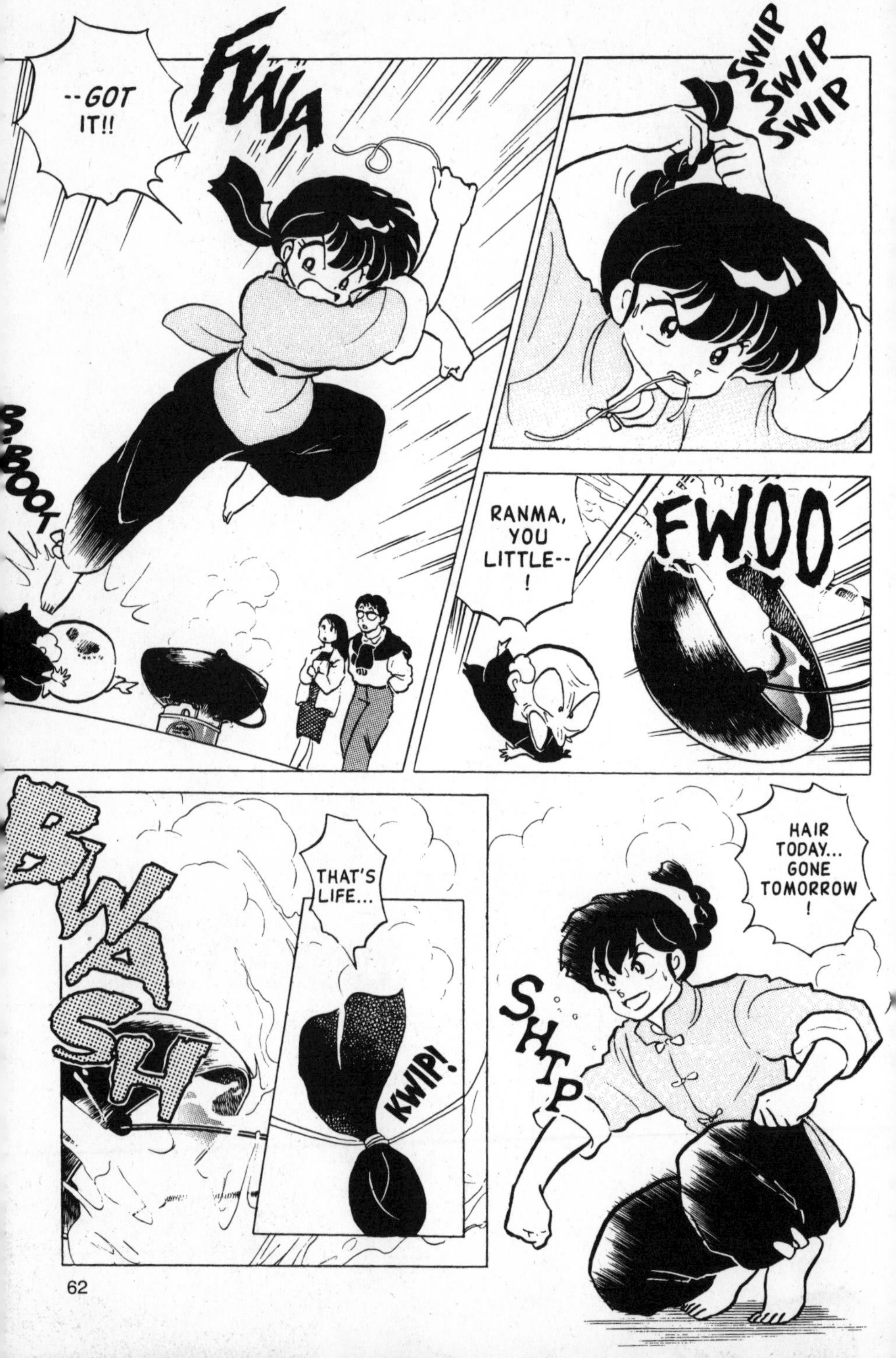

--GOT IT!!
FWA
B-BOOT
SWIP SWIP SWIP
RANMA, YOU LITTLE--!
FWOO
BWASH
THAT'S LIFE...
KWIP!
HAIR TODAY... GONE TOMORROW!
SHTP

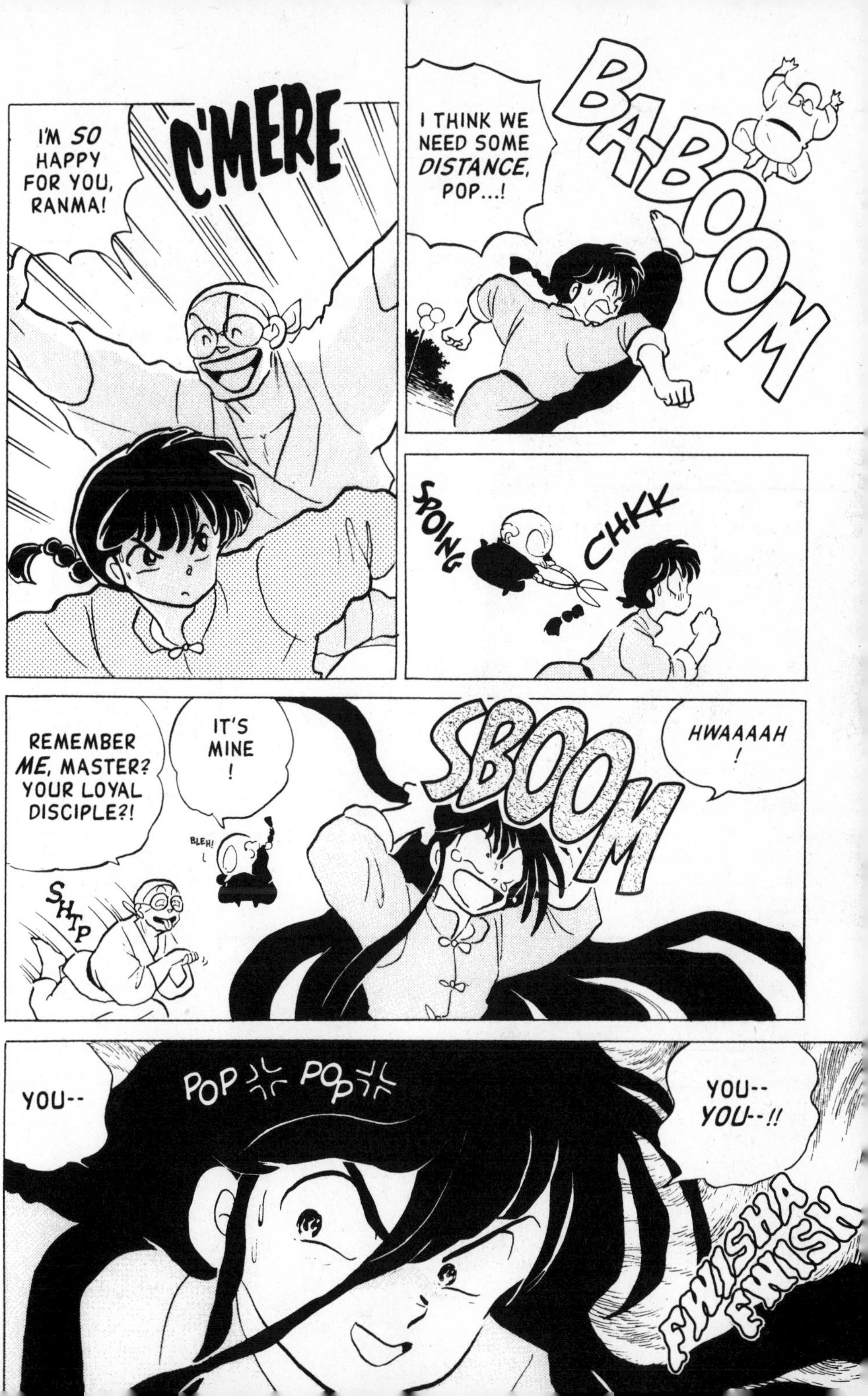
I'M SO HAPPY FOR YOU, RANMA!
C'MERE
I THINK WE NEED SOME DISTANCE, POP...!
BA-BOOM
SPOING
CHKK
REMEMBER ME, MASTER? YOUR LOYAL DISCIPLE?!
IT'S MINE!
BLEH!
SHTP
SBOOM
HWAAAAH!
YOU--
POP POP
YOU-- YOU--!!
FINISHA FINISH

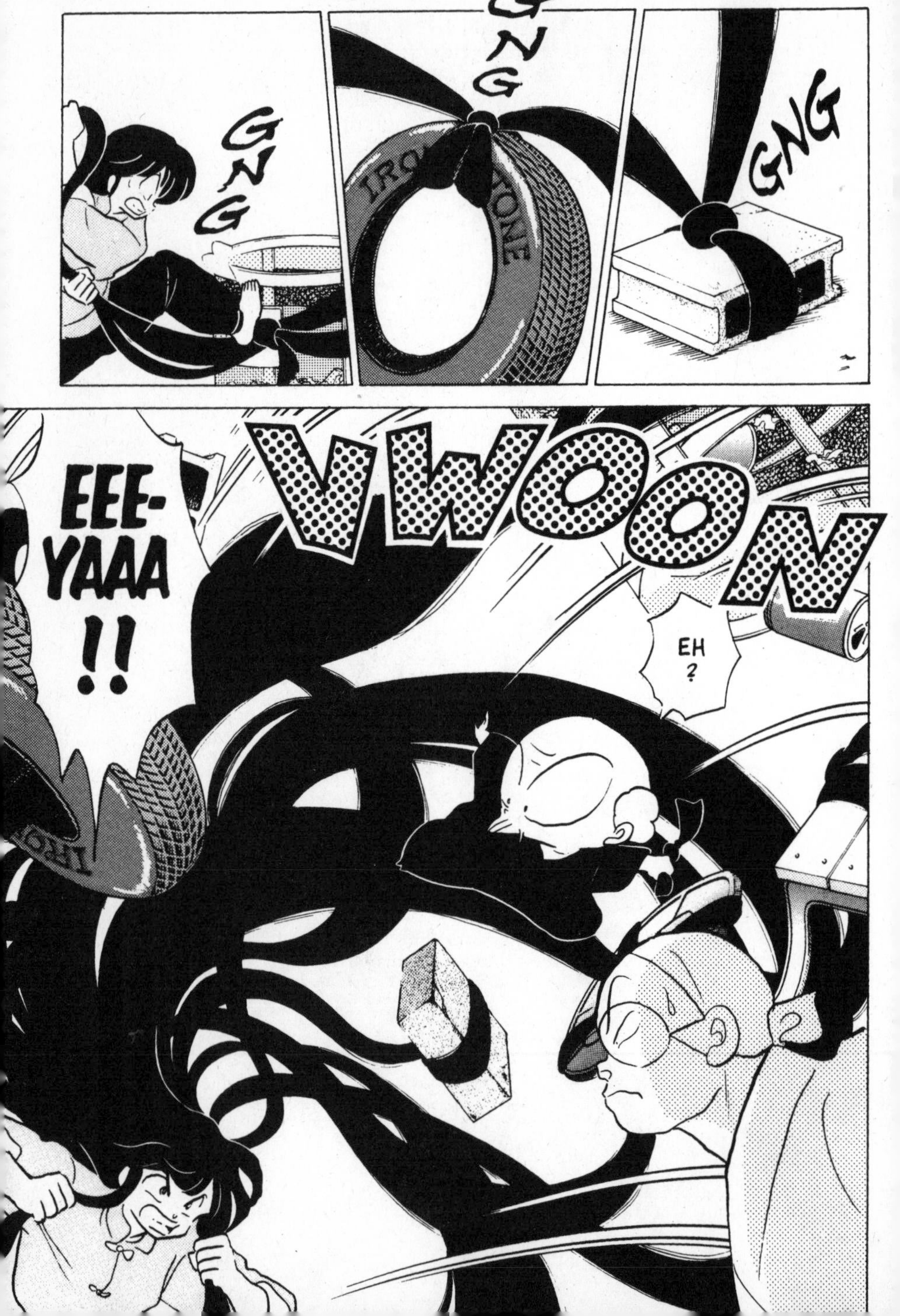
GNG
GNG
GNG
EEE-YAAA!!
VWOOON
EH?

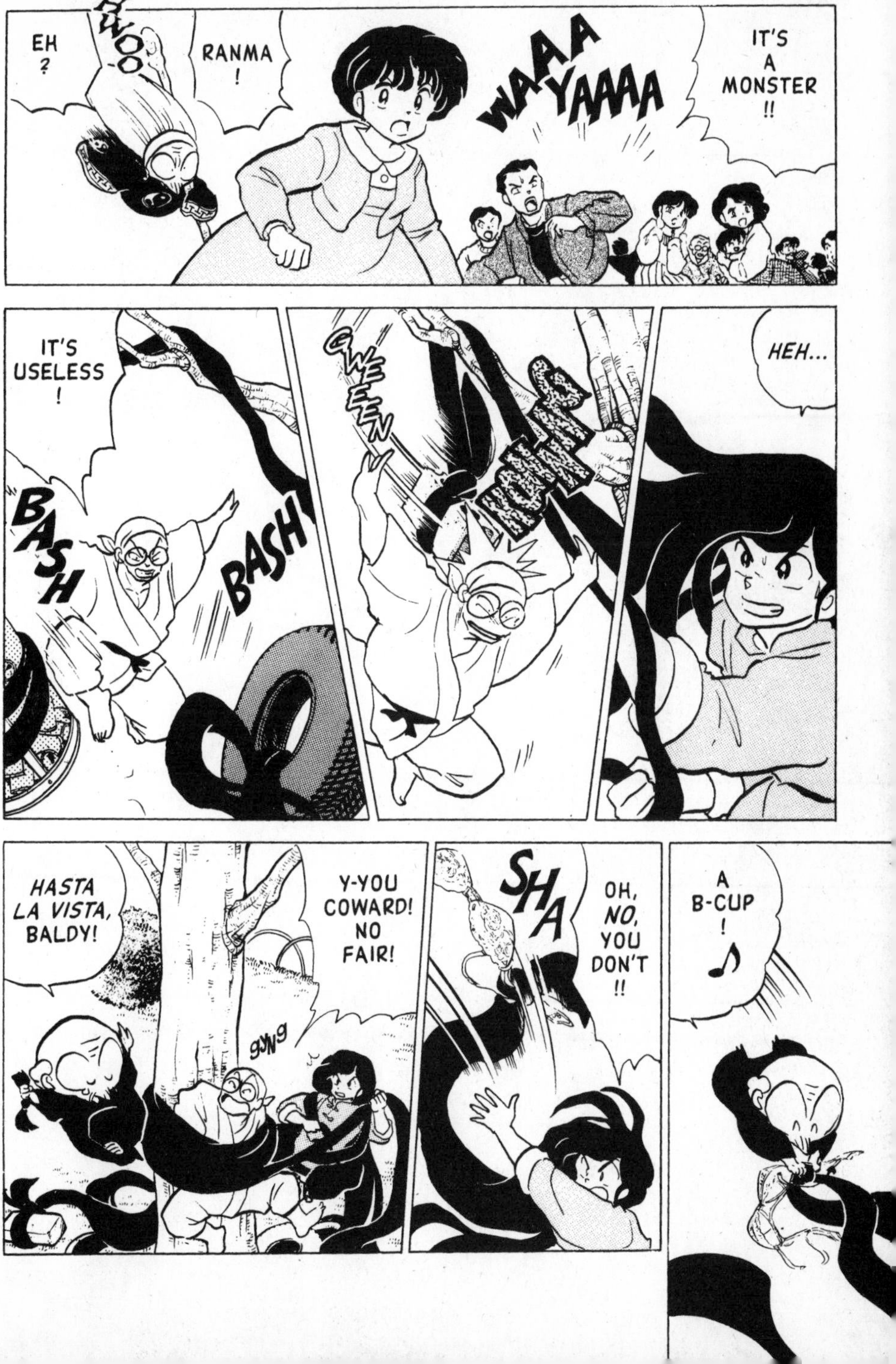
EH ?
SHWOO
RANMA !
WAAA YAAAA
IT'S A MONSTER !!
IT'S USELESS !
BASH
BASH
GWEEEN
HEH...
HASTA LA VISTA, BALDY!
Y-YOU COWARD! NO FAIR!
SHA
OH, NO, YOU DON'T !!
A B-CUP ! ♪

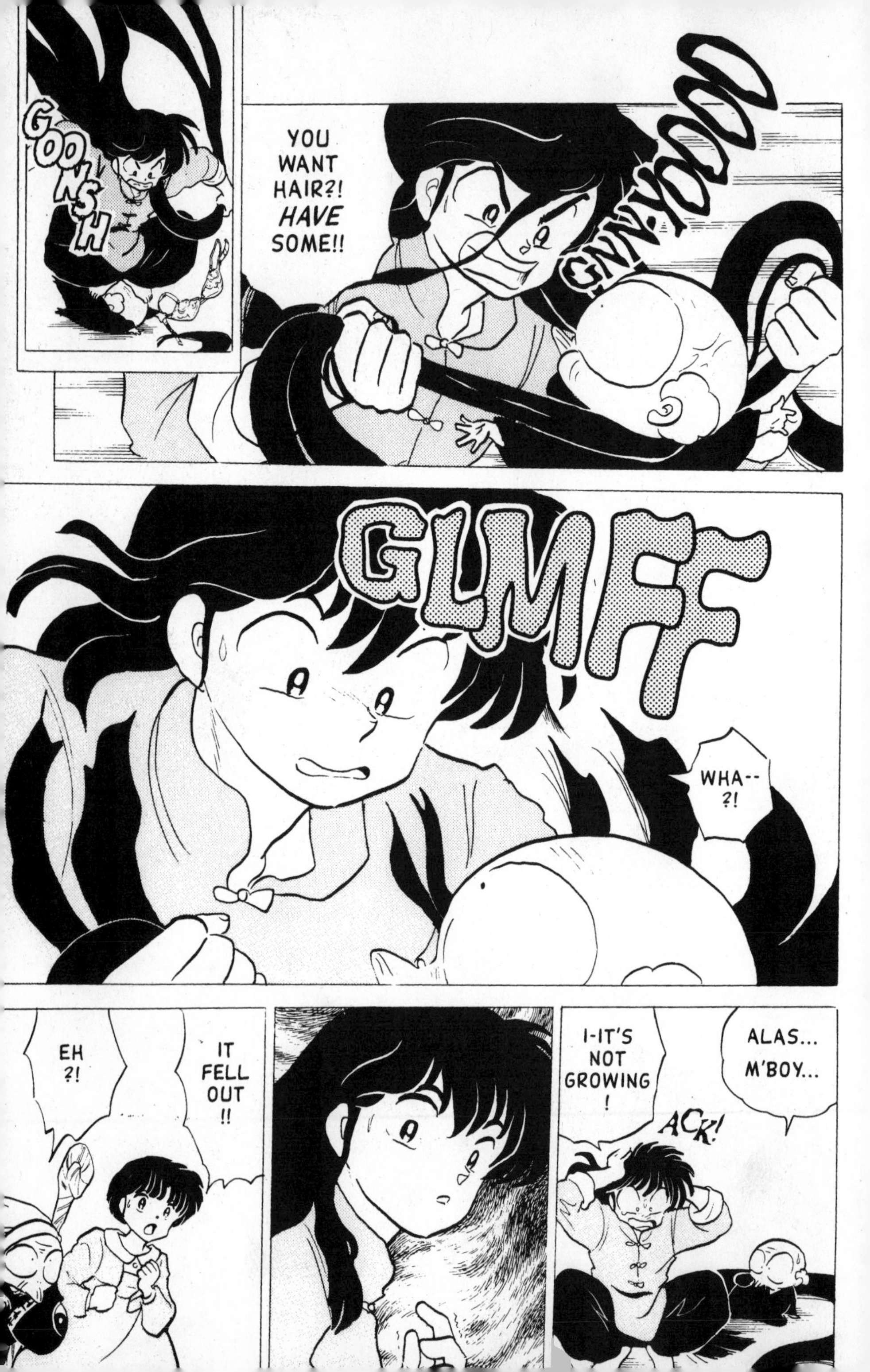
GOOONSH
YOU WANT HAIR?! HAVE SOME!!
GNNYOOOM
GLMFF
WHA--?!
EH?!
IT FELL OUT!!
I-IT'S NOT GROWING!
ACK!
ALAS... M'BOY...

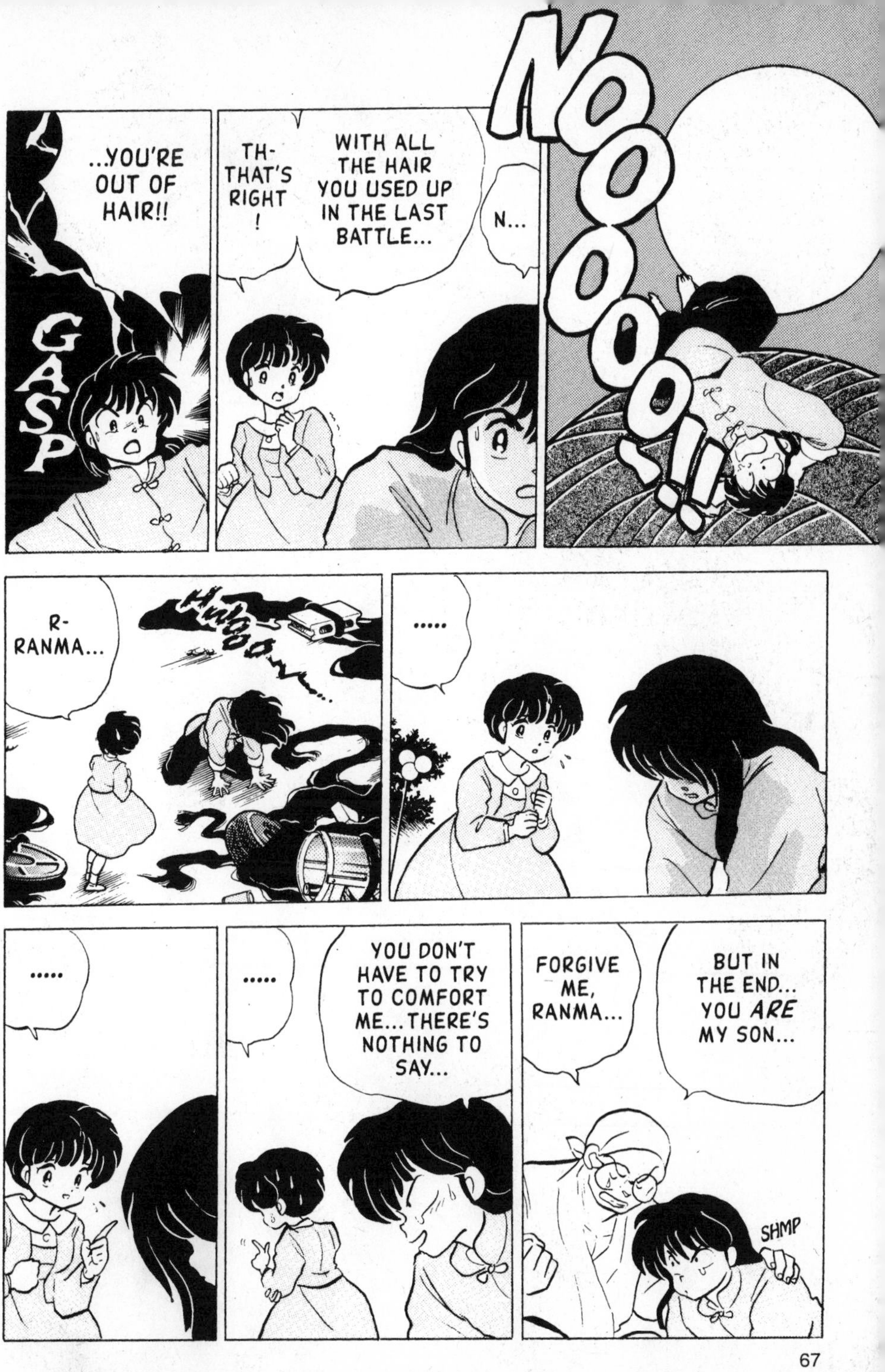

...YOU'RE OUT OF HAIR!!
GASP
TH- THAT'S RIGHT !
WITH ALL THE HAIR YOU USED UP IN THE LAST BATTLE...
N...
NOOOOO!!
R- RANMA...
.....
.....
.....
YOU DON'T HAVE TO TRY TO COMFORT ME...THERE'S NOTHING TO SAY...
FORGIVE ME, RANMA...
BUT IN THE END... YOU *ARE* MY SON...
SHMP

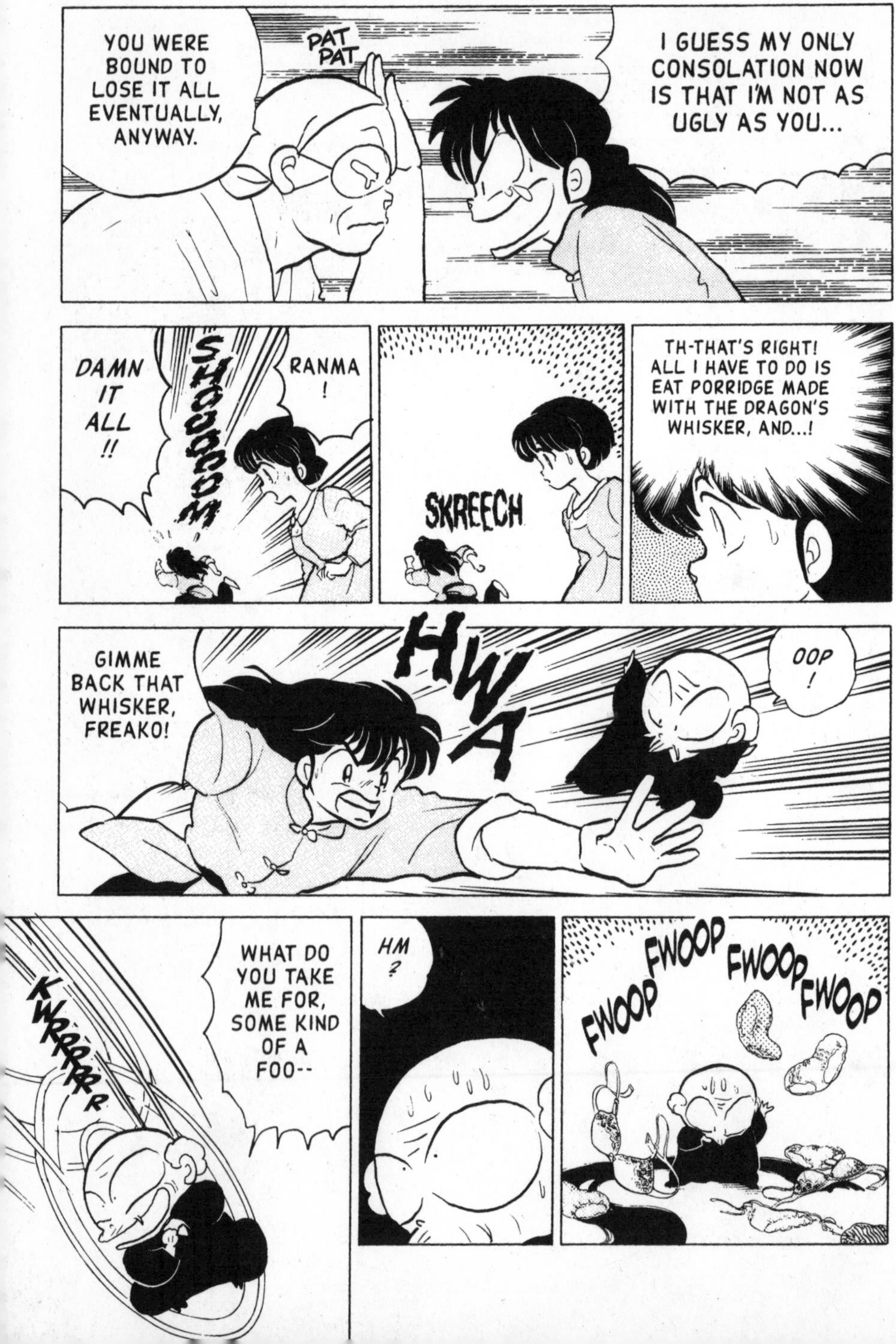
YOU WERE BOUND TO LOSE IT ALL EVENTUALLY, ANYWAY.
PAT PAT
I GUESS MY ONLY CONSOLATION NOW IS THAT I'M NOT AS UGLY AS YOU...
DAMN IT ALL !!
SHOOOOOOM
RANMA !
SKREECH
TH-THAT'S RIGHT! ALL I HAVE TO DO IS EAT PORRIDGE MADE WITH THE DRAGON'S WHISKER, AND...!
GIMME BACK THAT WHISKER, FREAKO!
HWA
OOP !
KWRRRRRR
WHAT DO YOU TAKE ME FOR, SOME KIND OF A FOO--
HM ?
FWOOP FWOOP FWOOP FWOOP

I LOST IT.

FFFFF FUMP

BOING

GOOD. IT'S NOT COMING OUT.

TUG TUG

IF YOU WERE TRULY OUT OF HAIR, THE REST WOULD HAVE PULLED OUT EASILY. THAT MEANS...

...THE EFFECT OF THE DRAGON'S WHISKER HAS WORN OFF!

REALLY ?!

HERE I'M TELLING HIM GREAT NEWS, AND HE ISN'T EVEN PAYING ATTENTION.

HE'S PASSED OUT.

GAAH...

FHOOP FHOOP

WHERE'S MY DRAGON'S WHISKER ?!

MEAN-WHILE...

CAT CAFÉ

DRAGON-WHISKER PORRIDGE ALL READY!

WAH HOO! LET'S DIG IN!

KOMP

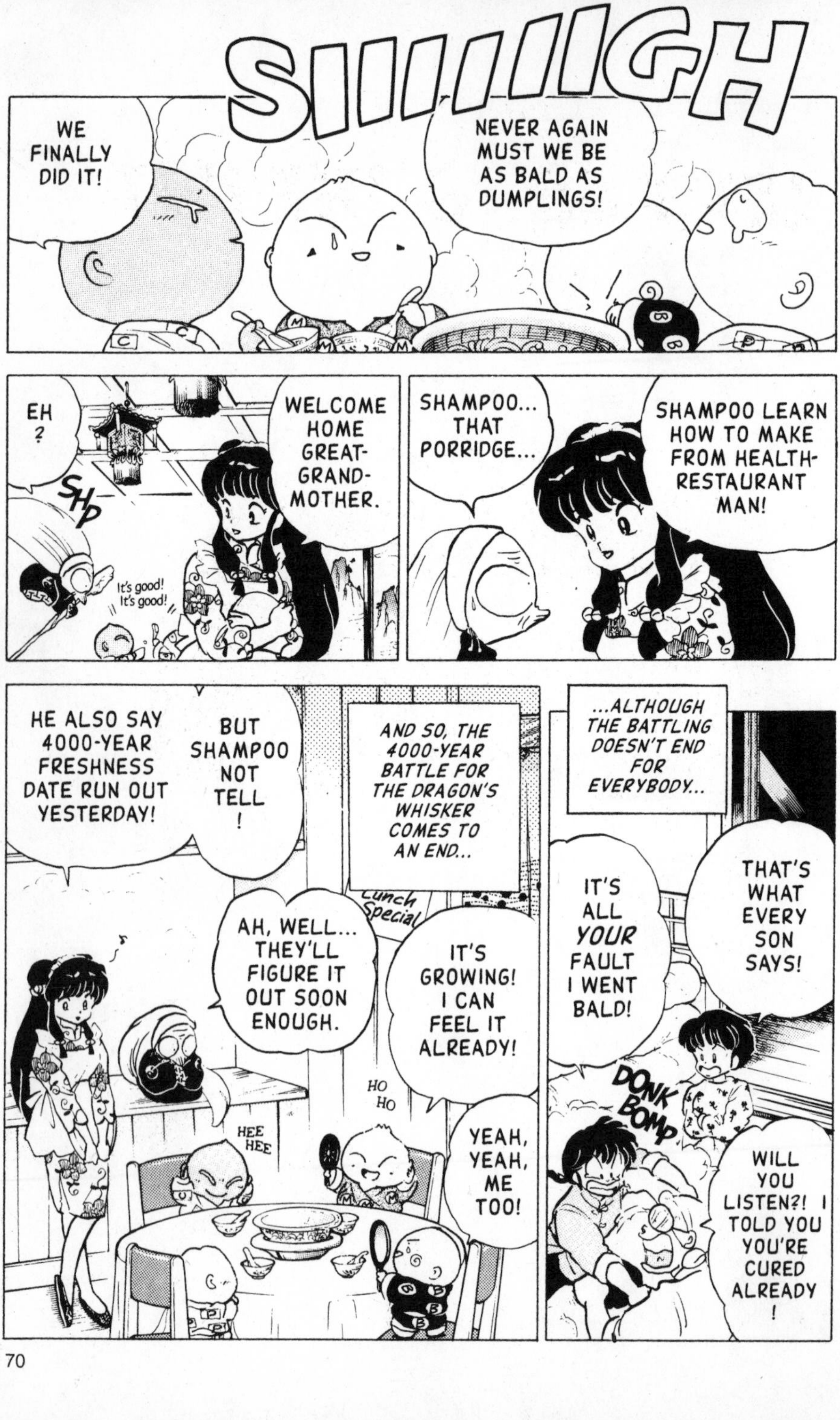
SIIIIIIGH
WE FINALLY DID IT!
NEVER AGAIN MUST WE BE AS BALD AS DUMPLINGS!
EH?
SHP
It's good! It's good!
WELCOME HOME GREAT-GRANDMOTHER.
SHAMPOO... THAT PORRIDGE...
SHAMPOO LEARN HOW TO MAKE FROM HEALTH-RESTAURANT MAN!
HE ALSO SAY 4000-YEAR FRESHNESS DATE RUN OUT YESTERDAY!
BUT SHAMPOO NOT TELL!
AH, WELL... THEY'LL FIGURE IT OUT SOON ENOUGH.
HEE HEE
HO HO
AND SO, THE 4000-YEAR BATTLE FOR THE DRAGON'S WHISKER COMES TO AN END...
Lunch Special
IT'S GROWING! I CAN FEEL IT ALREADY!
YEAH, YEAH, ME TOO!
...ALTHOUGH THE BATTLING DOESN'T END FOR EVERYBODY...
IT'S ALL YOUR FAULT I WENT BALD!
THAT'S WHAT EVERY SON SAYS!
DONK BOMP
WILL YOU LISTEN?! I TOLD YOU YOU'RE CURED ALREADY!

PART 5
LET'S GO TO THE HOT

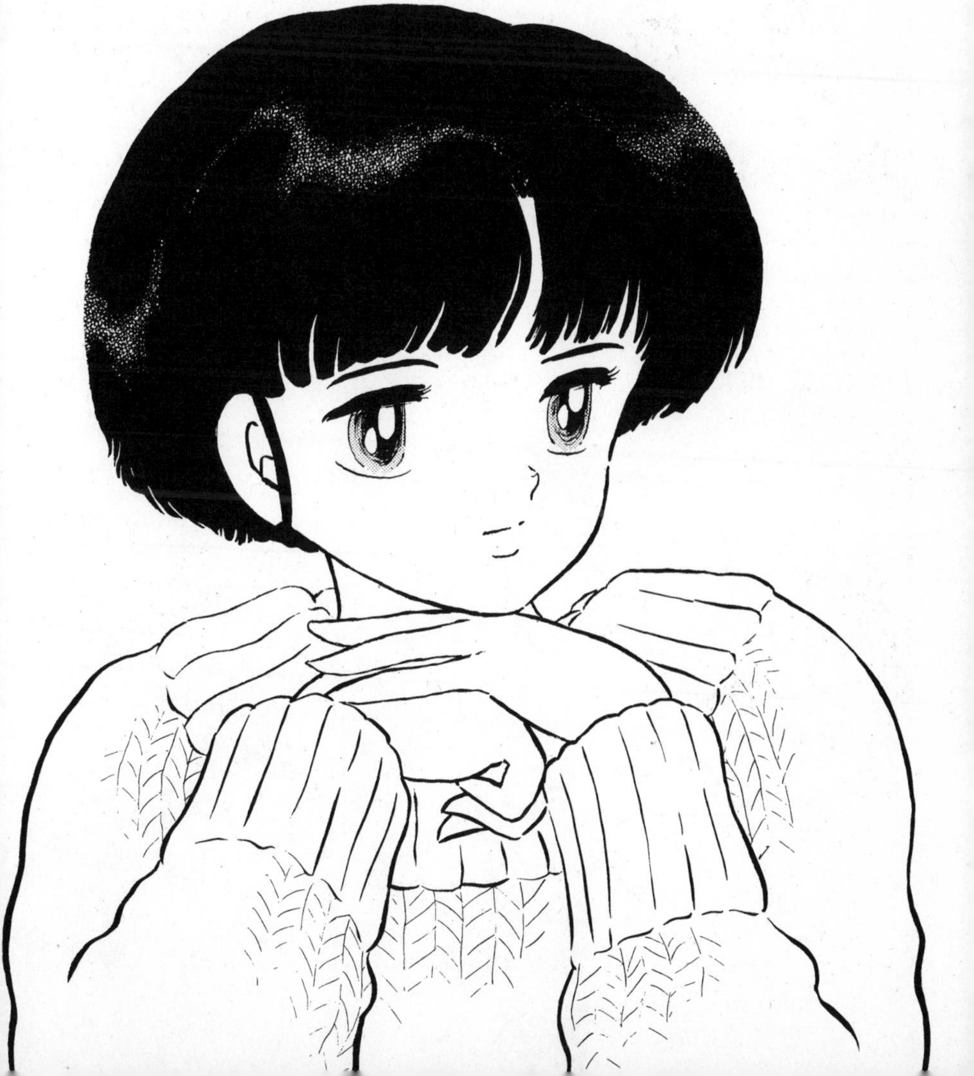

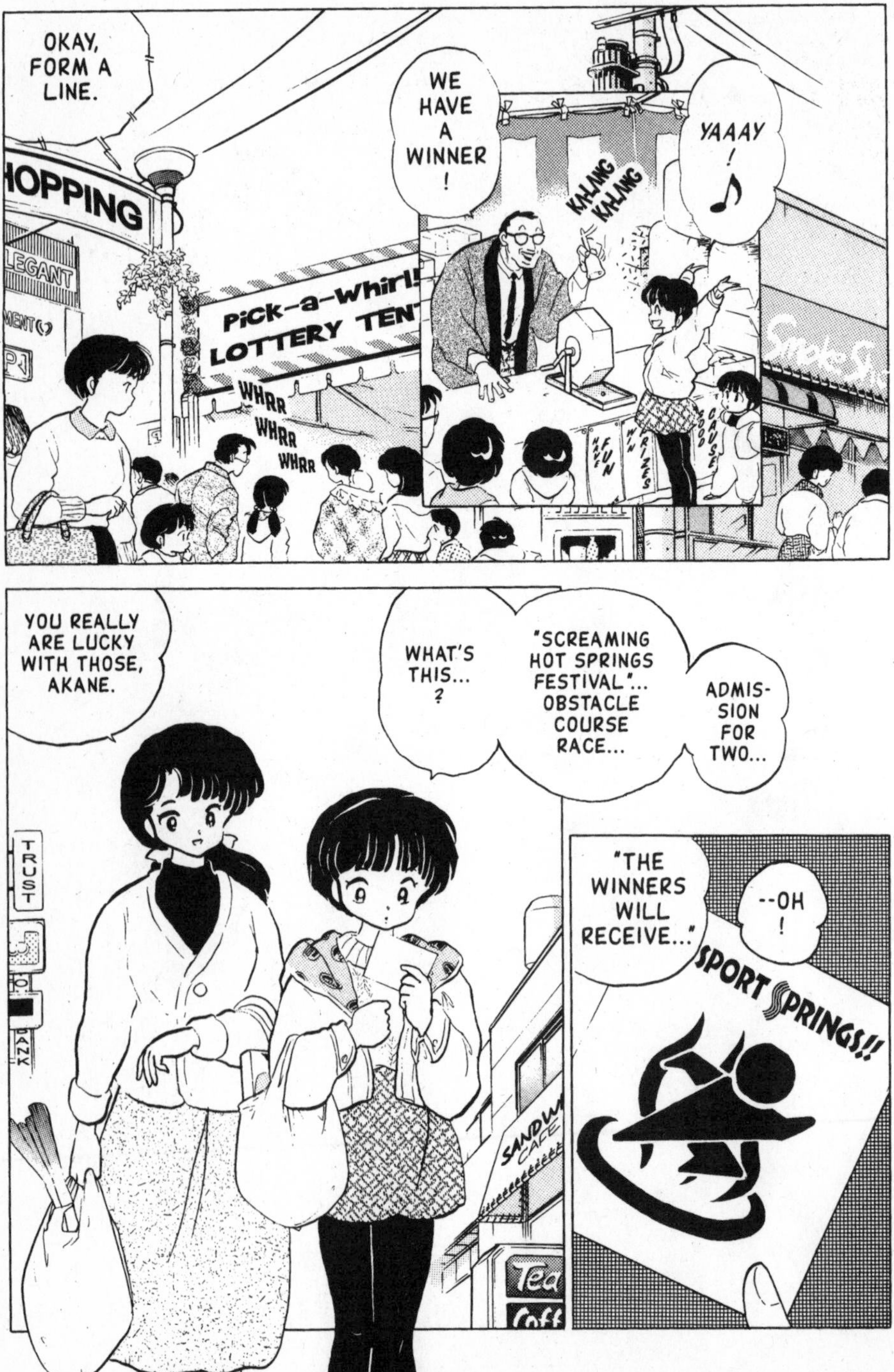
OKAY, FORM A LINE.
HOPPING
ELEGANT
Pick-a-Whirl! LOTTERY TENT
WHRR WHRR WHRR
WE HAVE A WINNER!
KALANG KALANG
YAAAY! ♪
HAVE FUN
WIN PRIZES
GOOD CAUSE
YOU REALLY ARE LUCKY WITH THOSE, AKANE.
WHAT'S THIS...?
"SCREAMING HOT SPRINGS FESTIVAL"... OBSTACLE COURSE RACE...
ADMIS-SION FOR TWO...
TRUST
BANK
"THE WINNERS WILL RECEIVE..."
--OH!
SPORT SPRINGS!!

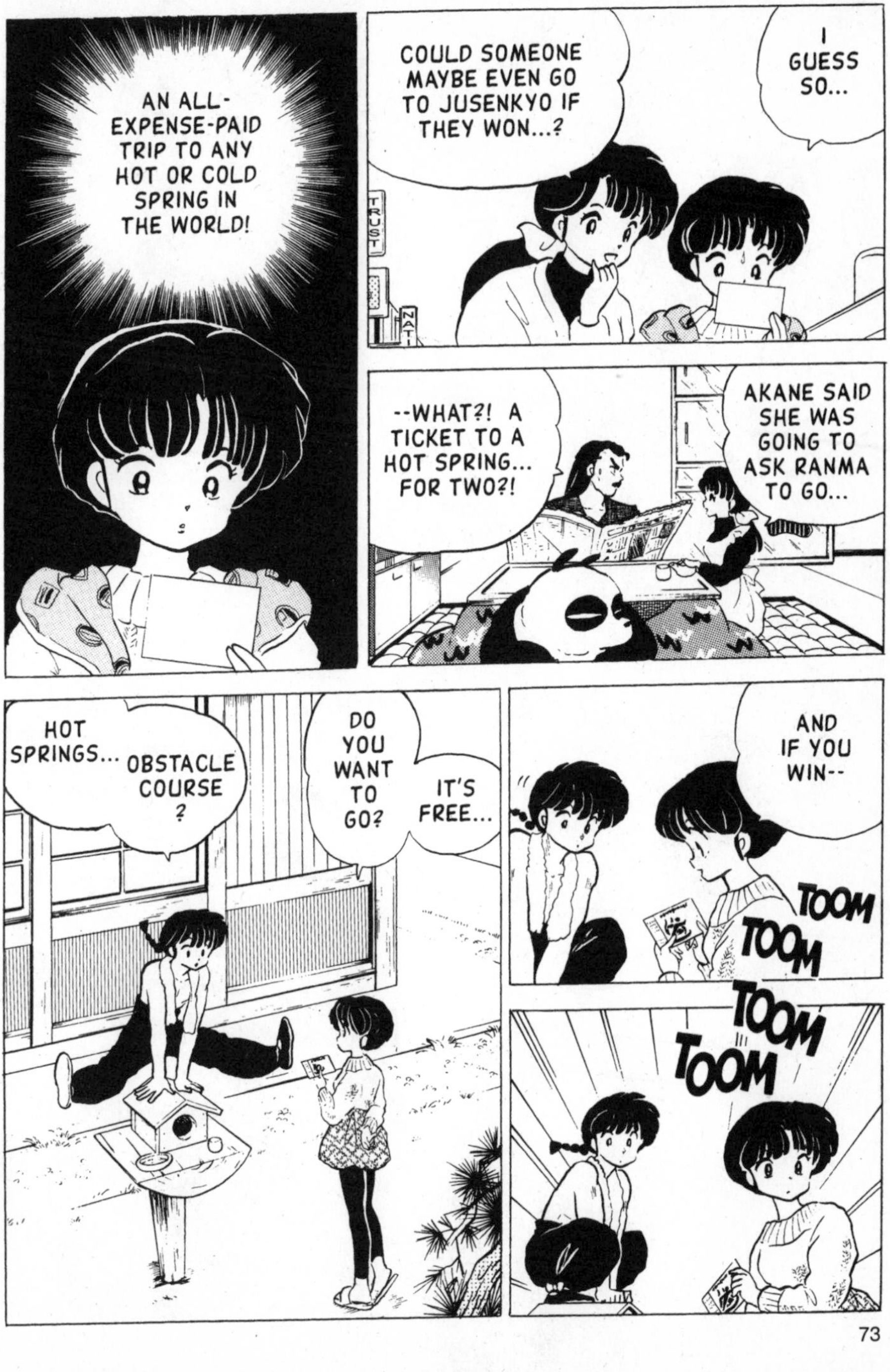
AN ALL-EXPENSE-PAID TRIP TO ANY HOT OR COLD SPRING IN THE WORLD!
COULD SOMEONE MAYBE EVEN GO TO JUSENKYO IF THEY WON...?
I GUESS SO...
TRUST
NATI
--WHAT?! A TICKET TO A HOT SPRING... FOR TWO?!
AKANE SAID SHE WAS GOING TO ASK RANMA TO GO...
HOT SPRINGS... OBSTACLE COURSE?
DO YOU WANT TO GO?
IT'S FREE...
AND IF YOU WIN--
TOOM
TOOM
TOOM
TOOM

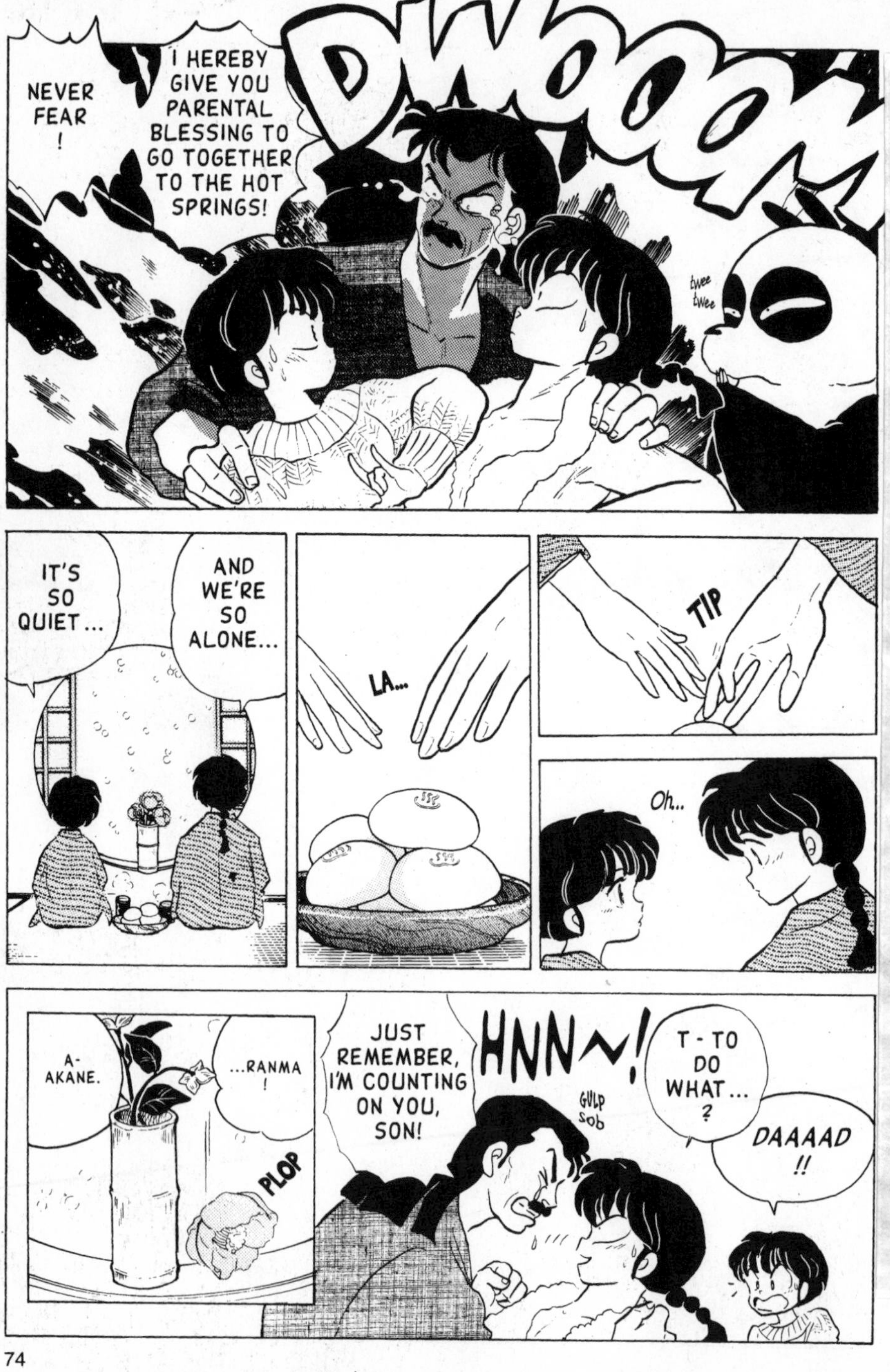
NEVER FEAR !
I HEREBY GIVE YOU PARENTAL BLESSING TO GO TOGETHER TO THE HOT SPRINGS!
DWOOOM
twee twee
IT'S SO QUIET...
AND WE'RE SO ALONE...
LA...
TIP
Oh...
A- AKANE.
...RANMA !
PLOP
JUST REMEMBER, I'M COUNTING ON YOU, SON!
HNN~!
GULP sob
T - TO DO WHAT... ?
DAAAAD !!

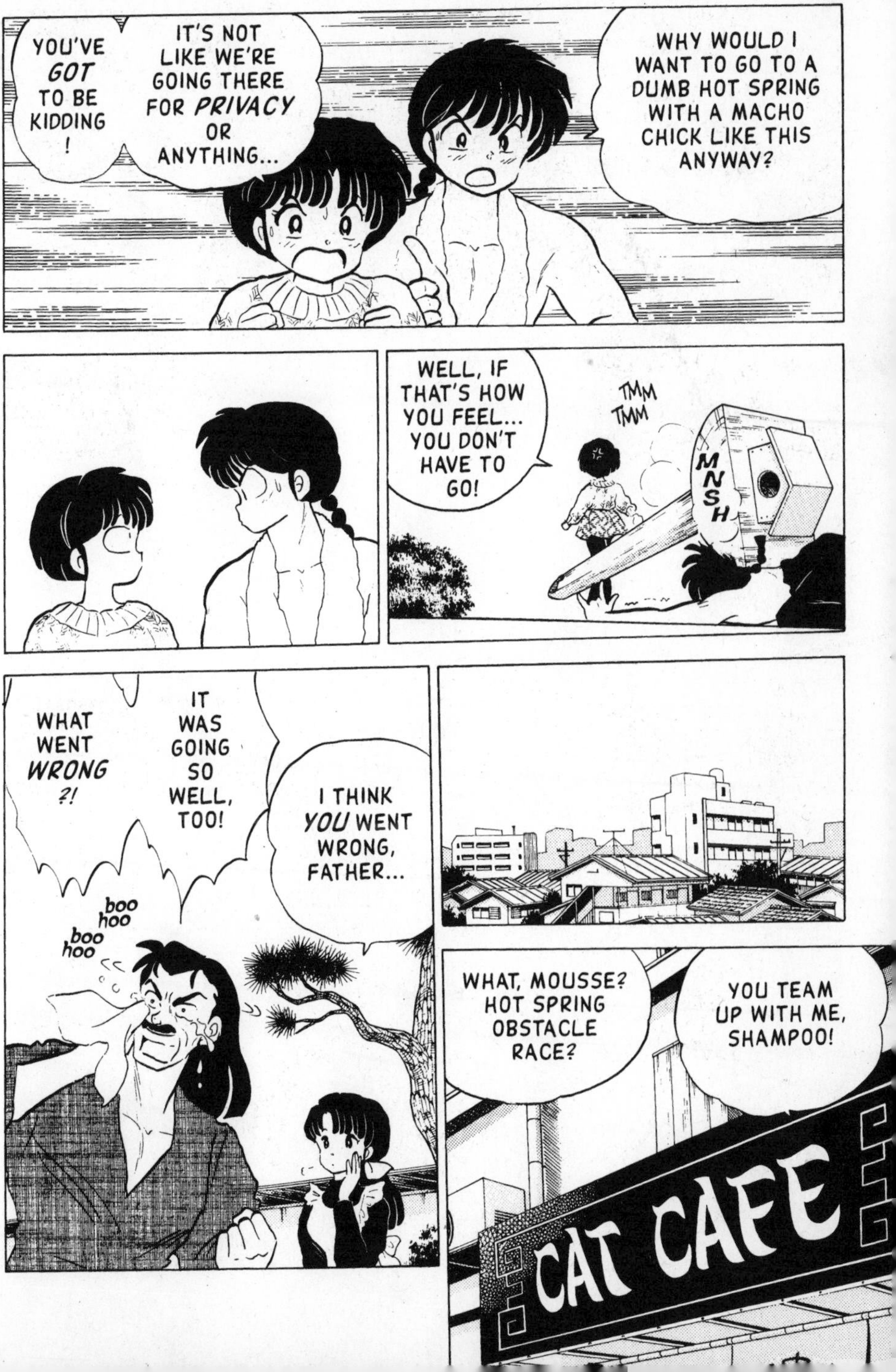
YOU'VE GOT TO BE KIDDING!
IT'S NOT LIKE WE'RE GOING THERE FOR PRIVACY OR ANYTHING...
WHY WOULD I WANT TO GO TO A DUMB HOT SPRING WITH A MACHO CHICK LIKE THIS ANYWAY?
WELL, IF THAT'S HOW YOU FEEL... YOU DON'T HAVE TO GO!
TMM TMM
MNSH
WHAT WENT WRONG?!
IT WAS GOING SO WELL, TOO!
I THINK YOU WENT WRONG, FATHER...
boo hoo boo hoo
WHAT, MOUSSE? HOT SPRING OBSTACLE RACE?
YOU TEAM UP WITH ME, SHAMPOO!
CAT CAFE

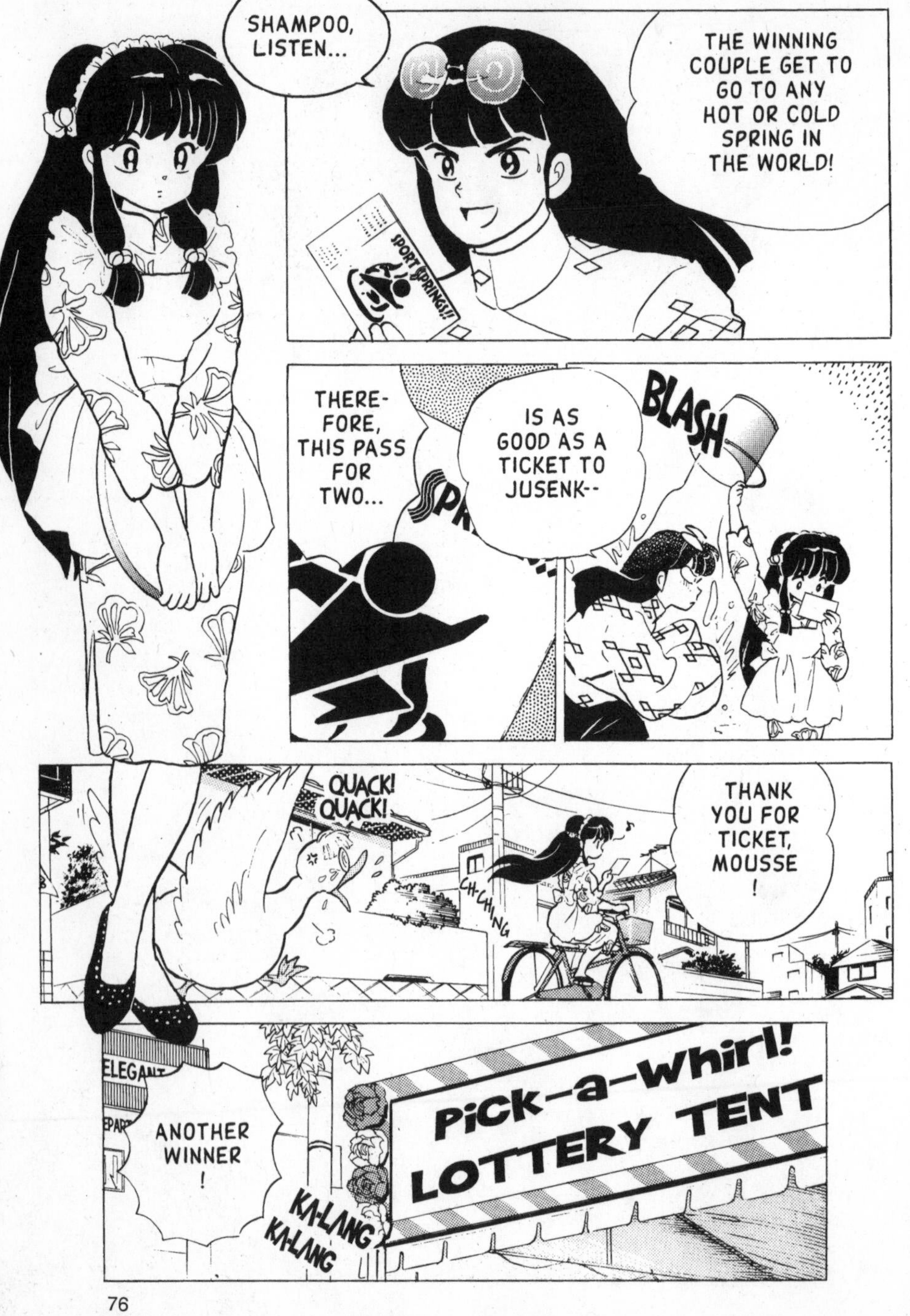
SHAMPOO, LISTEN...
THE WINNING COUPLE GET TO GO TO ANY HOT OR COLD SPRING IN THE WORLD!
SPORT SPRINGS!!
THERE-FORE, THIS PASS FOR TWO...
IS AS GOOD AS A TICKET TO JUSENK--
BLASH
QUACK! QUACK!
CH-CHING
THANK YOU FOR TICKET, MOUSSE !
ANOTHER WINNER !
KA-LANG KA-LANG
Pick-a-Whirl! LOTTERY TENT

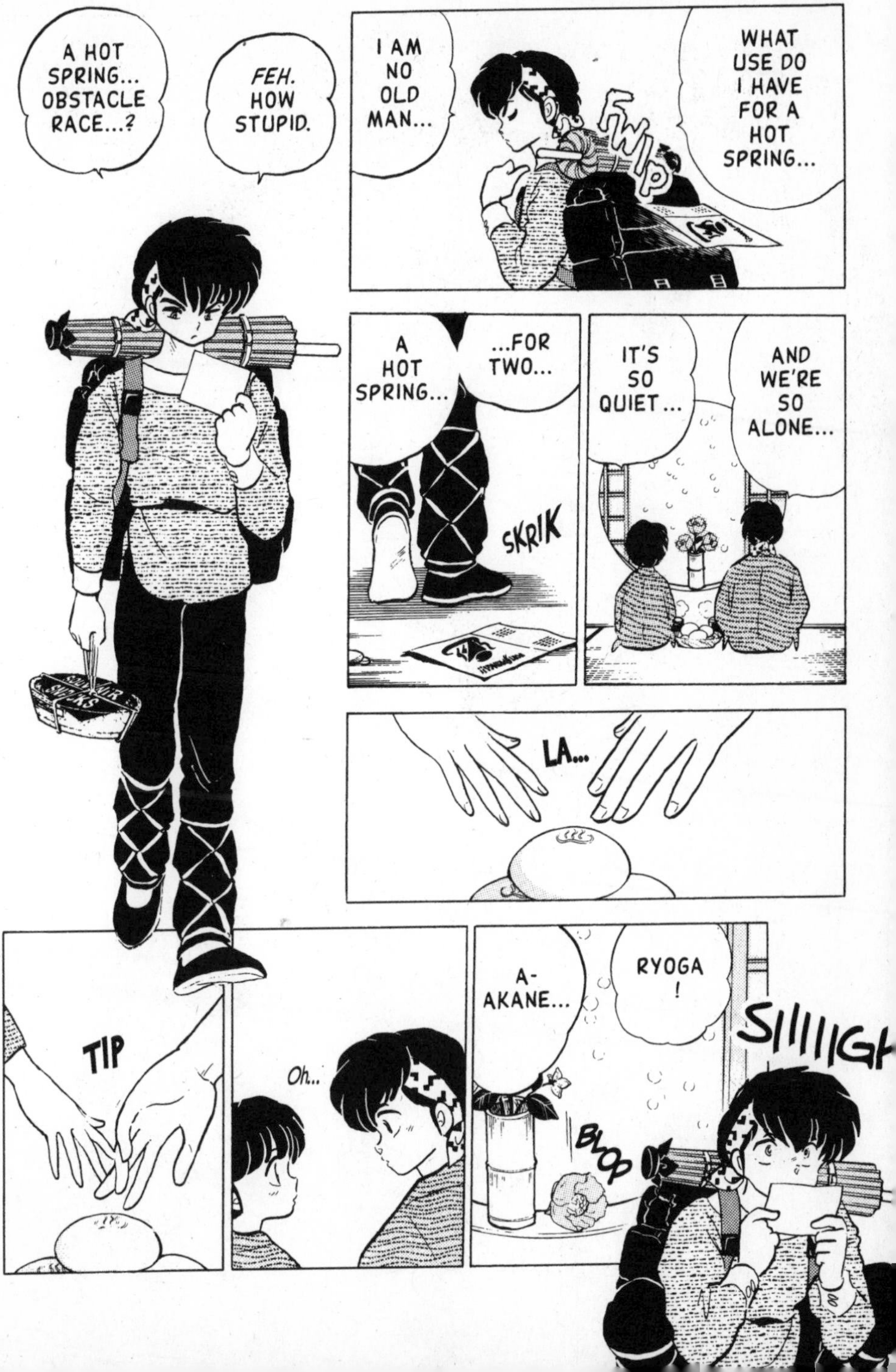
A HOT SPRING... OBSTACLE RACE...?
FEH. HOW STUPID.
I AM NO OLD MAN...
FWIP
WHAT USE DO I HAVE FOR A HOT SPRING...
A HOT SPRING...
...FOR TWO...
SKRIK
IT'S SO QUIET...
AND WE'RE SO ALONE...
LA...
TIP
Oh...
A- AKANE...
RYOGA !
BLOOP
SIIIIGH

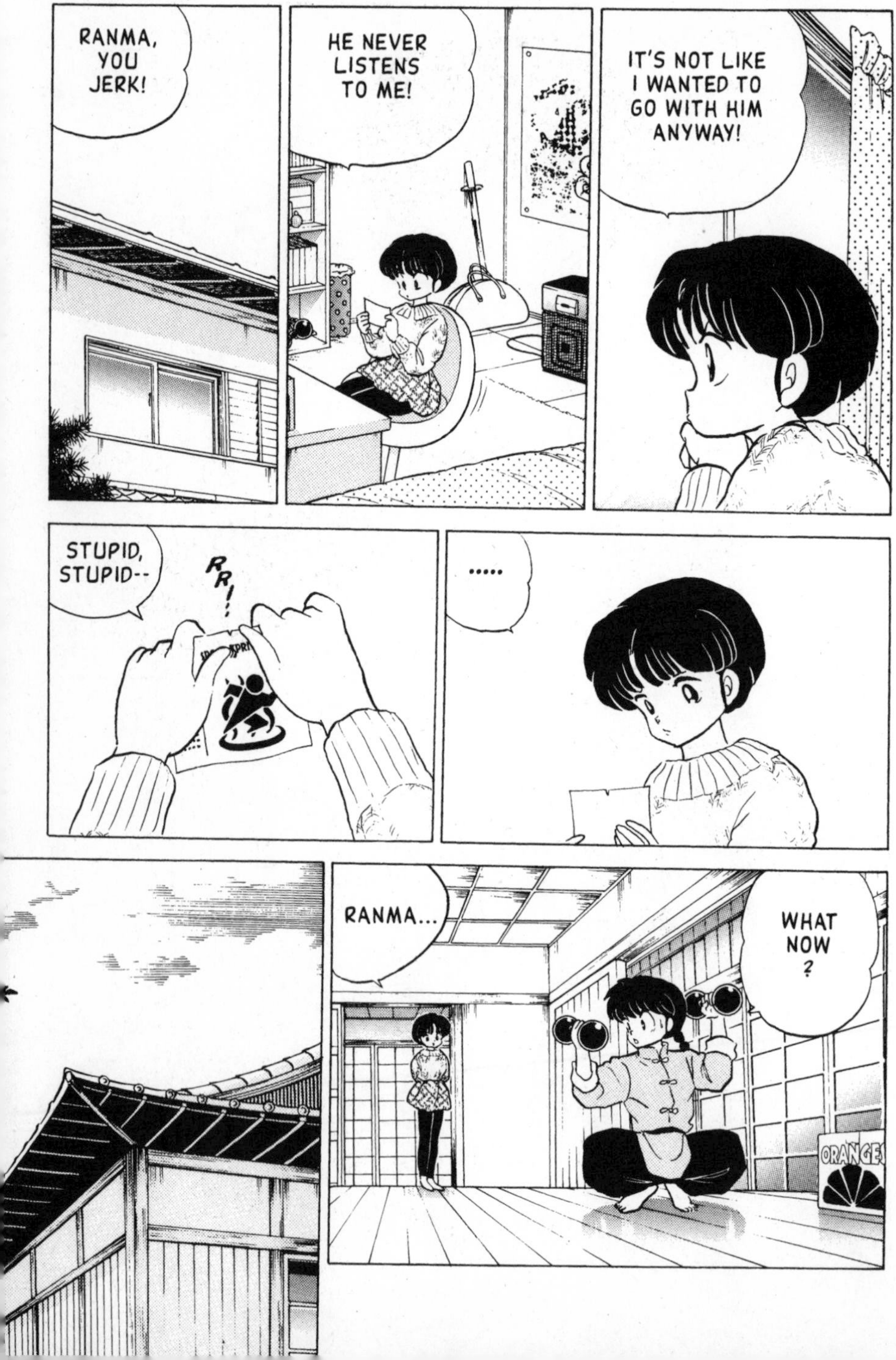
RANMA, YOU JERK!
HE NEVER LISTENS TO ME!
IT'S NOT LIKE I WANTED TO GO WITH HIM ANYWAY!
STUPID, STUPID--
RRI!
.....
RANMA...
WHAT NOW?
ORANGES

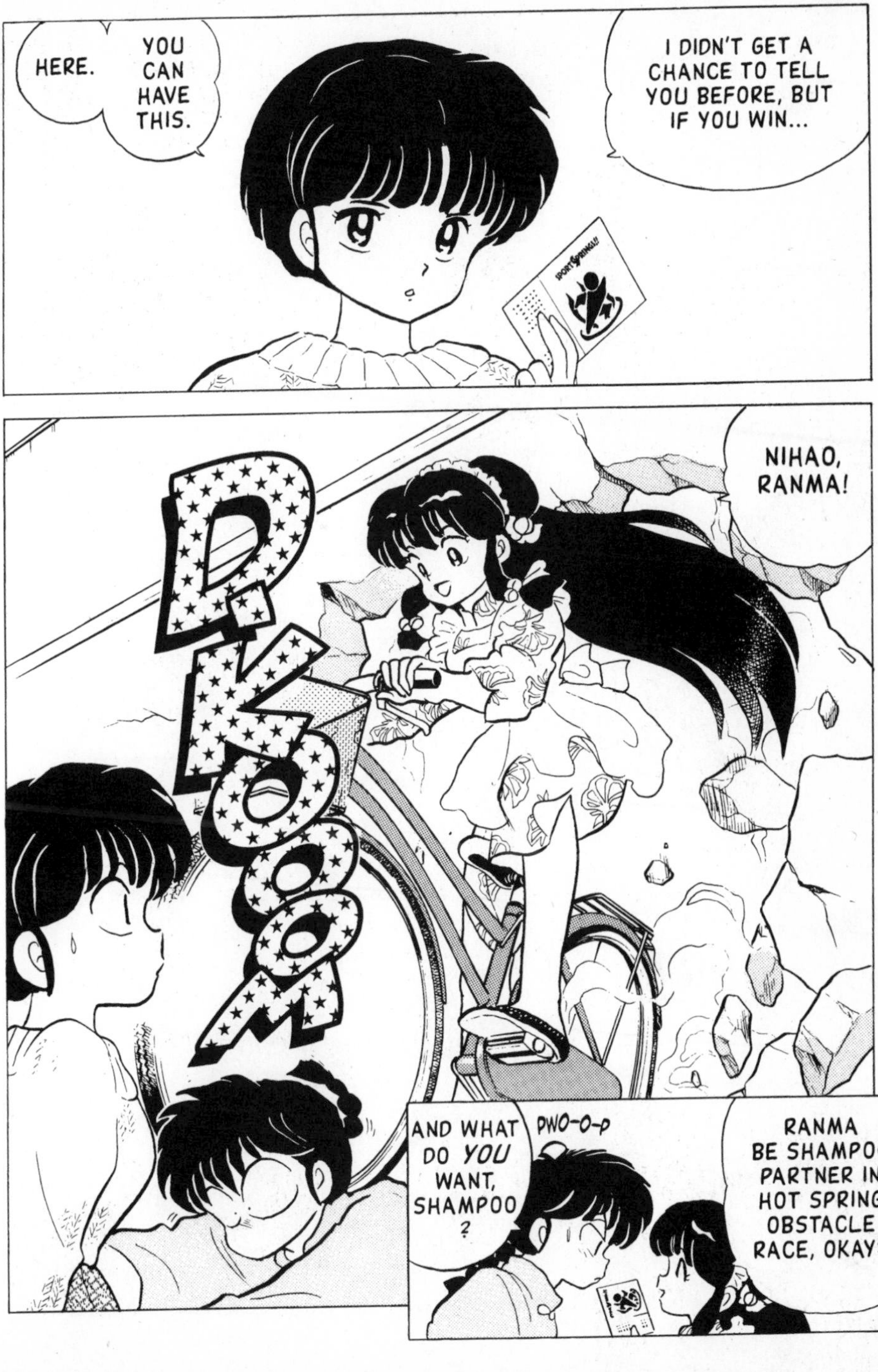
HERE.
YOU CAN HAVE THIS.
I DIDN'T GET A CHANCE TO TELL YOU BEFORE, BUT IF YOU WIN...
DKOOOOM
NIHAO, RANMA!
AND WHAT DO *YOU* WANT, SHAMPOO?
PWO-O-P
RANMA BE SHAMPOO PARTNER IN HOT SPRING OBSTACLE RACE, OKAY?

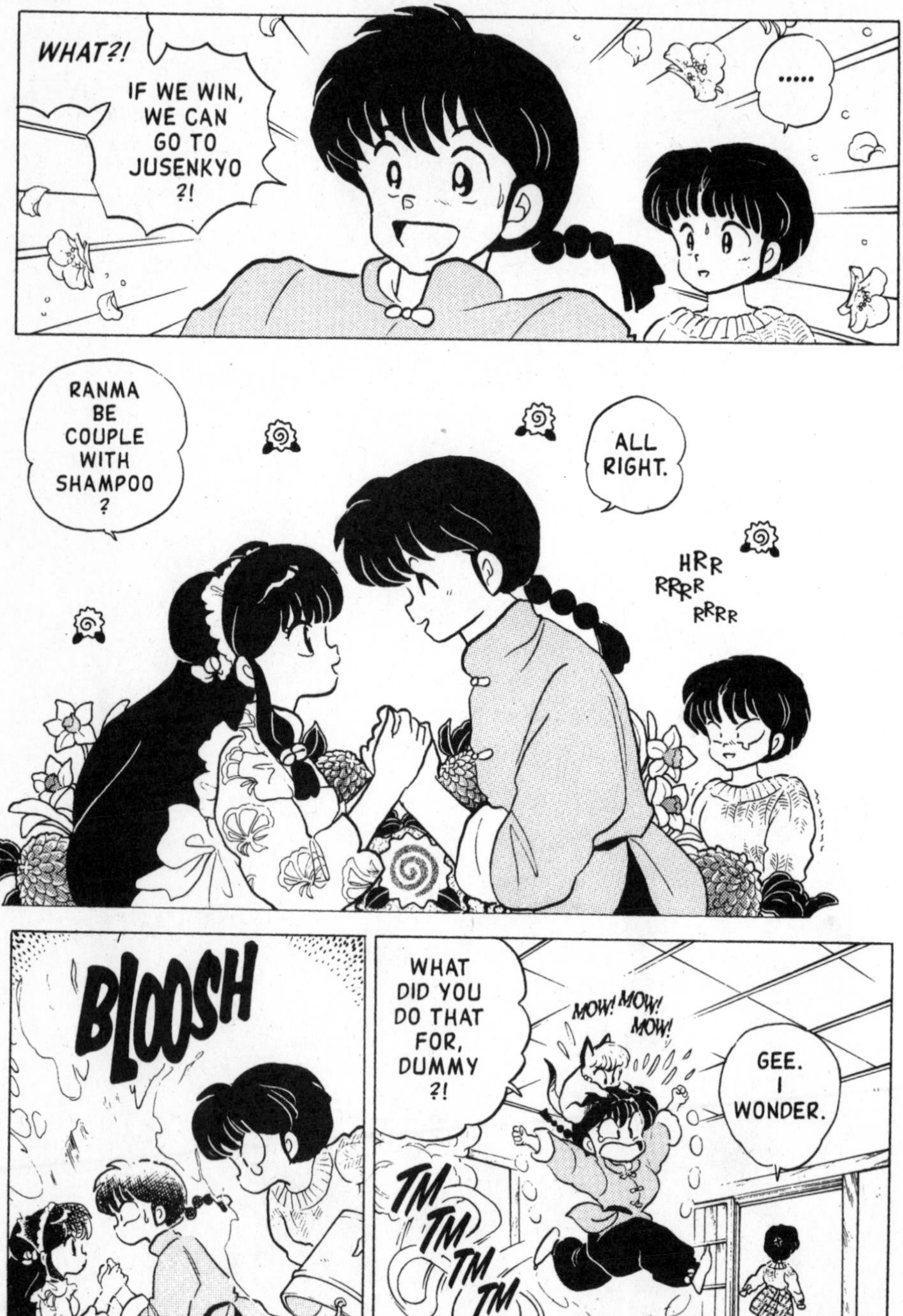
WHAT?!
IF WE WIN, WE CAN GO TO JUSENKYO ?!
......
RANMA BE COUPLE WITH SHAMPOO ?
ALL RIGHT.
HRR RRRR RRRR
BLOOSH
WHAT DID YOU DO THAT FOR, DUMMY ?!
MOW! MOW! MOW!
GEE. I WONDER.
TM TM TM TM

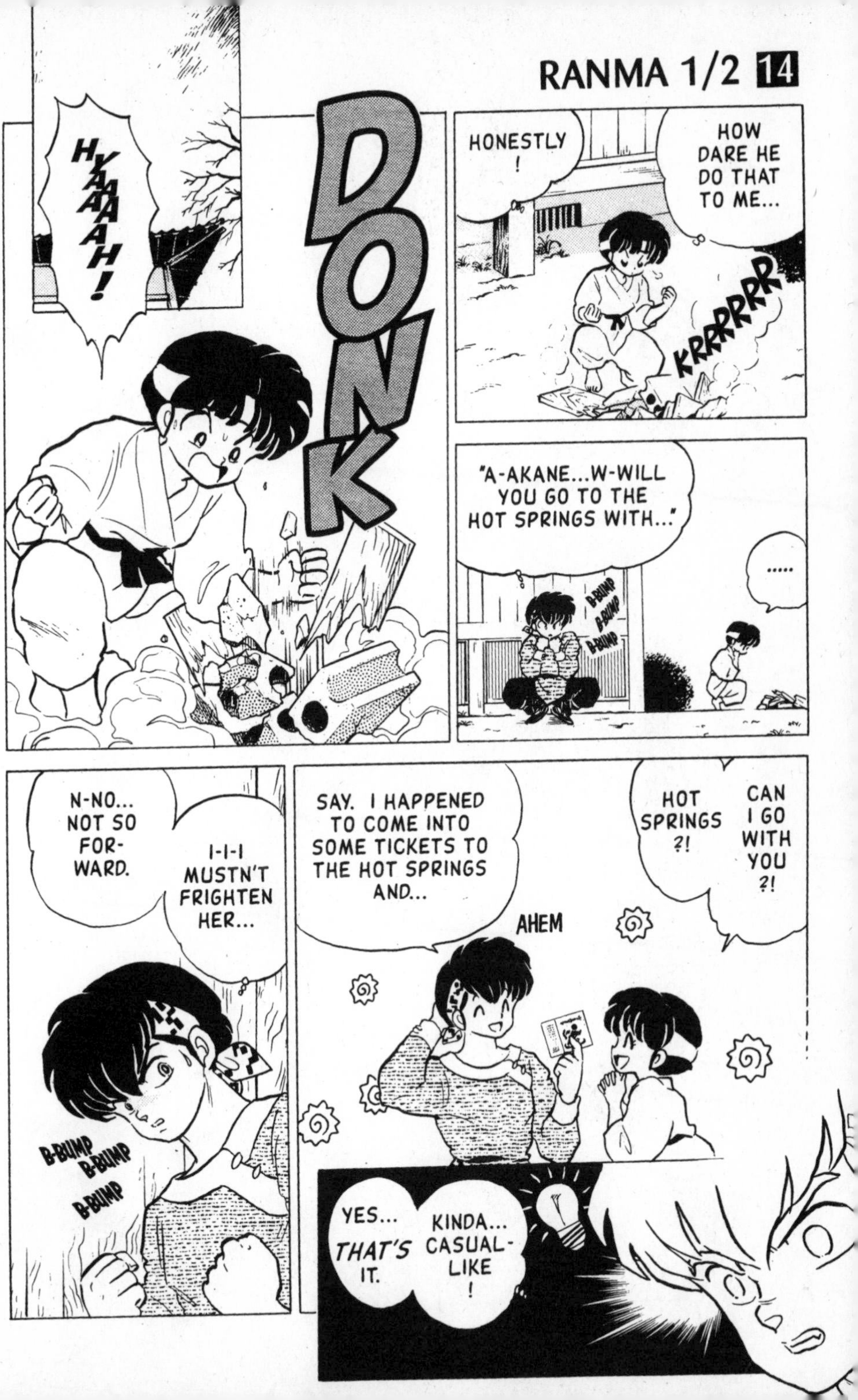
HYAAAAAH!
DONK
HONESTLY!
HOW DARE HE DO THAT TO ME...
KRRRRRR
"A-AKANE...W-WILL YOU GO TO THE HOT SPRINGS WITH..."
B-BUMP B-BUMP B-BUMP
.....
N-NO... NOT SO FOR-WARD.
I-I-I MUSTN'T FRIGHTEN HER...
B-BUMP B-BUMP B-BUMP
SAY. I HAPPENED TO COME INTO SOME TICKETS TO THE HOT SPRINGS AND...
AHEM
HOT SPRINGS ?!
CAN I GO WITH YOU ?!
YES... THAT'S IT.
KINDA... CASUAL-LIKE!

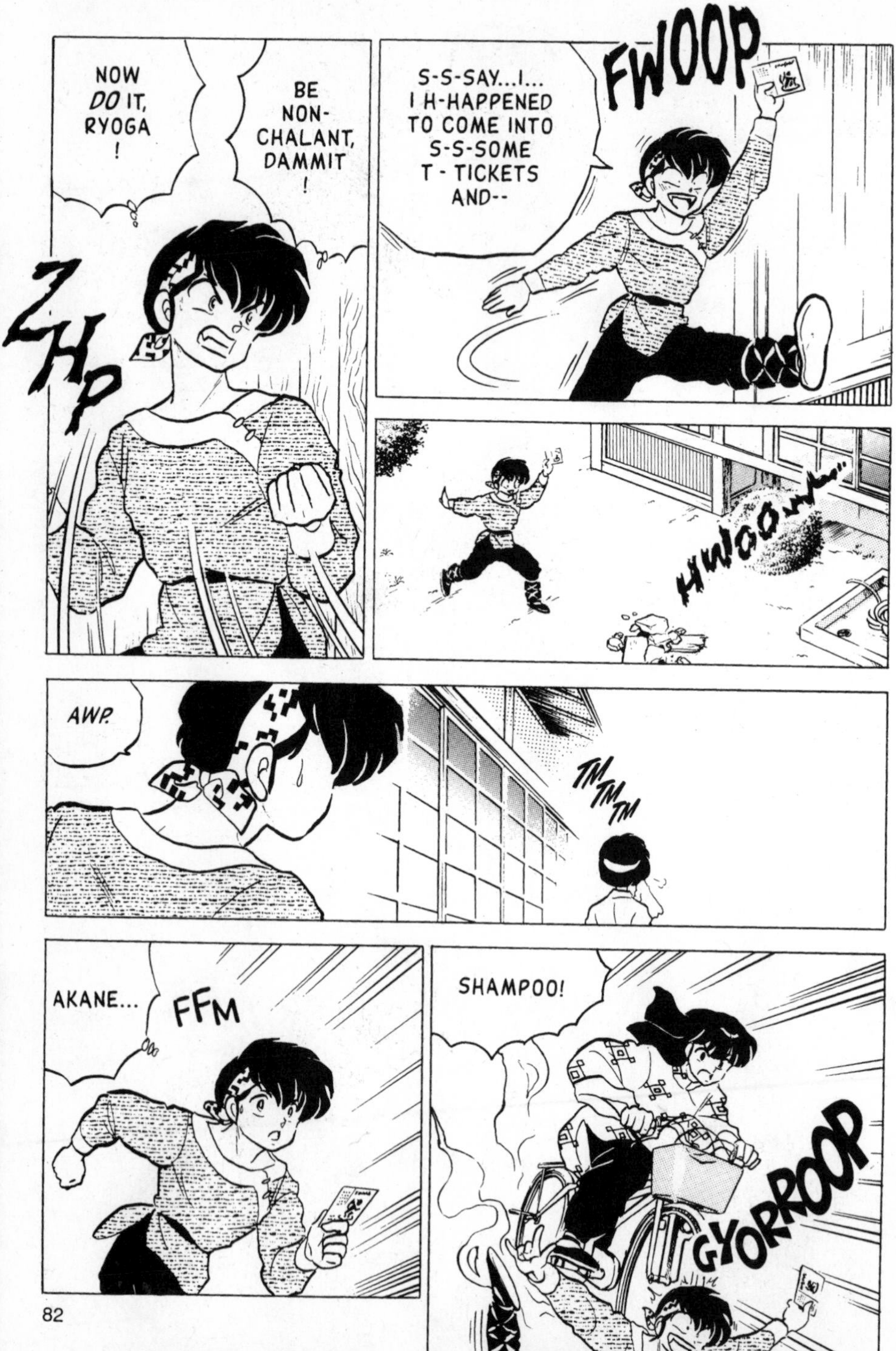
NOW DO IT, RYOGA!
BE NONCHALANT, DAMMIT!
ZHP
S-S-SAY...I... I H-HAPPENED TO COME INTO S-S-SOME T-TICKETS AND--
FWOOP
HWOOM...
AWP.
TM TM TM
AKANE...
FFM
SHAMPOO!
GYORROOP

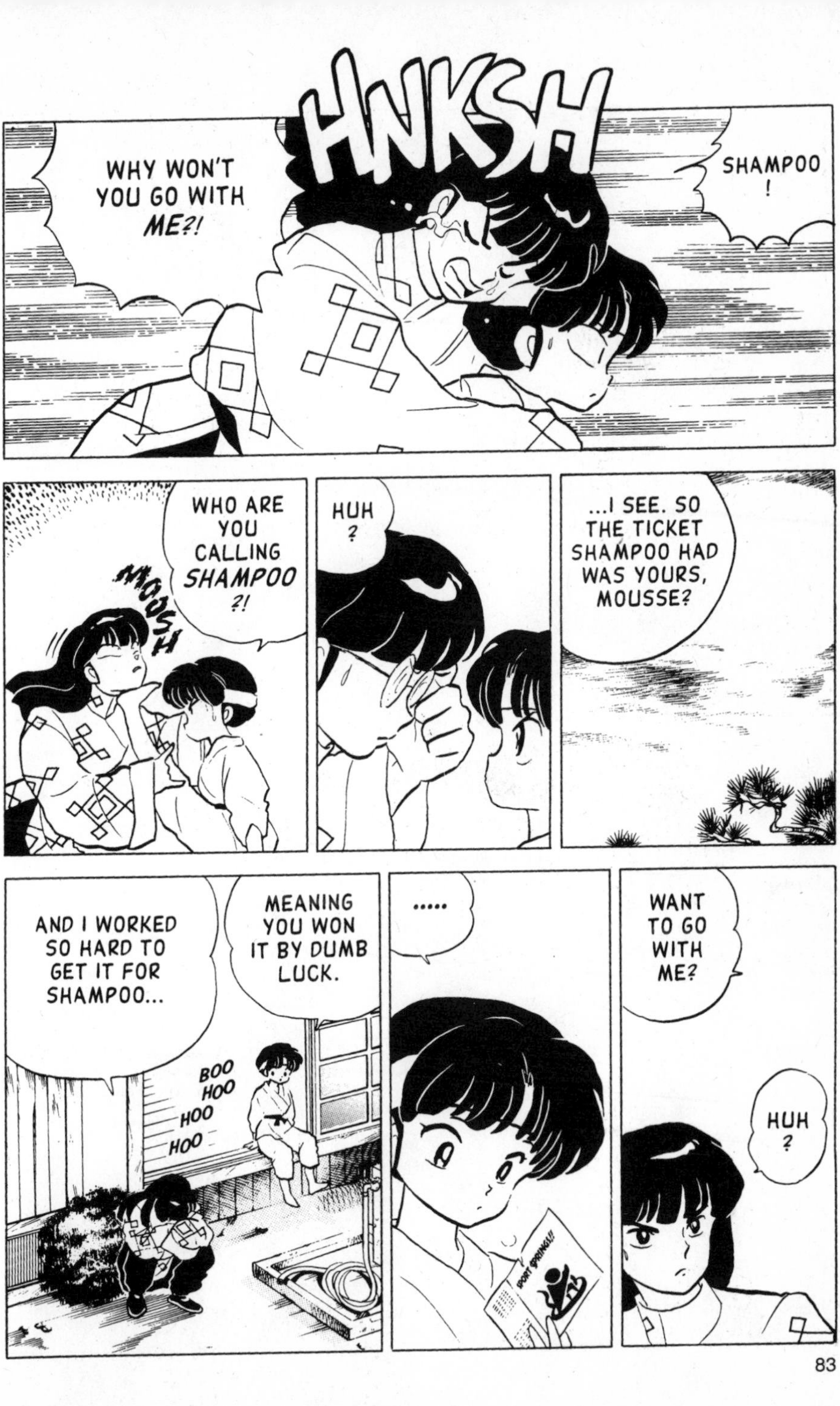
HNKSH
WHY WON'T YOU GO WITH ME?!
SHAMPOO!
WHO ARE YOU CALLING SHAMPOO?!
MOOSH
HUH?
...I SEE. SO THE TICKET SHAMPOO HAD WAS YOURS, MOUSSE?
AND I WORKED SO HARD TO GET IT FOR SHAMPOO...
MEANING YOU WON IT BY DUMB LUCK.
BOO HOO HOO HOO
.....
WANT TO GO WITH ME?
HUH?

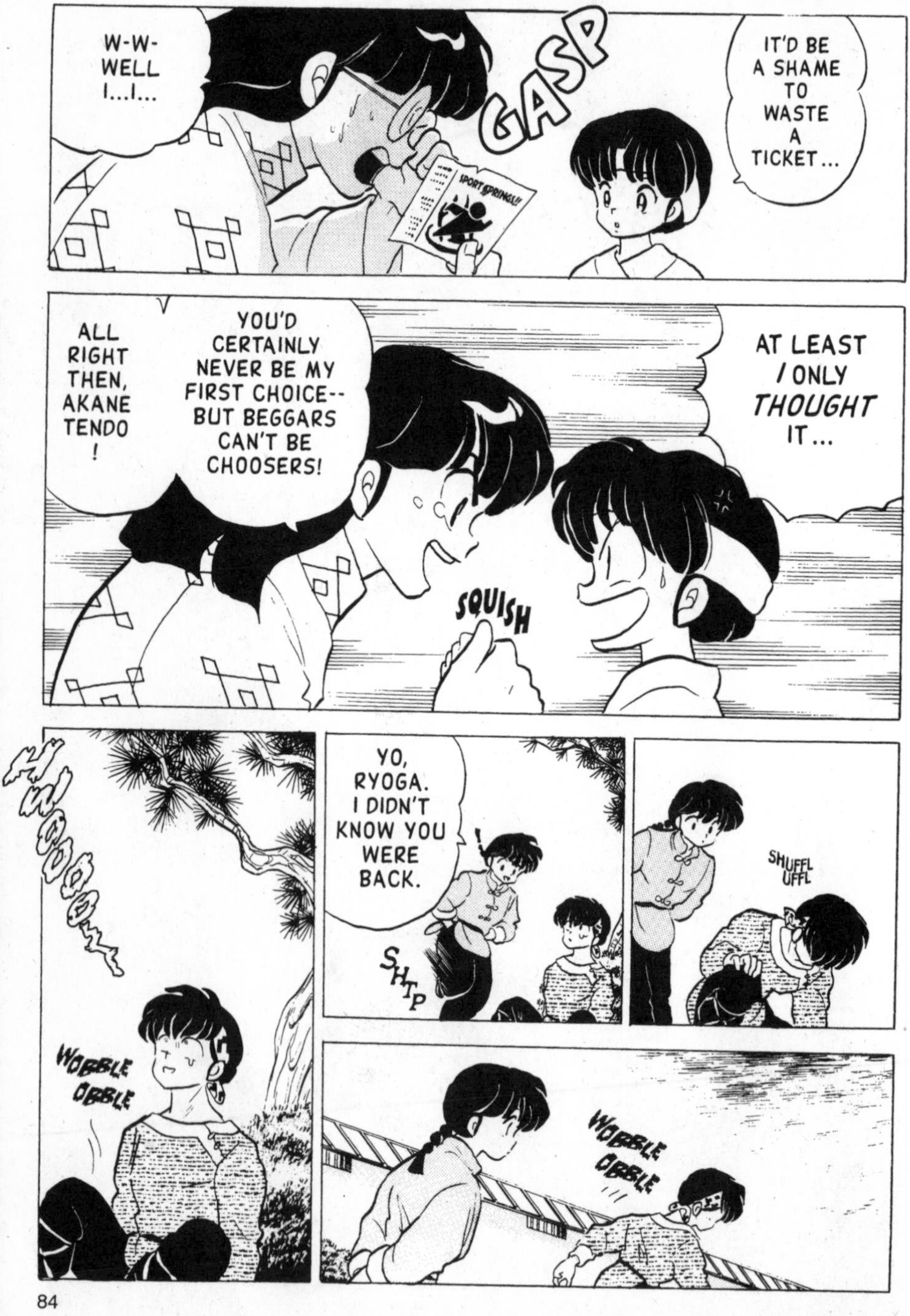
W-W-WELL I...I...
GASP
IT'D BE A SHAME TO WASTE A TICKET...
ALL RIGHT THEN, AKANE TENDO!
YOU'D CERTAINLY NEVER BE MY FIRST CHOICE--BUT BEGGARS CAN'T BE CHOOSERS!
AT LEAST I ONLY *THOUGHT* IT...
SQUISH
HWOOOOM
WOBBLE OBBLE
YO, RYOGA. I DIDN'T KNOW YOU WERE BACK.
SHTP
SHUFFL UFFL
WOBBLE OBBLE

WHAT'S THE MATTER, MAN? YOU GET DUMPED OR SOMETHING?

TWIK

RRRR--!

ULP.

HOW CAN YOU KNOW WHAT I FEEL?!

...I DON'T.

BONK

FWOOOM

SIGH

STUMBL

WHY COULDN'T I SAY IT?

IT SHOULD BE SO EASY.

mumbl umbl

SPORT SPRINGS!

PLEASE !!

I WANT YOU TO GO...

...TO THE HOT SPRINGS WITH ME!!

VWAH

HOT SPRINGS!
OBSTACLE RACE!
COUPLES FUN!

SPORT SPRINGS!!

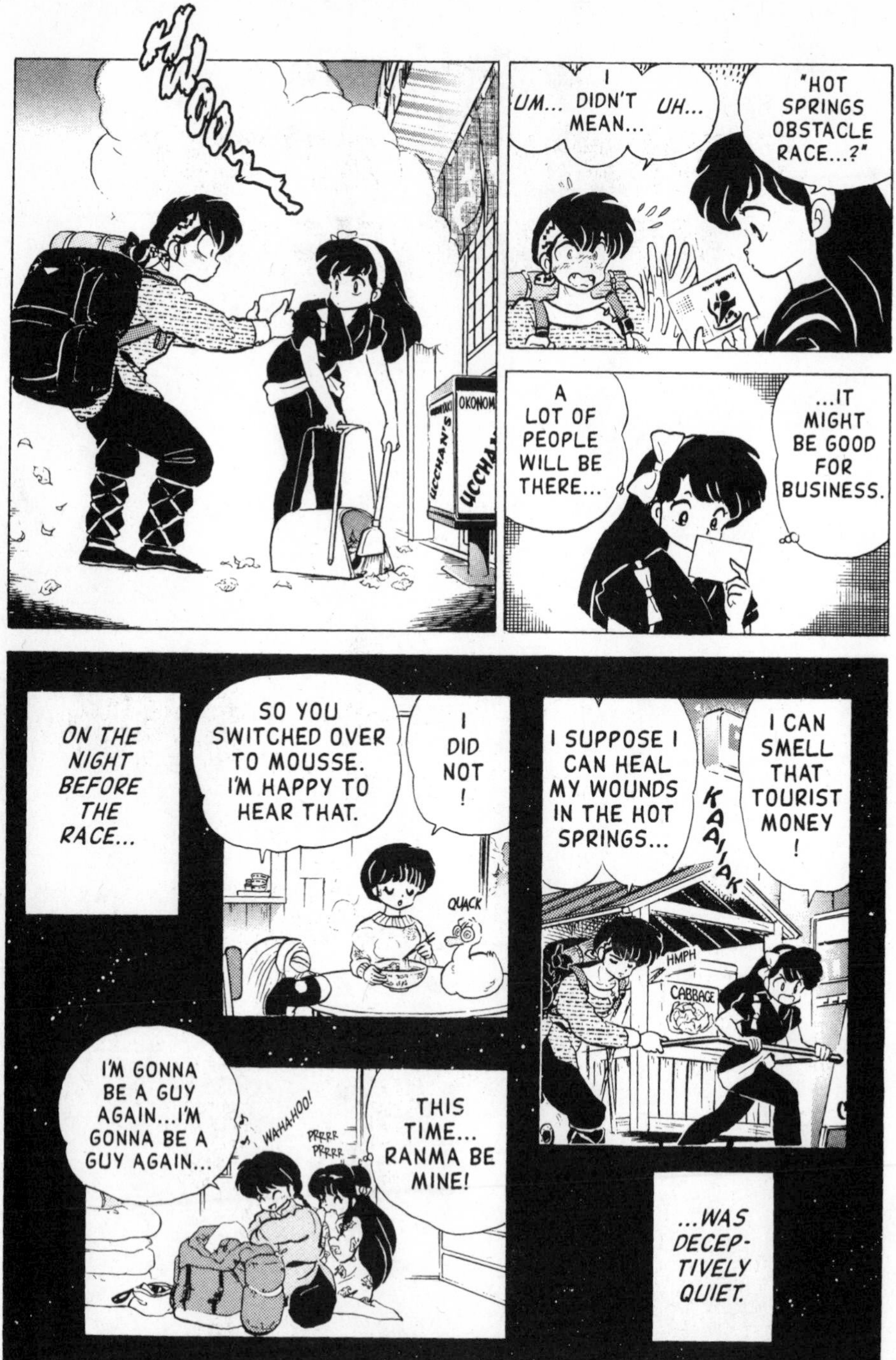
OKONOMI
UCCHAN'S
UM... I DIDN'T MEAN... UH...
"HOT SPRINGS OBSTACLE RACE...?"
A LOT OF PEOPLE WILL BE THERE...
...IT MIGHT BE GOOD FOR BUSINESS.
ON THE NIGHT BEFORE THE RACE...
SO YOU SWITCHED OVER TO MOUSSE. I'M HAPPY TO HEAR THAT.
I DID NOT!
QUACK
I SUPPOSE I CAN HEAL MY WOUNDS IN THE HOT SPRINGS...
I CAN SMELL THAT TOURIST MONEY!
KAAAIAK
HMPH
CABBAGE
I'M GONNA BE A GUY AGAIN...I'M GONNA BE A GUY AGAIN...
WAHA-HOO!
PRRRR PRRRR
THIS TIME... RANMA BE MINE!
...WAS DECEPTIVELY QUIET.

PART 6
SCREAMIN' AT THE HOT SPRINGS!

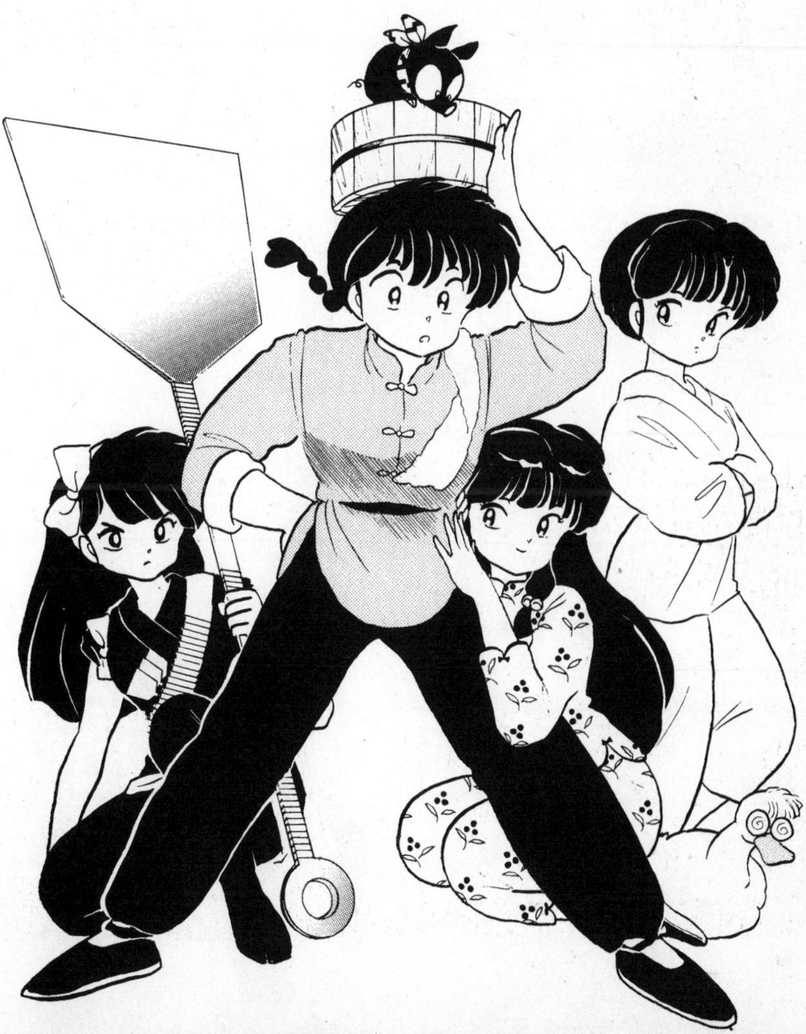

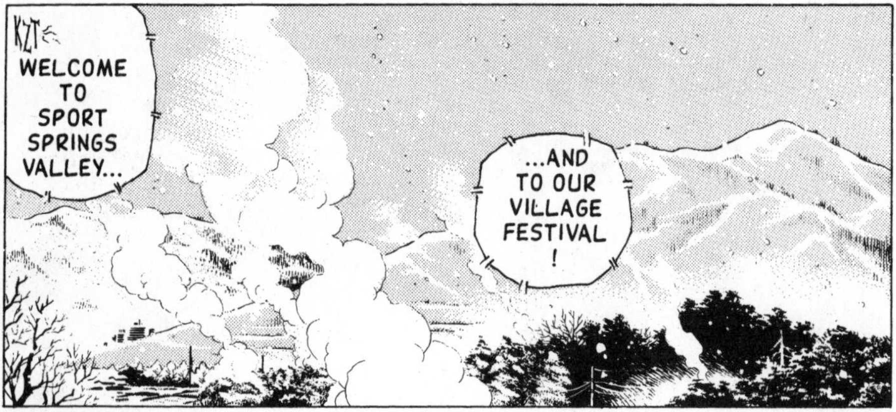
KZT
WELCOME TO SPORT SPRINGS VALLEY...
...AND TO OUR VILLAGE FESTIVAL !

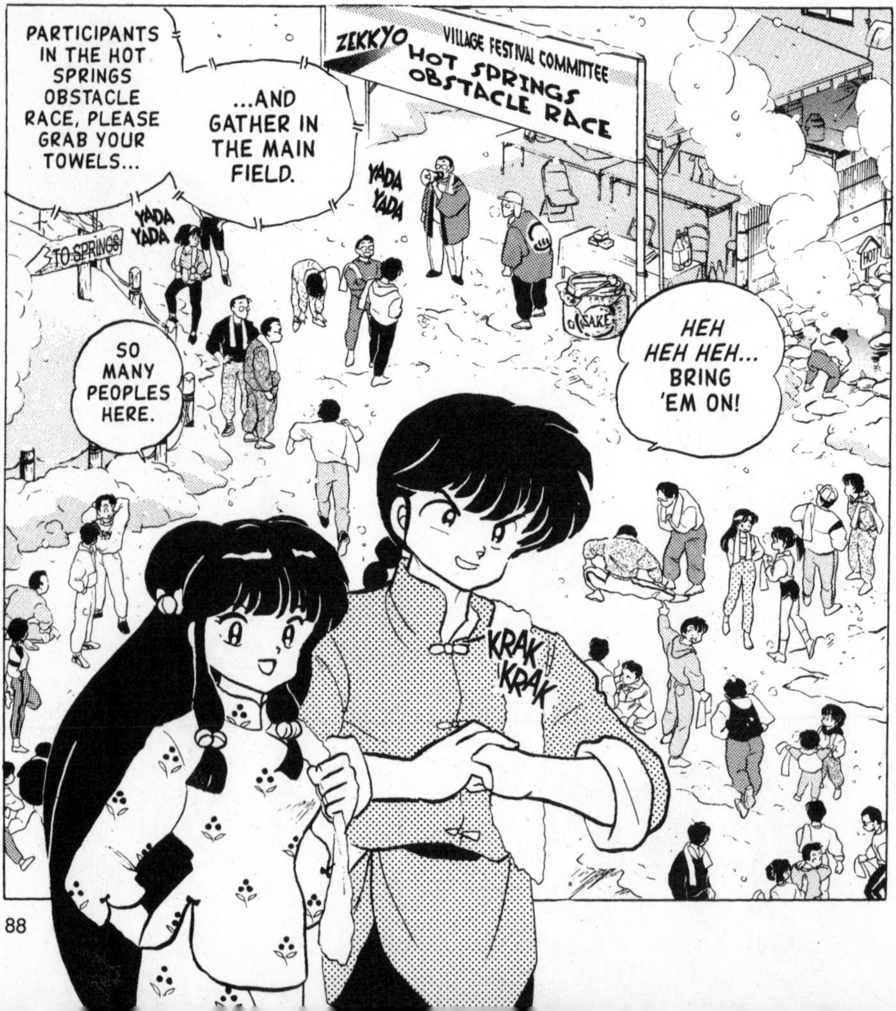
ZEKKYO VILLAGE FESTIVAL COMMITTEE
HOT SPRINGS OBSTACLE RACE
PARTICIPANTS IN THE HOT SPRINGS OBSTACLE RACE, PLEASE GRAB YOUR TOWELS...
...AND GATHER IN THE MAIN FIELD.
YADA YADA
YADA YADA
TO SPRINGS
SAKE
HOT
SO MANY PEOPLES HERE.
HEH HEH HEH... BRING 'EM ON!
KRAK KRAK

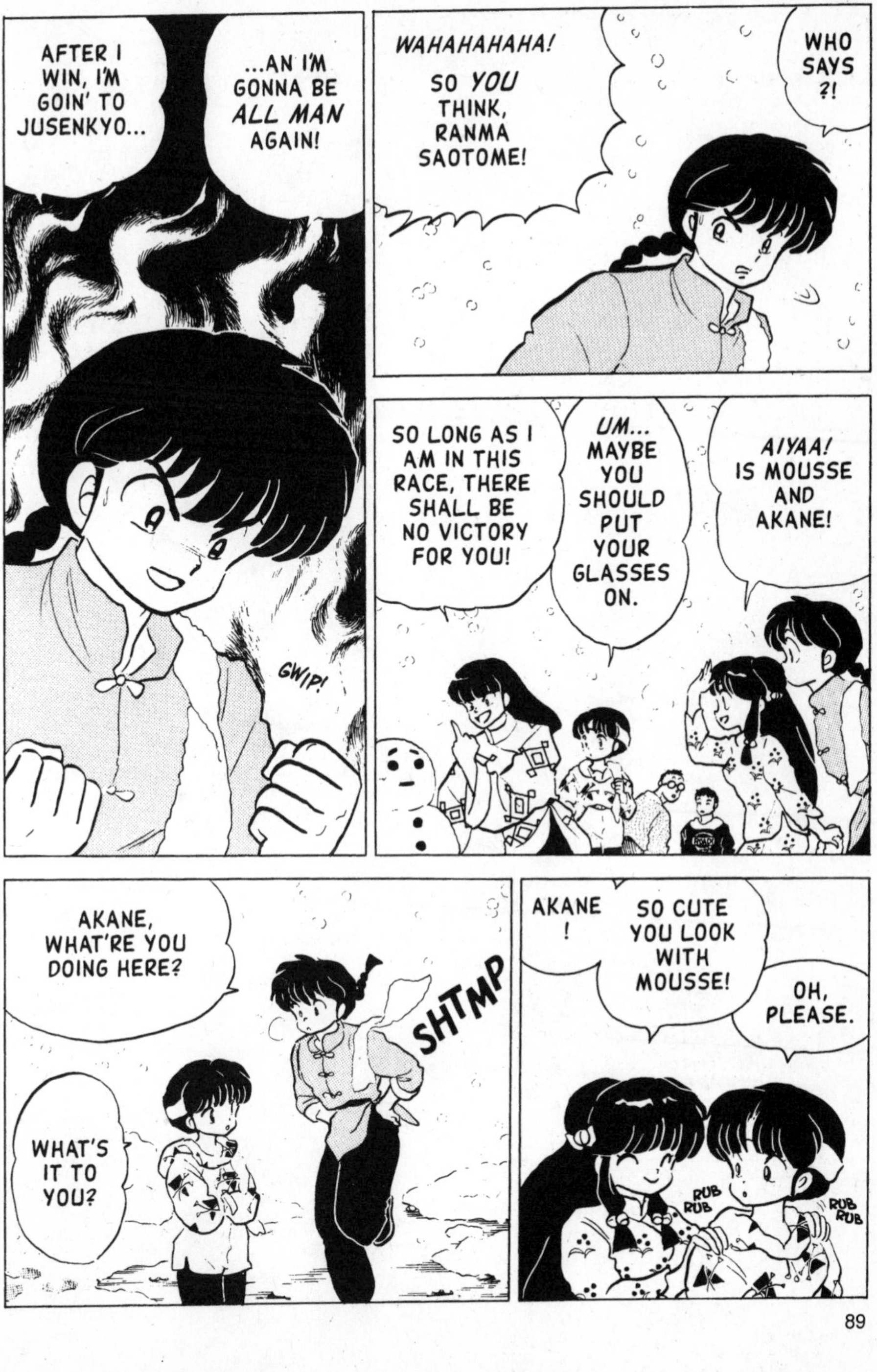
AFTER I WIN, I'M GOIN' TO JUSENKYO...
...AN I'M GONNA BE ALL MAN AGAIN!
GWIP!
WAHAHAHAHA!
SO YOU THINK, RANMA SAOTOME!
WHO SAYS ?!
SO LONG AS I AM IN THIS RACE, THERE SHALL BE NO VICTORY FOR YOU!
UM... MAYBE YOU SHOULD PUT YOUR GLASSES ON.
AIYAA! IS MOUSSE AND AKANE!
AKANE, WHAT'RE YOU DOING HERE?
SHTMP
WHAT'S IT TO YOU?
AKANE !
SO CUTE YOU LOOK WITH MOUSSE!
OH, PLEASE.
RUB RUB
RUB RUB

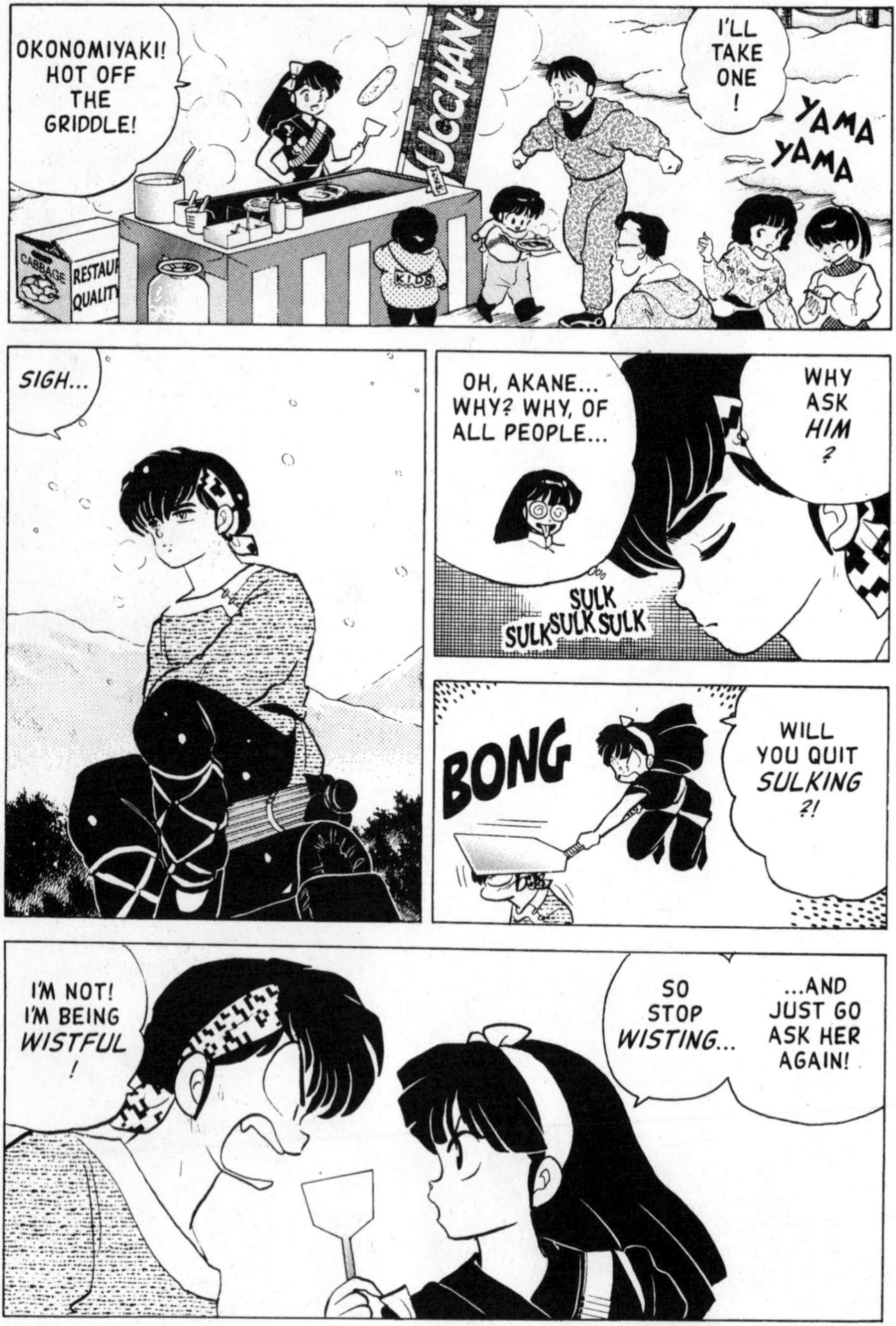
OKONOMIYAKI! HOT OFF THE GRIDDLE!
UCCHAN'S
CABBAGE
RESTAUR QUALITY
KIDS
I'LL TAKE ONE!
YAMA YAMA
SIGH...
OH, AKANE... WHY? WHY, OF ALL PEOPLE...
WHY ASK HIM?
SULK SULK SULK SULK
BONG
WILL YOU QUIT SULKING?!
I'M NOT! I'M BEING WISTFUL!
SO STOP WISTING...
...AND JUST GO ASK HER AGAIN!

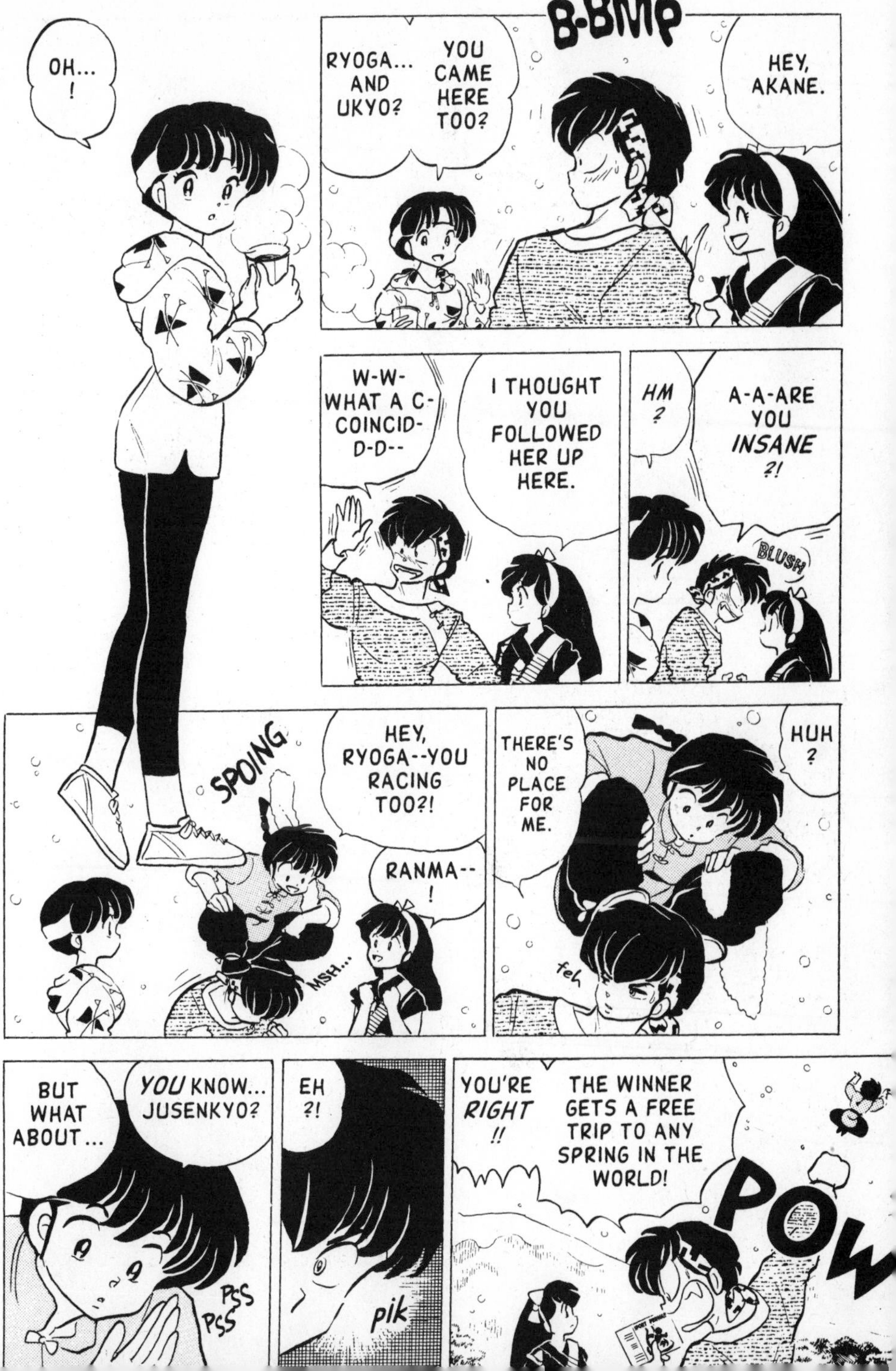
OH... !
RYOGA... AND UKYO?
YOU CAME HERE TOO?
B-BMP
HEY, AKANE.
W-W-WHAT A C-COINCID-D-D--
I THOUGHT YOU FOLLOWED HER UP HERE.
HM?
A-A-ARE YOU INSANE?!
BLUSH
SPOING
HEY, RYOGA--YOU RACING TOO?!
RANMA--!
MSH...
THERE'S NO PLACE FOR ME.
HUH?
feh
BUT WHAT ABOUT...
YOU KNOW... JUSENKYO?
PSS PSS
EH?!
pik
YOU'RE RIGHT!!
THE WINNER GETS A FREE TRIP TO ANY SPRING IN THE WORLD!
POW

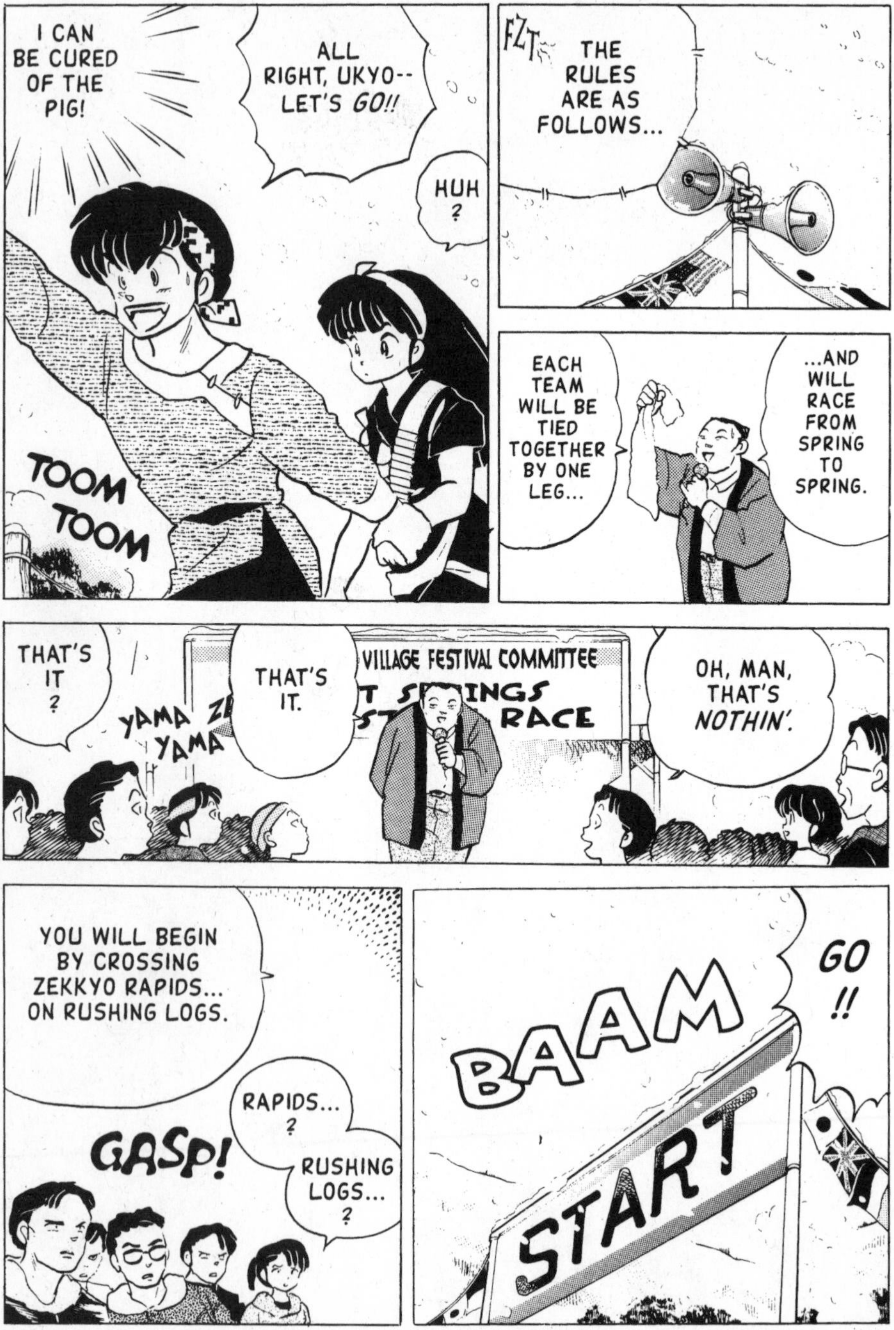

I CAN BE CURED OF THE PIG!
ALL RIGHT, UKYO-- LET'S *GO!!*
HUH ?
TOOM TOOM
FZT
THE RULES ARE AS FOLLOWS...
EACH TEAM WILL BE TIED TOGETHER BY ONE LEG...
...AND WILL RACE FROM SPRING TO SPRING.
THAT'S IT ?
YAMA YAMA
THAT'S IT.
VILLAGE FESTIVAL COMMITTEE
RACE
OH, MAN, THAT'S *NOTHIN'*.
YOU WILL BEGIN BY CROSSING ZEKKYO RAPIDS... ON RUSHING LOGS.
RAPIDS... ?
GASP!
RUSHING LOGS... ?
BAAM
GO !!
START

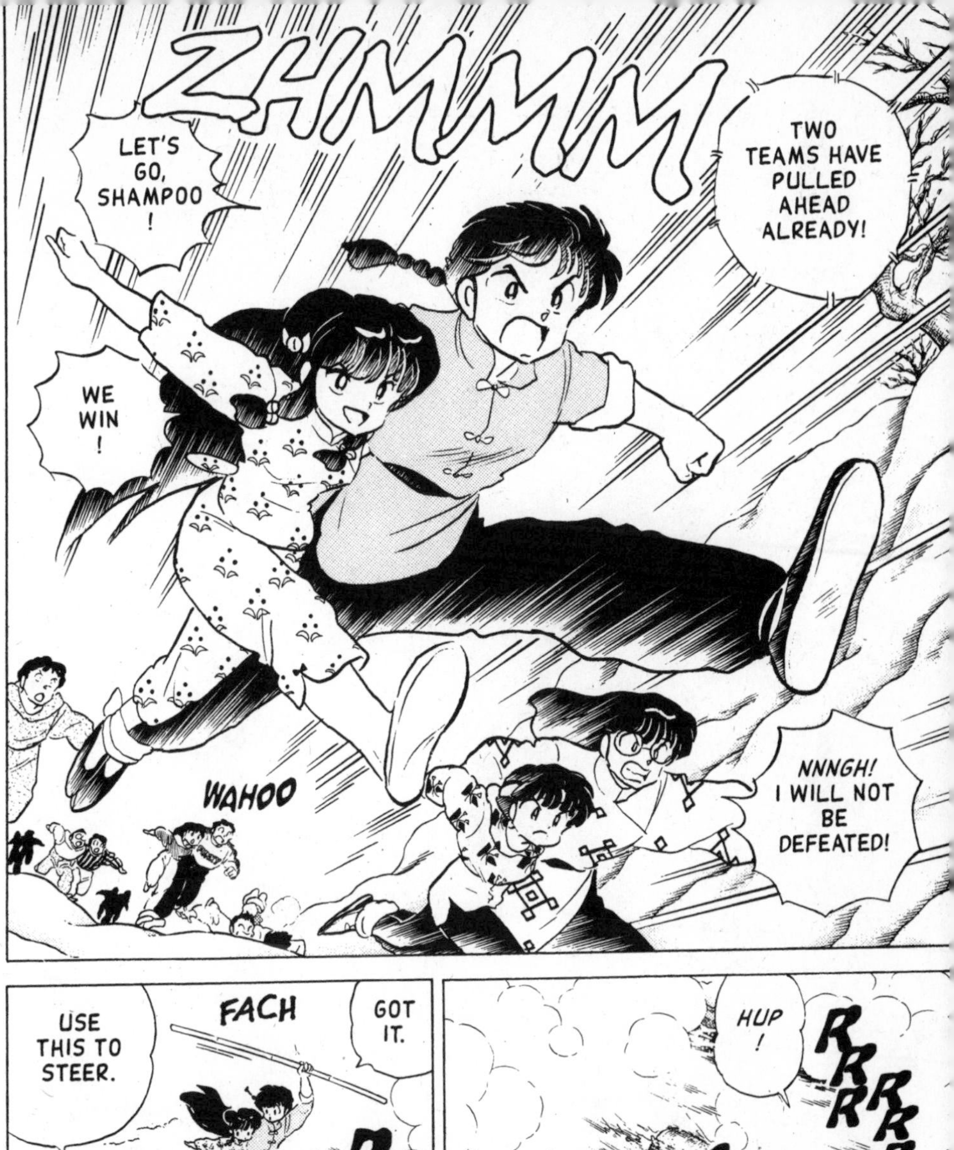
ZHMMM
LET'S GO, SHAMPOO!
TWO TEAMS HAVE PULLED AHEAD ALREADY!
WE WIN!
WAHOO
NNNGH! I WILL NOT BE DEFEATED!

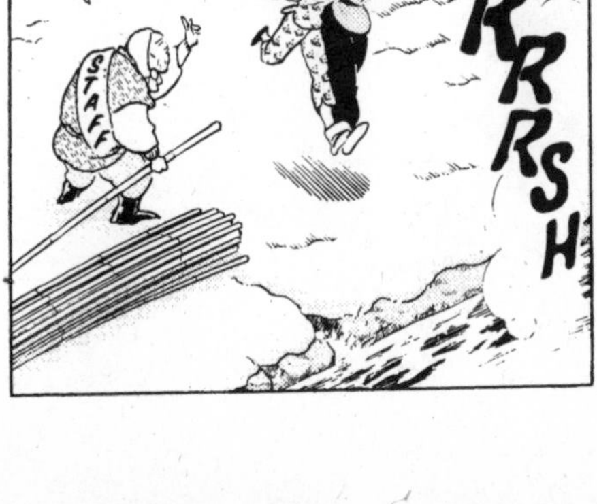
USE THIS TO STEER.
FACH
GOT IT.
RRRSH

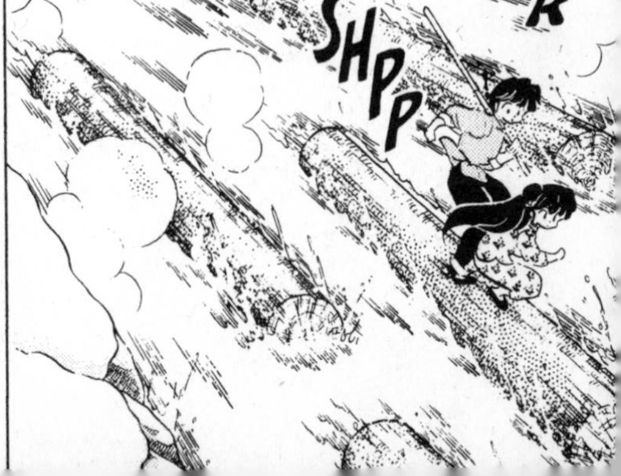
HUP!
RRRRRR
SHPP

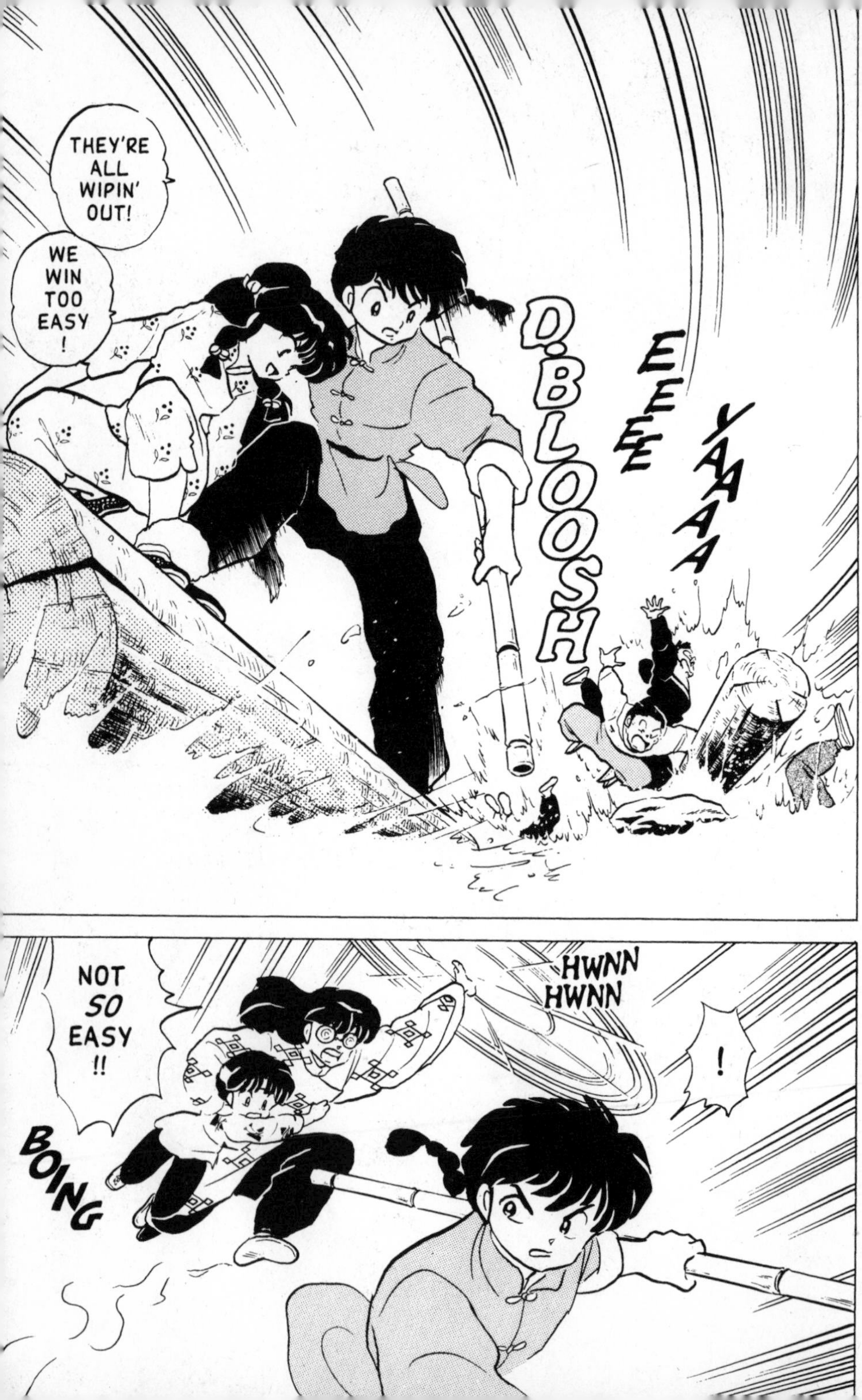
THEY'RE ALL WIPIN' OUT!
WE WIN TOO EASY!
DBLOOOSH
EEEE
YAAAA
NOT SO EASY!!
HWNN HWNN
!
BOING

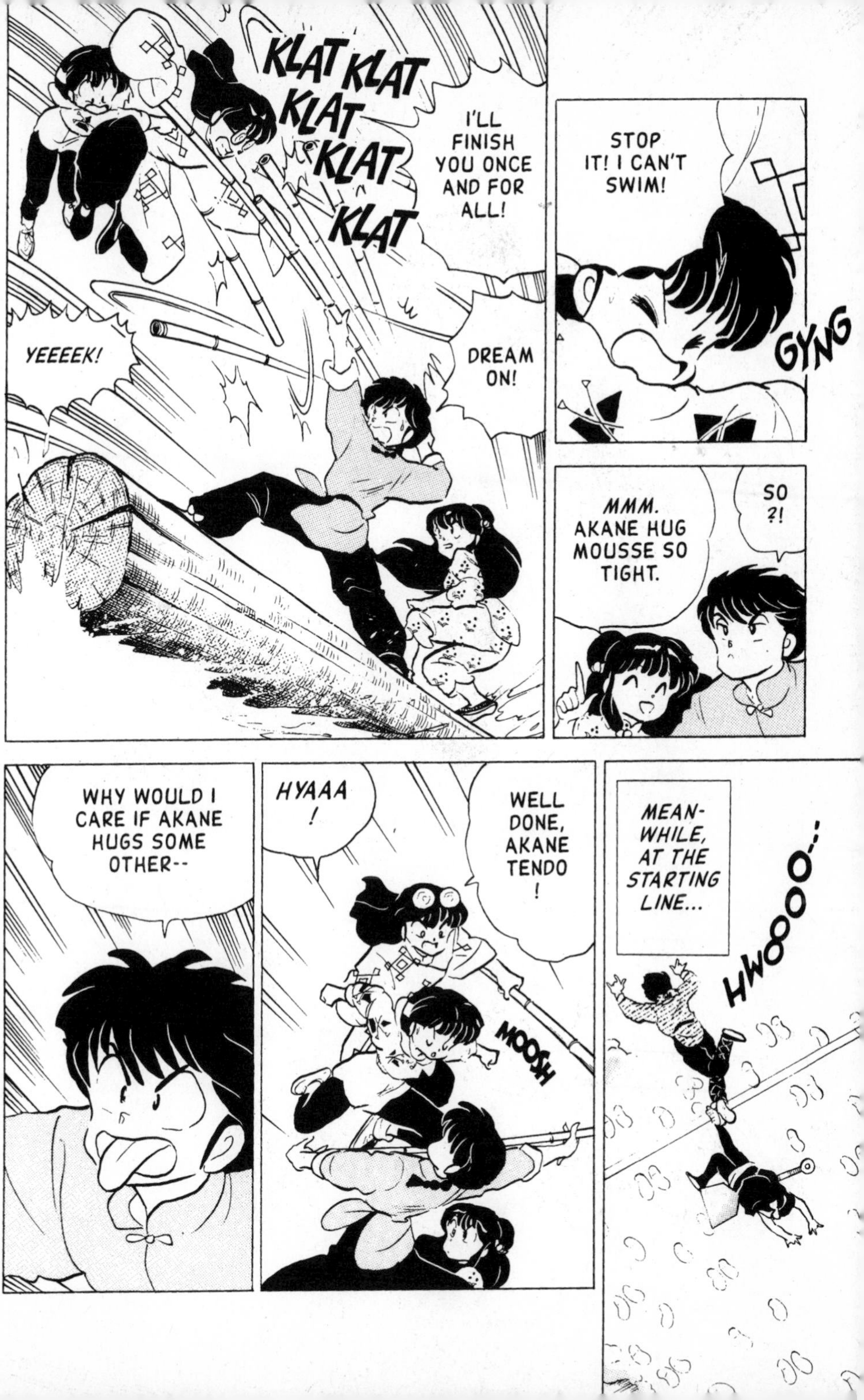
STOP IT! I CAN'T SWIM!
GYNG
MMM. AKANE HUG MOUSSE SO TIGHT.
SO ?!
KLAT KLAT KLAT KLAT KLAT
I'LL FINISH YOU ONCE AND FOR ALL!
DREAM ON!
YEEEEK!
MEAN-WHILE, AT THE STARTING LINE...
HWOOOO...
WELL DONE, AKANE TENDO!
HYAAA!
MOOSH
WHY WOULD I CARE IF AKANE HUGS SOME OTHER--

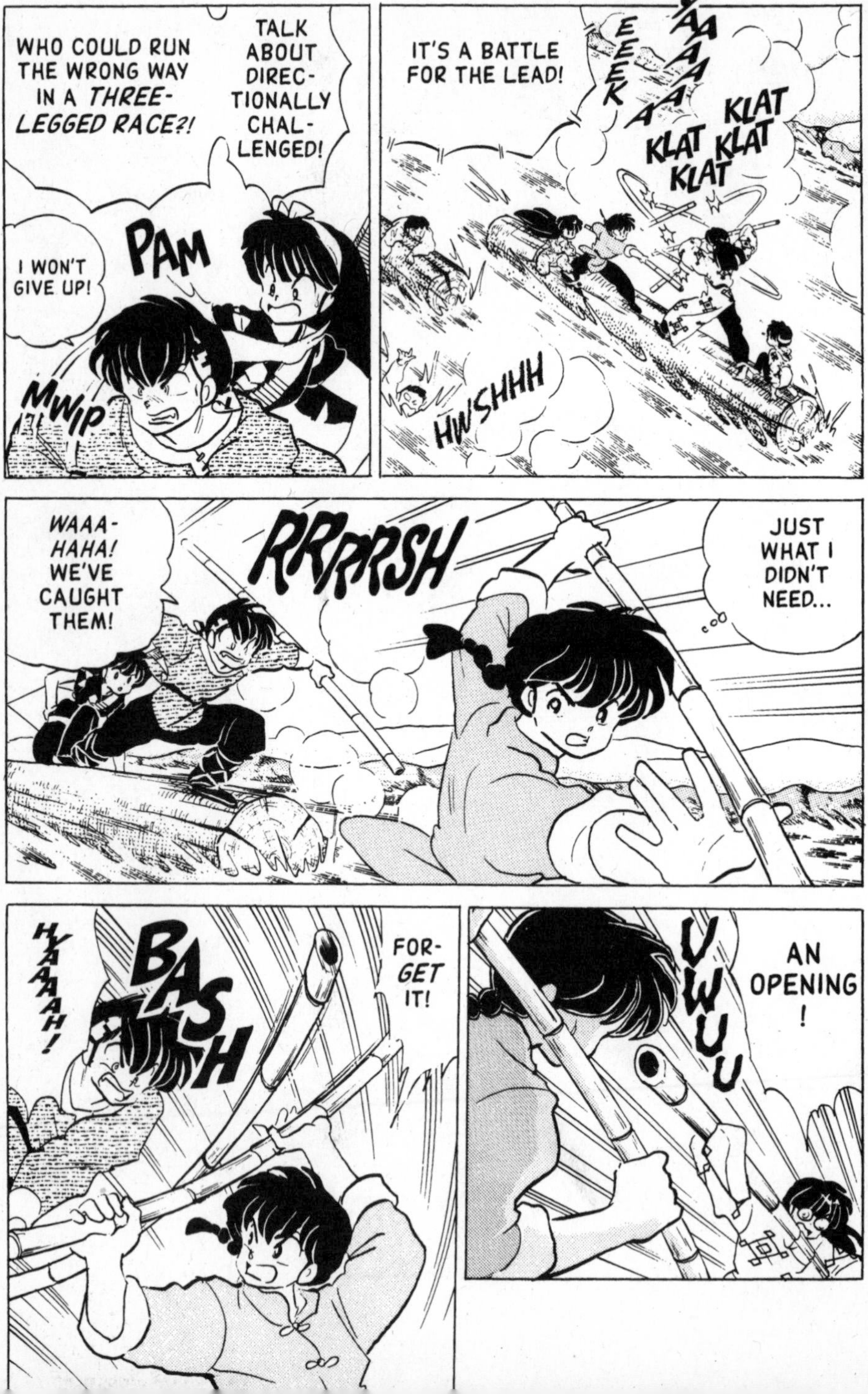
WHO COULD RUN THE WRONG WAY IN A *THREE-LEGGED RACE?!*
TALK ABOUT DIREC-TIONALLY CHAL-LENGED!
PAM
I WON'T GIVE UP!
MWIP
IT'S A BATTLE FOR THE LEAD!
EEEEK
YAAAAA
KLAT KLAT KLAT KLAT KLAT
HWSHHH
WAAA-HAHA! WE'VE CAUGHT THEM!
RRRRSH
JUST WHAT I DIDN'T NEED...
HYAAAAH!
BASH
FOR-*GET* IT!
VWUU
AN OPENING!

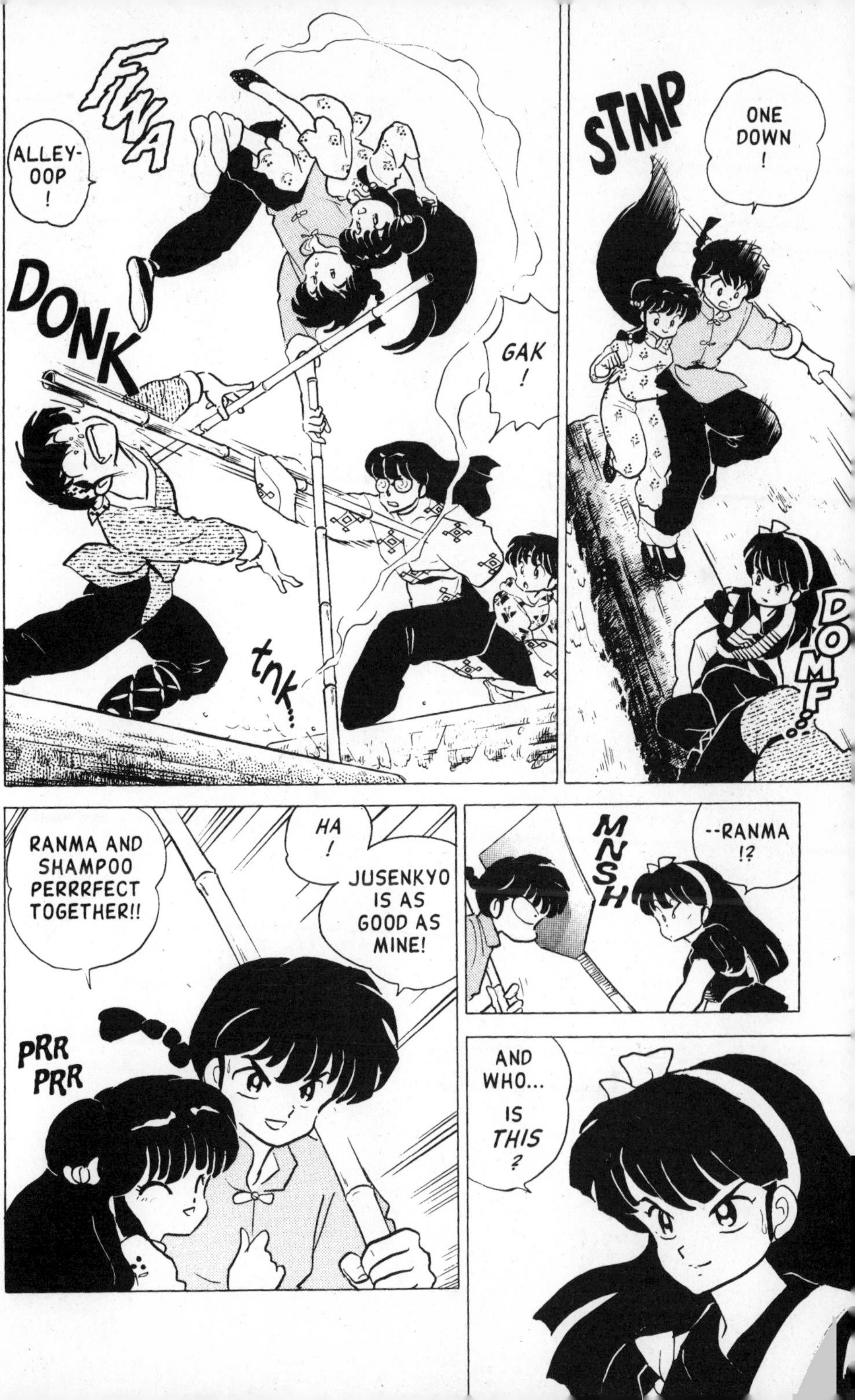
FWA
ALLEY-OOP!
DONK
GAK!
tnk...
STMP
ONE DOWN!
DOMF...
RANMA AND SHAMPOO PERRRFECT TOGETHER!!
HA!
JUSENKYO IS AS GOOD AS MINE!
PRR PRR
MNSH
--RANMA!?
AND WHO... IS THIS?

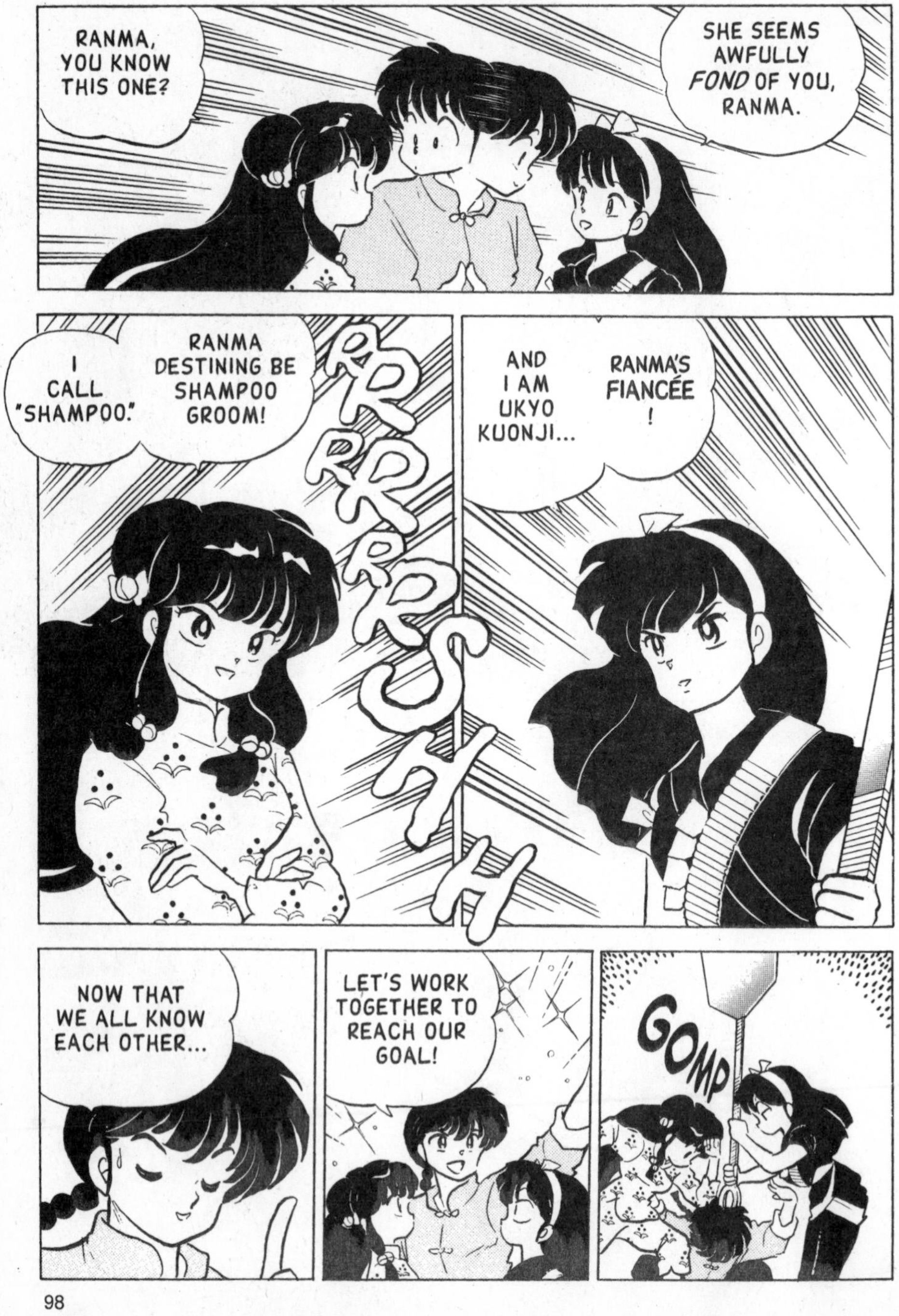
RANMA, YOU KNOW THIS ONE?
SHE SEEMS AWFULLY *FOND* OF YOU, RANMA.
I CALL "SHAMPOO."
RANMA DESTINING BE SHAMPOO GROOM!
RRRRRSH
AND I AM UKYO KUONJI...
RANMA'S FIANCÉE!
NOW THAT WE ALL KNOW EACH OTHER...
LET'S WORK TOGETHER TO REACH OUR GOAL!
GOMP

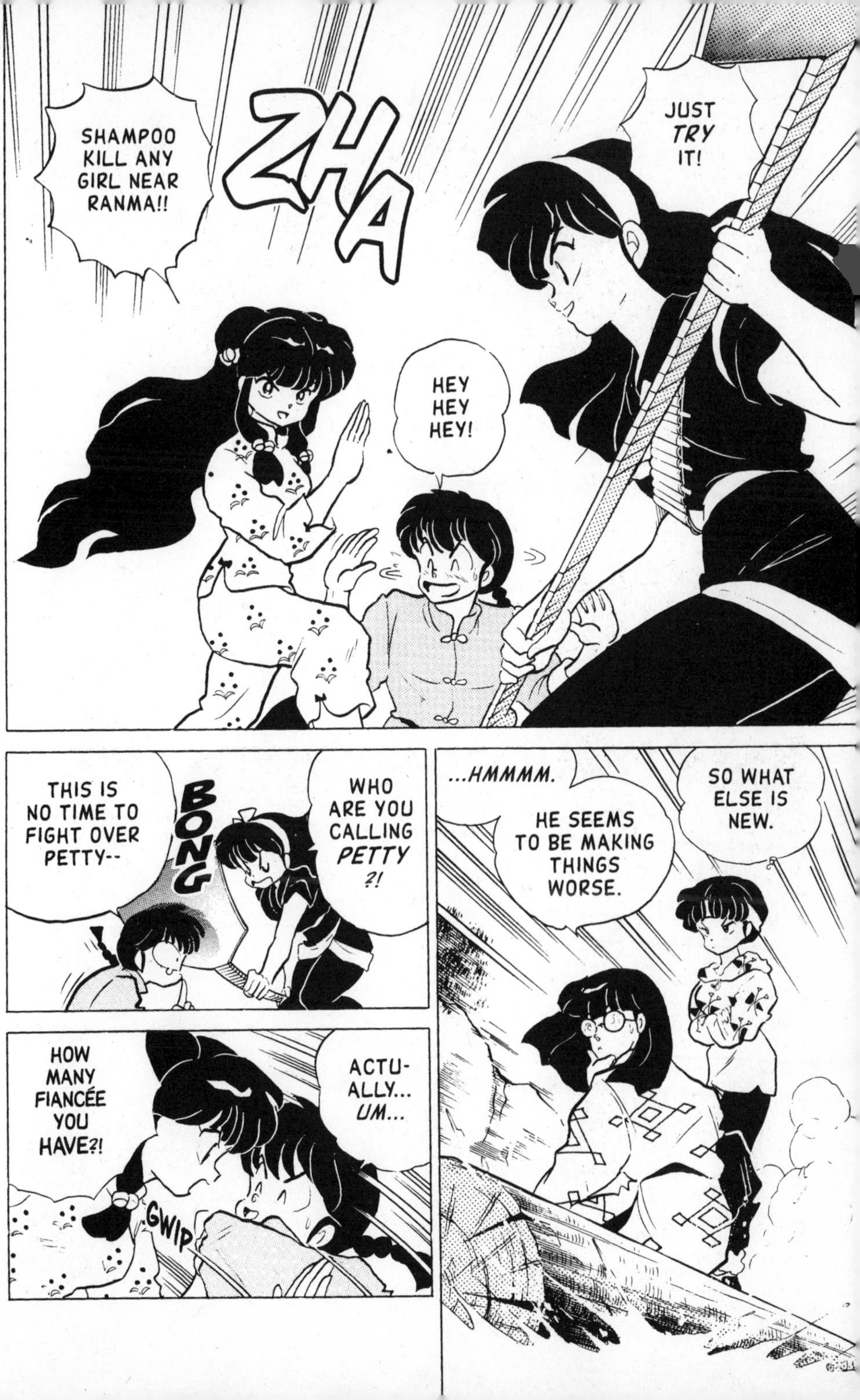

SHAMPOO KILL ANY GIRL NEAR RANMA!!
ZHA
JUST TRY IT!
HEY HEY HEY!
THIS IS NO TIME TO FIGHT OVER PETTY--
BONG
WHO ARE YOU CALLING PETTY ?!
...HMMMM.
SO WHAT ELSE IS NEW.
HE SEEMS TO BE MAKING THINGS WORSE.
HOW MANY FIANCÉE YOU HAVE?!
ACTU-ALLY... UM...
GWIP

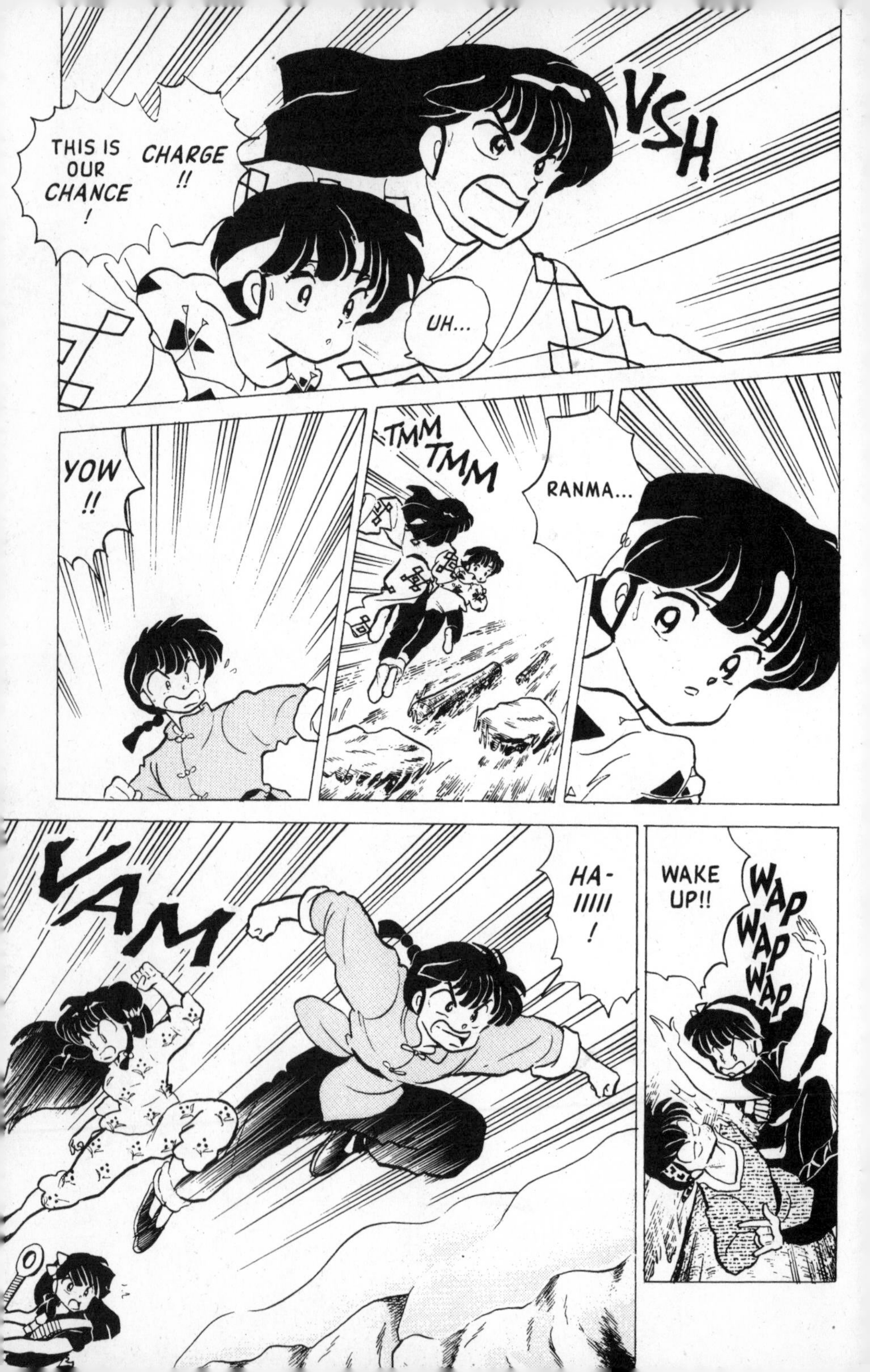
THIS IS OUR CHANCE !
CHARGE !!
VSH
UH...
YOW !!
TMM TMM
RANMA...
VAM
HA-IIIII !
WAKE UP!!
WAP WAP WAP WAP

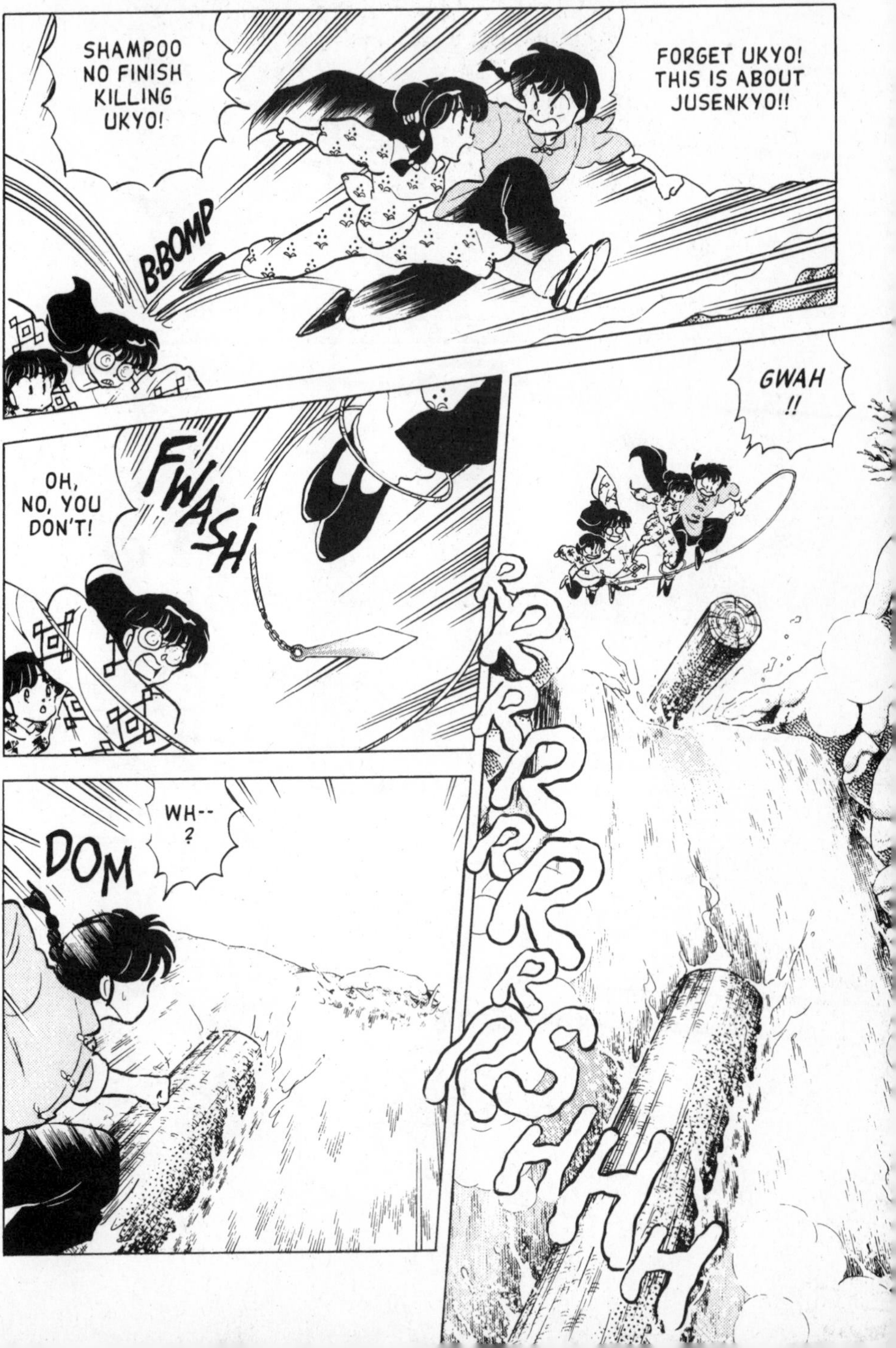
SHAMPOO NO FINISH KILLING UKYO!
FORGET UKYO! THIS IS ABOUT JUSENKYO!!
B-BOMP
OH, NO, YOU DON'T!
FWASH
WH-- ?
DOM
GWAH !!
RRRRRRRSHHHH

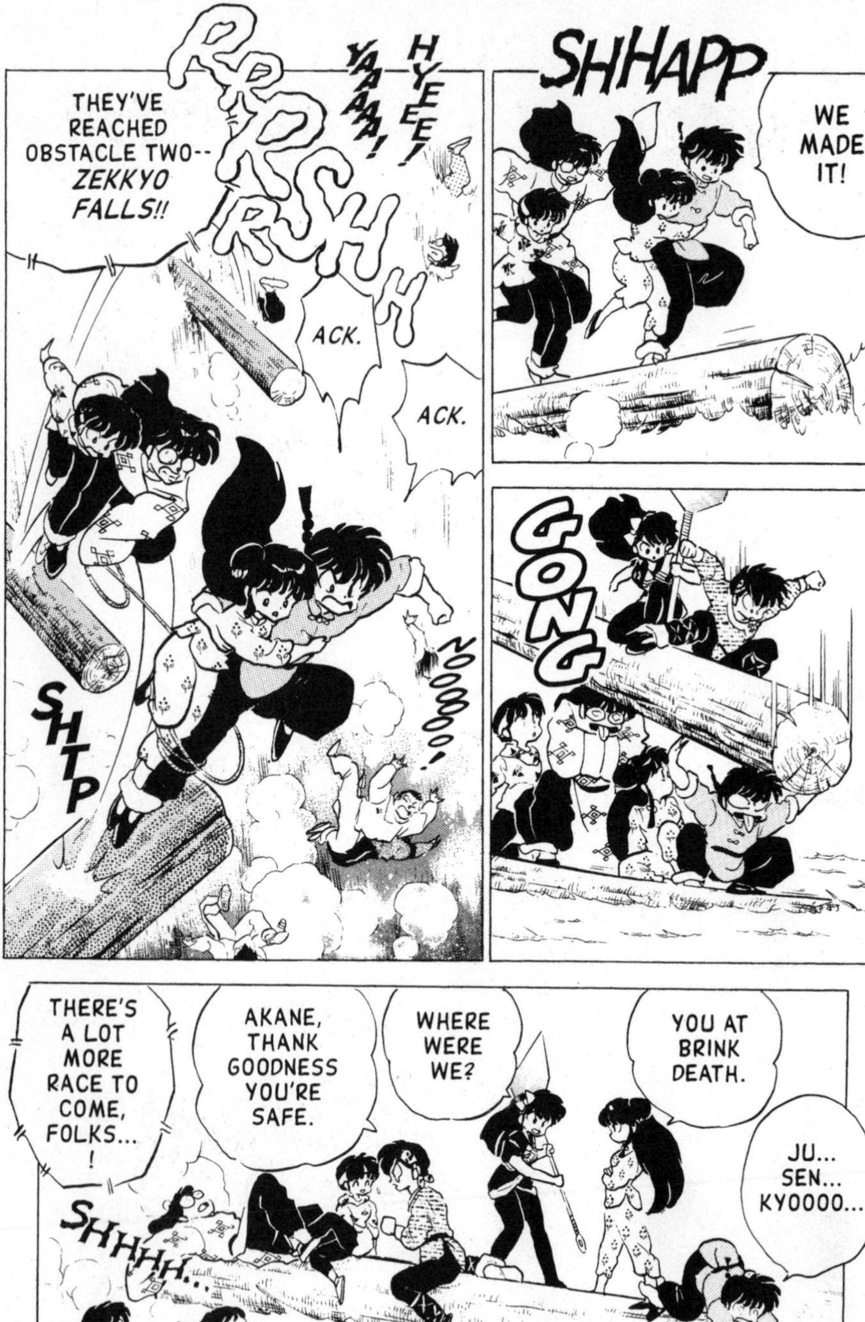
RRRRSHHH
YAAAAA!
HYEEE!
THEY'VE REACHED OBSTACLE TWO-- ZEKKYO FALLS!!
ACK.
ACK.
SHTP
NOOOOOOO!
SHHAPP
WE MADE IT!
GONG
THERE'S A LOT MORE RACE TO COME, FOLKS... !
AKANE, THANK GOODNESS YOU'RE SAFE.
WHERE WERE WE?
YOU AT BRINK DEATH.
JU... SEN... KYOOOO...
SHHHH...

PART 7
THREE-LEG SCRAMBLE

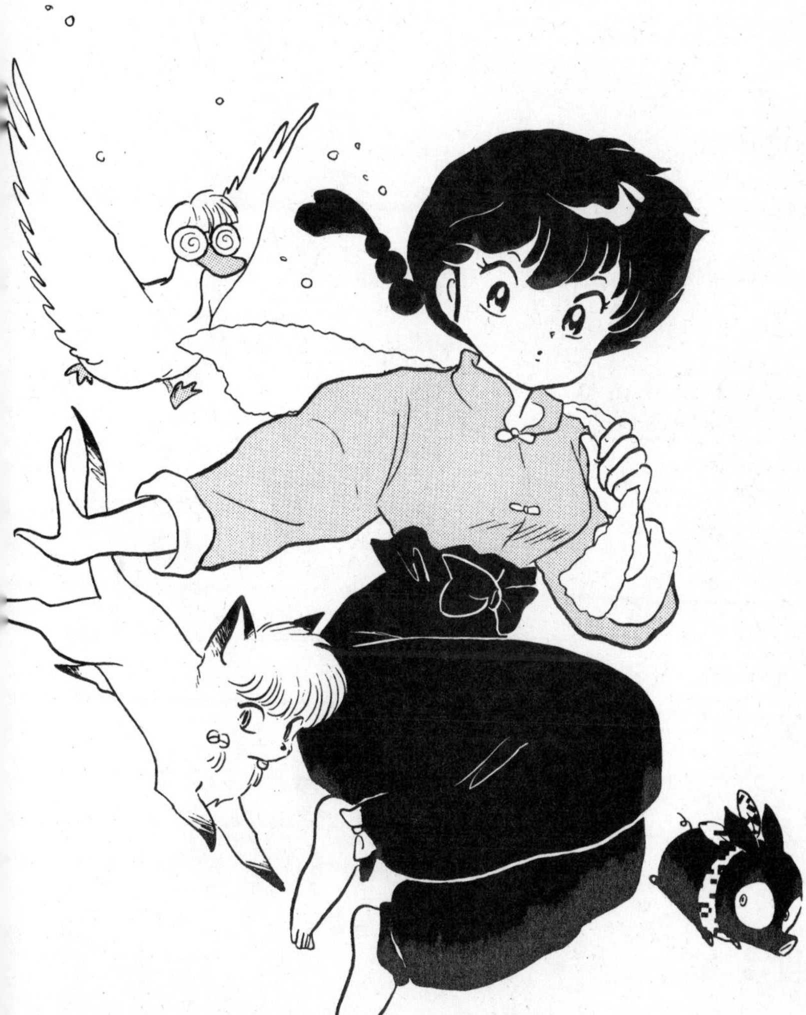

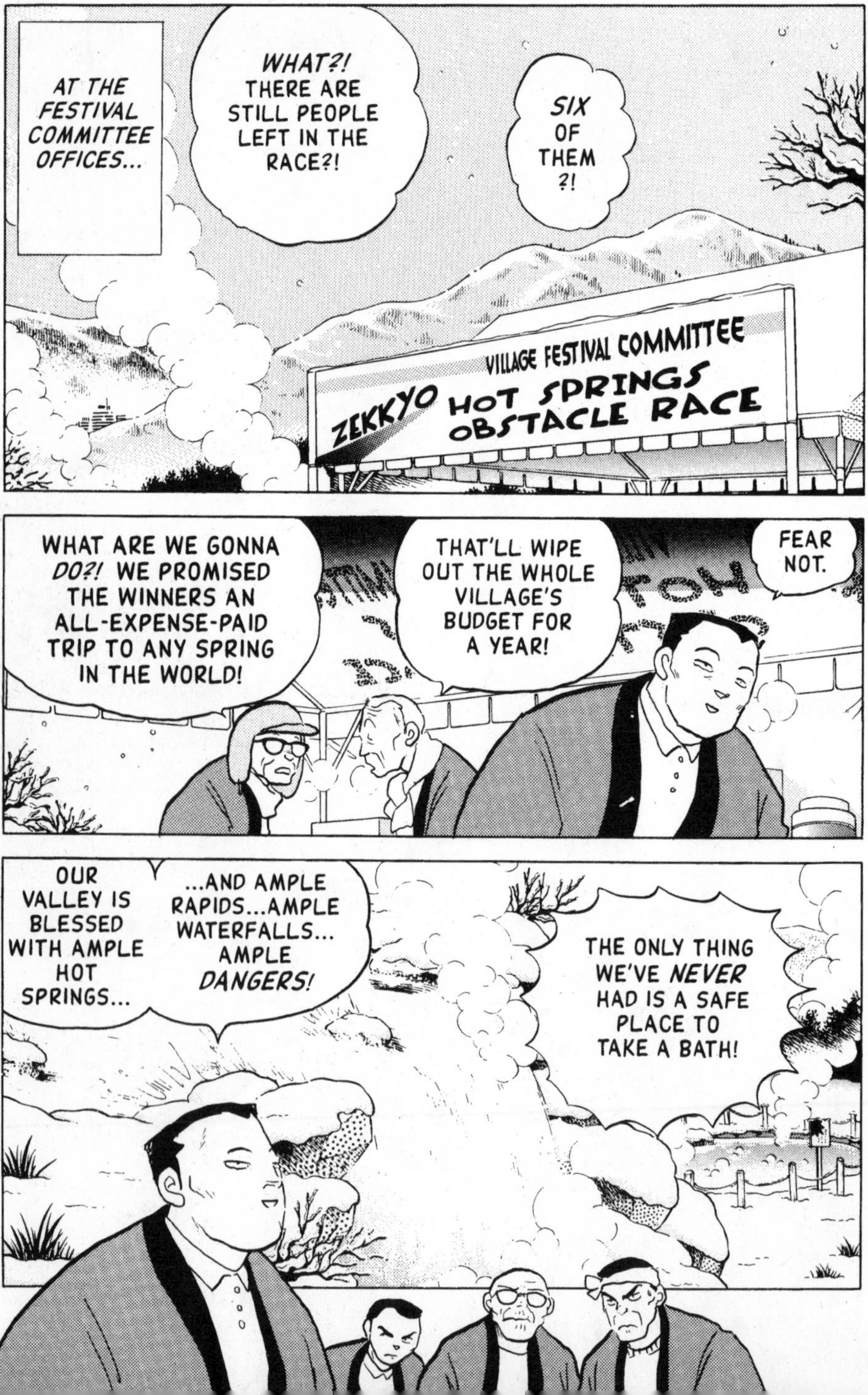
AT THE FESTIVAL COMMITTEE OFFICES...
WHAT?! THERE ARE STILL PEOPLE LEFT IN THE RACE?!
SIX OF THEM ?!
VILLAGE FESTIVAL COMMITTEE
ZEKKYO HOT SPRINGS OBSTACLE RACE
WHAT ARE WE GONNA *DO?!* WE PROMISED THE WINNERS AN ALL-EXPENSE-PAID TRIP TO ANY SPRING IN THE WORLD!
THAT'LL WIPE OUT THE WHOLE VILLAGE'S BUDGET FOR A YEAR!
FEAR NOT.
OUR VALLEY IS BLESSED WITH AMPLE HOT SPRINGS...
...AND AMPLE RAPIDS...AMPLE WATERFALLS... AMPLE *DANGERS!*
THE ONLY THING WE'VE *NEVER* HAD IS A SAFE PLACE TO TAKE A BATH!

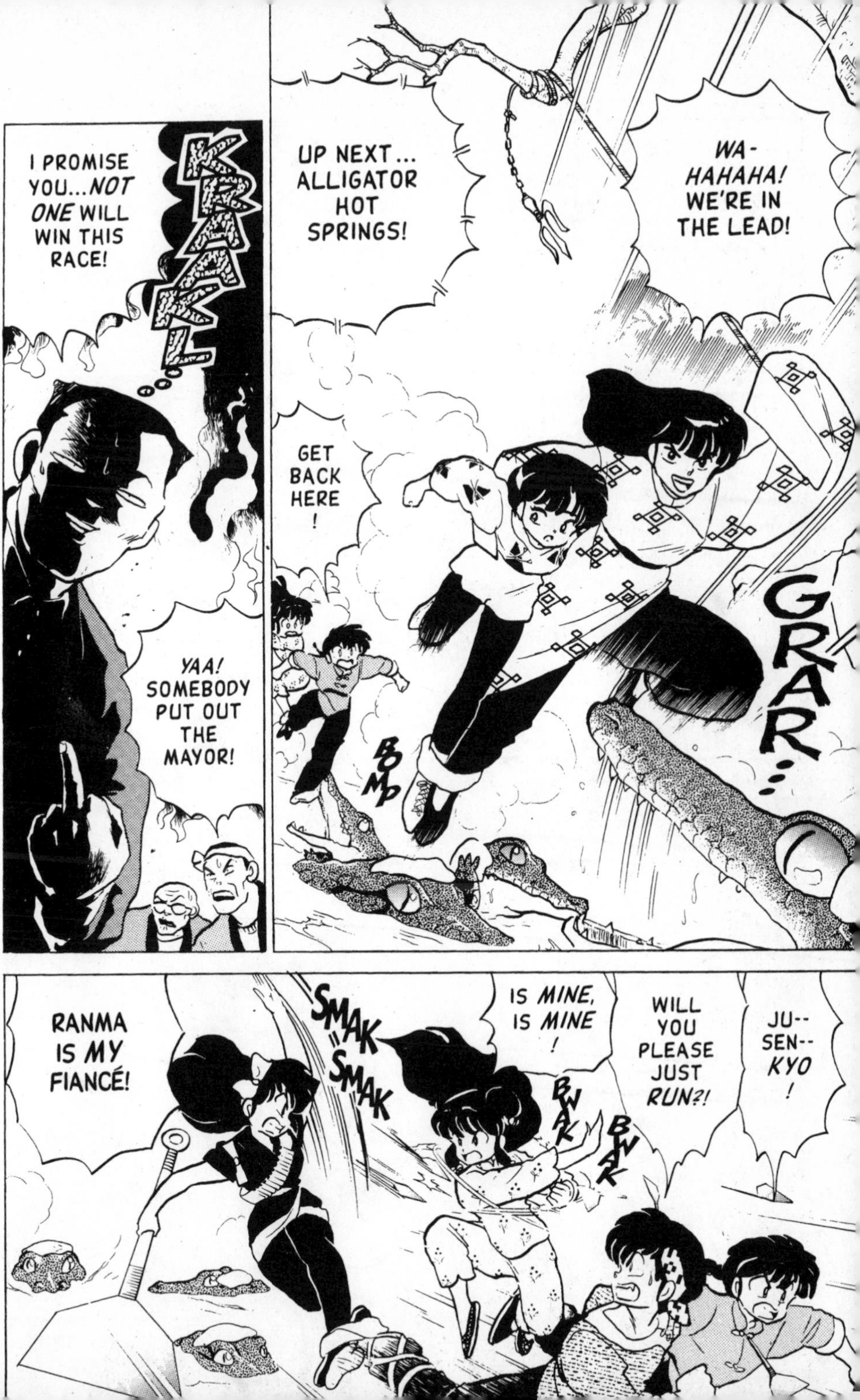
I PROMISE YOU...NOT ONE WILL WIN THIS RACE!
KRAKL
YAA! SOMEBODY PUT OUT THE MAYOR!
UP NEXT... ALLIGATOR HOT SPRINGS!
WA-HAHAHA! WE'RE IN THE LEAD!
GET BACK HERE!
BOMP
GRAR...
RANMA IS MY FIANCÉ!
SMAK SMAK
IS MINE, IS MINE!
BWAK BWAK
WILL YOU PLEASE JUST RUN?!
JU-- SEN-- KYO!

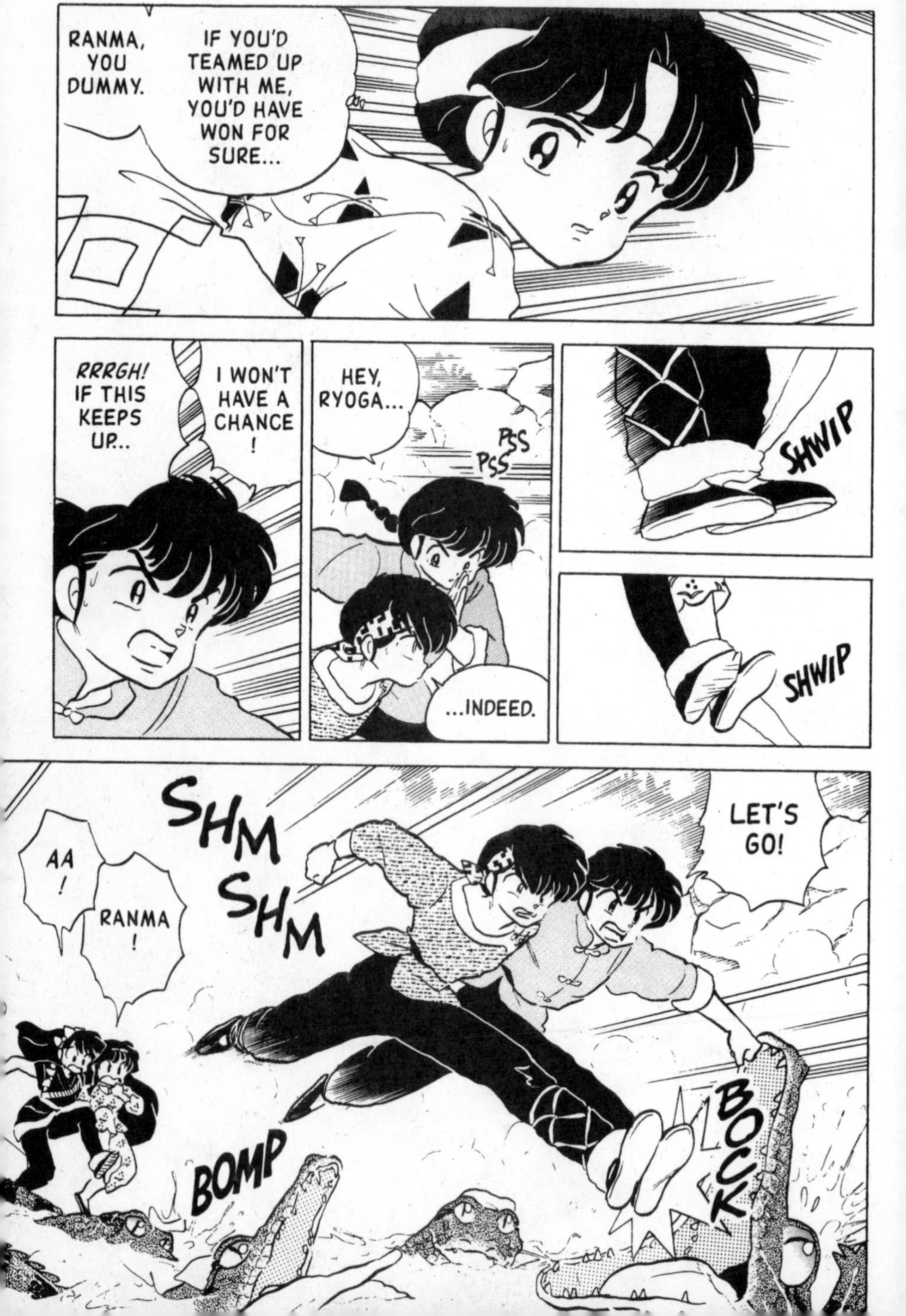
RANMA, YOU DUMMY.
IF YOU'D TEAMED UP WITH ME, YOU'D HAVE WON FOR SURE...
RRRGH! IF THIS KEEPS UP...
I WON'T HAVE A CHANCE !
HEY, RYOGA...
PSS PSS
...INDEED.
SHWIP
SHWIP
SHM SHM
AA !
RANMA !
LET'S GO!
BOMP
BOCK

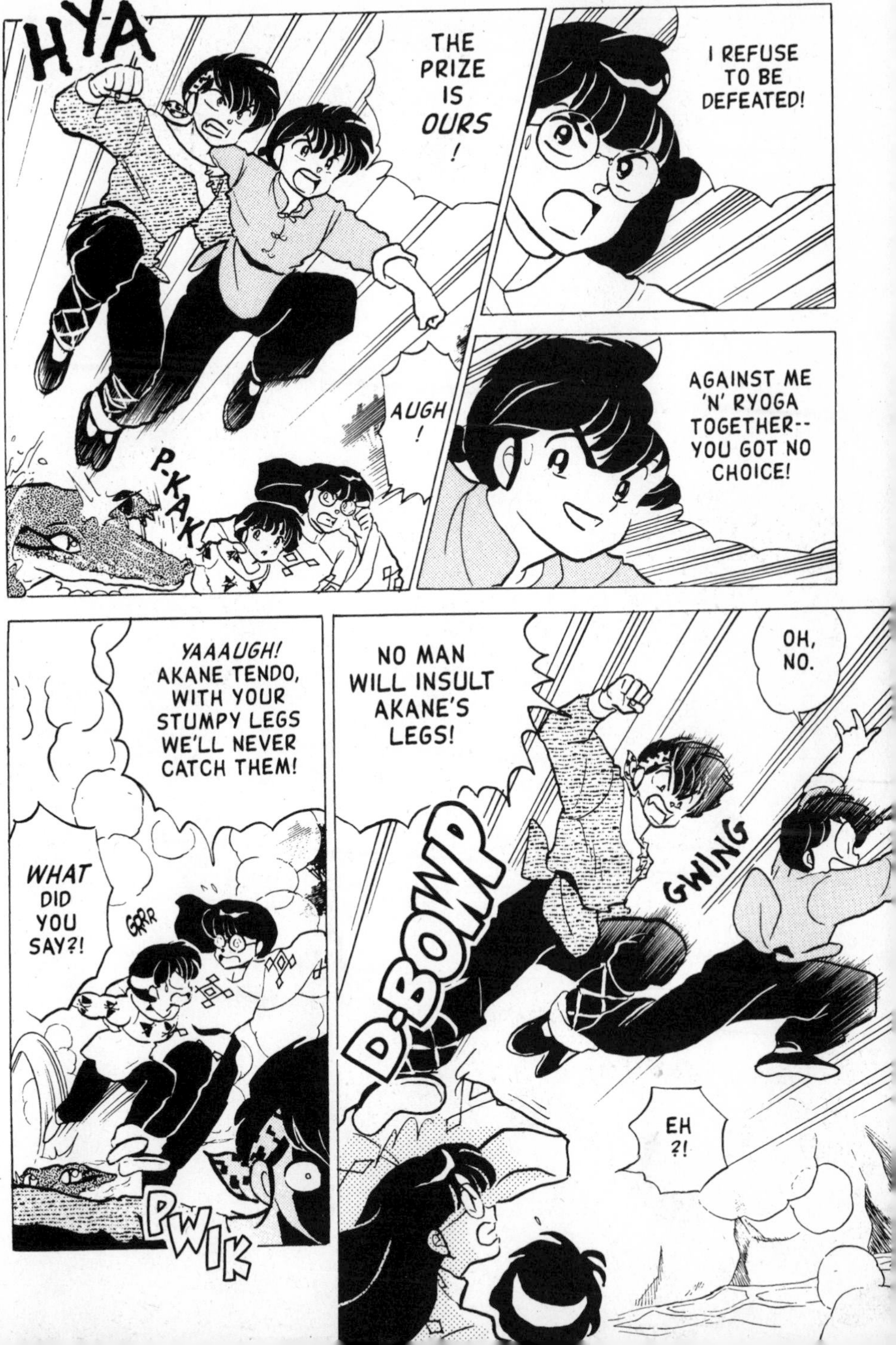
HYA
THE PRIZE IS OURS!
P-KAK
AUGH!
I REFUSE TO BE DEFEATED!
AGAINST ME 'N' RYOGA TOGETHER-- YOU GOT NO CHOICE!
YAAAUGH! AKANE TENDO, WITH YOUR STUMPY LEGS WE'LL NEVER CATCH THEM!
WHAT DID YOU SAY?!
GRRR
PWIK
NO MAN WILL INSULT AKANE'S LEGS!
OH, NO.
D-BOWP
GWING
EH?!

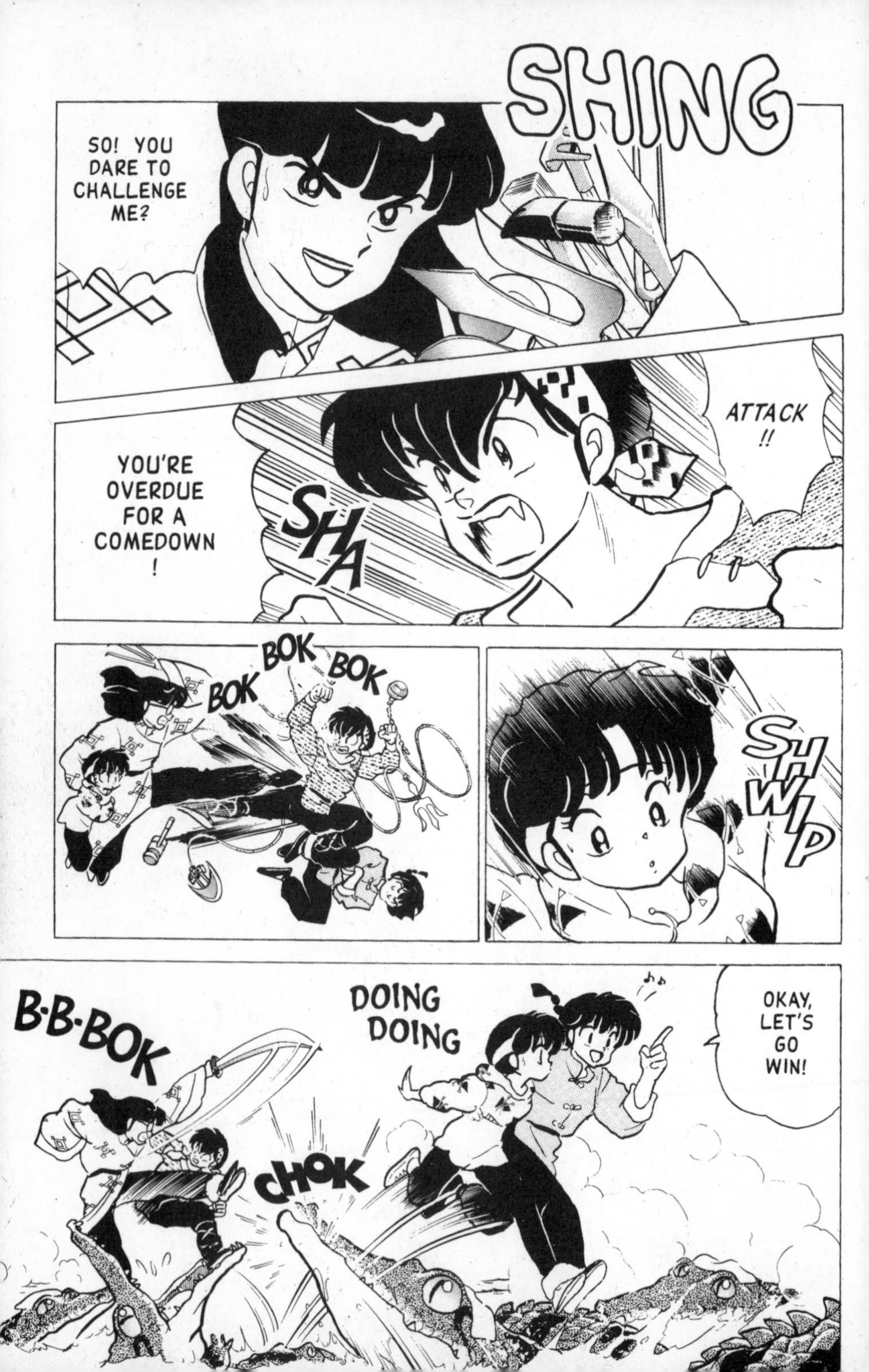
SHING
SO! YOU DARE TO CHALLENGE ME?
YOU'RE OVERDUE FOR A COMEDOWN !
SHA
ATTACK !!
BOK
BOK
BOK
SHWIP
B-B-BOK
CHOK
DOING DOING
OKAY, LET'S GO WIN!

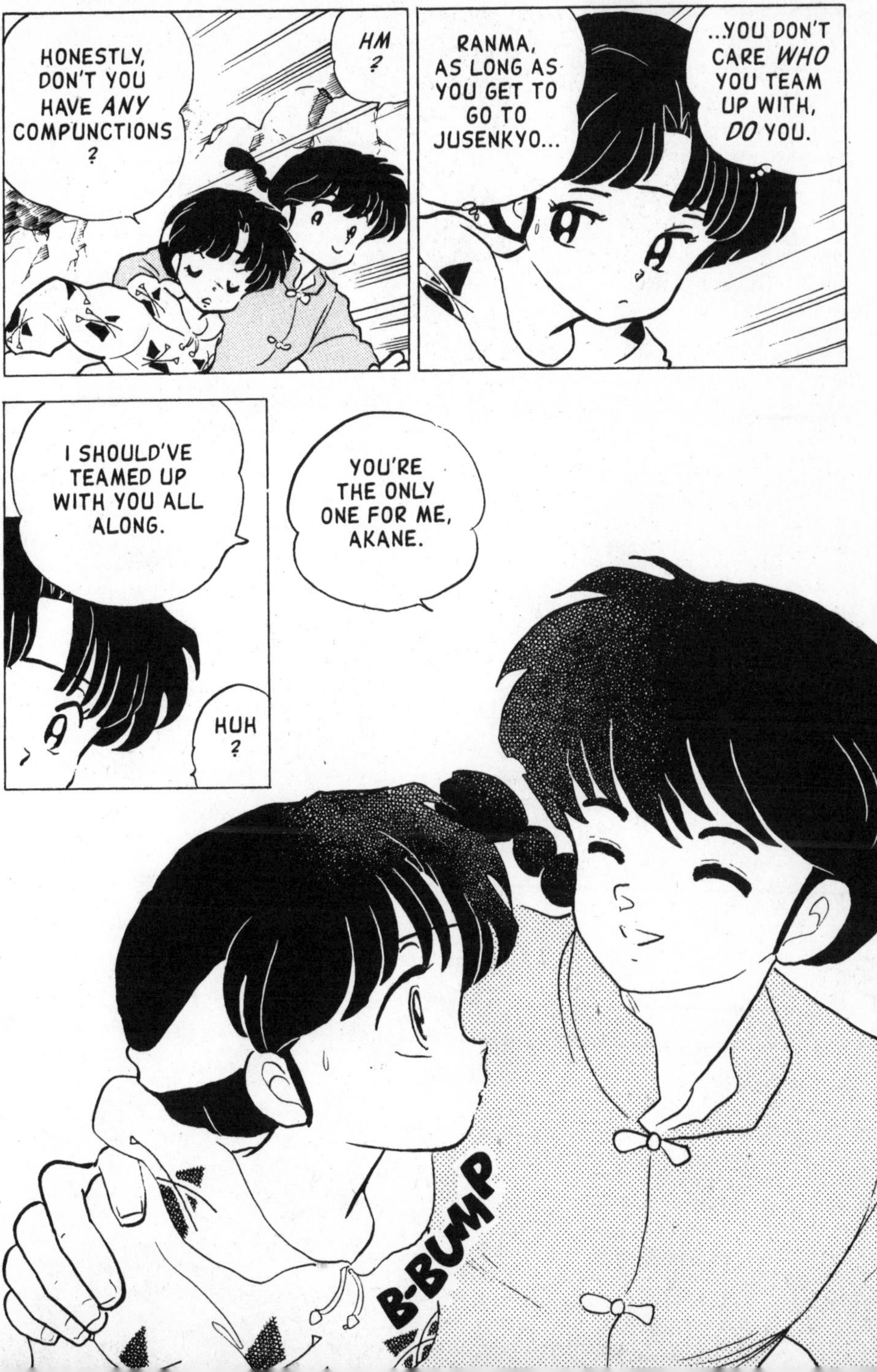
HONESTLY, DON'T YOU HAVE *ANY* COMPUNCTIONS ?
HM ?
RANMA, AS LONG AS YOU GET TO GO TO JUSENKYO...
...YOU DON'T CARE *WHO* YOU TEAM UP WITH, *DO* YOU.
I SHOULD'VE TEAMED UP WITH YOU ALL ALONG.
HUH ?
YOU'RE THE ONLY ONE FOR ME, AKANE.
B-BUMP

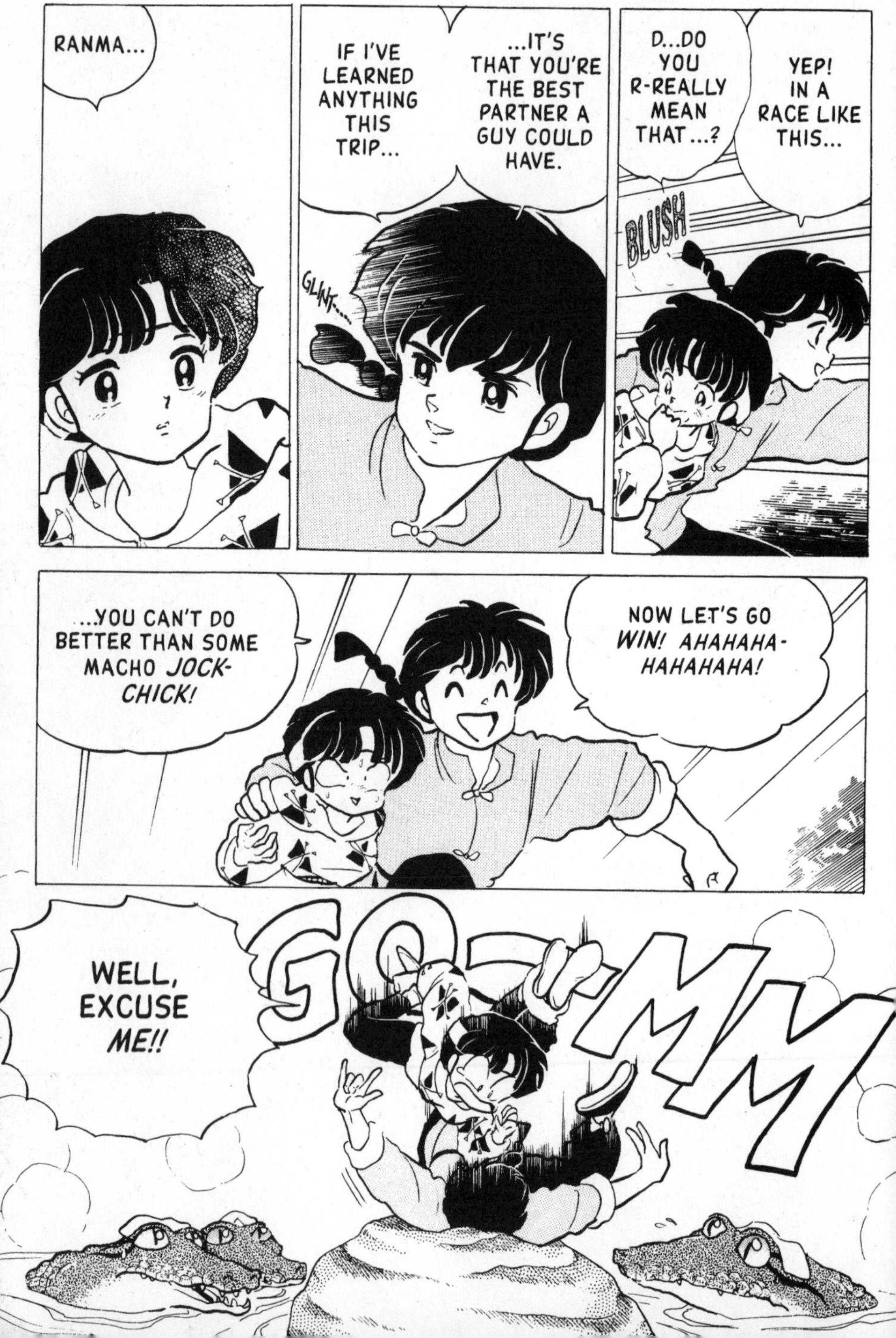
RANMA...
IF I'VE LEARNED ANYTHING THIS TRIP...
...IT'S THAT YOU'RE THE BEST PARTNER A GUY COULD HAVE.
GLINT...
D...DO YOU R-REALLY MEAN THAT...?
YEP! IN A RACE LIKE THIS...
BLUSH
...YOU CAN'T DO BETTER THAN SOME MACHO *JOCK-CHICK!*
NOW LET'S GO *WIN! AHAHAHA-HAHAHAHA!*
WELL, EXCUSE *ME!!*
GO-MM

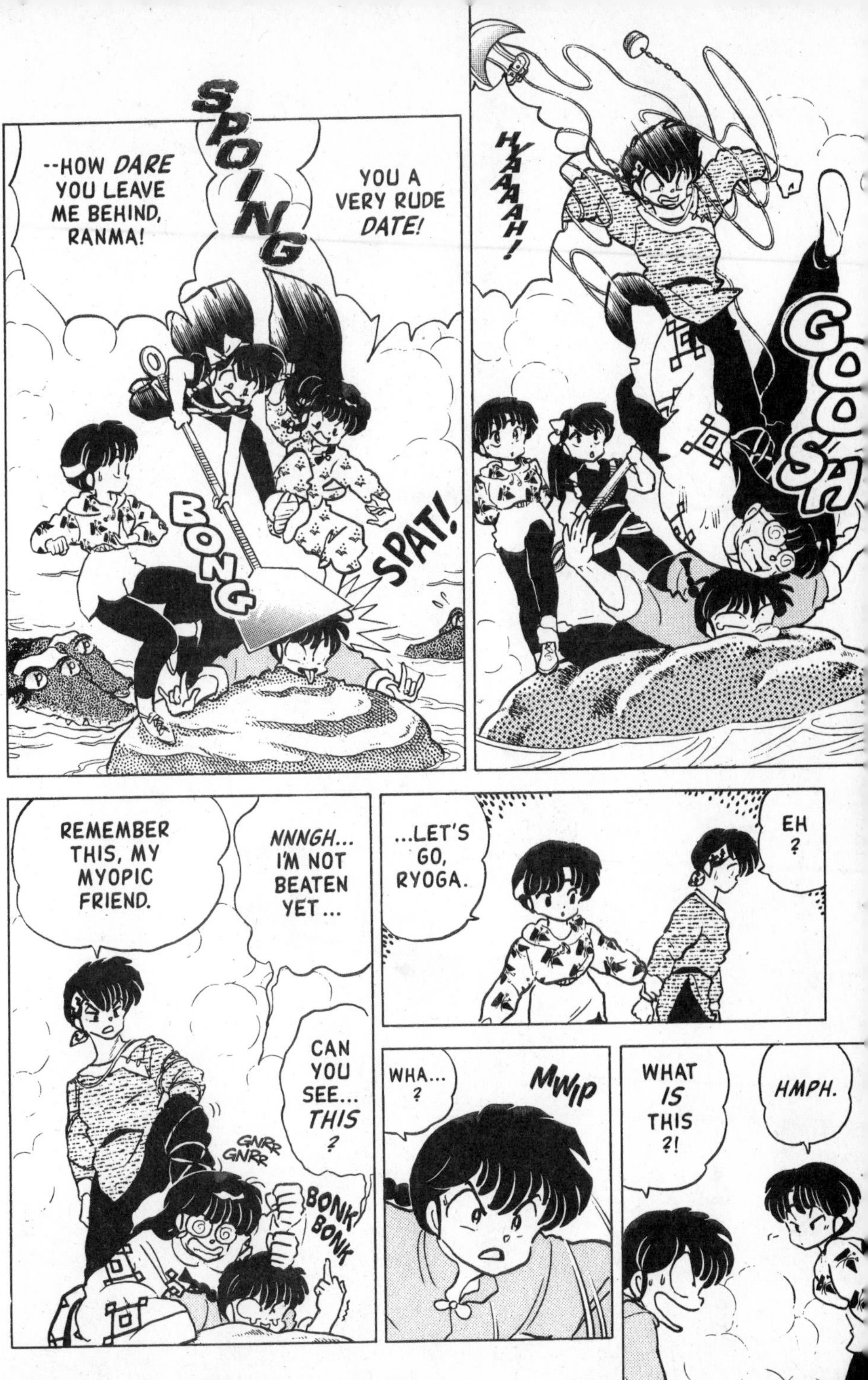
--HOW DARE YOU LEAVE ME BEHIND, RANMA!
SPOING
YOU A VERY RUDE DATE!
BONG
SPAT!
HYAAAAH!
GOOOSH
REMEMBER THIS, MY MYOPIC FRIEND.
NNNGH... I'M NOT BEATEN YET...
CAN YOU SEE... THIS?
GNRR GNRR
BONK BONK
...LET'S GO, RYOGA.
EH?
WHA...?
MWIP
WHAT IS THIS?!
HMPH.

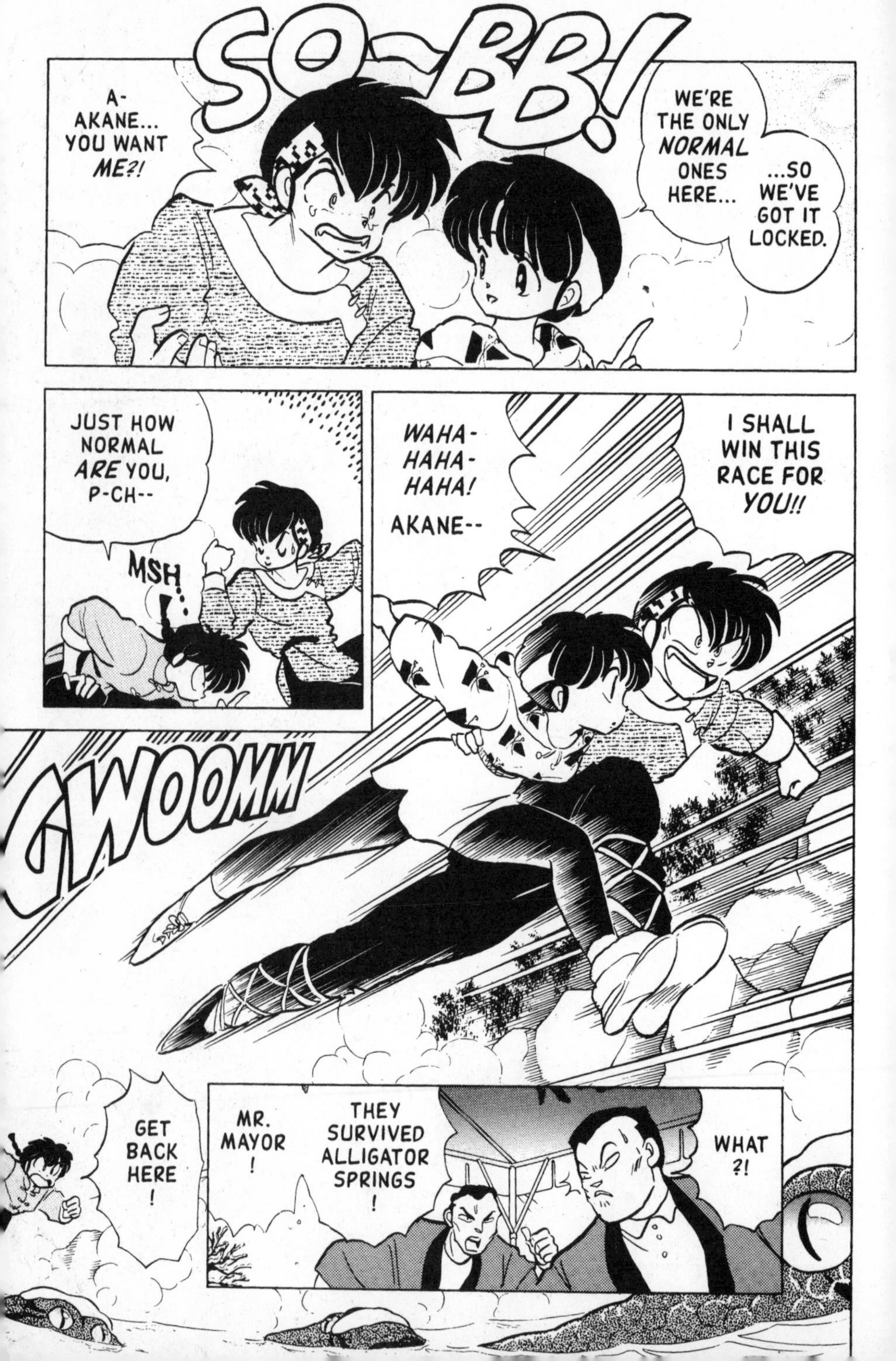
SO-BB!
A-AKANE... YOU WANT ME?!
WE'RE THE ONLY NORMAL ONES HERE...
...SO WE'VE GOT IT LOCKED.
JUST HOW NORMAL ARE YOU, P-CH--
MSH
WAHA-HAHA-HAHA! AKANE--
I SHALL WIN THIS RACE FOR YOU!!
GWOOMM
GET BACK HERE!
MR. MAYOR!
THEY SURVIVED ALLIGATOR SPRINGS!
WHAT?!

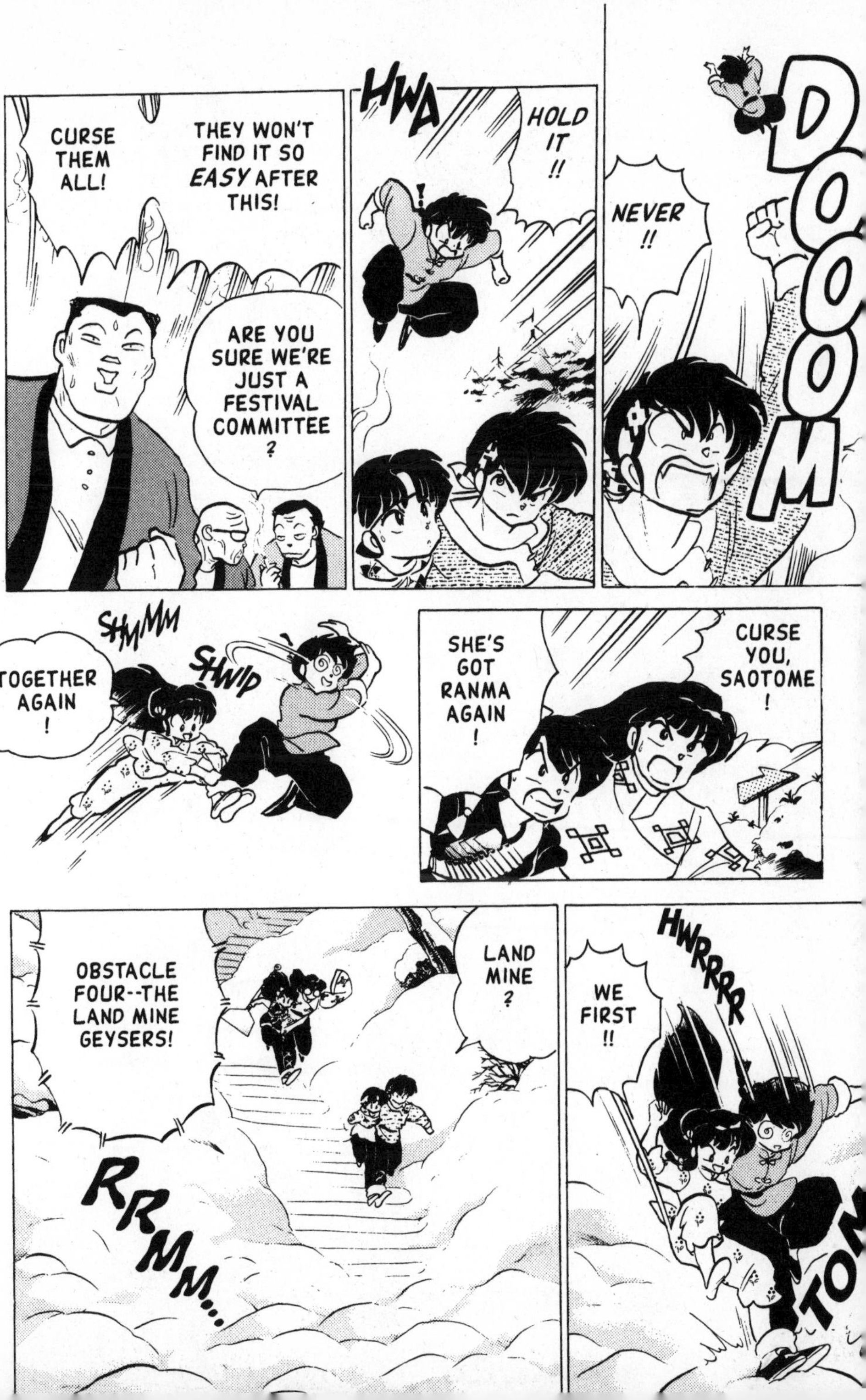
CURSE THEM ALL!
THEY WON'T FIND IT SO EASY AFTER THIS!
ARE YOU SURE WE'RE JUST A FESTIVAL COMMITTEE ?
HWA
HOLD IT !!
NEVER !!
DOOOOOM
SHMMM
TOGETHER AGAIN !
SHWIP
SHE'S GOT RANMA AGAIN !
CURSE YOU, SAOTOME !
OBSTACLE FOUR--THE LAND MINE GEYSERS!
LAND MINE ?
RRMM...
HWRRRRR
WE FIRST !!
TON

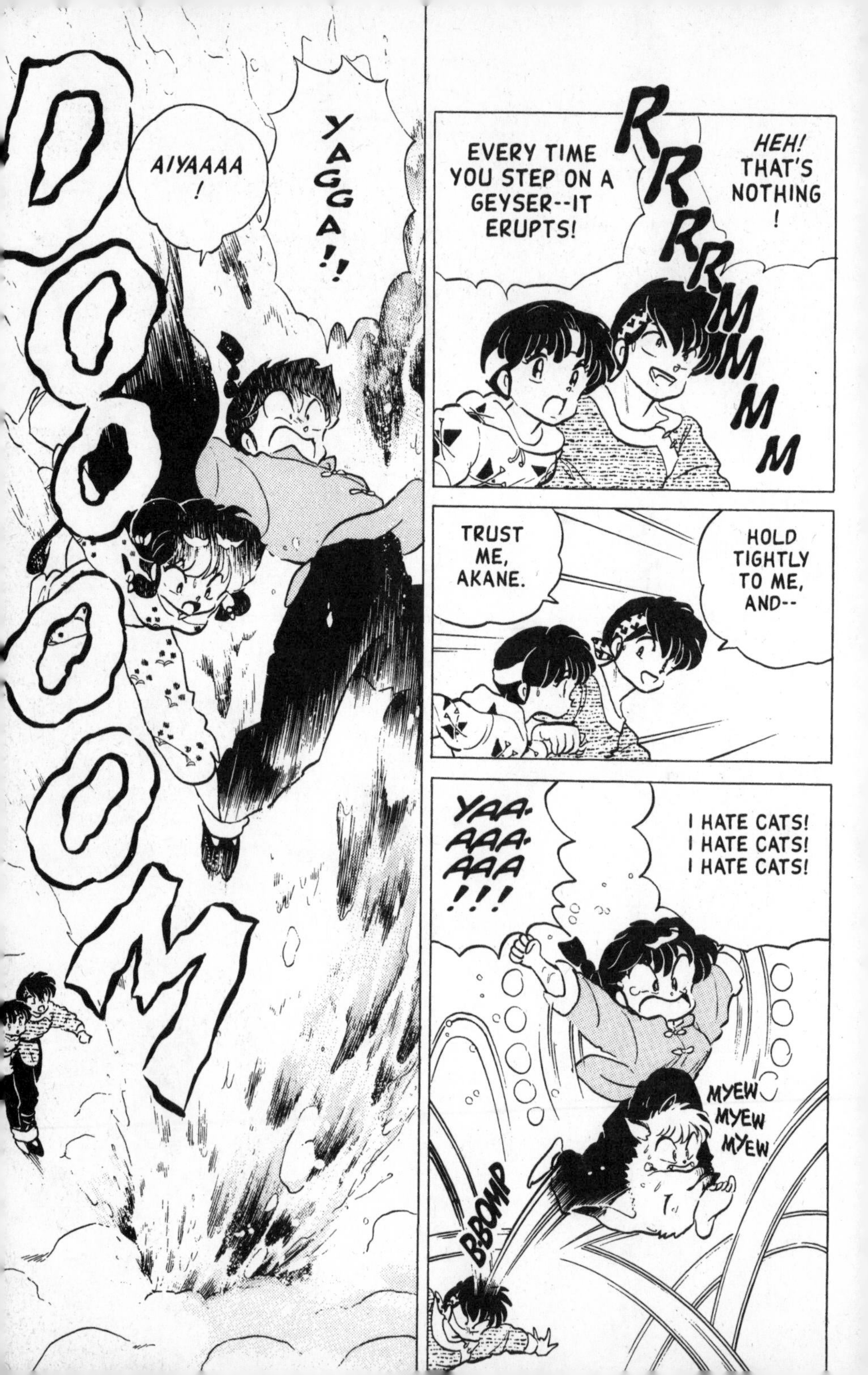
DOOOOOOM
AIYAAAA!
YAGGA!!
EVERY TIME YOU STEP ON A GEYSER--IT ERUPTS!
RRRRRMMMMM
HEH! THAT'S NOTHING!
TRUST ME, AKANE.
HOLD TIGHTLY TO ME, AND--
YAA-AAA-AAA!!!
I HATE CATS! I HATE CATS! I HATE CATS!
MYEW MYEW MYEW
BBOMP

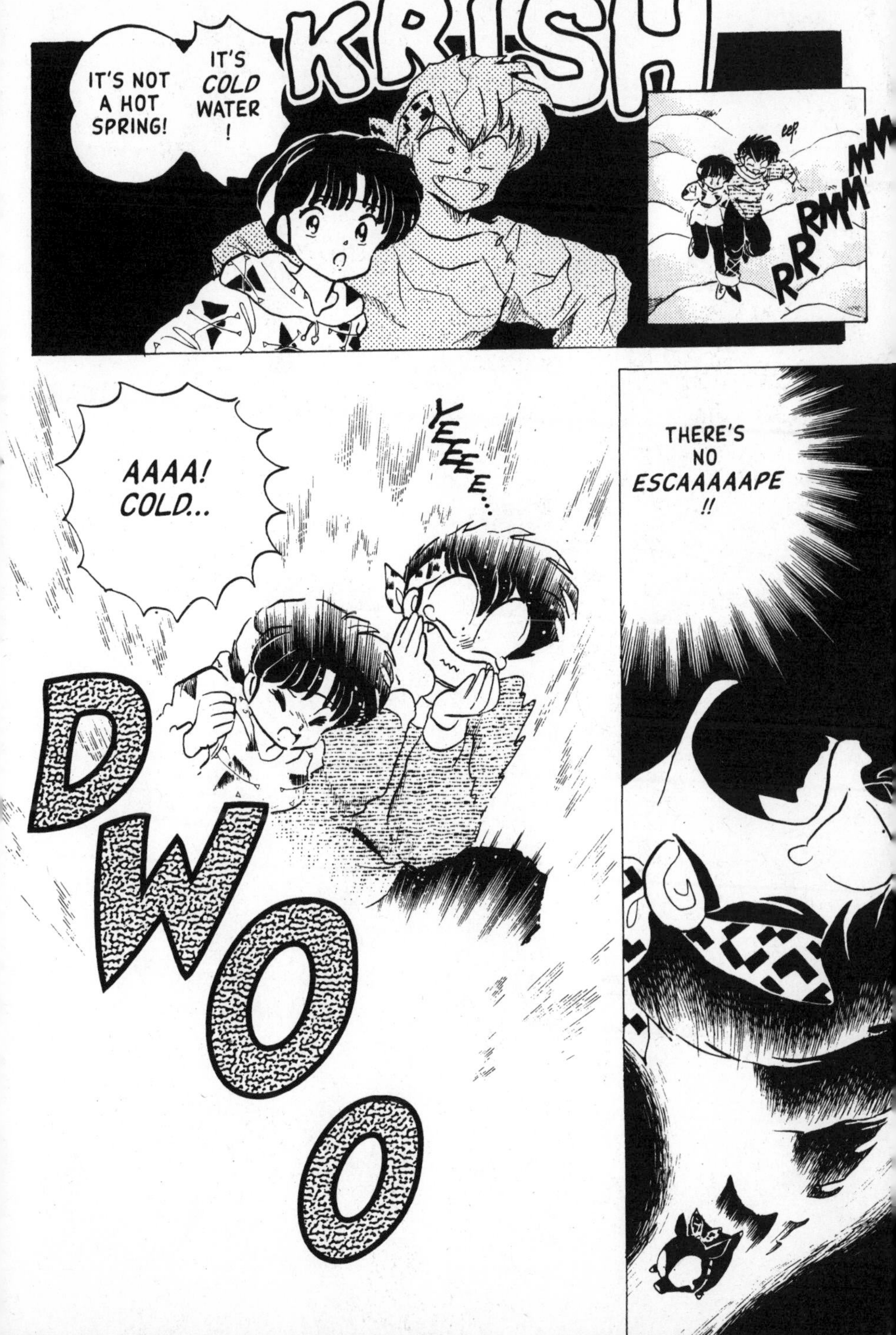

IT'S NOT A HOT SPRING!
IT'S COLD WATER !
KRISH
eep.
RRRMMMMM
AAAA! COLD...
YEEEE...
DWOOO
THERE'S NO ESCAAAAAPE !!

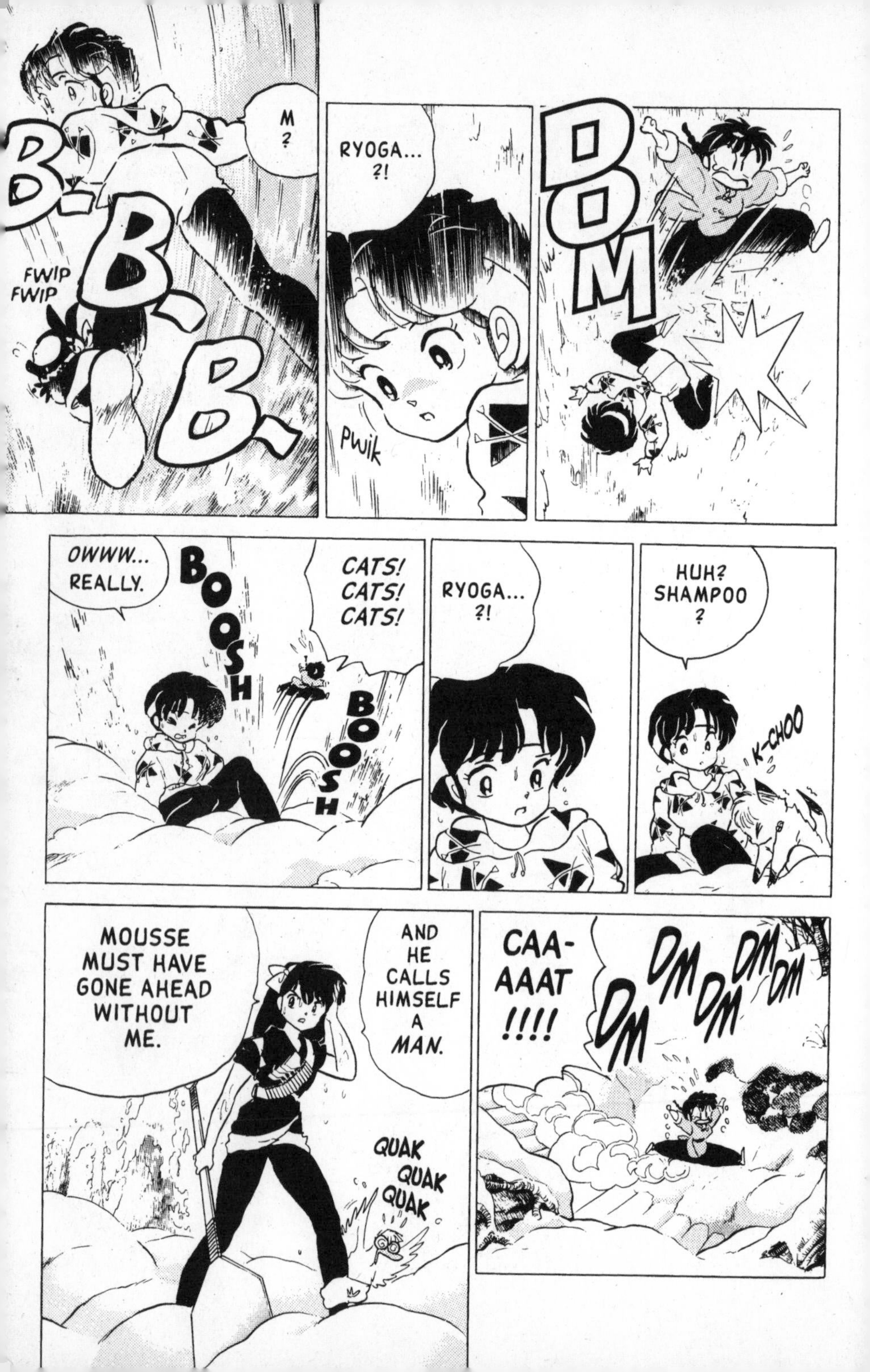
B-B-B-B-
FWIP FWIP
M ?
RYOGA... ?!
PWIK
DOM
OWWW... REALLY.
BOOSH
CATS! CATS! CATS!
BOOSH
RYOGA... ?!
HUH? SHAMPOO ?
K-CHOO
MOUSSE MUST HAVE GONE AHEAD WITHOUT ME.
AND HE CALLS HIMSELF A MAN.
QUAK QUAK QUAK
CAA-AAAT !!!!
DM DM DM DM DM DM DM

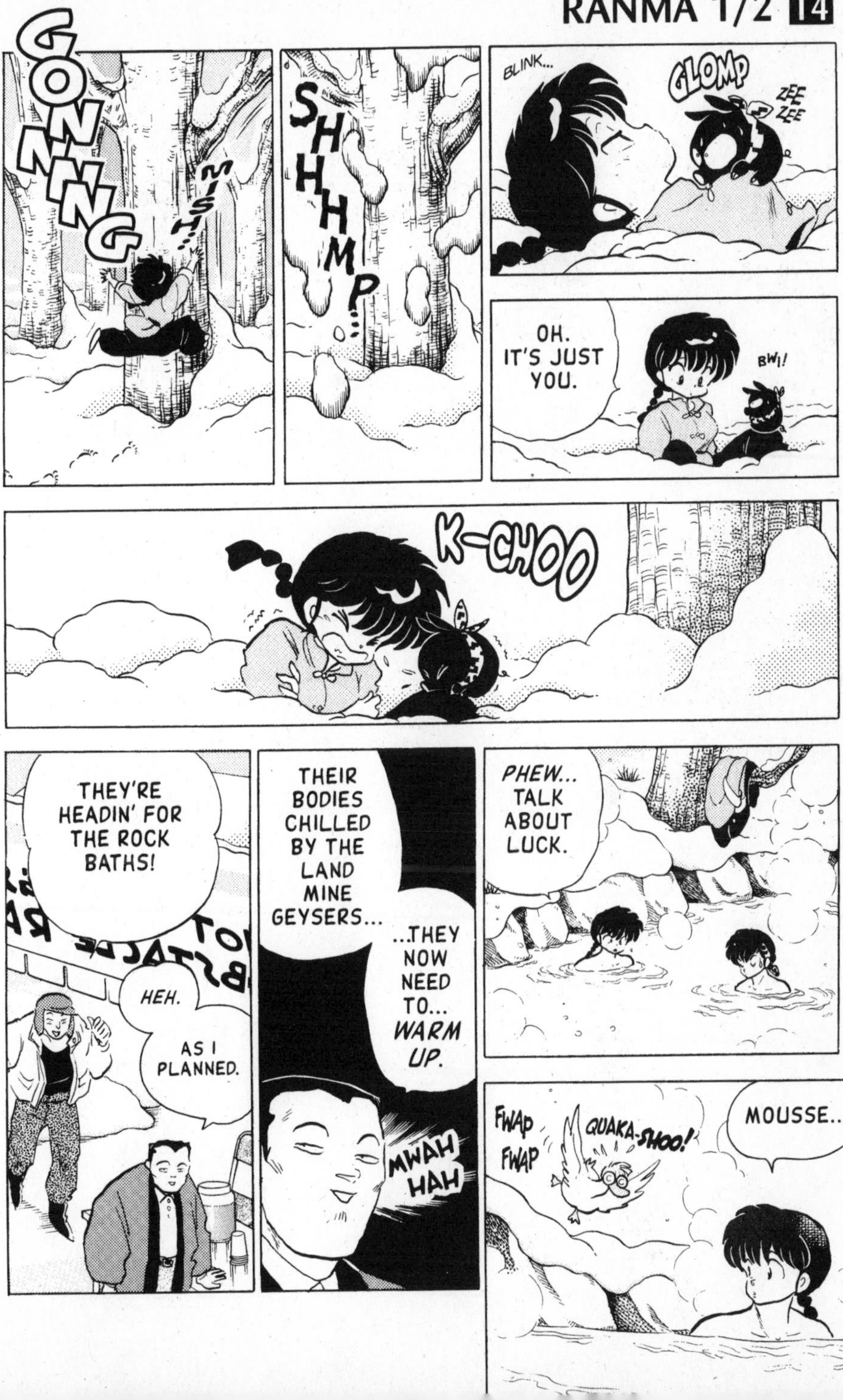
GONNNNG
MISH...
SHHHMP...
BLINK...
GLOMP
ZEE ZEE
OH. IT'S JUST YOU.
BWI!
K-CHOO
THEY'RE HEADIN' FOR THE ROCK BATHS!
HEH.
AS I PLANNED.
THEIR BODIES CHILLED BY THE LAND MINE GEYSERS...
...THEY NOW NEED TO... WARM UP.
MWAH HAH
PHEW... TALK ABOUT LUCK.
FWAP FWAP
QUAKA-SHOO!
MOUSSE...

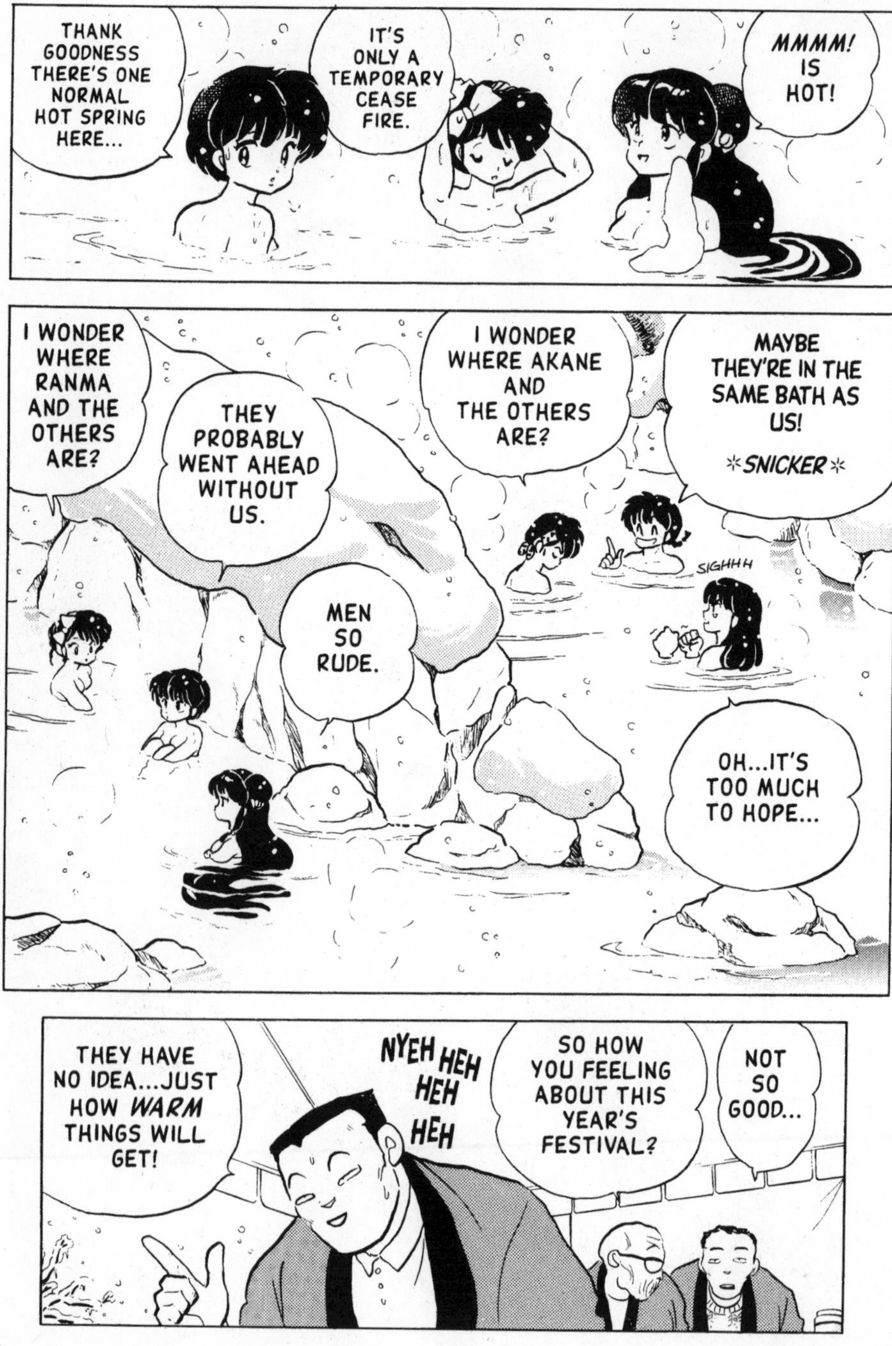
THANK GOODNESS THERE'S ONE NORMAL HOT SPRING HERE...
IT'S ONLY A TEMPORARY CEASE FIRE.
MMMM! IS HOT!
I WONDER WHERE RANMA AND THE OTHERS ARE?
THEY PROBABLY WENT AHEAD WITHOUT US.
MEN SO RUDE.
I WONDER WHERE AKANE AND THE OTHERS ARE?
MAYBE THEY'RE IN THE SAME BATH AS US!
SNICKER
SIGHHH
OH...IT'S TOO MUCH TO HOPE...
THEY HAVE NO IDEA...JUST HOW WARM THINGS WILL GET!
NYEH HEH HEH HEH
SO HOW YOU FEELING ABOUT THIS YEAR'S FESTIVAL?
NOT SO GOOD...

PART 8
HOT BATH!

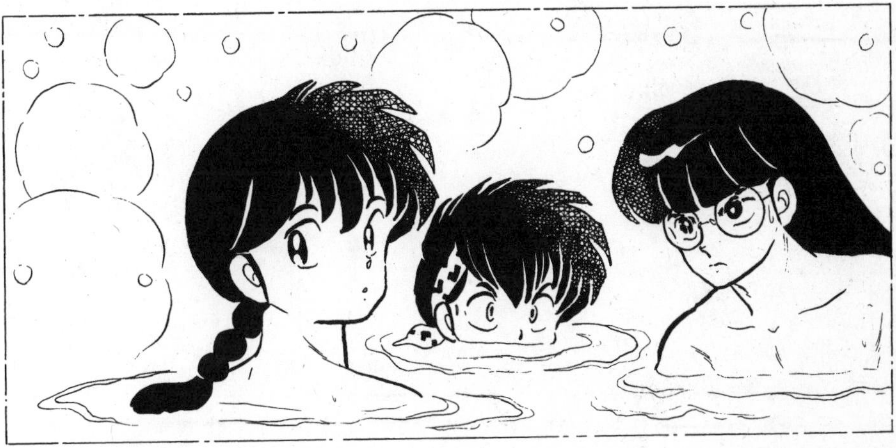

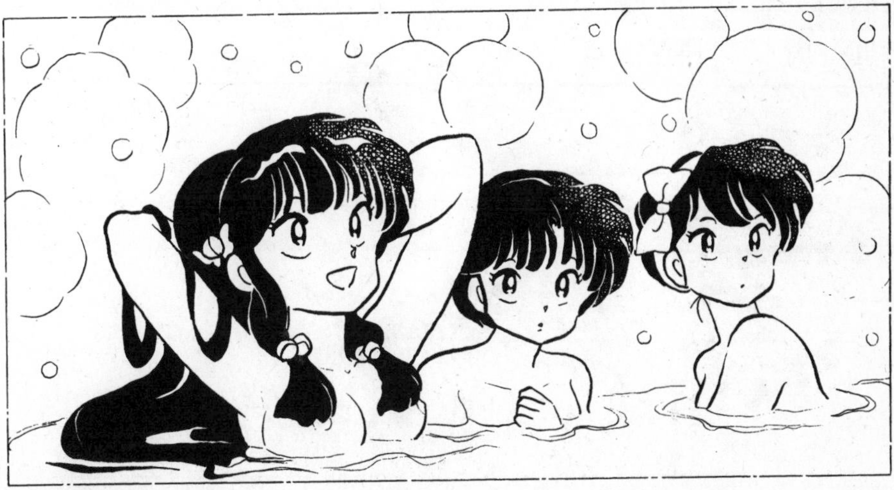

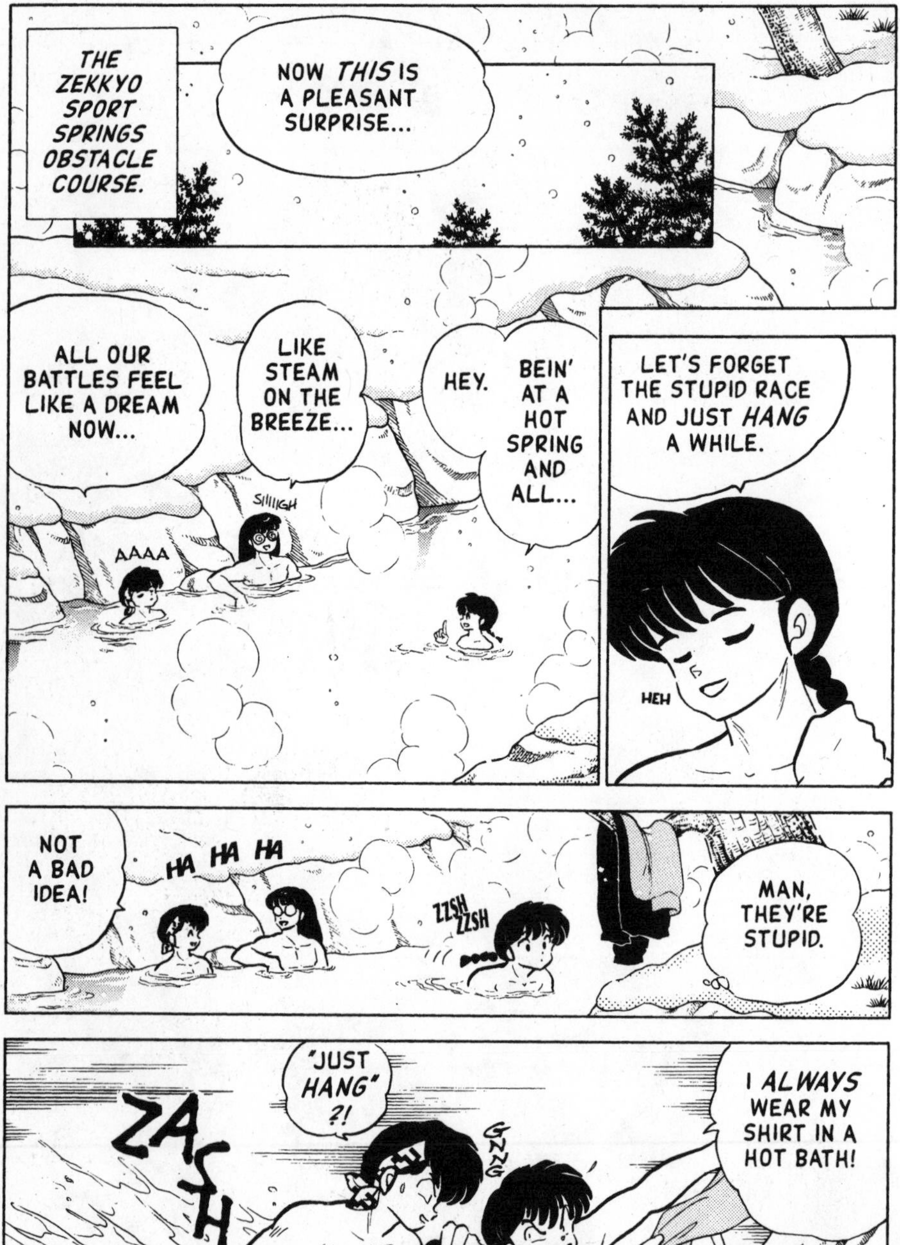
THE ZEKKYO SPORT SPRINGS OBSTACLE COURSE.
NOW THIS IS A PLEASANT SURPRISE...
ALL OUR BATTLES FEEL LIKE A DREAM NOW...
LIKE STEAM ON THE BREEZE...
SIIIIGH
AAAA
HEY.
BEIN' AT A HOT SPRING AND ALL...
LET'S FORGET THE STUPID RACE AND JUST HANG A WHILE.
HEH
NOT A BAD IDEA!
HA HA HA
ZZSH ZZSH
MAN, THEY'RE STUPID.
ZASH
"JUST HANG" ?!
GNNG
I ALWAYS WEAR MY SHIRT IN A HOT BATH!

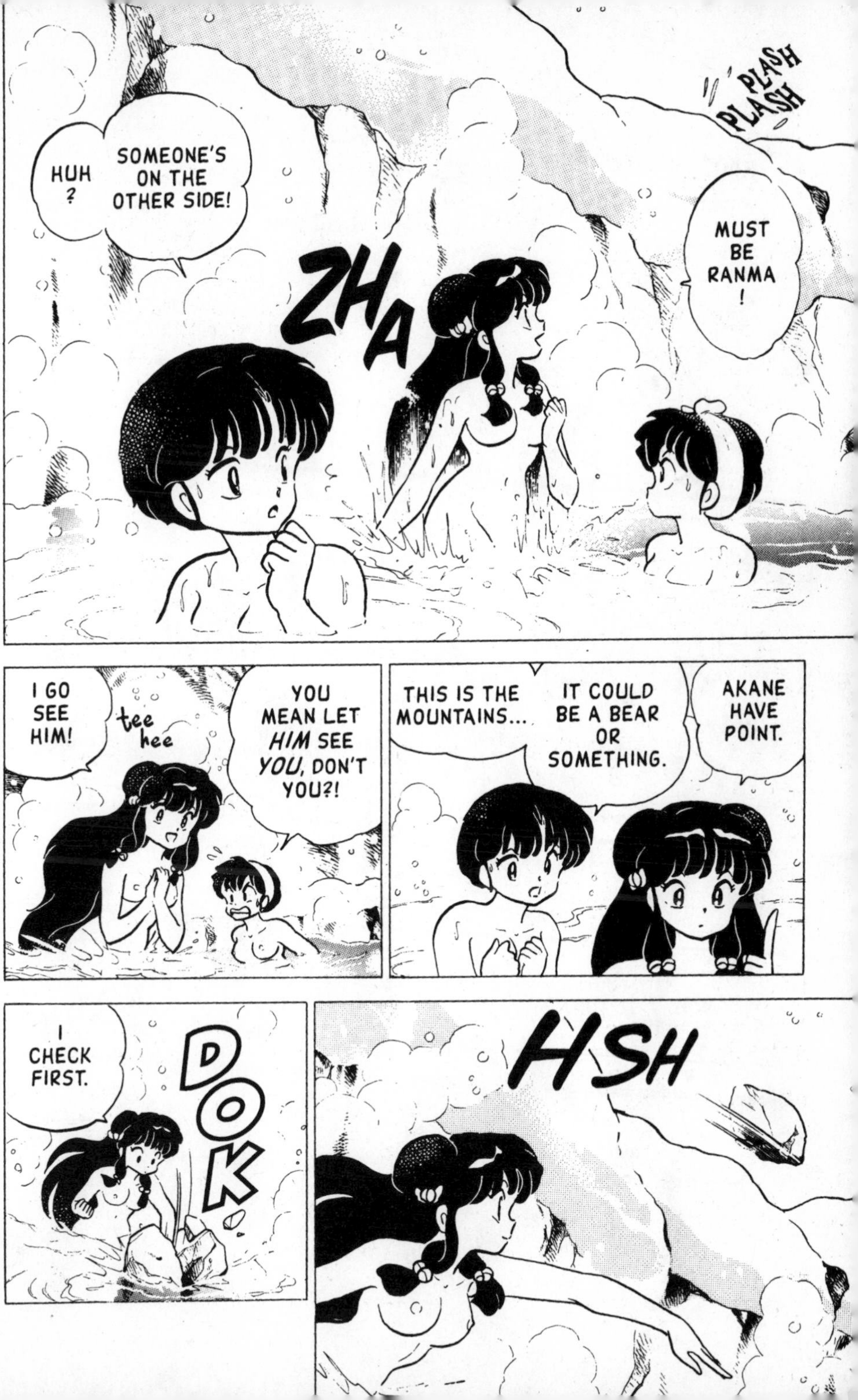
HUH ?
SOMEONE'S ON THE OTHER SIDE!
PLASH PLASH
ZHA
MUST BE RANMA !
I GO SEE HIM!
tee hee
YOU MEAN LET *HIM* SEE *YOU*, DON'T YOU?!
THIS IS THE MOUNTAINS...
IT COULD BE A BEAR OR SOMETHING.
AKANE HAVE POINT.
I CHECK FIRST.
DOK
HSH

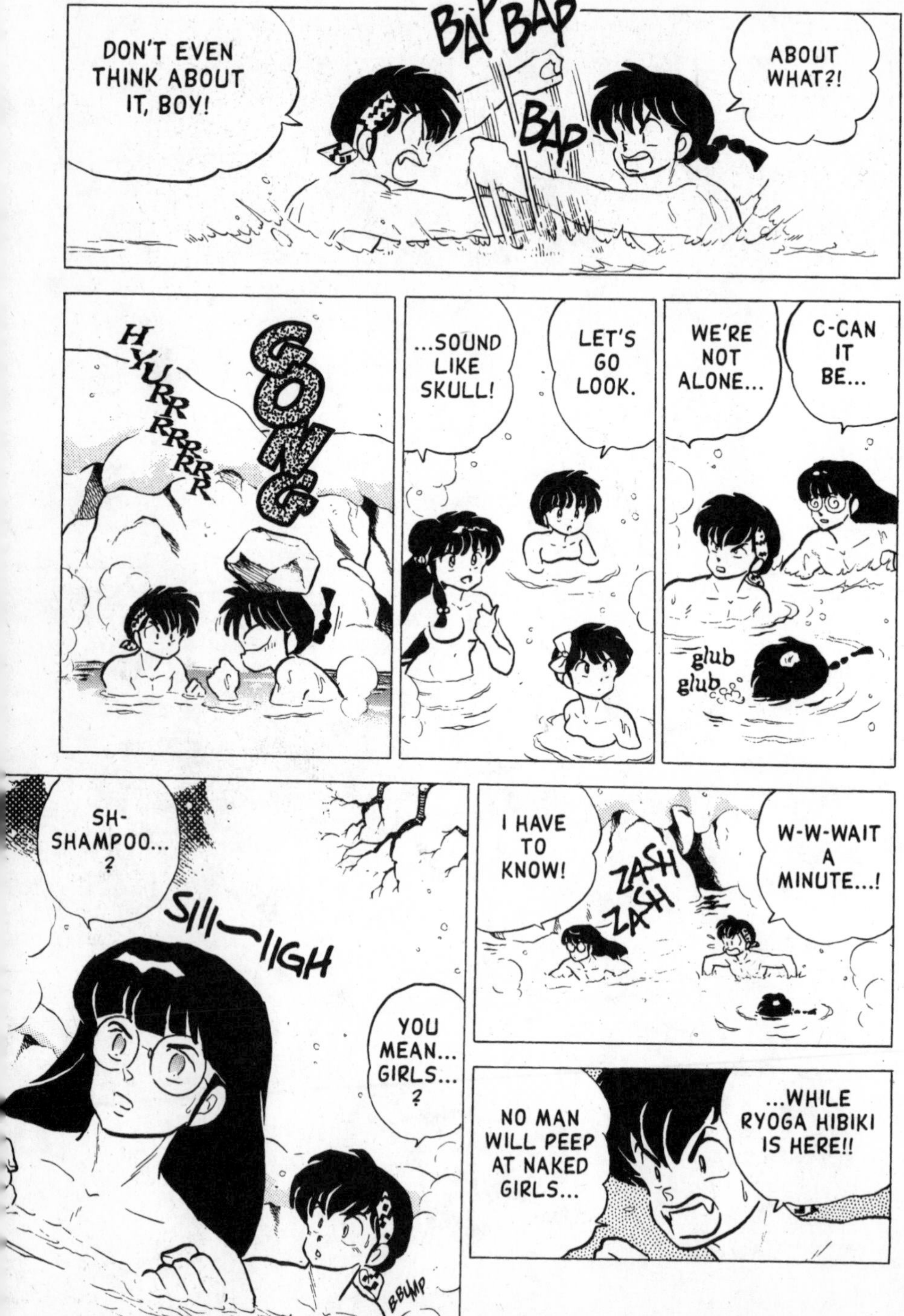

DON'T EVEN THINK ABOUT IT, BOY!
BAP BAP
BAP
ABOUT WHAT?!
HYURRRRRRRRR
GONG
...SOUND LIKE SKULL!
LET'S GO LOOK.
WE'RE NOT ALONE...
C-CAN IT BE...
glub glub
SH-SHAMPOO...?
SIII—IIGH
YOU MEAN... GIRLS...?
B-BUMP
I HAVE TO KNOW!
ZASH ZASH
W-W-WAIT A MINUTE...!
NO MAN WILL PEEP AT NAKED GIRLS...
...WHILE RYOGA HIBIKI IS HERE!!

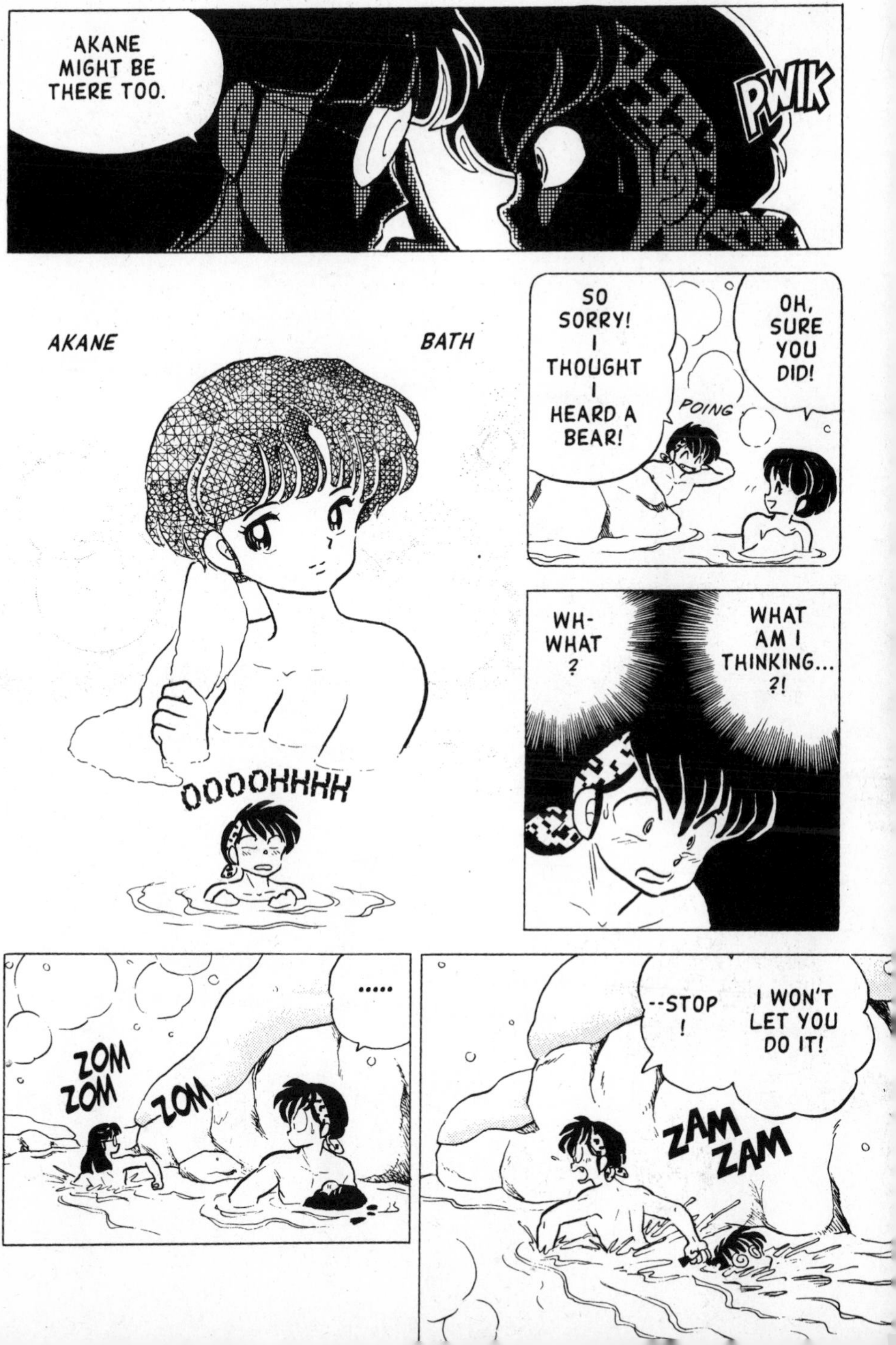
AKANE MIGHT BE THERE TOO.
PWIK
AKANE
BATH
OOOOHHHH
SO SORRY! I THOUGHT I HEARD A BEAR!
POING
OH, SURE YOU DID!
WH-WHAT?
WHAT AM I THINKING...?!
ZOM ZOM
ZOM
.....
--STOP!
I WON'T LET YOU DO IT!
ZAM ZAM

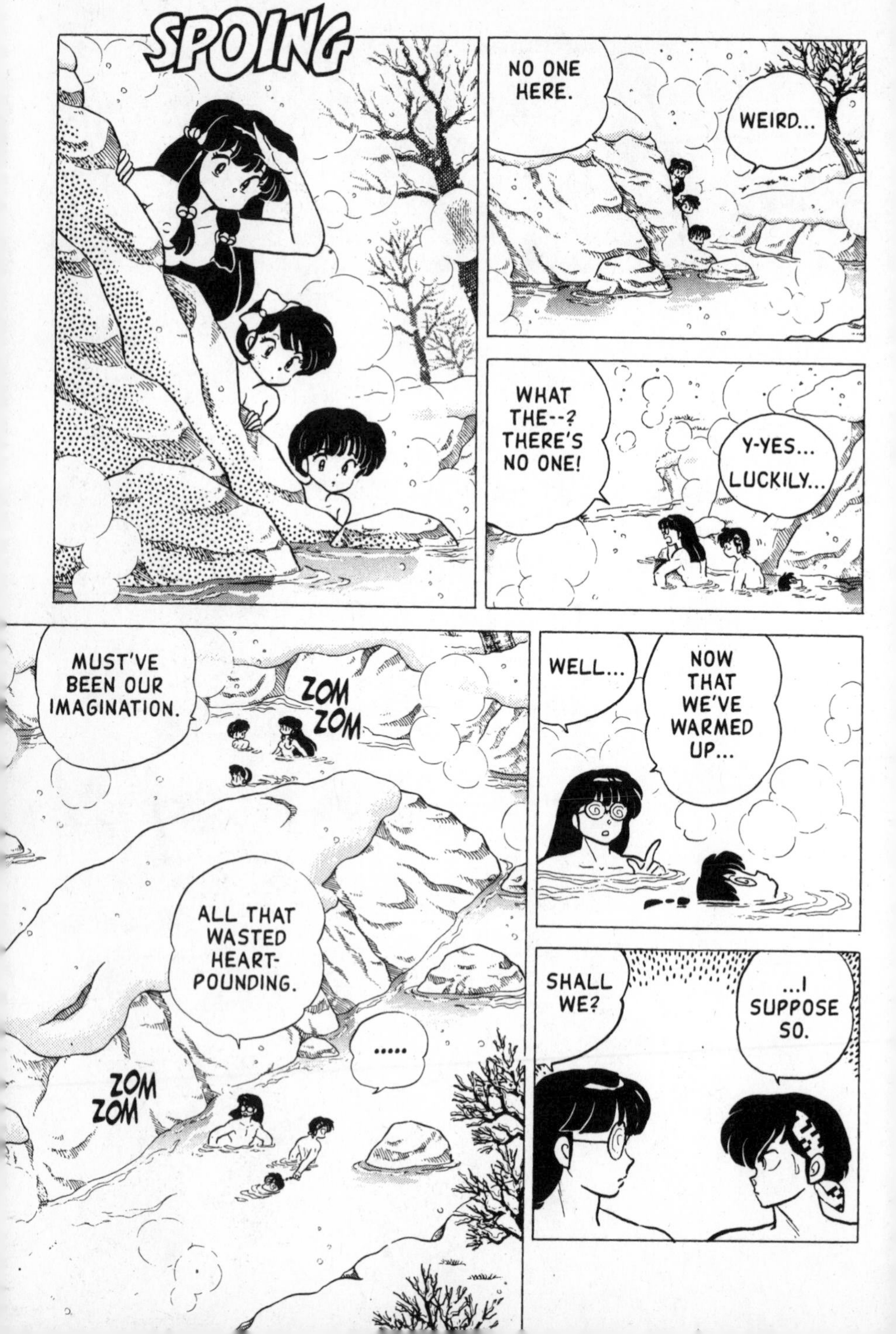
SPOING
NO ONE HERE.
WEIRD...
WHAT THE--? THERE'S NO ONE!
Y-YES... LUCKILY...
MUST'VE BEEN OUR IMAGINATION.
ZOM ZOM
ALL THAT WASTED HEART-POUNDING.
.....
ZOM ZOM
WELL...
NOW THAT WE'VE WARMED UP...
SHALL WE?
...I SUPPOSE SO.

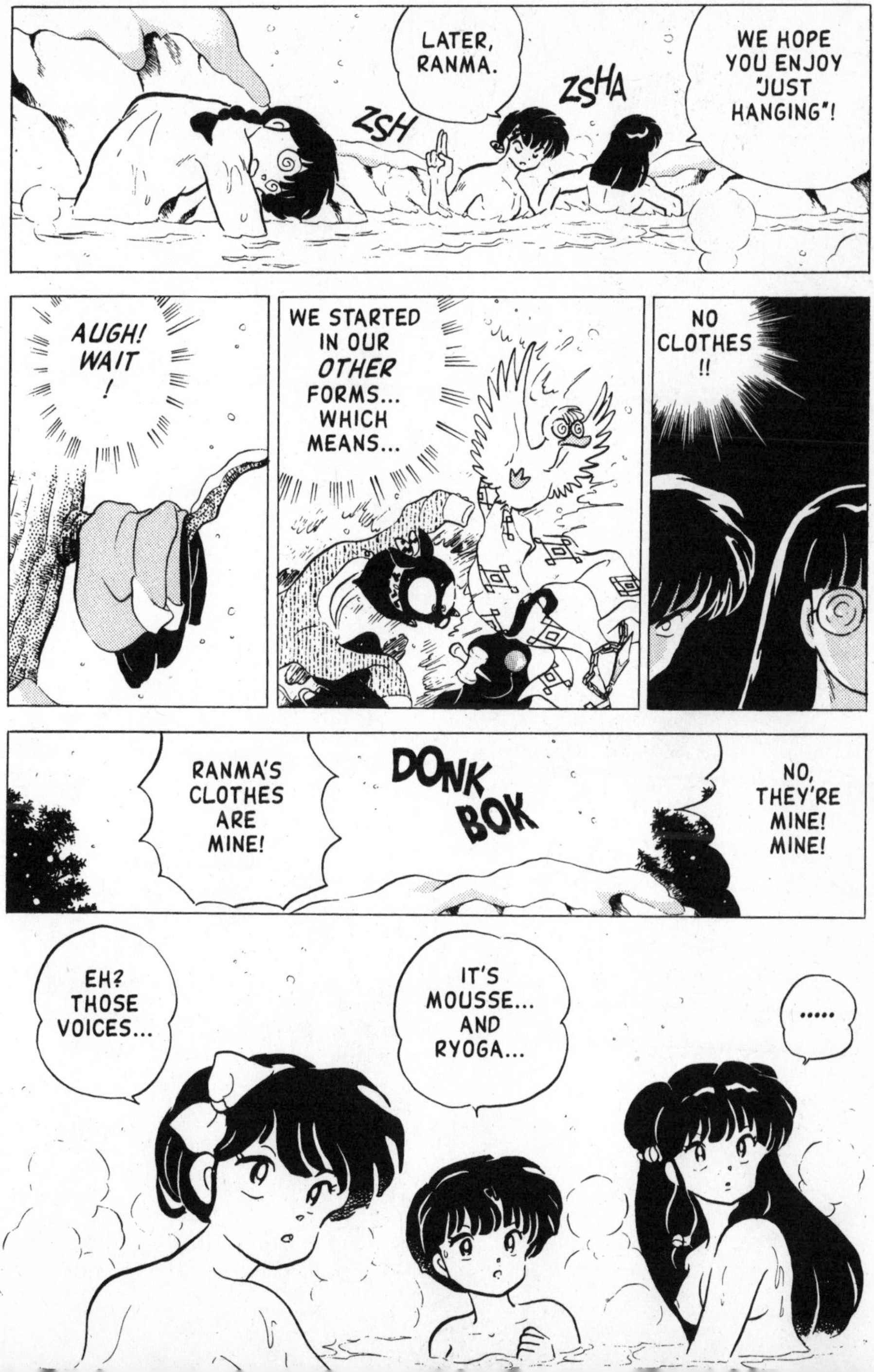
ZSH
LATER, RANMA.
ZSHA
WE HOPE YOU ENJOY "JUST HANGING"!
AUGH! WAIT !
WE STARTED IN OUR OTHER FORMS... WHICH MEANS...
NO CLOTHES !!
RANMA'S CLOTHES ARE MINE!
DONK
BOK
NO, THEY'RE MINE! MINE!
EH? THOSE VOICES...
IT'S MOUSSE... AND RYOGA...
......

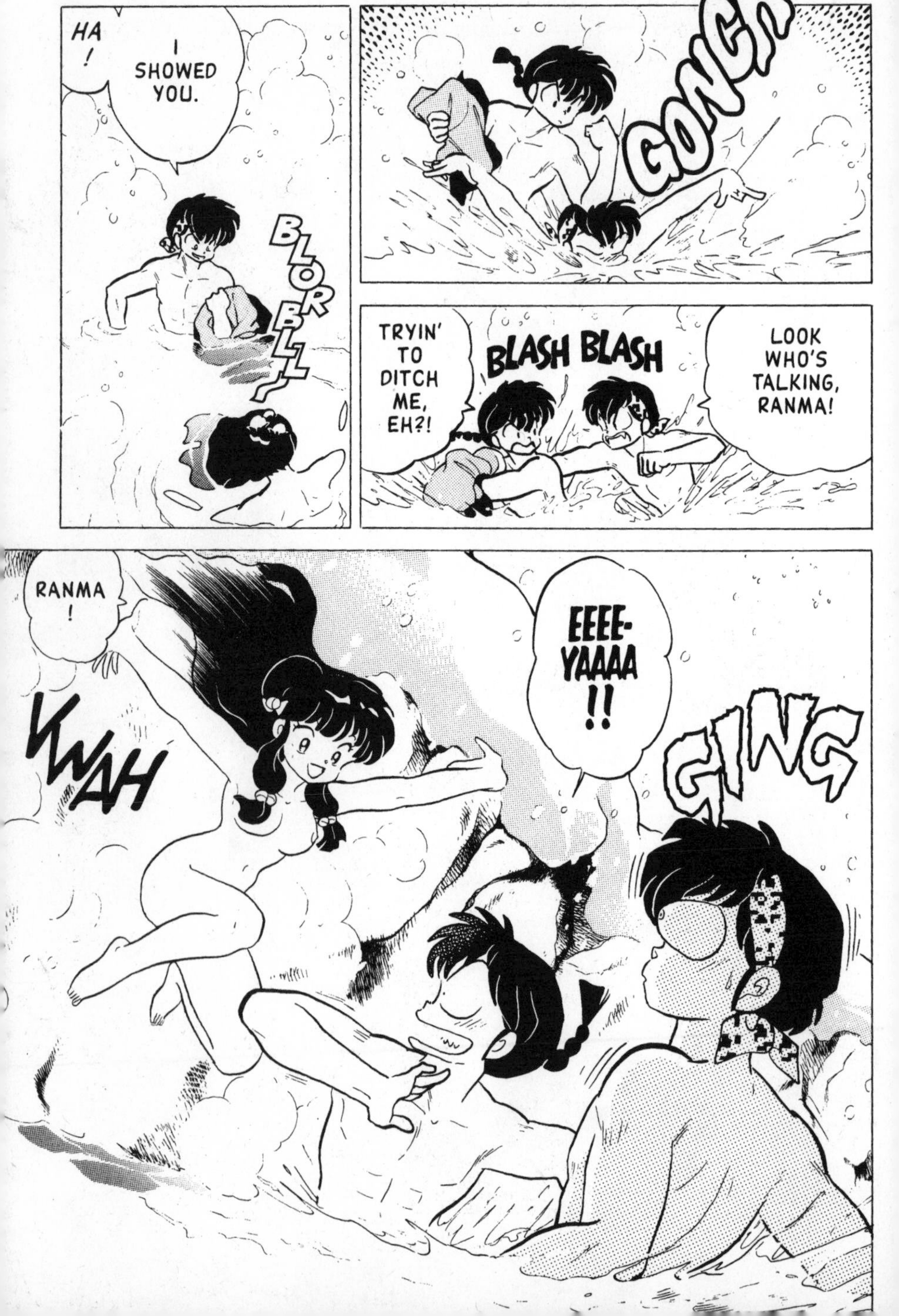

HA!
I SHOWED YOU.
BLORBLLL
GONCH
TRYIN' TO DITCH ME, EH?!
BLASH BLASH
LOOK WHO'S TALKING, RANMA!
RANMA!
KWAH
EEEE-YAAAA!!
GING

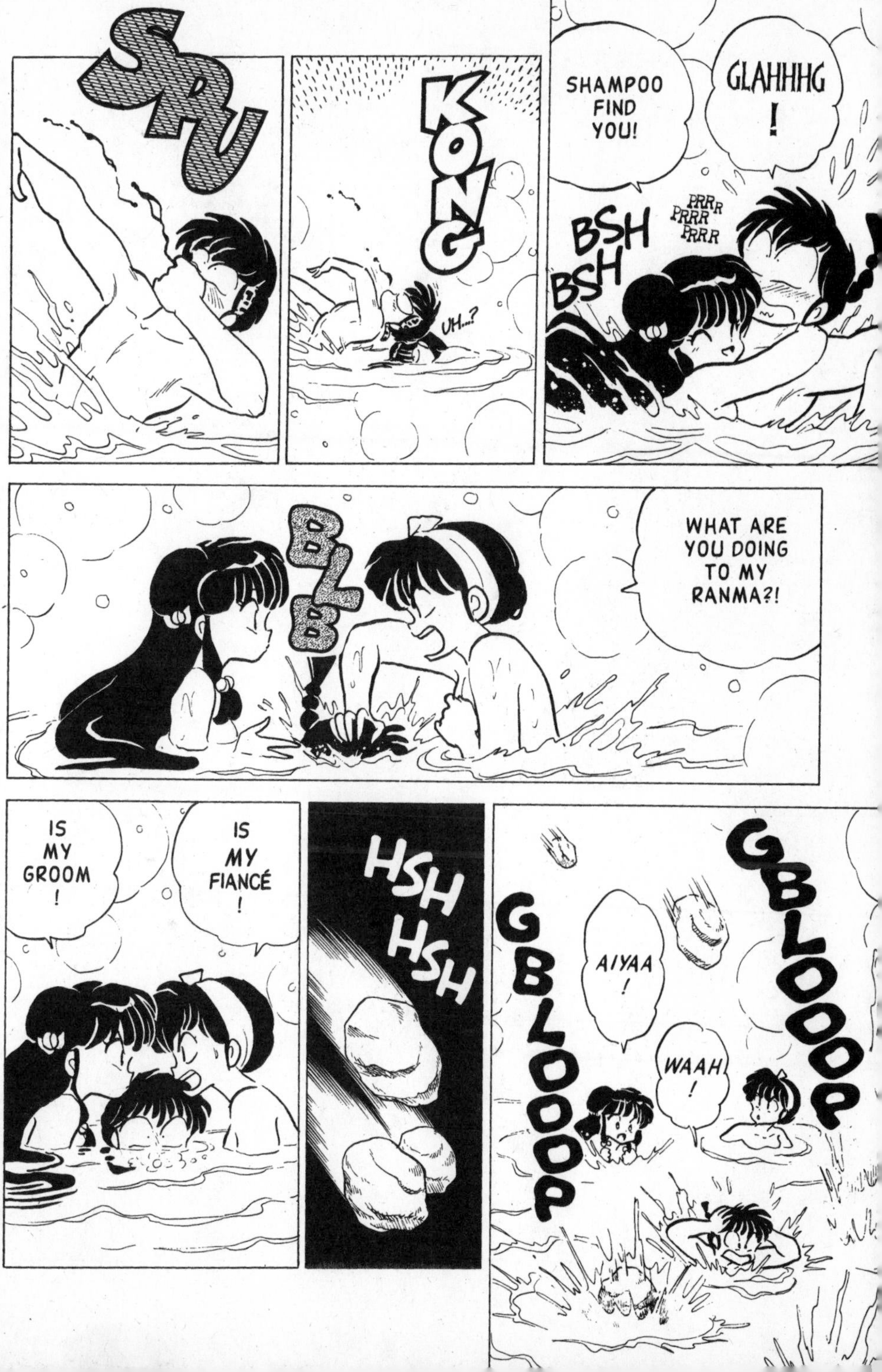
SRU
KONG
UH...?
SHAMPOO FIND YOU!
GLAHHHG!
BSH BSH
PRRR PRRR PRRR
BLB
WHAT ARE YOU DOING TO MY RANMA?!
IS MY GROOM!
IS MY FIANCÉ!
HSH HSH
GBLOOOP
AIYAA!
WAAH!
GBLOOOP

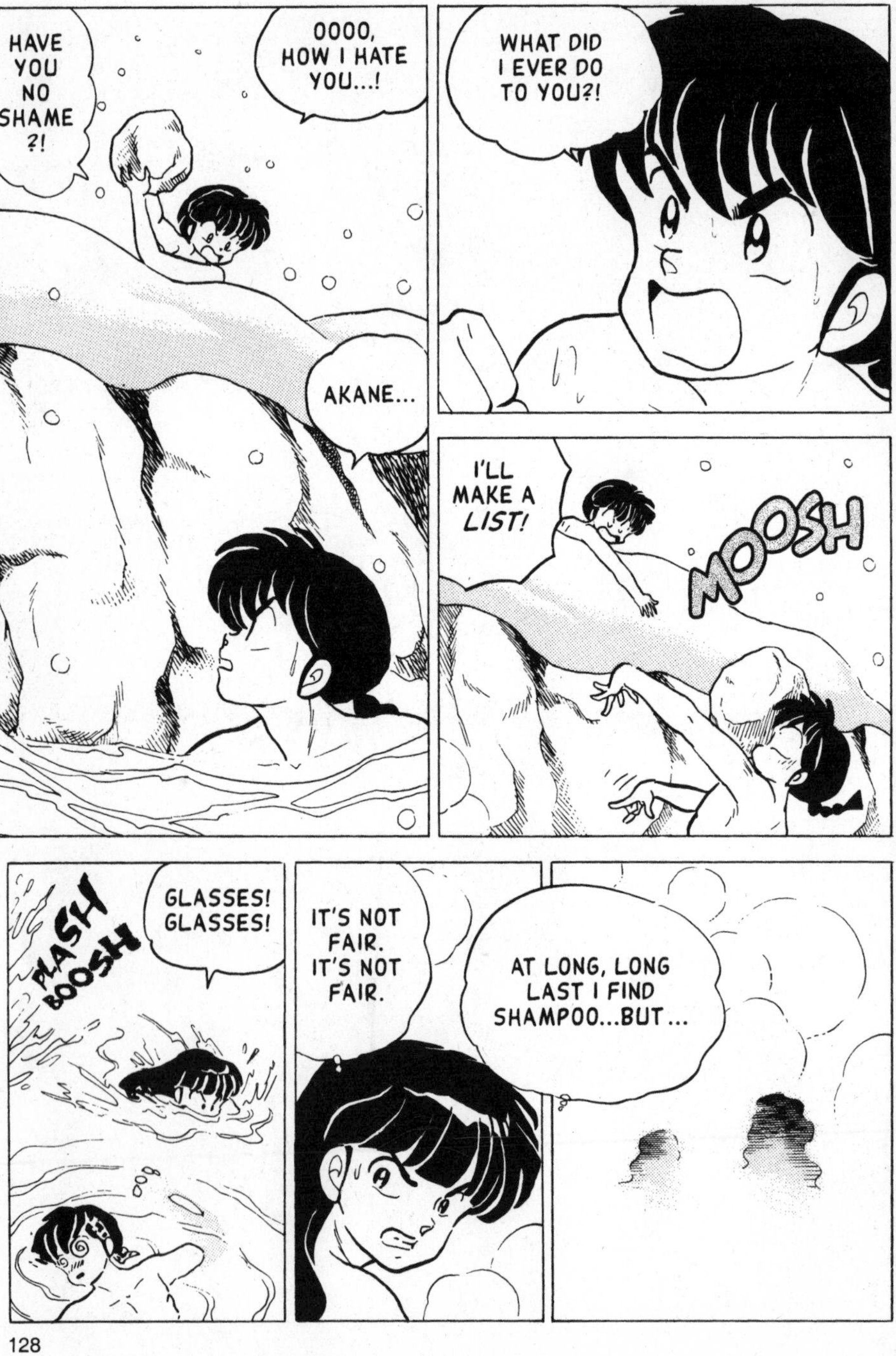
HAVE YOU NO SHAME ?!
OOOO, HOW I HATE YOU...!
AKANE...
WHAT DID I EVER DO TO YOU?!
I'LL MAKE A LIST!
MOOSH
PLASH
BOOSH
GLASSES! GLASSES!
IT'S NOT FAIR. IT'S NOT FAIR.
AT LONG, LONG LAST I FIND SHAMPOO...BUT...

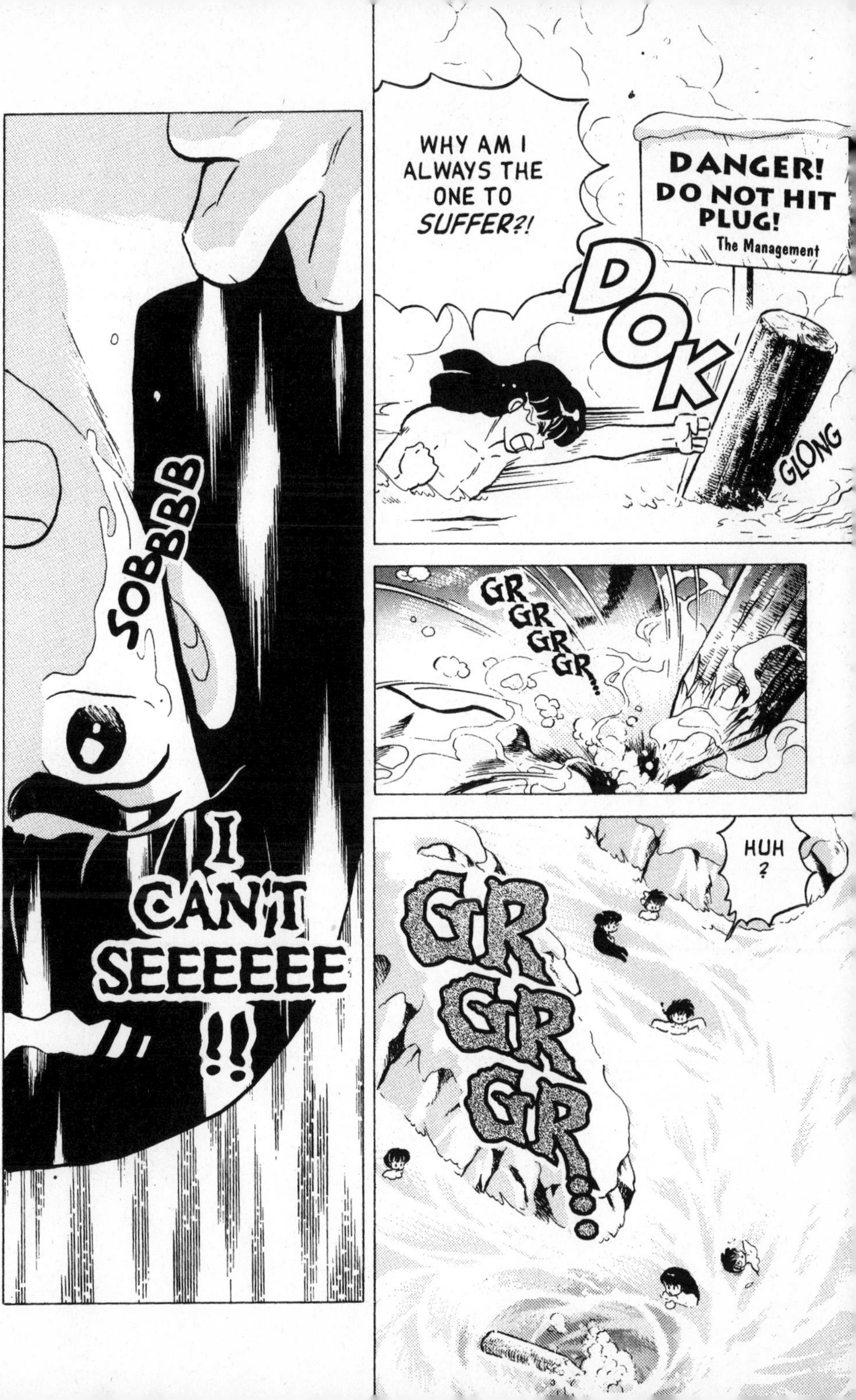
WHY AM I ALWAYS THE ONE TO *SUFFER?!*
DANGER! DO NOT HIT PLUG!
The Management
DOK
GLONG
GR GR GR GR...
HUH ?
GR GR GR!!
SOBBBB
I CAN'T SEEEEEE!!

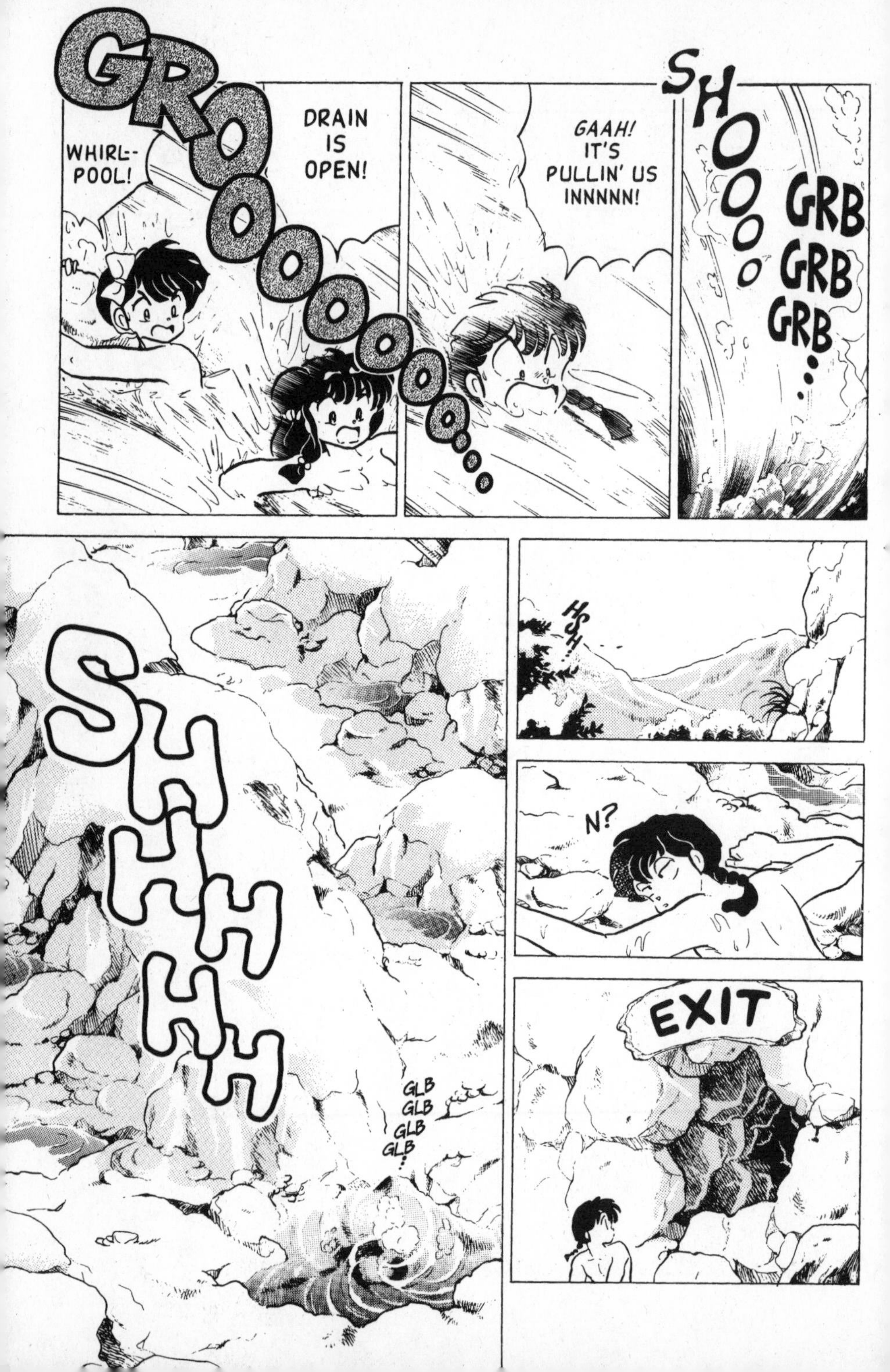
GROOOOOOOOOO...
WHIRL-POOL!
DRAIN IS OPEN!
GAAH! IT'S PULLIN' US INNNNN!
SHOOOO
GRB GRB GRB...
SHHHHHHHH
GLB GLB GLB GLB...
HSH...
N?
EXIT

I'M...THE ONLY ONE HERE...

HA-SHOOO!

HUH ?

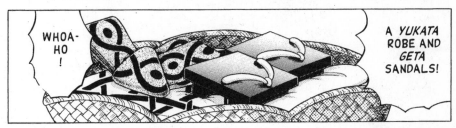

WHOA-HO !

A *YUKATA* ROBE AND *GETA* SANDALS!

KUH-LANK

HUH?

WHAZZAT SOUND ?

ZUNG

TH-THIS ROBE...

...HAS CHAINS SEWN INTO IT!

ZNG!

UGH !

ZNG!

EVEN THE *OBI* SASH IS FULLA LEAD...

AND THE *GETA* ARE IRON!

CHING

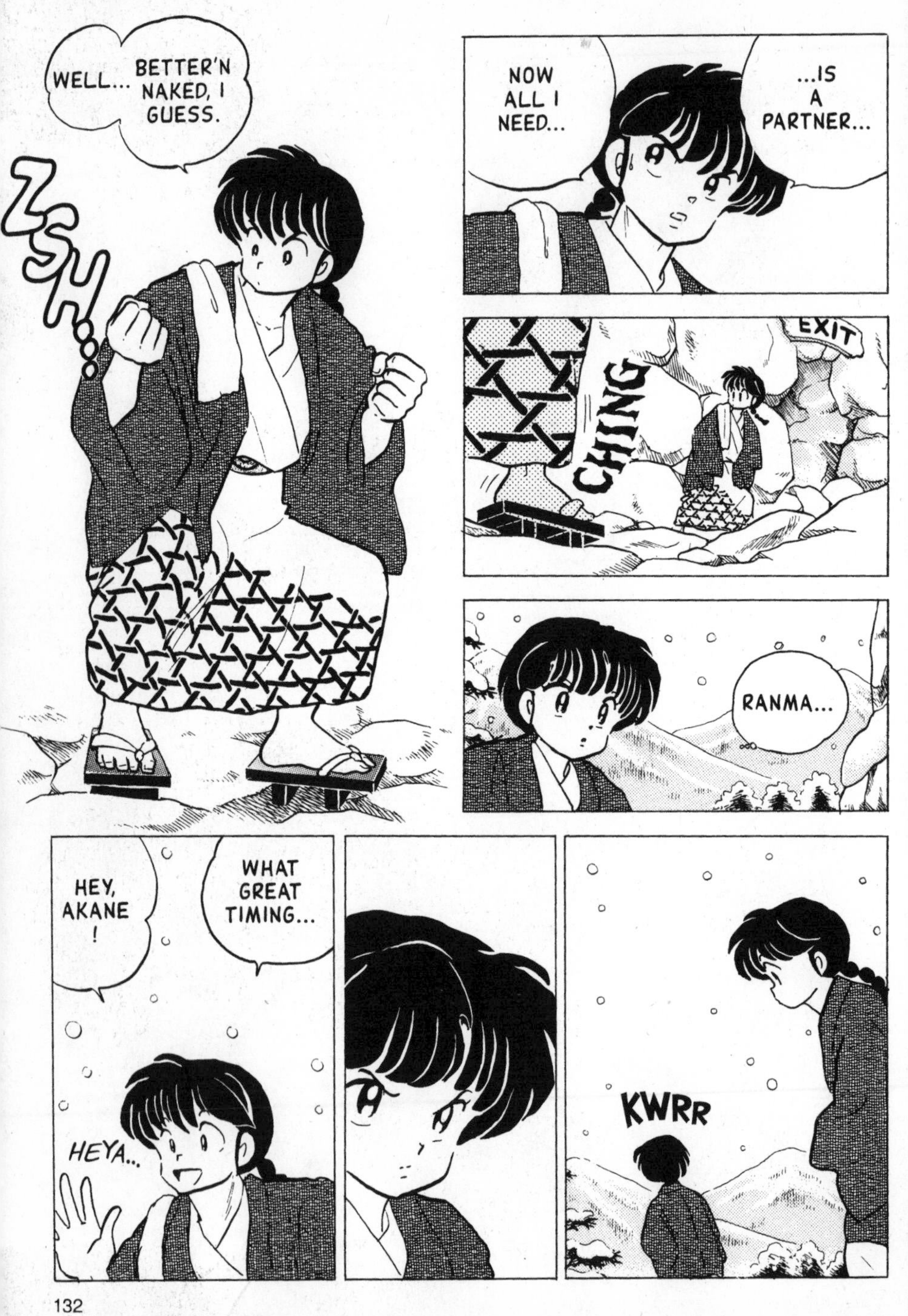
WELL... BETTER'N NAKED, I GUESS.
ZSH...
NOW ALL I NEED...
...IS A PARTNER...
CHING
EXIT
RANMA...
HEY, AKANE!
WHAT GREAT TIMING...
HEYA...
KWRR

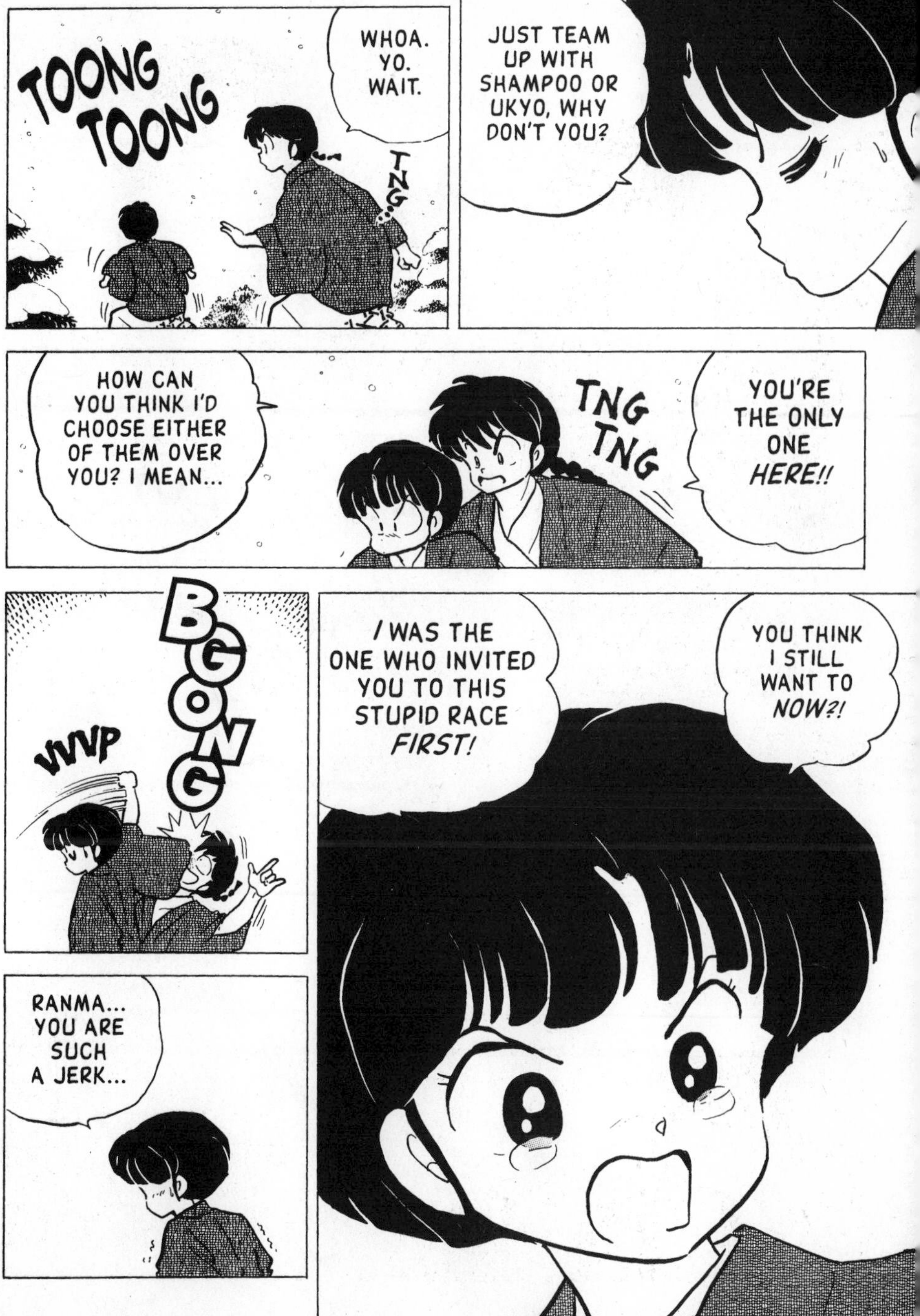
TOONG TOONG
WHOA. YO. WAIT.
TNG
JUST TEAM UP WITH SHAMPOO OR UKYO, WHY DON'T YOU?
HOW CAN YOU THINK I'D CHOOSE EITHER OF THEM OVER YOU? I MEAN...
TNG TNG
YOU'RE THE ONLY ONE *HERE!!*
VVVP
BGONG
I WAS THE ONE WHO INVITED YOU TO THIS STUPID RACE *FIRST!*
YOU THINK I STILL WANT TO *NOW?!*
RANMA... YOU ARE SUCH A JERK...

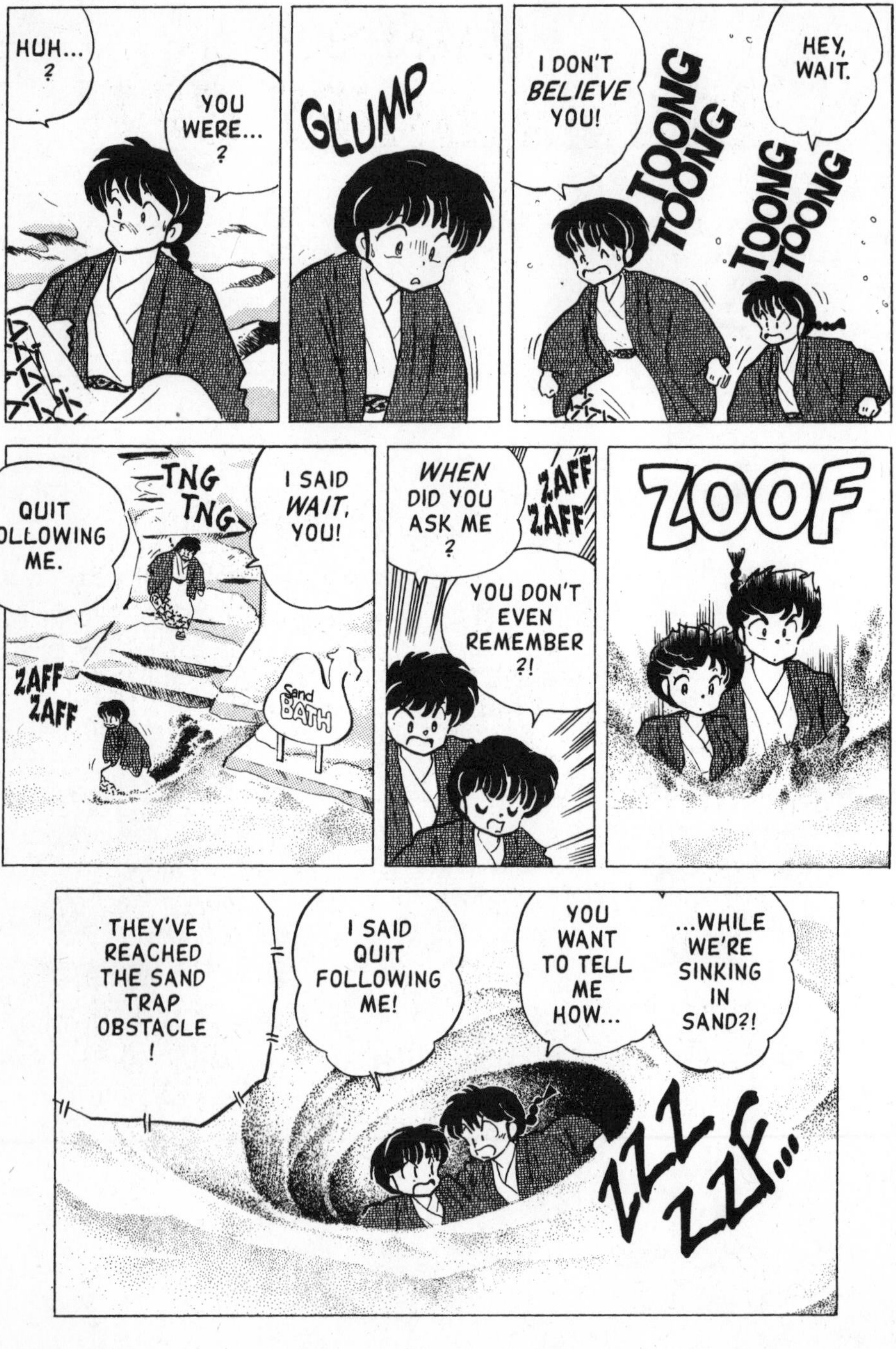
HUH...?
YOU WERE...?
GLUMP
I DON'T BELIEVE YOU!
TOONG TOONG
HEY, WAIT.
TOONG TOONG
QUIT FOLLOWING ME.
TNG TNG
I SAID WAIT, YOU!
ZAFF ZAFF
Sand BATH
WHEN DID YOU ASK ME?
ZAFF ZAFF
YOU DON'T EVEN REMEMBER?!
ZOOF
THEY'VE REACHED THE SAND TRAP OBSTACLE!
I SAID QUIT FOLLOWING ME!
YOU WANT TO TELL ME HOW...
...WHILE WE'RE SINKING IN SAND?!
ZZZ ZZF...

PART 9
RANMA GIVES UP?!

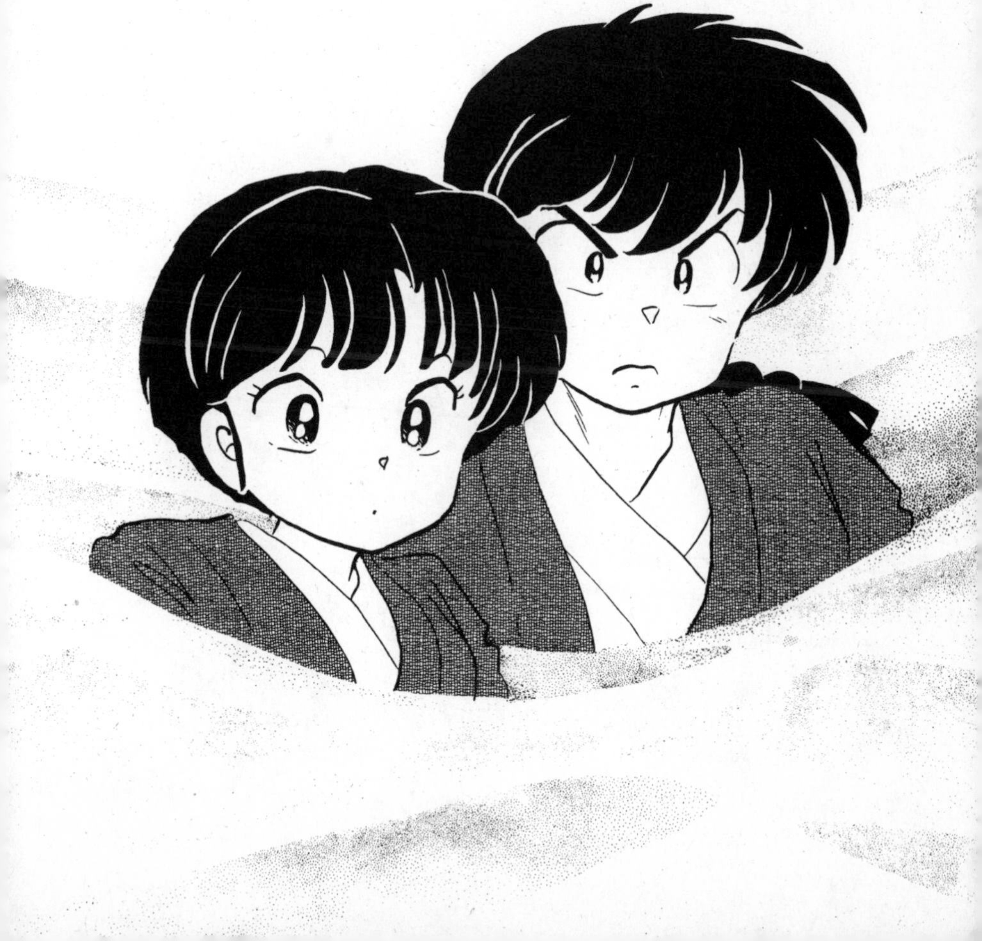

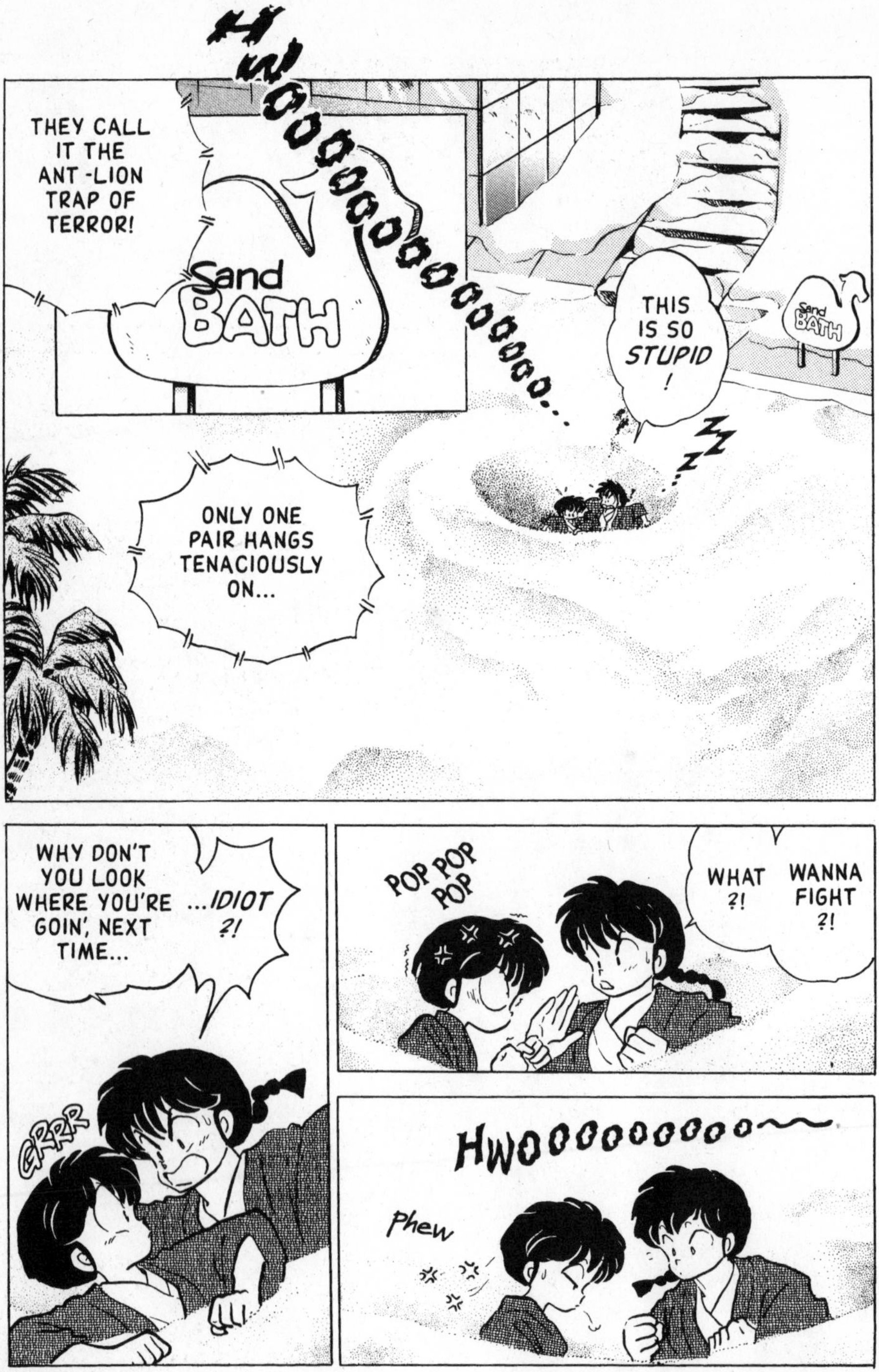
HWOOOOOOOOOOOOOOOOO...
THEY CALL IT THE ANT-LION TRAP OF TERROR!
Sand BATH
THIS IS SO STUPID!
Sand BATH
ZZZ...
ONLY ONE PAIR HANGS TENACIOUSLY ON...
WHY DON'T YOU LOOK WHERE YOU'RE GOIN', NEXT TIME...
...IDIOT?!
GRRR
POP POP POP
WHAT?!
WANNA FIGHT?!
HWOOOOOOOOOO~~
Phew

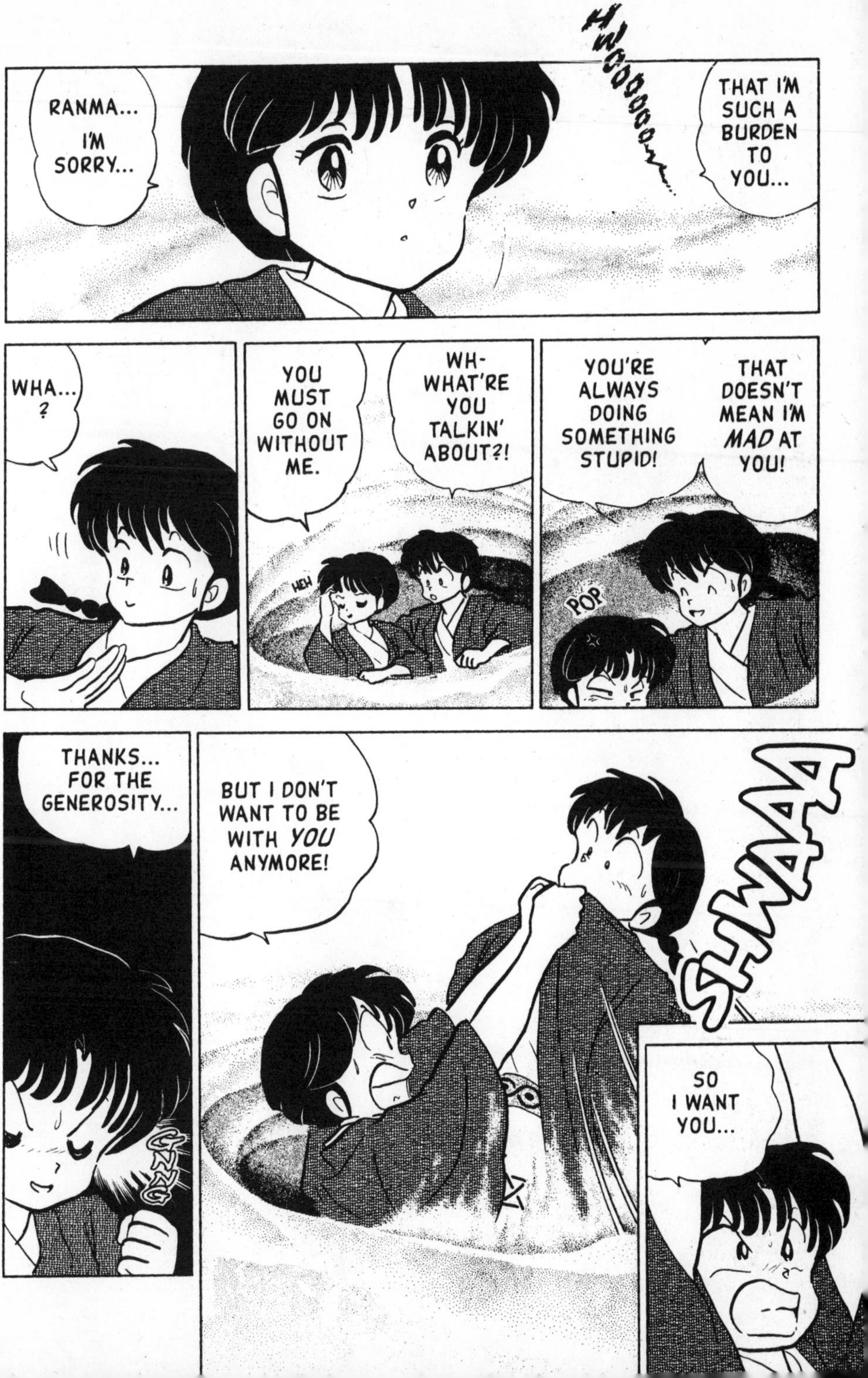
RANMA... I'M SORRY...
HWOOOOOOOOOOOO...
THAT I'M SUCH A BURDEN TO YOU...
WHA...?
YOU MUST GO ON WITHOUT ME.
WH-WHAT'RE YOU TALKIN' ABOUT?!
HEH
YOU'RE ALWAYS DOING SOMETHING STUPID!
THAT DOESN'T MEAN I'M *MAD* AT YOU!
POP
THANKS... FOR THE GENEROSITY...
GNNG
BUT I DON'T WANT TO BE WITH *YOU* ANYMORE!
SHWAAA
SO I WANT YOU...

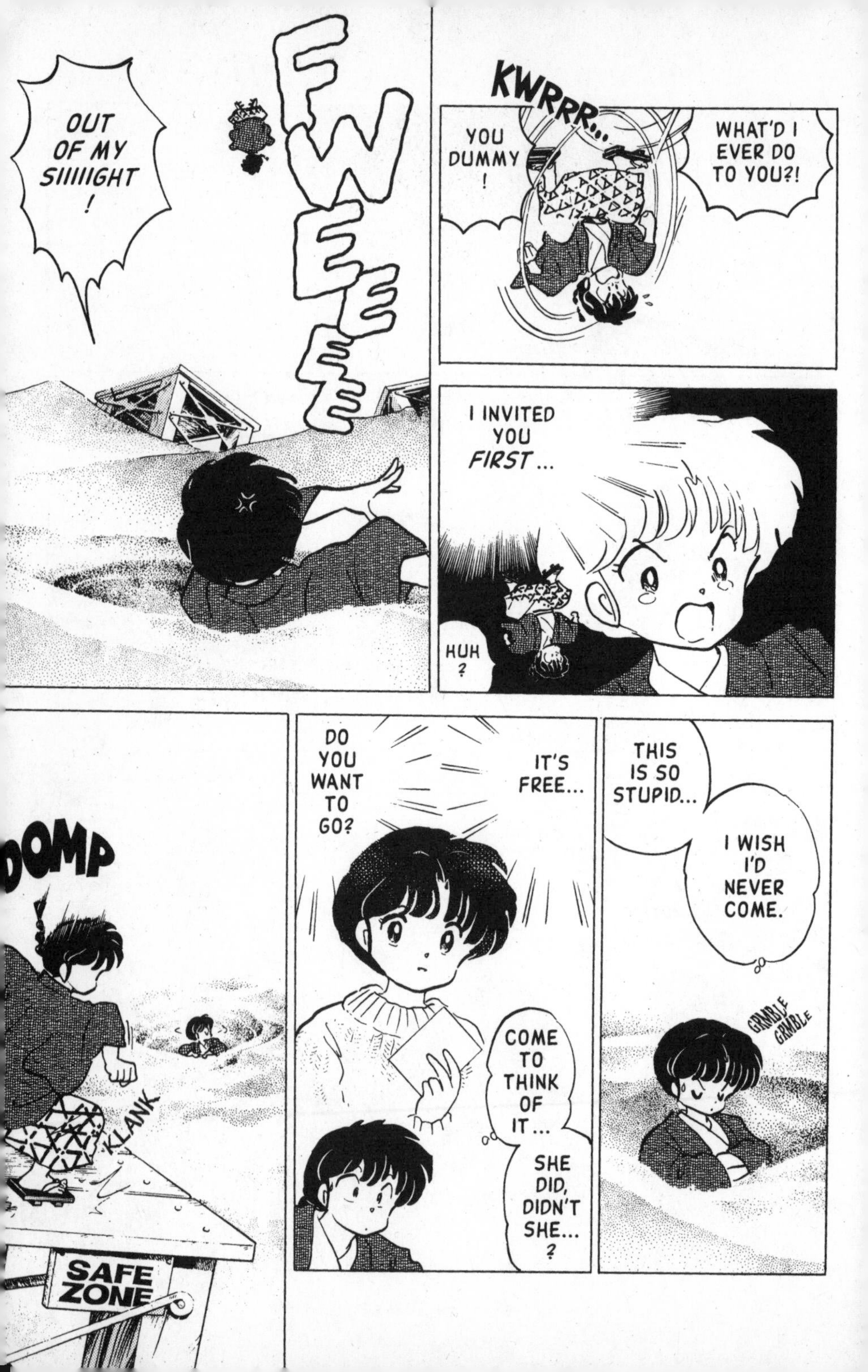
OUT OF MY SIIIIIGHT!
FWEEEE
KWRRR...
YOU DUMMY!
WHAT'D I EVER DO TO YOU?!
I INVITED YOU *FIRST*...
HUH?
DOMP
KLANK
SAFE ZONE
DO YOU WANT TO GO?
IT'S FREE...
COME TO THINK OF IT...
SHE DID, DIDN'T SHE...?
THIS IS SO STUPID...
I WISH I'D NEVER COME.
GRMBLE GRMBLE

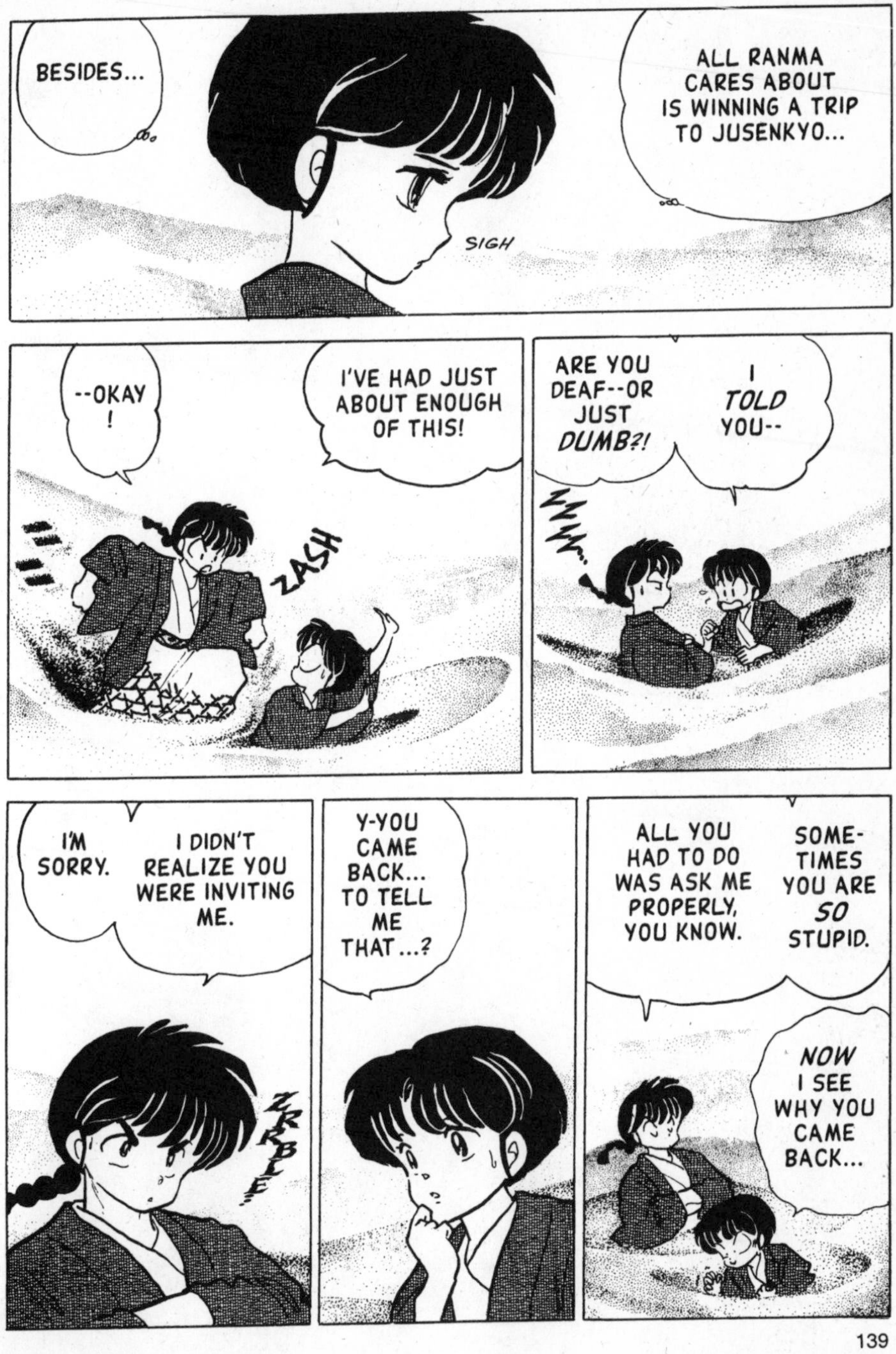
BESIDES...
ALL RANMA CARES ABOUT IS WINNING A TRIP TO JUSENKYO...
SIGH
--OKAY!
I'VE HAD JUST ABOUT ENOUGH OF THIS!
ZASH
ARE YOU DEAF--OR JUST DUMB?!
I TOLD YOU--
I'M SORRY.
I DIDN'T REALIZE YOU WERE INVITING ME.
ZRRBLE...
Y-YOU CAME BACK... TO TELL ME THAT...?
ALL YOU HAD TO DO WAS ASK ME PROPERLY, YOU KNOW.
SOMETIMES YOU ARE SO STUPID.
NOW I SEE WHY YOU CAME BACK...

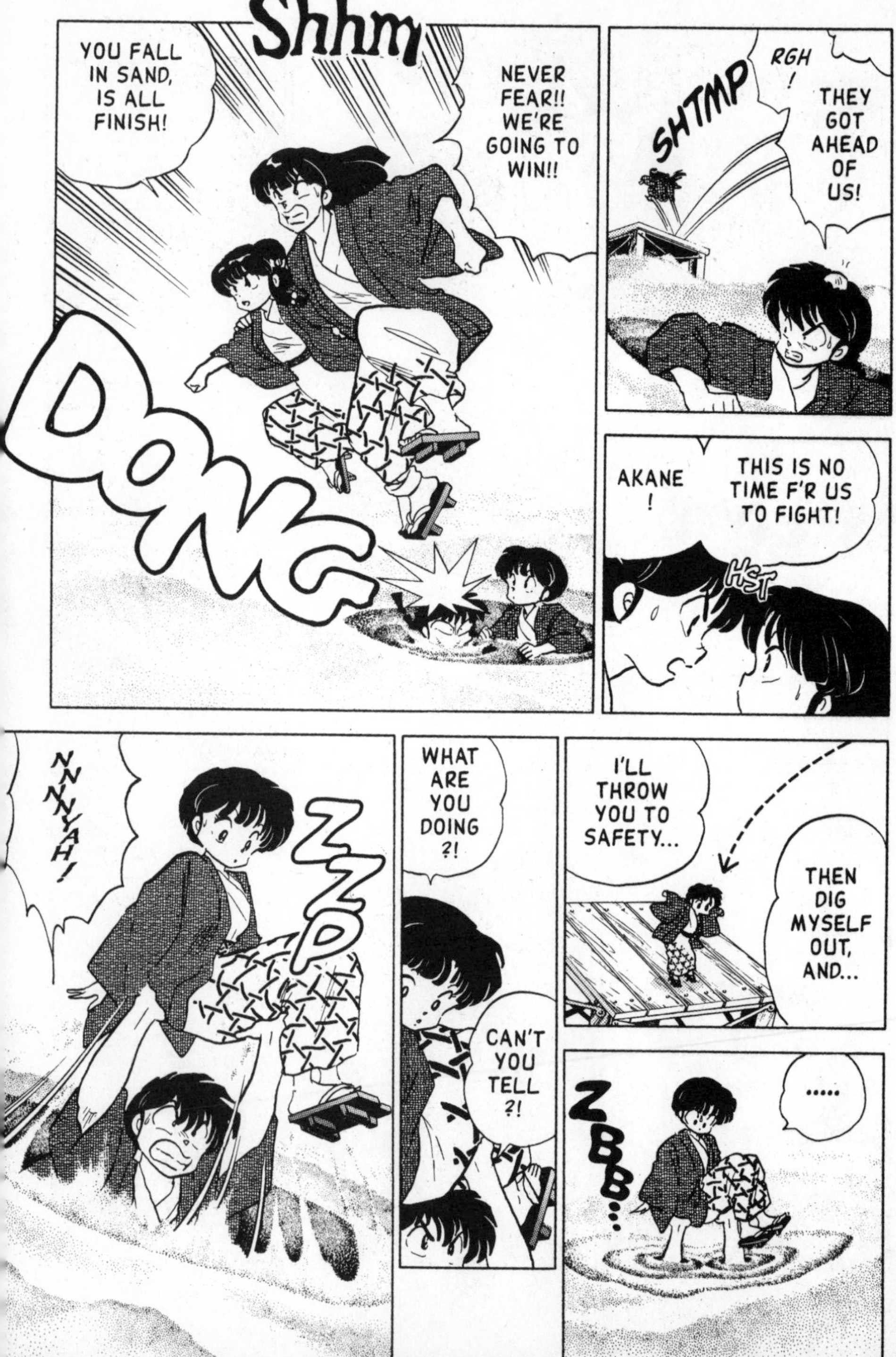
Shhm
YOU FALL IN SAND, IS ALL FINISH!
NEVER FEAR!! WE'RE GOING TO WIN!!
DONG
SHTMP
RGH!
THEY GOT AHEAD OF US!
AKANE!
THIS IS NO TIME F'R US TO FIGHT!
HST
NNNYAH!
ZZZP
WHAT ARE YOU DOING?!
CAN'T YOU TELL?!
I'LL THROW YOU TO SAFETY...
THEN DIG MYSELF OUT, AND...
ZBB...
.....

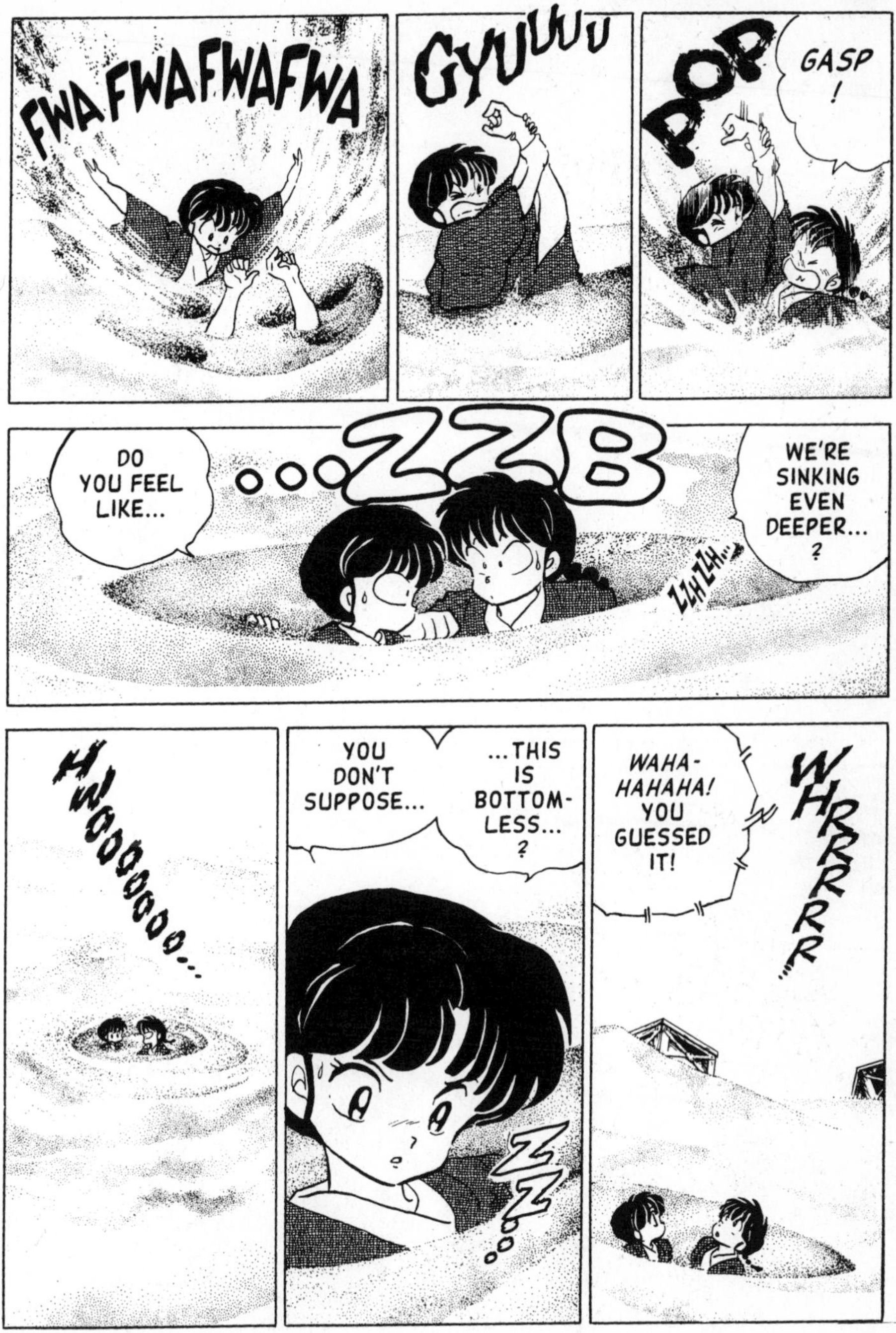
FWAFWAFWAFWA
GYUUUU
POP
GASP!
DO YOU FEEL LIKE...
...ZZB
ZZHZZH...
WE'RE SINKING EVEN DEEPER...?
HWOOOOOOO...
YOU DON'T SUPPOSE...
...THIS IS BOTTOMLESS...?
ZZZ
WAHAHAHAHA! YOU GUESSED IT!
WHRRRRR...

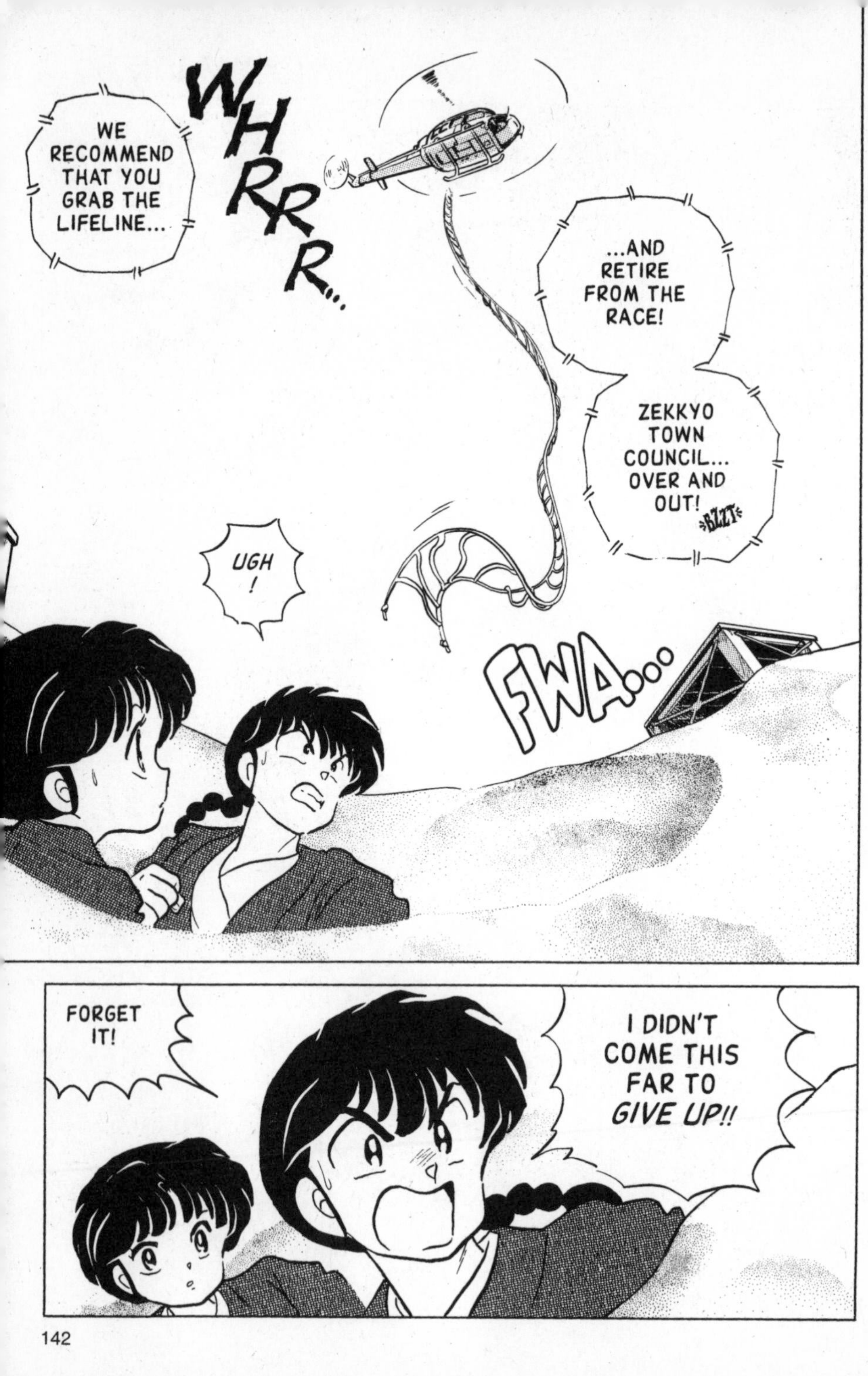
WE RECOMMEND THAT YOU GRAB THE LIFELINE...
WHRRR...
...AND RETIRE FROM THE RACE!
ZEKKYO TOWN COUNCIL... OVER AND OUT!
BZZT
UGH!
FWA...
FORGET IT!
I DIDN'T COME THIS FAR TO GIVE UP!!

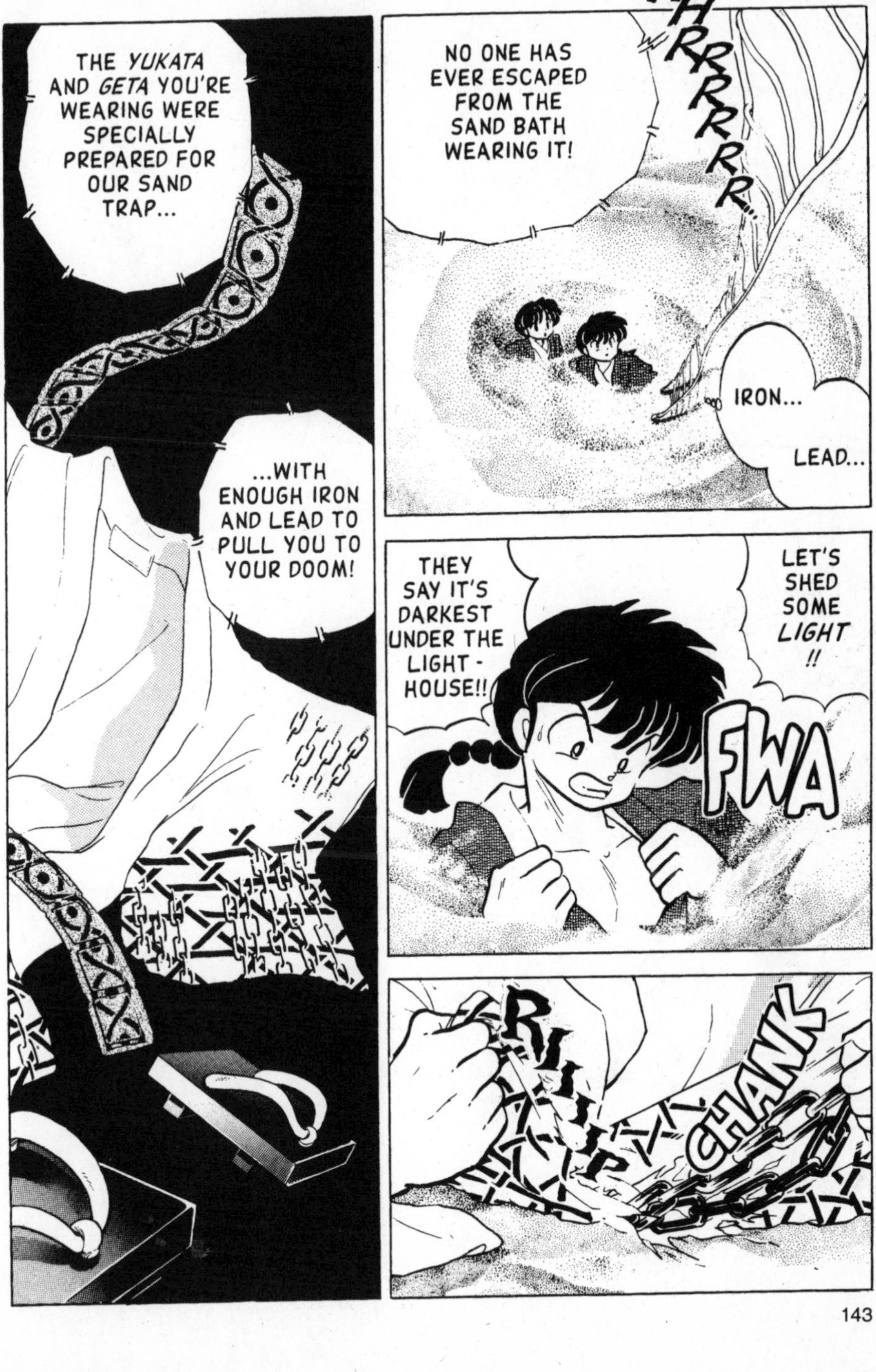
THE *YUKATA* AND *GETA* YOU'RE WEARING WERE SPECIALLY PREPARED FOR OUR SAND TRAP...
...WITH ENOUGH IRON AND LEAD TO PULL YOU TO YOUR DOOM!
WHRRRRRR...
NO ONE HAS EVER ESCAPED FROM THE SAND BATH WEARING IT!
IRON...
LEAD...
THEY SAY IT'S DARKEST UNDER THE LIGHT-HOUSE!!
LET'S SHED SOME *LIGHT* !!
FWA
RIIIIP
CHANK

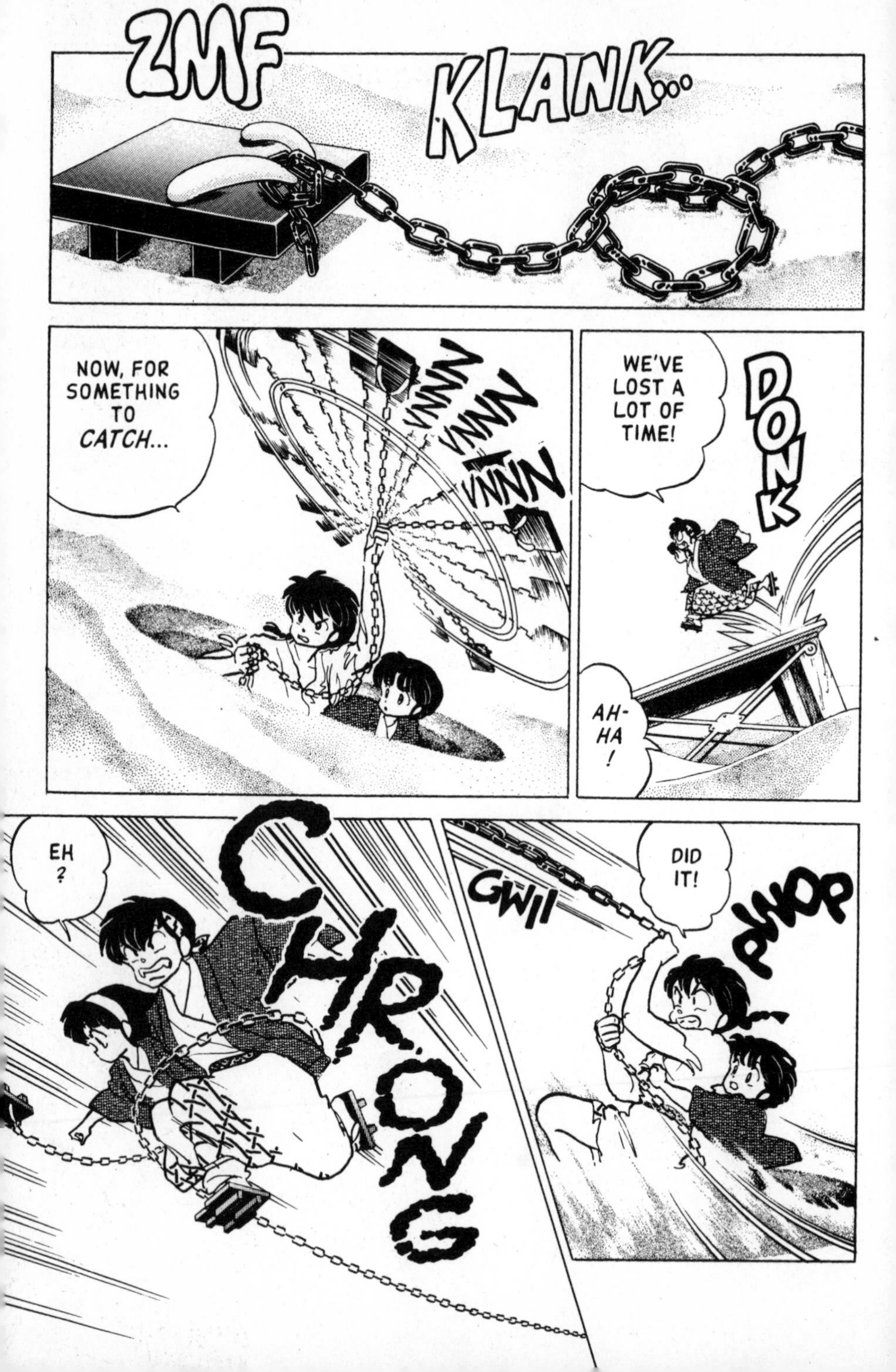
ZMF
KLANK...
NOW, FOR SOMETHING TO CATCH...
VNNN VNNN VNNN
WE'VE LOST A LOT OF TIME!
DONK
AH-HA!
EH?
CHRONG
GWII
DID IT!
PWOP

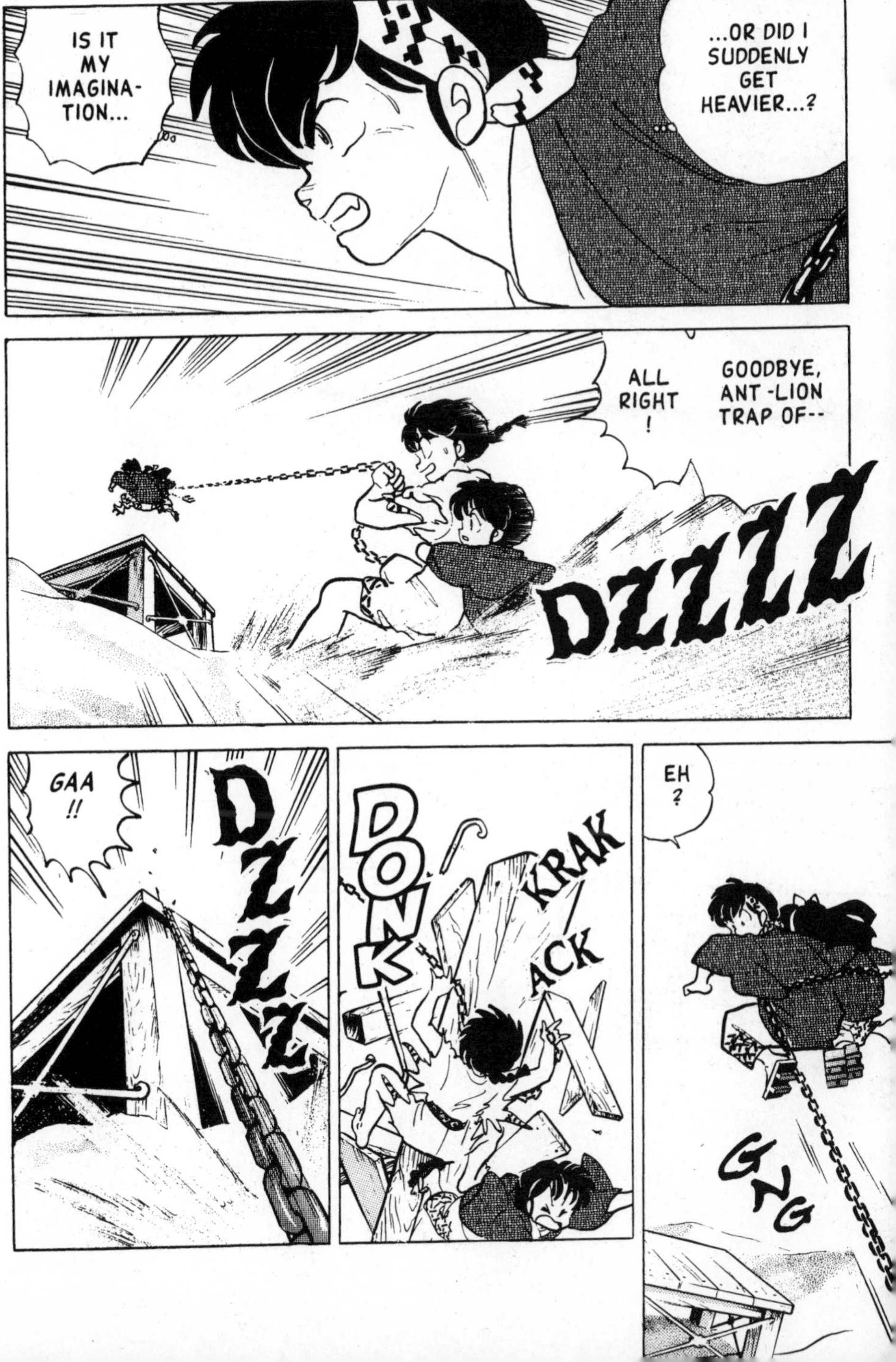
IS IT MY IMAGINATION...
...OR DID I SUDDENLY GET HEAVIER...?
ALL RIGHT!
GOODBYE, ANT-LION TRAP OF--
DZZZZZ
GAA!!
DZZZZ
DONK
KRAK
ACK
EH?
GNG

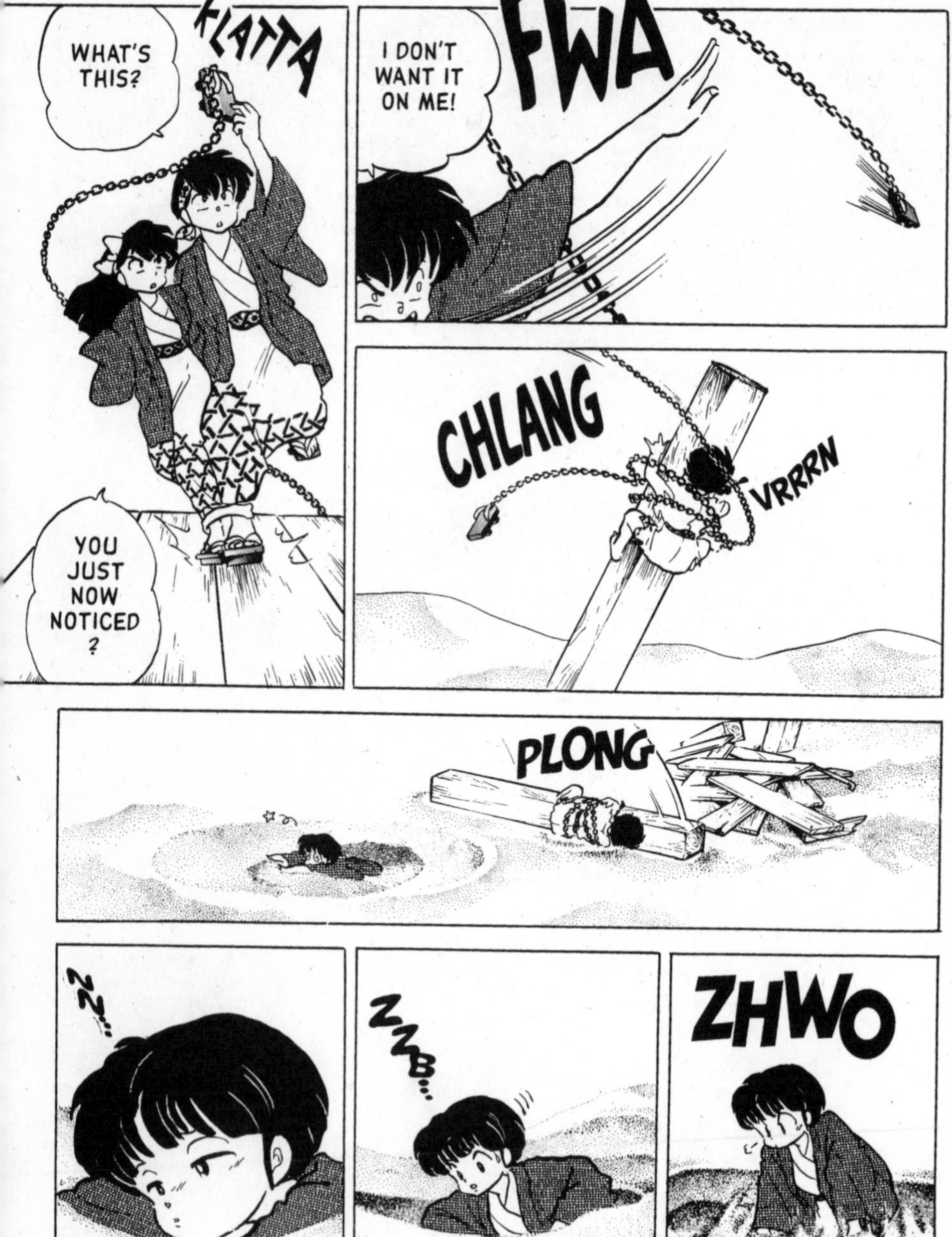
WHAT'S THIS?
KLATTA
YOU JUST NOW NOTICED?
I DON'T WANT IT ON ME!
FWA
CHLANG
VRRRN
PLONG
ZZZ...
ZZB...
ZHWO

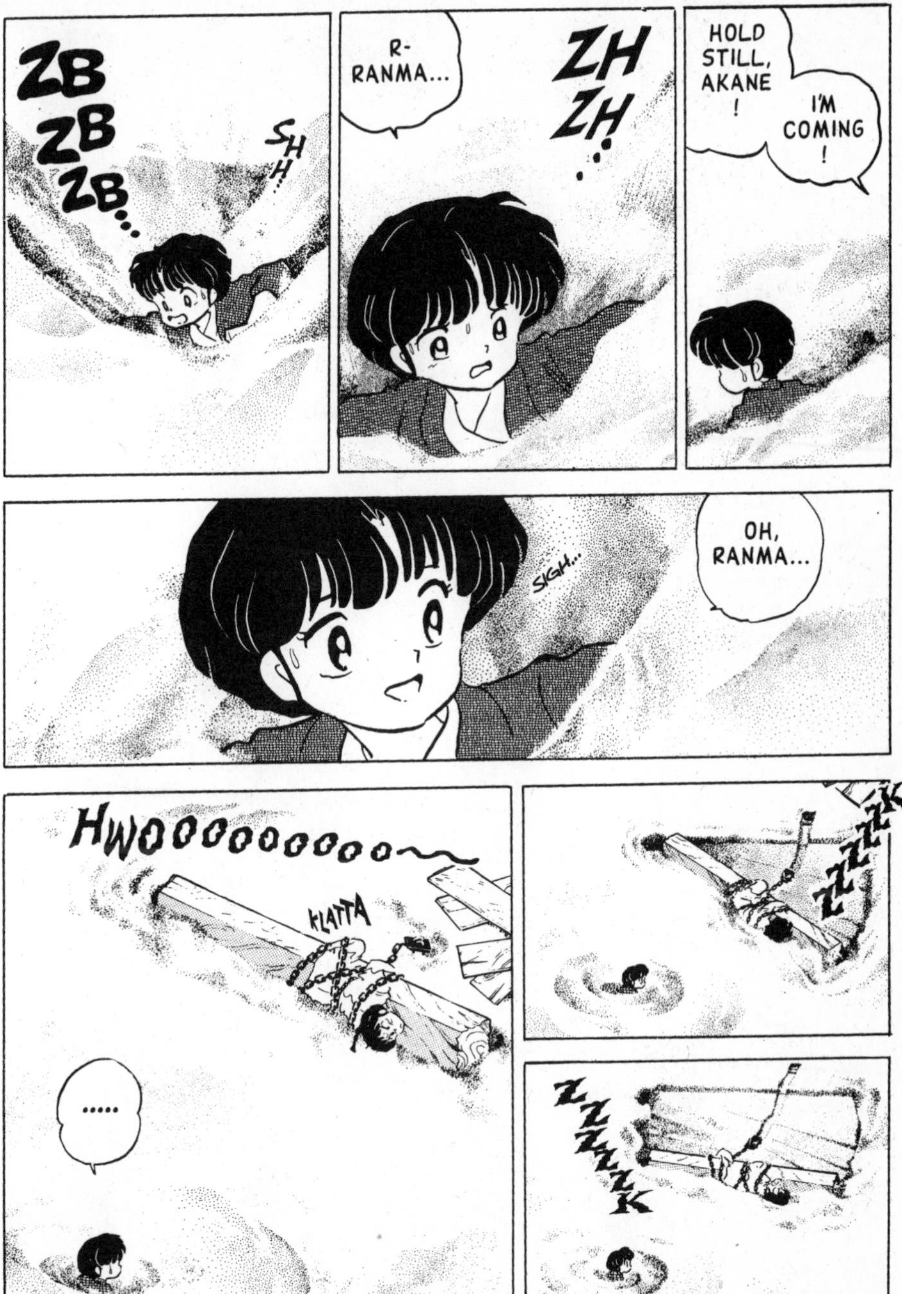
ZB ZB ZB...
SHH...
R- RANMA...
ZH ZH...
HOLD STILL, AKANE!
I'M COMING!
SIGH...
OH, RANMA...
HWOOOOOOOOOO~~
KLATTA
......
ZZZZZK
ZZZZZZK

ZzZ...

RANMA...

DON'T
SINK
!

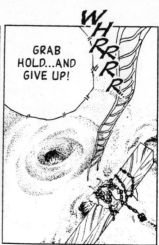

GRAB
HOLD...AND
GIVE UP!

WHRRR

WHRRR

OH
MAN,
OH
MAN-
N-N...

I'M
SORRY,
AKANE...

I CAN'T
HELP
YOU
LIKE
THIS.

GRAB
THE LIFE-
LINE!

RANMA...

YOU...
YOU...

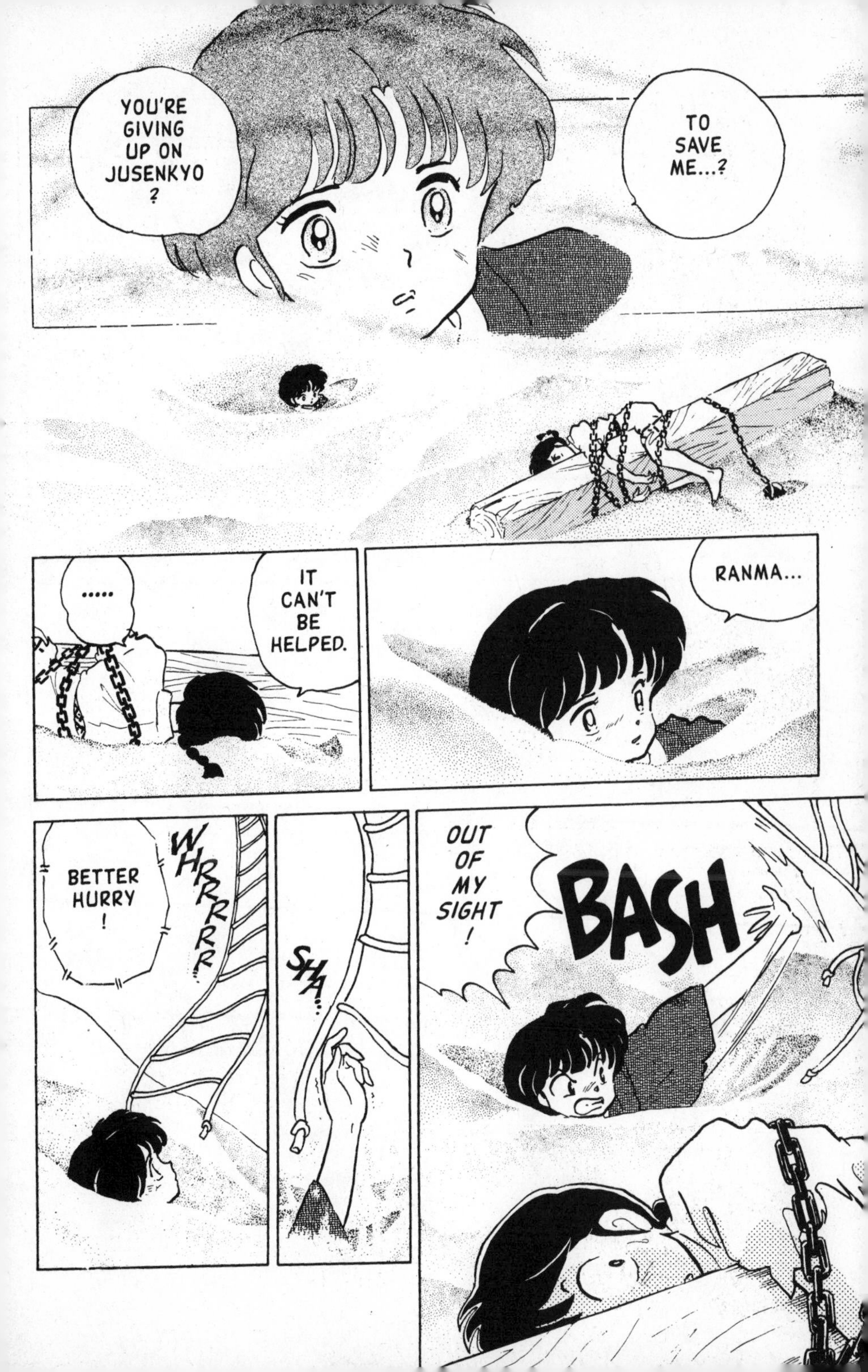
YOU'RE GIVING UP ON JUSENKYO?
TO SAVE ME...?
......
IT CAN'T BE HELPED.
RANMA...
BETTER HURRY!
WHRRRRR
SHA
OUT OF MY SIGHT!
BASH

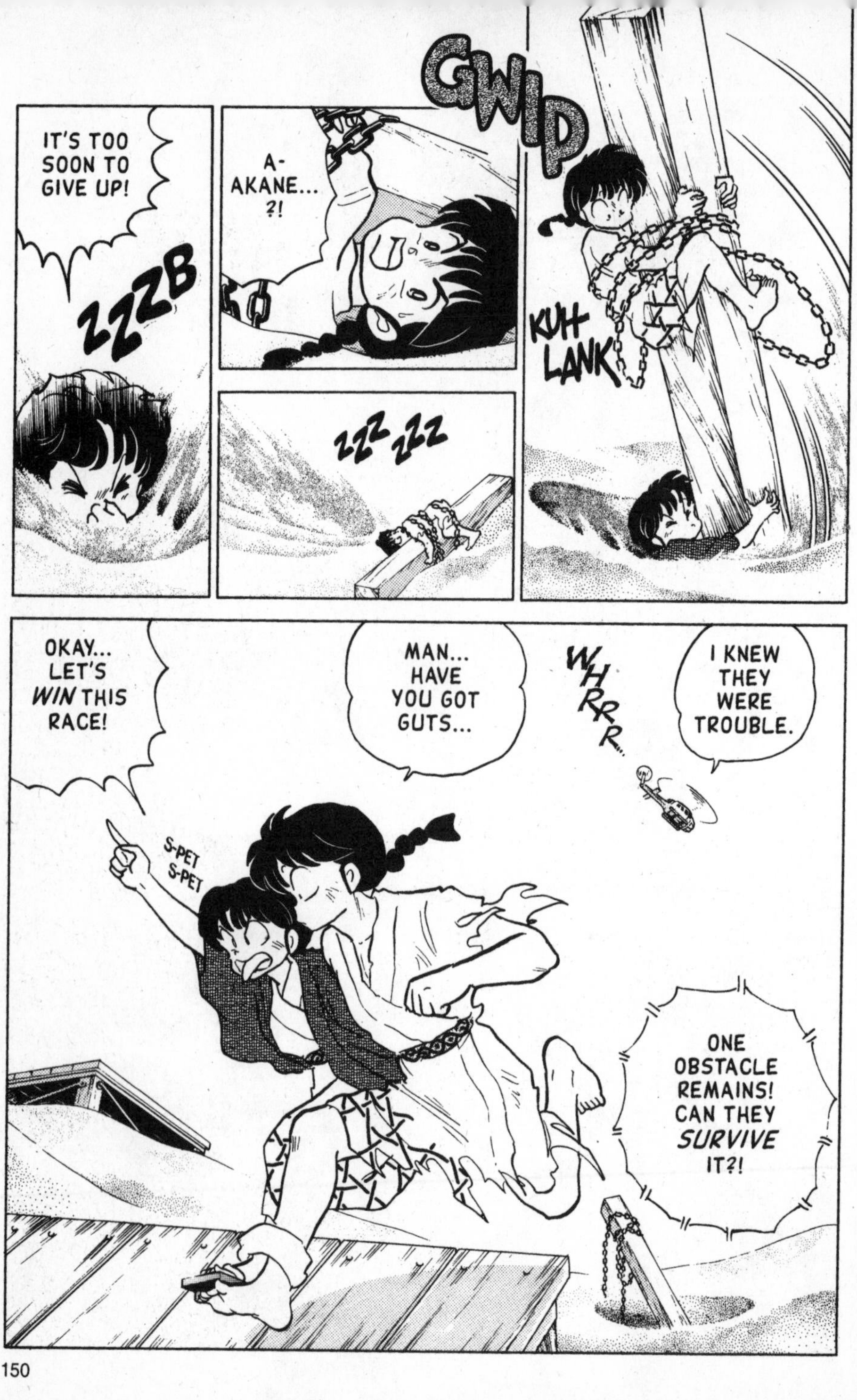
IT'S TOO SOON TO GIVE UP!
ZZZB
A- AKANE... ?!
ZZZ ZZZ
GWIP
KUH LANK
OKAY... LET'S *WIN* THIS RACE!
MAN... HAVE YOU GOT GUTS...
WHRRR...
I KNEW THEY WERE TROUBLE.
S-PET S-PET
ONE OBSTACLE REMAINS! CAN THEY *SURVIVE* IT?!

PART 10
THE FINAL CHOICE

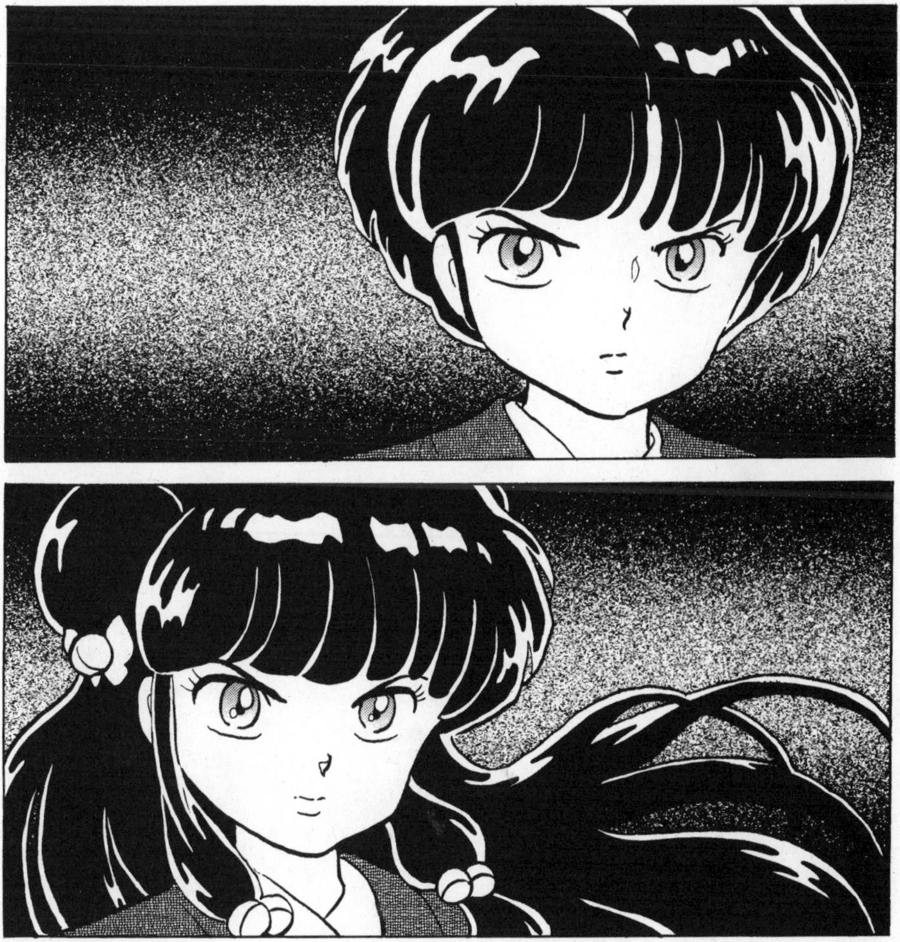

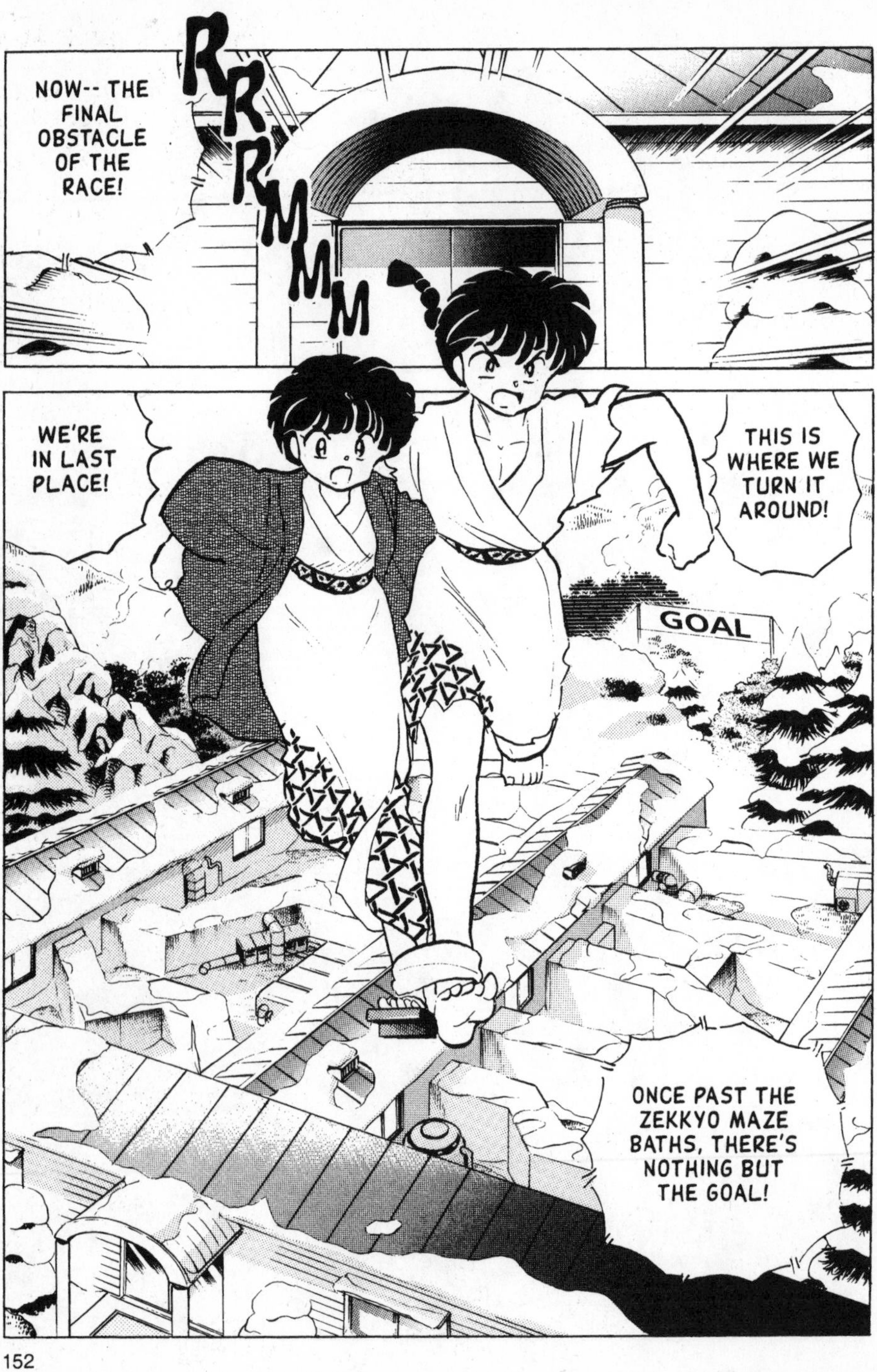
RRRMMMM
NOW-- THE FINAL OBSTACLE OF THE RACE!
WE'RE IN LAST PLACE!
THIS IS WHERE WE TURN IT AROUND!
GOAL
ONCE PAST THE ZEKKYO MAZE BATHS, THERE'S NOTHING BUT THE GOAL!

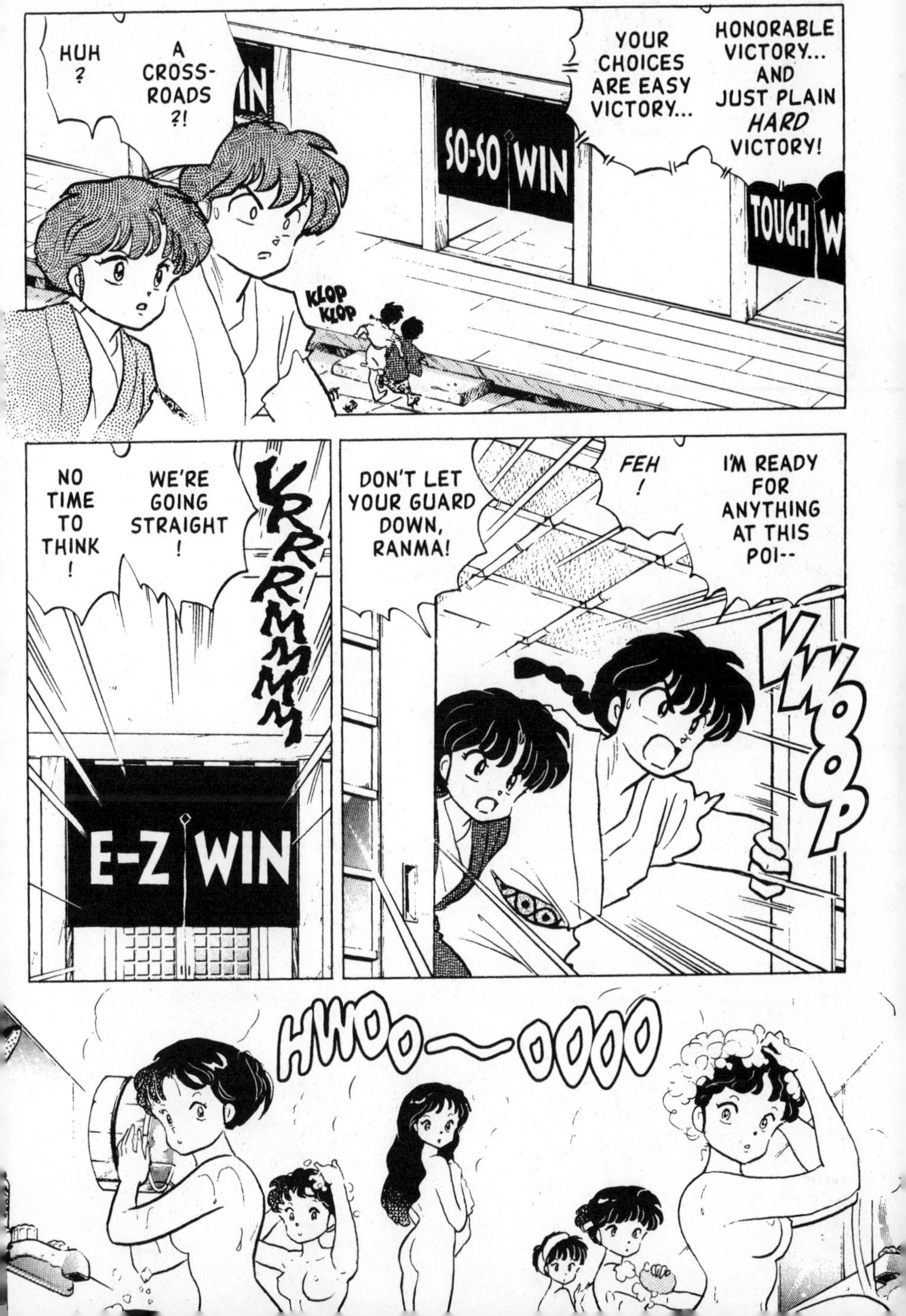
HUH ?
A CROSS-ROADS ?!
SO-SO WIN
YOUR CHOICES ARE EASY VICTORY...
HONORABLE VICTORY... AND JUST PLAIN HARD VICTORY!
TOUGH W
KLOP KLOP
NO TIME TO THINK !
WE'RE GOING STRAIGHT !
VRRRMMMM
E-Z WIN
DON'T LET YOUR GUARD DOWN, RANMA!
FEH !
I'M READY FOR ANYTHING AT THIS POI--
VWOOOP
HWOO～OOOO

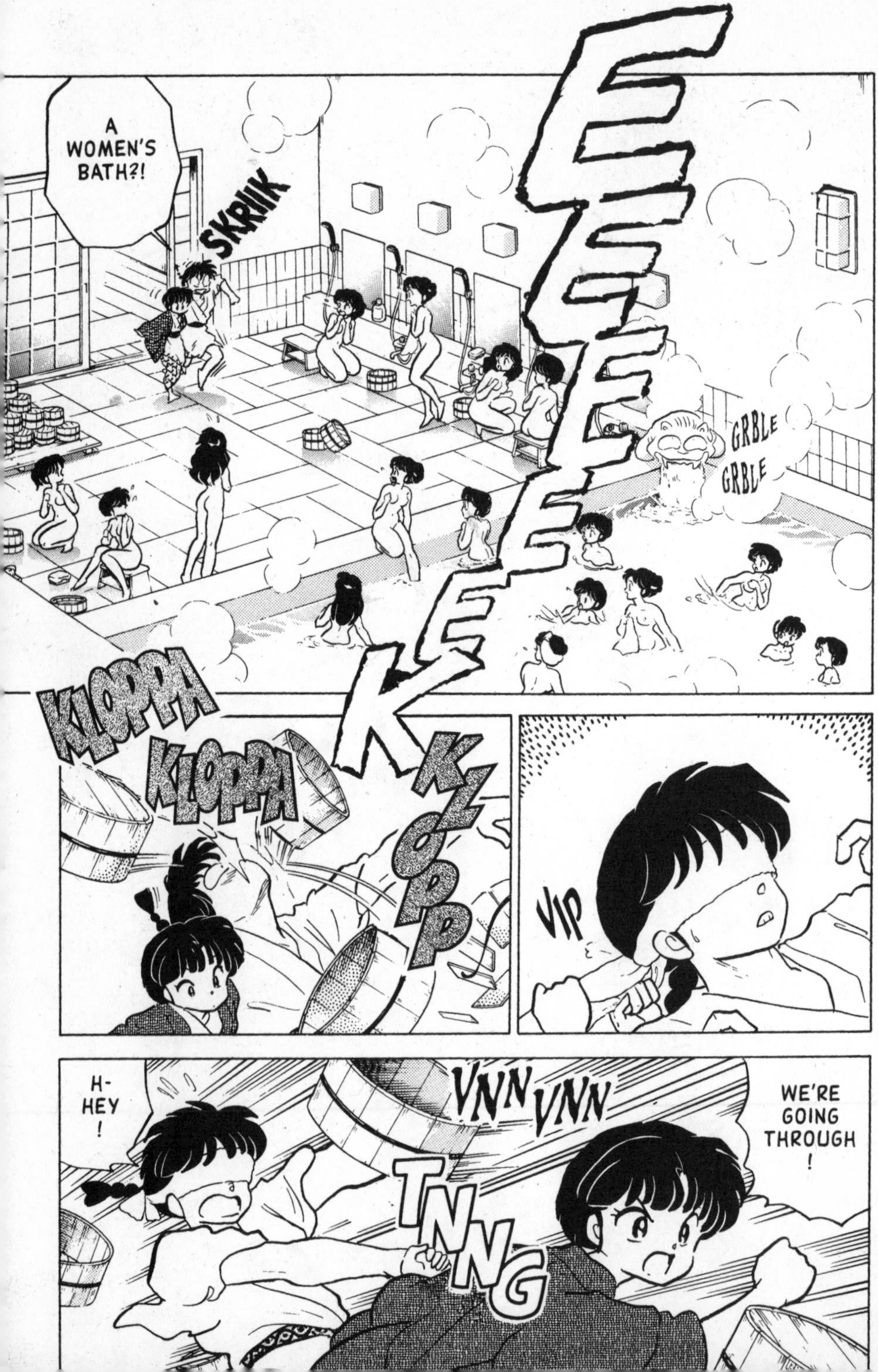
A WOMEN'S BATH?!
SKRIIK
EEEEEEEEEK
GRBLE GRBLE
KLOPPA
KLOPPA
KLOPP
VIP
H-HEY!
VNN VNN
TNNG
WE'RE GOING THROUGH!

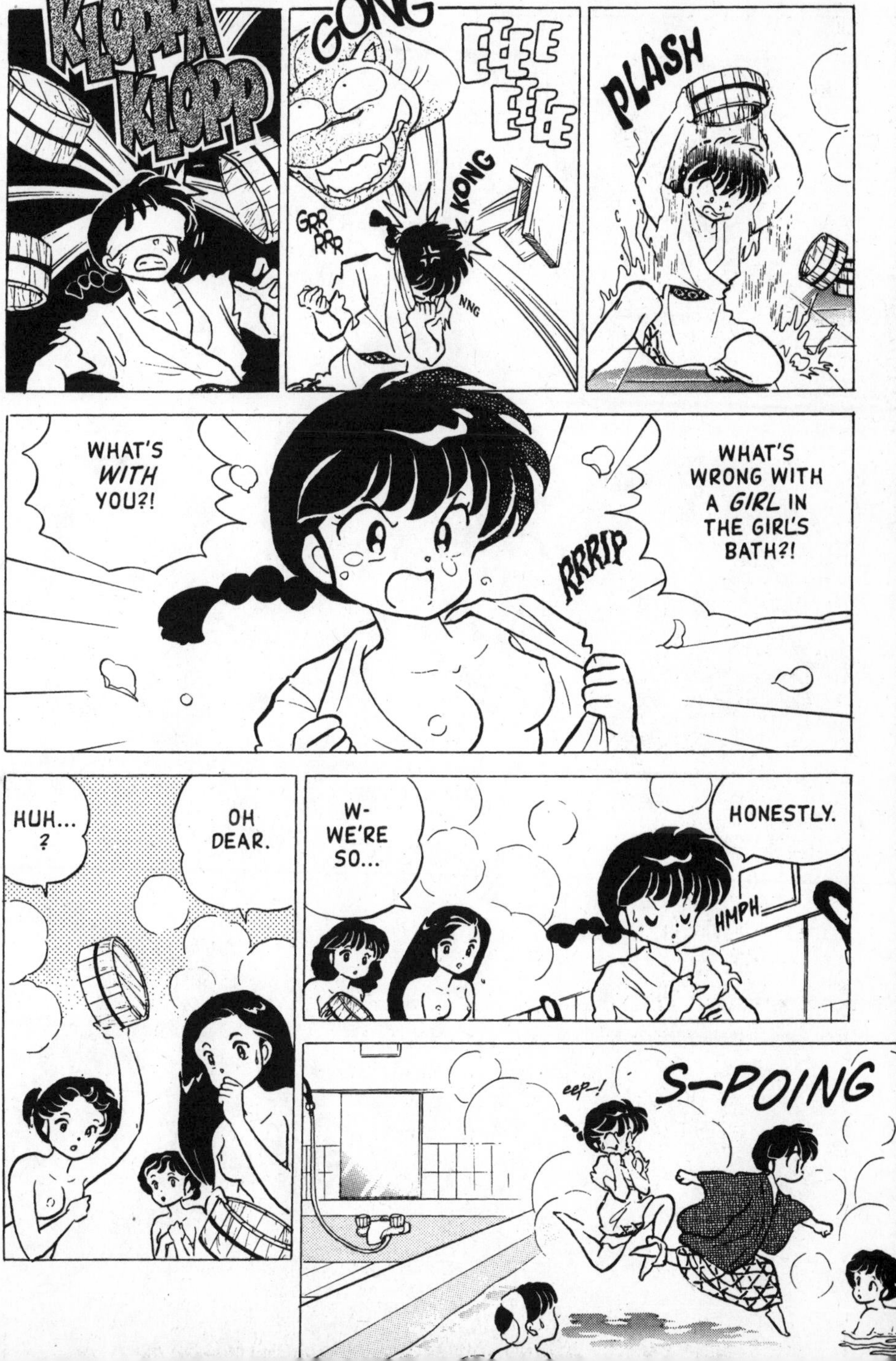
KLOPPA KLOPP
GONG
EEEE EEEE
KONG
GRR RRR
NNG
PLASH
WHAT'S WITH YOU?!
RRRIP
WHAT'S WRONG WITH A GIRL IN THE GIRL'S BATH?!
HUH...?
OH DEAR.
W- WE'RE SO...
HONESTLY.
HMPH
eep-!
S-POING

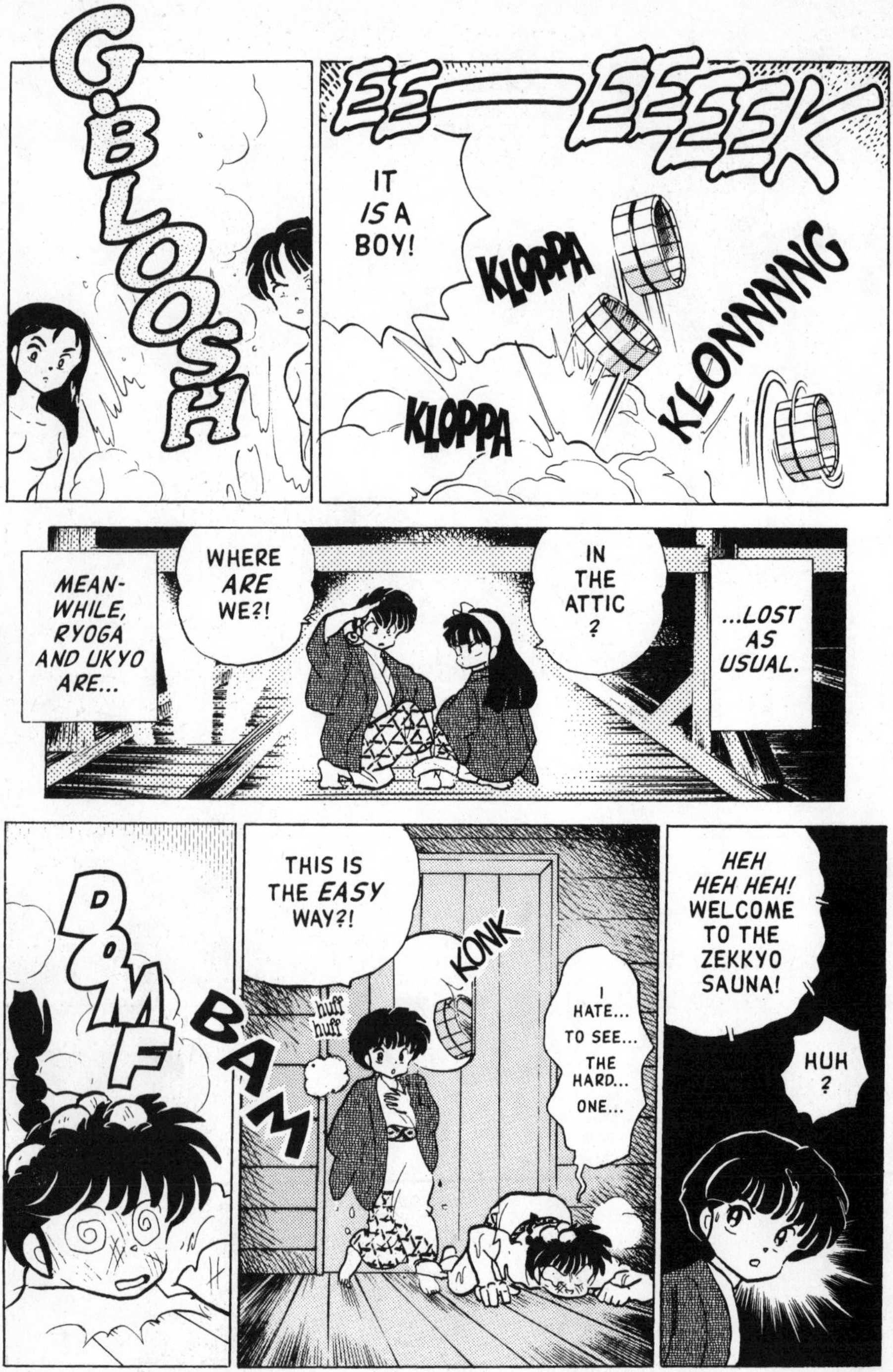
G-BLOOSH
EE—EEEEK
IT IS A BOY!
KLOPPA
KLOPPA
KLONNNNG
MEAN-WHILE, RYOGA AND UKYO ARE...
WHERE ARE WE?!
IN THE ATTIC?
...LOST AS USUAL.
DOMF
BAM
THIS IS THE EASY WAY?!
KONK
huff huff
I HATE... TO SEE... THE HARD... ONE...
HEH HEH HEH! WELCOME TO THE ZEKKYO SAUNA!
HUH?

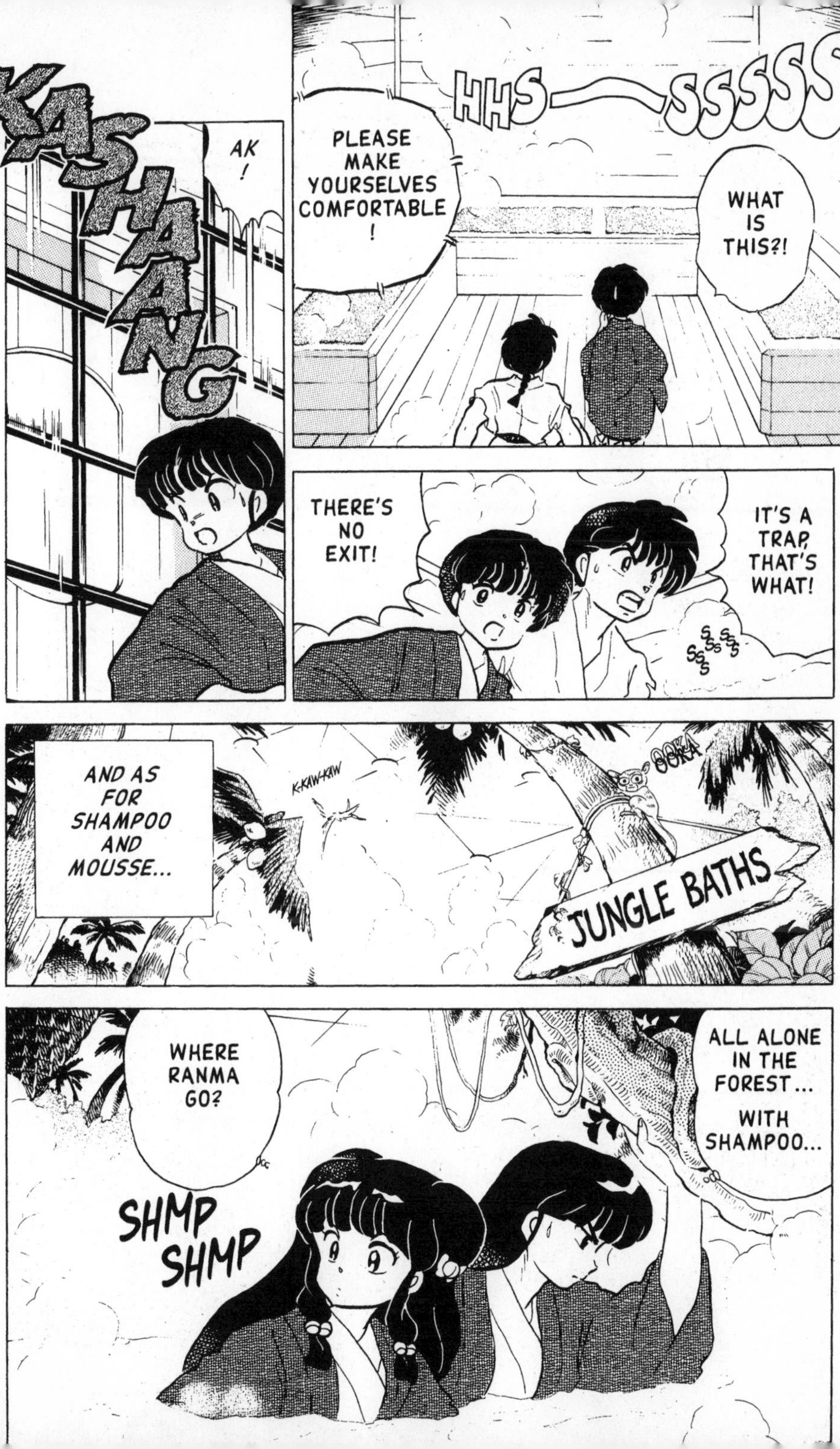
KASHANG
AK!
HHS—SSSSS
PLEASE MAKE YOURSELVES COMFORTABLE!
WHAT IS THIS?!
THERE'S NO EXIT!
IT'S A TRAP, THAT'S WHAT!
AND AS FOR SHAMPOO AND MOUSSE...
K-KAW-KAW
OOKA
JUNGLE BATHS
WHERE RANMA GO?
ALL ALONE IN THE FOREST... WITH SHAMPOO...
SHMP SHMP

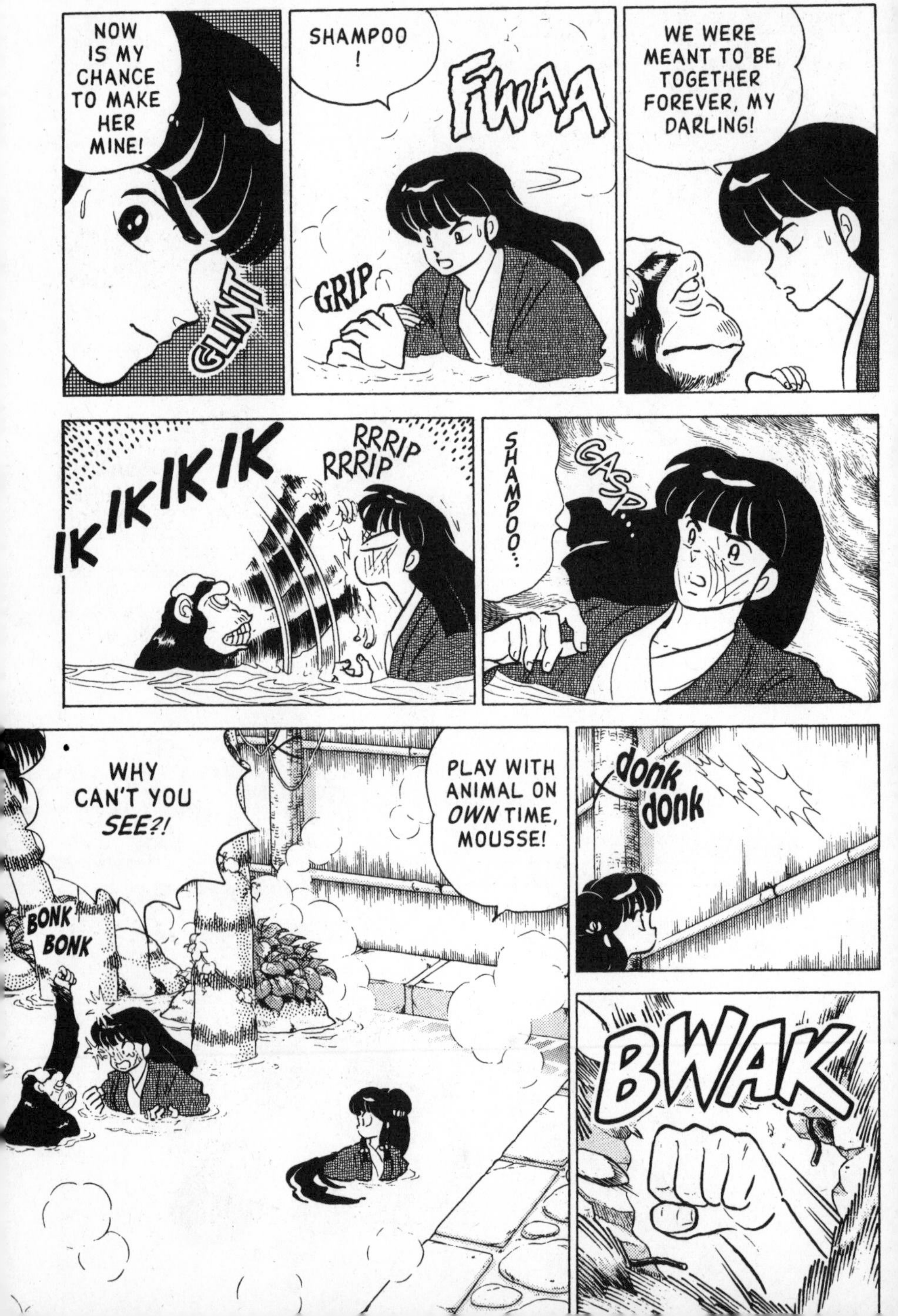

NOW IS MY CHANCE TO MAKE HER MINE!
GLINT
SHAMPOO!
FWAA
GRIP
WE WERE MEANT TO BE TOGETHER FOREVER, MY DARLING!
IK IK IK IK IK
RRRIP RRRIP
SHAMPOO...
GASP
WHY CAN'T YOU *SEE?!*
BONK BONK
PLAY WITH ANIMAL ON *OWN* TIME, MOUSSE!
donk donk
BWAK

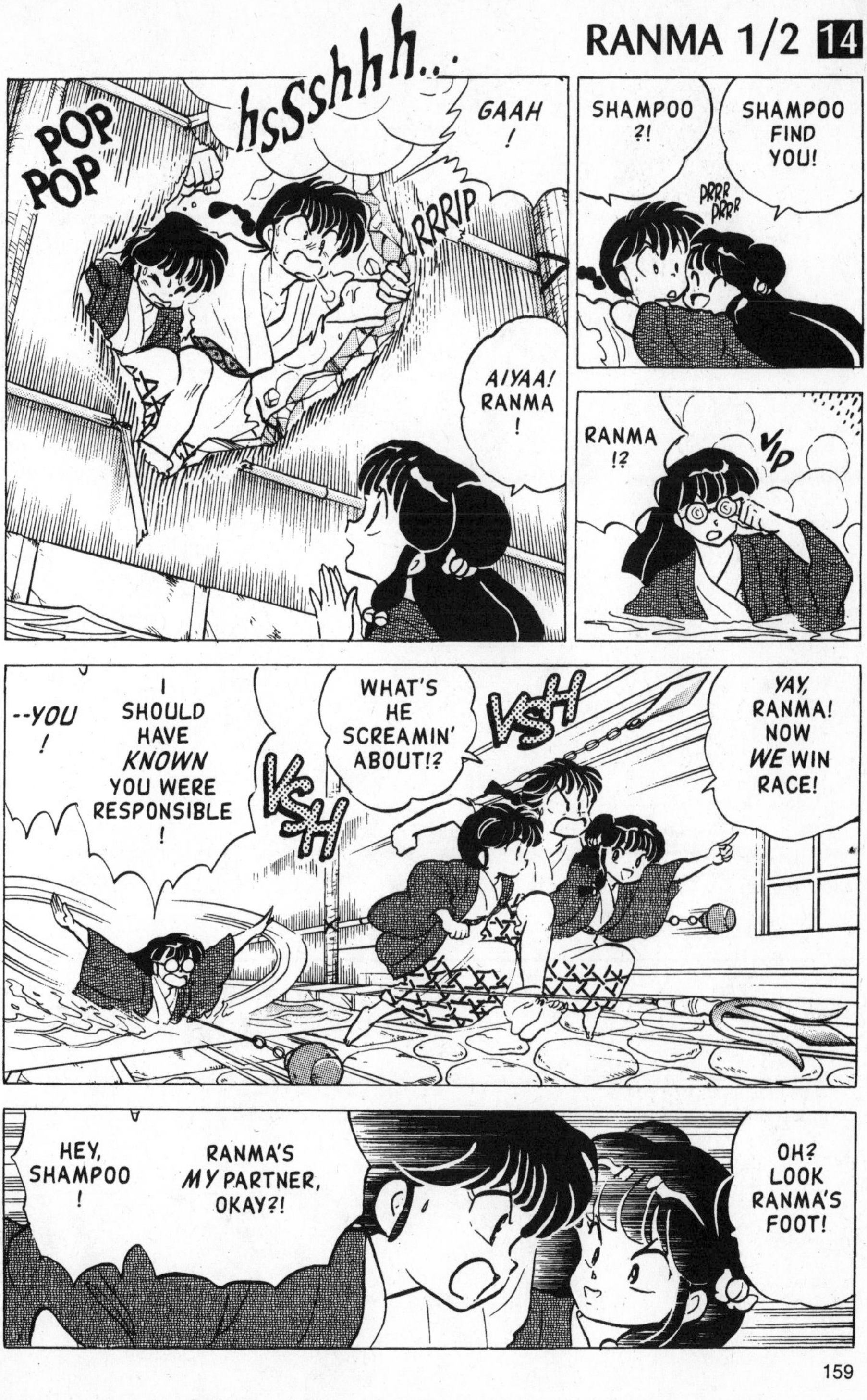
hsSshhh...
POP POP
GAAH!
RRRIP
AIYAA! RANMA!
SHAMPOO ?!
PRRR PRRR
SHAMPOO FIND YOU!
RANMA !?
VIP
--YOU!
I SHOULD HAVE KNOWN YOU WERE RESPONSIBLE!
VSH
WHAT'S HE SCREAMIN' ABOUT!?
VSH
YAY, RANMA! NOW WE WIN RACE!
HEY, SHAMPOO!
RANMA'S MY PARTNER, OKAY?!
OH? LOOK RANMA'S FOOT!

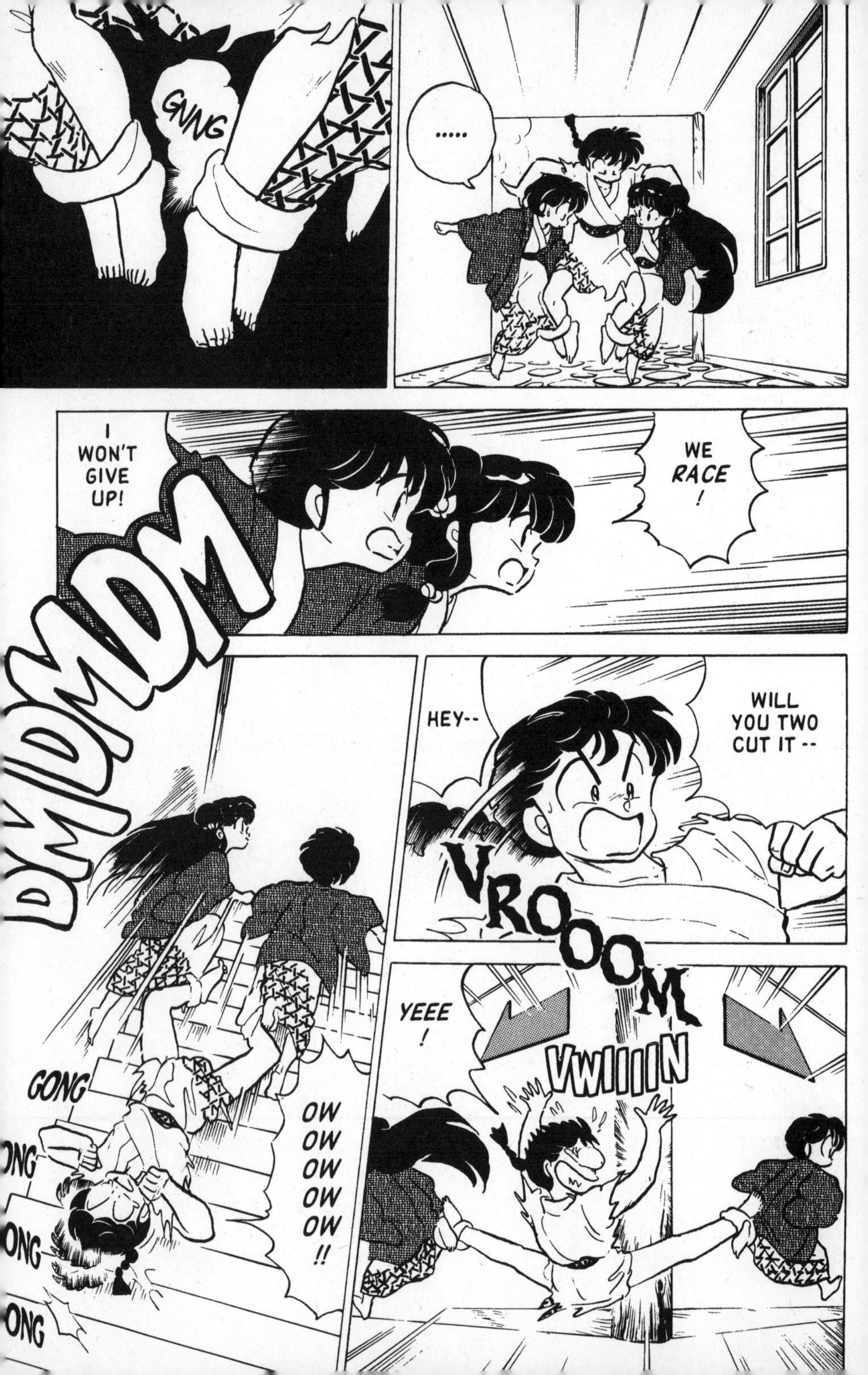
GNNG
......
I WON'T GIVE UP!
WE RACE !
DMDMDM
GONG
ONG
ONG
ONG
ONG
OW OW OW OW OW !!
HEY--
WILL YOU TWO CUT IT --
VROOOOM
YEEE !
VWIIIIN

MUSH

TSK TSK... EVEN I FEEL A LITTLE BAD...

CONK

RANMA, COME WITH SHAMPOO!

NO! YOU COME WITH ME!

LET GO!

YOU HURTING RANMA!

ING

YOU'RE THE ONE HURTING HIM!

GNG GNG GNG

AIEEEEE

GNG GNG

H-Help me...

WAIT! I REMEMBER!

I'VE HEARD THIS TALE!

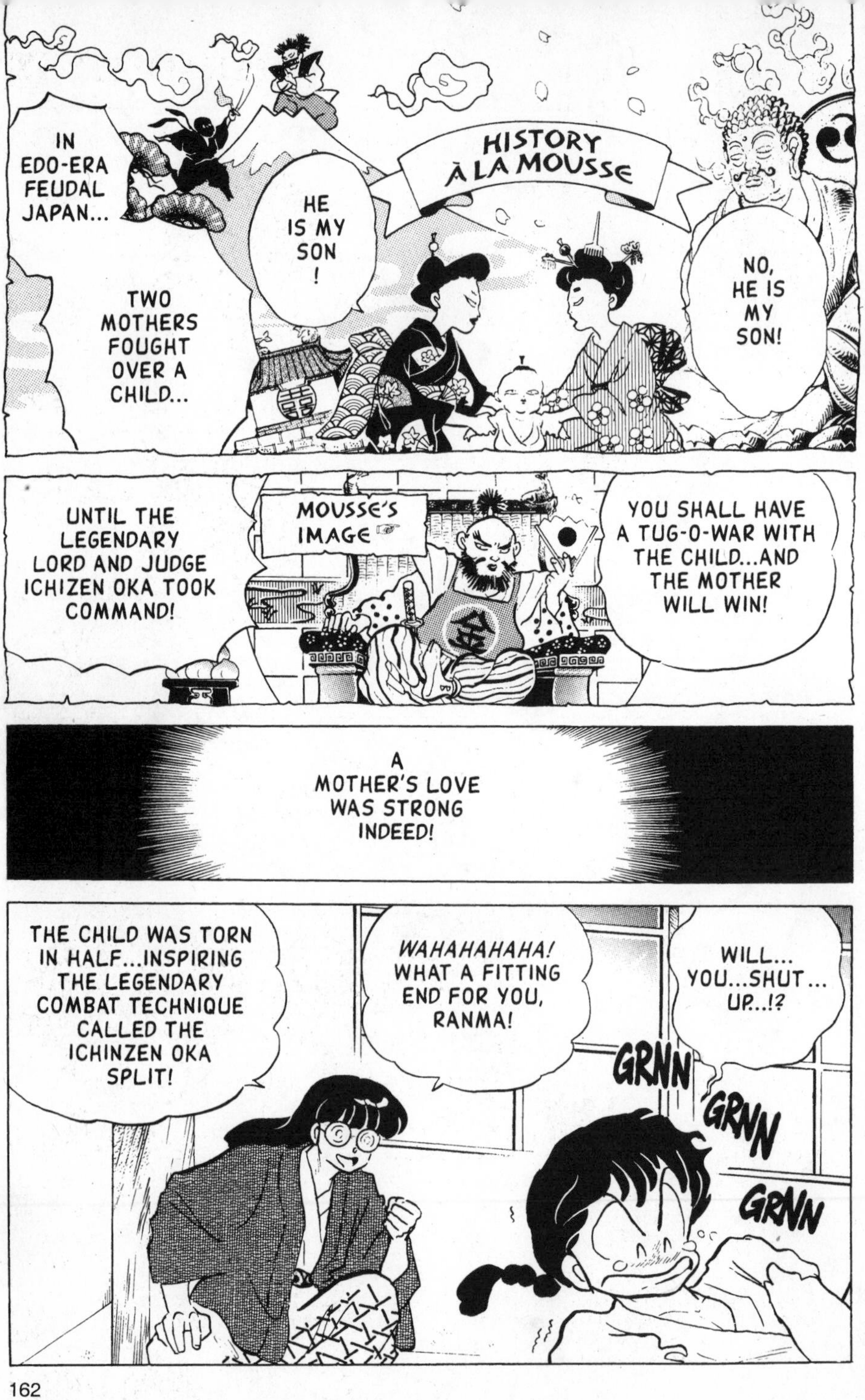

IN EDO-ERA FEUDAL JAPAN...
TWO MOTHERS FOUGHT OVER A CHILD...
HE IS MY SON!
HISTORY À LA MOUSSE
NO, HE IS MY SON!
UNTIL THE LEGENDARY LORD AND JUDGE ICHIZEN OKA TOOK COMMAND!
MOUSSE'S IMAGE
YOU SHALL HAVE A TUG-O-WAR WITH THE CHILD...AND THE MOTHER WILL WIN!
A MOTHER'S LOVE WAS STRONG INDEED!
THE CHILD WAS TORN IN HALF...INSPIRING THE LEGENDARY COMBAT TECHNIQUE CALLED THE ICHINZEN OKA SPLIT!
WAHAHAHAHA! WHAT A FITTING END FOR YOU, RANMA!
WILL... YOU...SHUT... UP...!?
GRNN
GRNN
GRNN

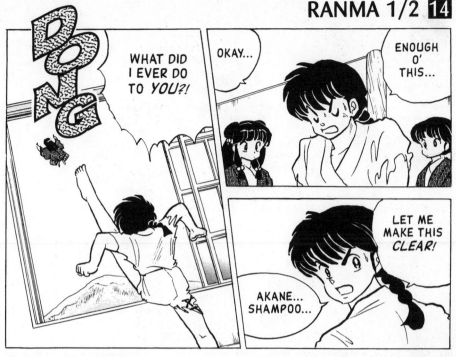

DOING

WHAT DID I EVER DO TO *YOU?!*

OKAY...

ENOUGH O' THIS...

LET ME MAKE THIS *CLEAR!*

AKANE... SHAMPOO...

THE ONLY THING I CARE ABOUT IS WINNING THIS RACE AND GOING TO JUSENKYO.

THIS ISN'T A PARTY... IT ISN'T A PROM...

IT DOESN'T MATTER *WHO* I PAIR UP WITH.

AM I MAKING MYSELF CLEAR?

SO LET'S STOP FIGHTING OVER *NOTHING,* OKAY?

geez

OKAY RANMA.

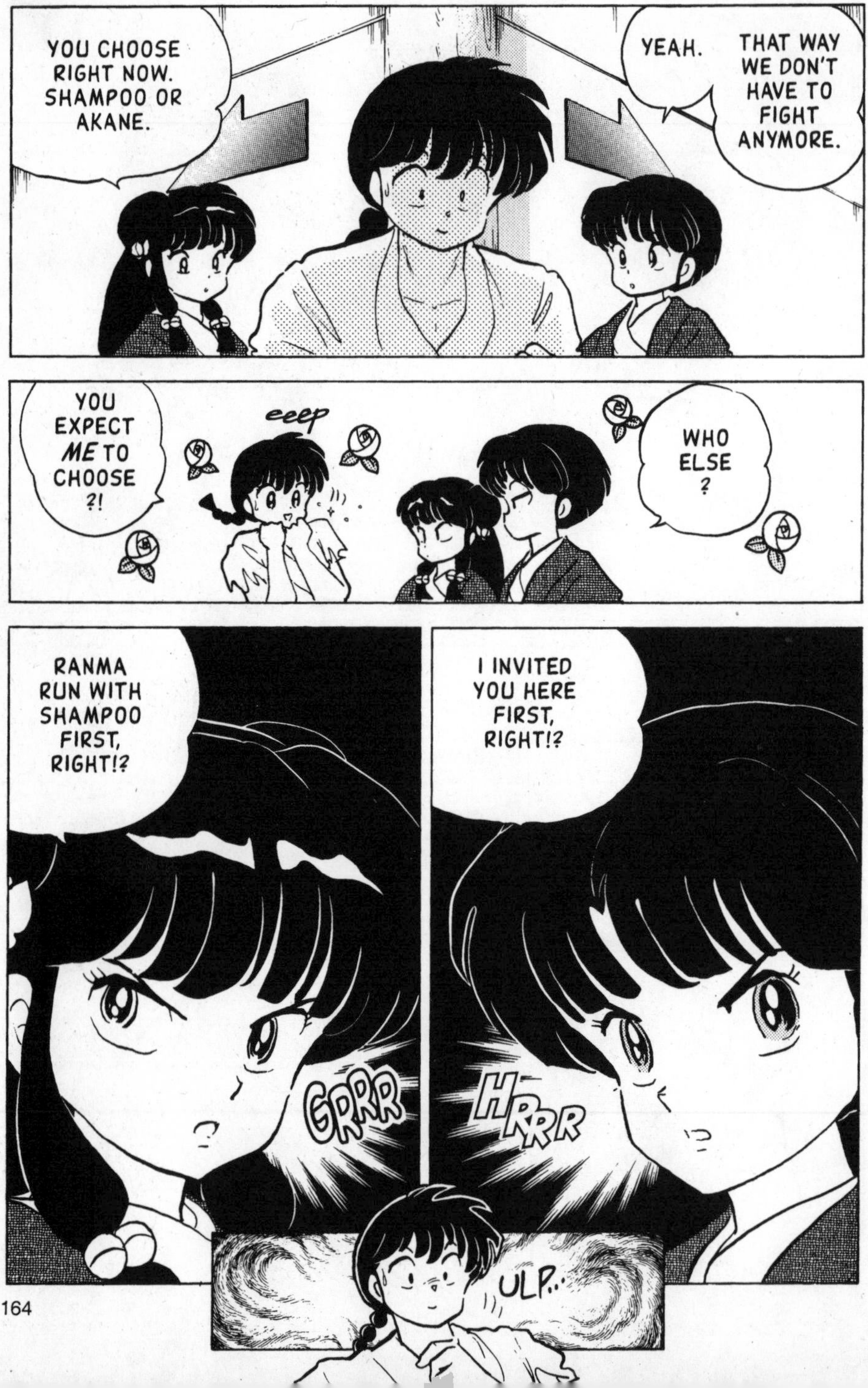
YOU CHOOSE RIGHT NOW. SHAMPOO OR AKANE.
YEAH.
THAT WAY WE DON'T HAVE TO FIGHT ANYMORE.
YOU EXPECT *ME* TO CHOOSE ?!
eeep
WHO ELSE ?
RANMA RUN WITH SHAMPOO FIRST, RIGHT!?
GRRR
I INVITED YOU HERE FIRST, RIGHT!?
HRRR
ULP...

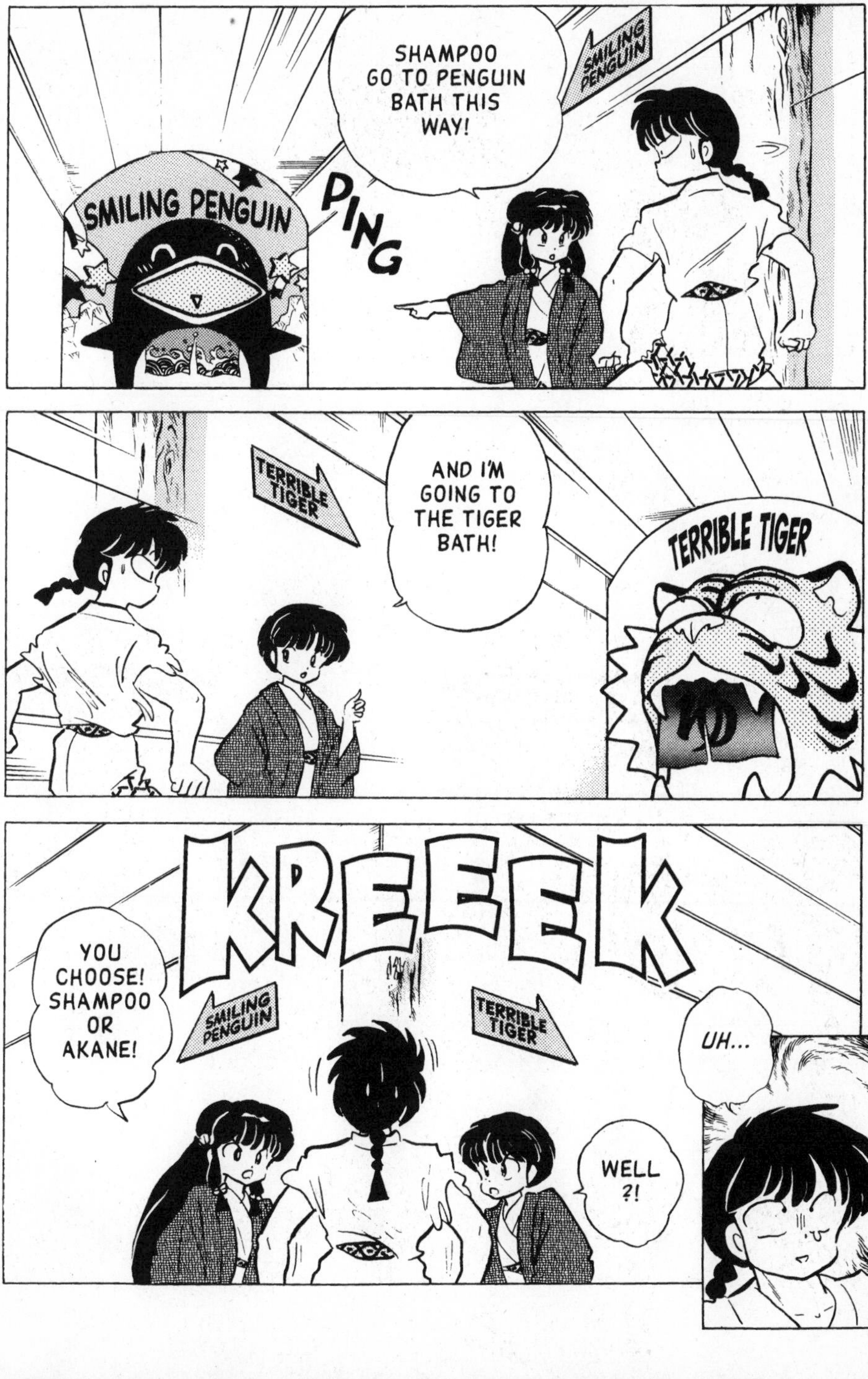
SMILING PENGUIN
PING
SHAMPOO GO TO PENGUIN BATH THIS WAY!
SMILING PENGUIN
TERRIBLE TIGER
AND I'M GOING TO THE TIGER BATH!
TERRIBLE TIGER
KREEEK
YOU CHOOSE! SHAMPOO OR AKANE!
SMILING PENGUIN
TERRIBLE TIGER
WELL ?!
UH...

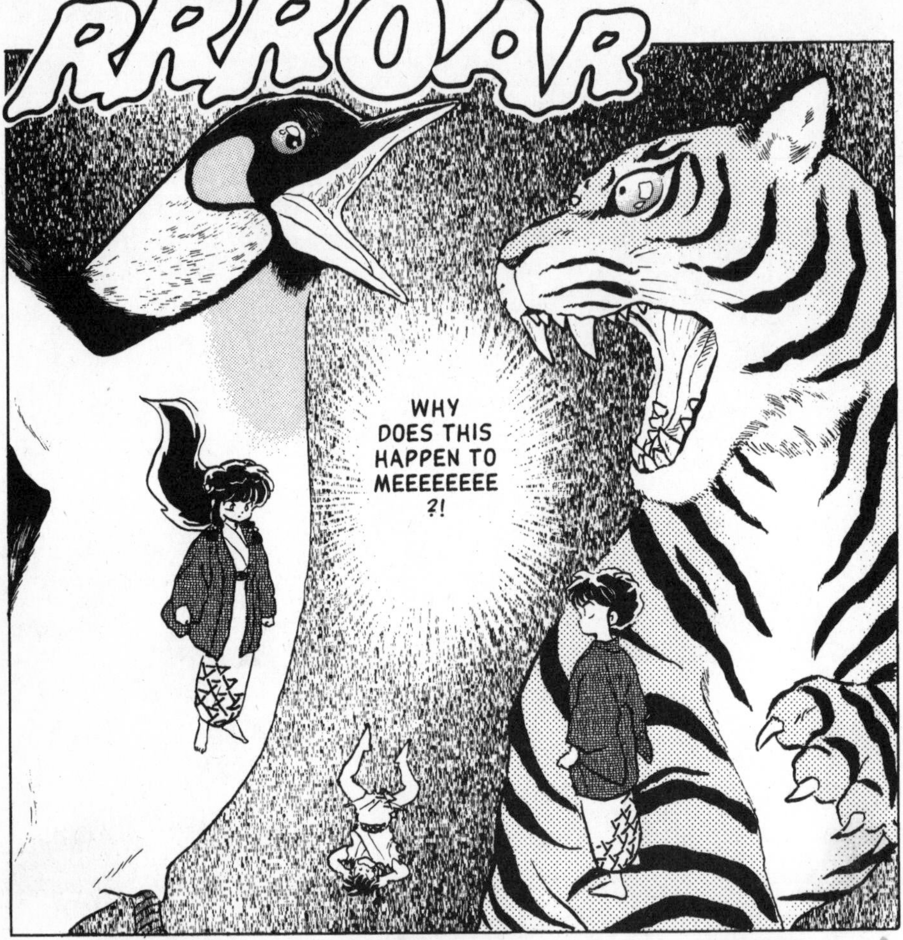
RRROAR
WHY DOES THIS HAPPEN TO MEEEEEEEE ?!

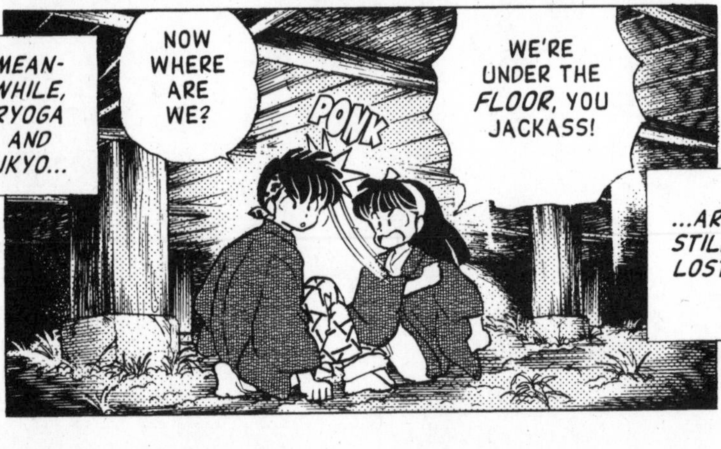
MEAN-WHILE, RYOGA AND UKYO...
NOW WHERE ARE WE?
PONK
WE'RE UNDER THE FLOOR, YOU JACKASS!
...ARE STILL LOST.

PART 12
A GOAL TOO FAR

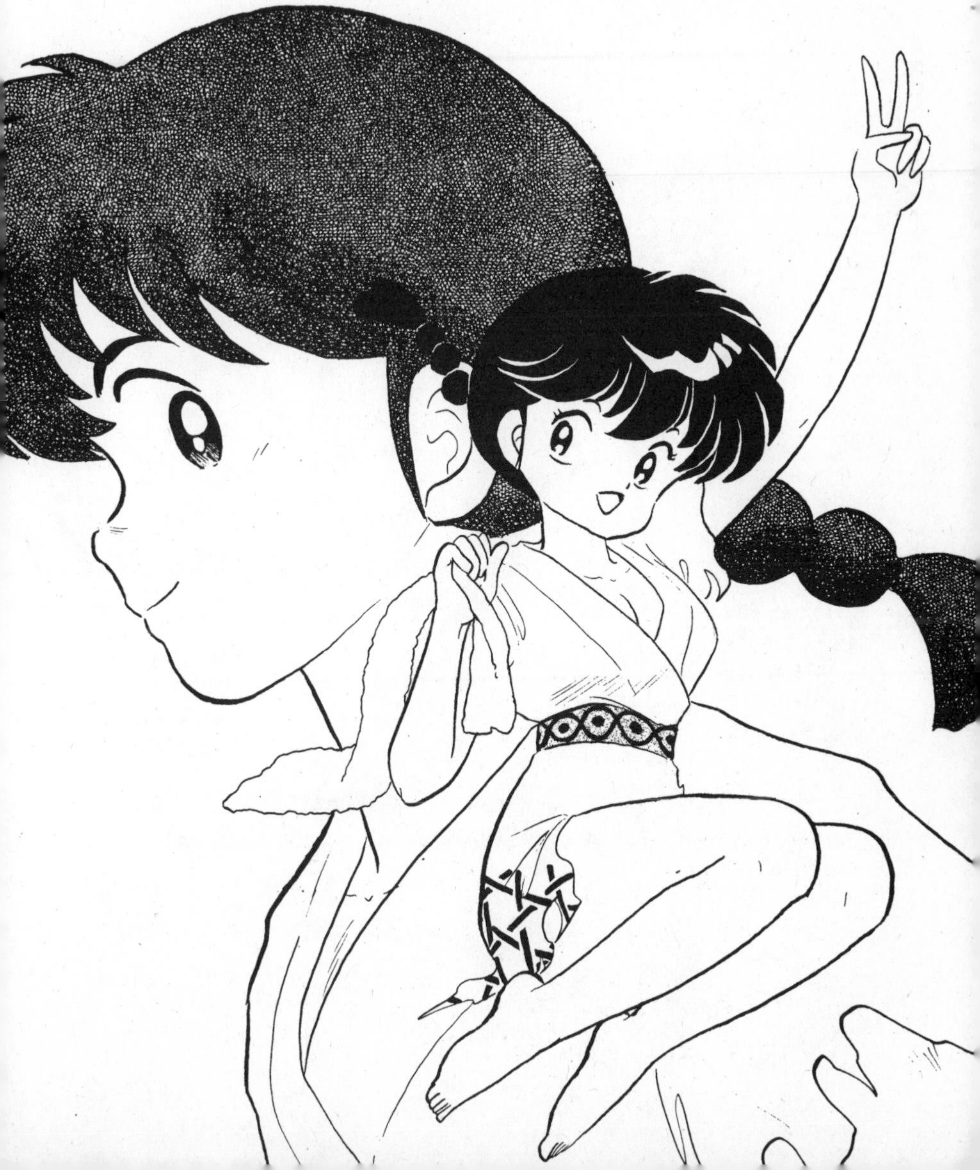

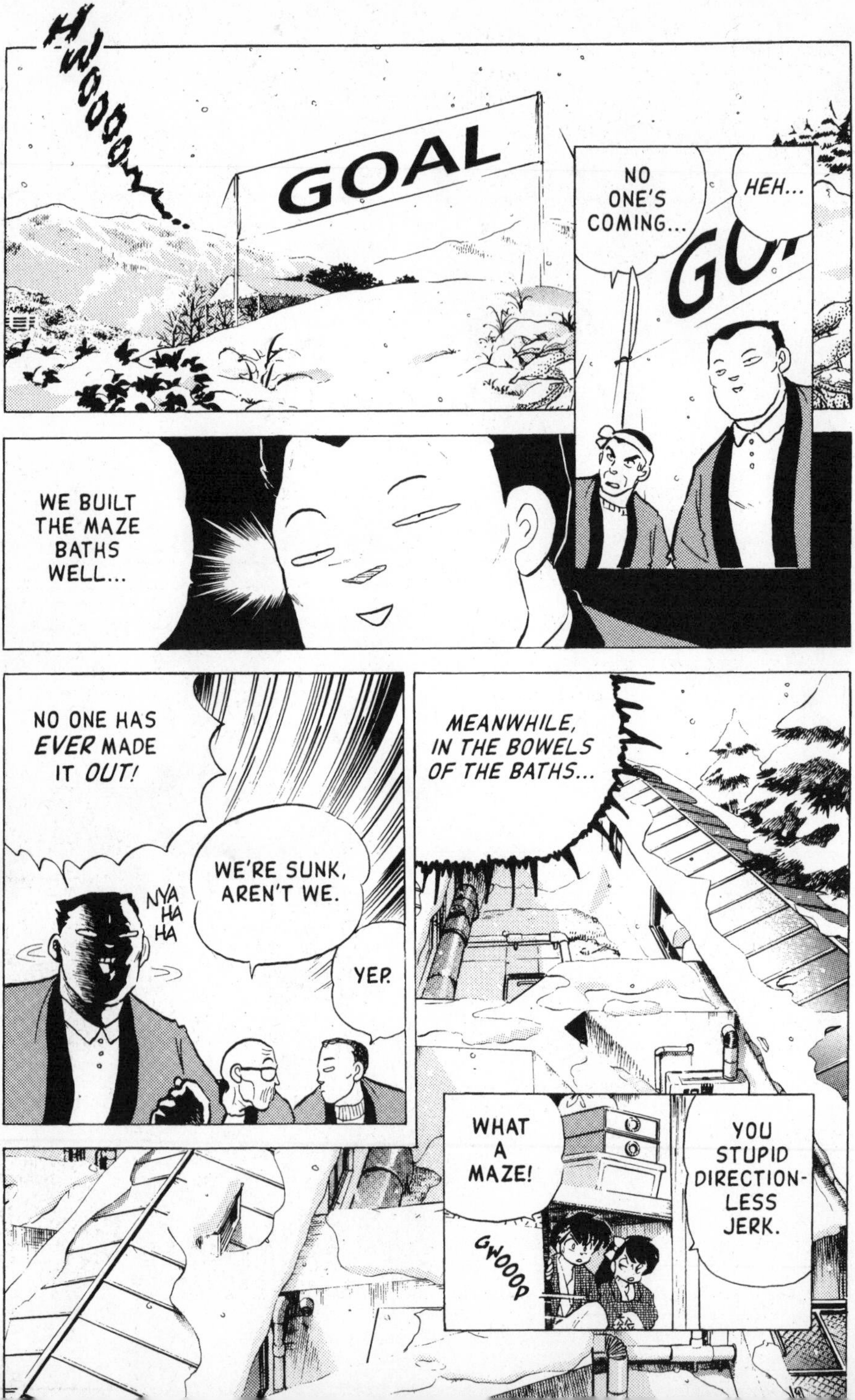
HWOOOOM...
GOAL
NO ONE'S COMING...
HEH...
GO
WE BUILT THE MAZE BATHS WELL...
NO ONE HAS *EVER* MADE IT *OUT!*
NYA HA HA HA
WE'RE SUNK, AREN'T WE.
YEP.
MEANWHILE, IN THE BOWELS OF THE BATHS...
WHAT A MAZE!
GWOOOP
YOU STUPID DIRECTION-LESS JERK.

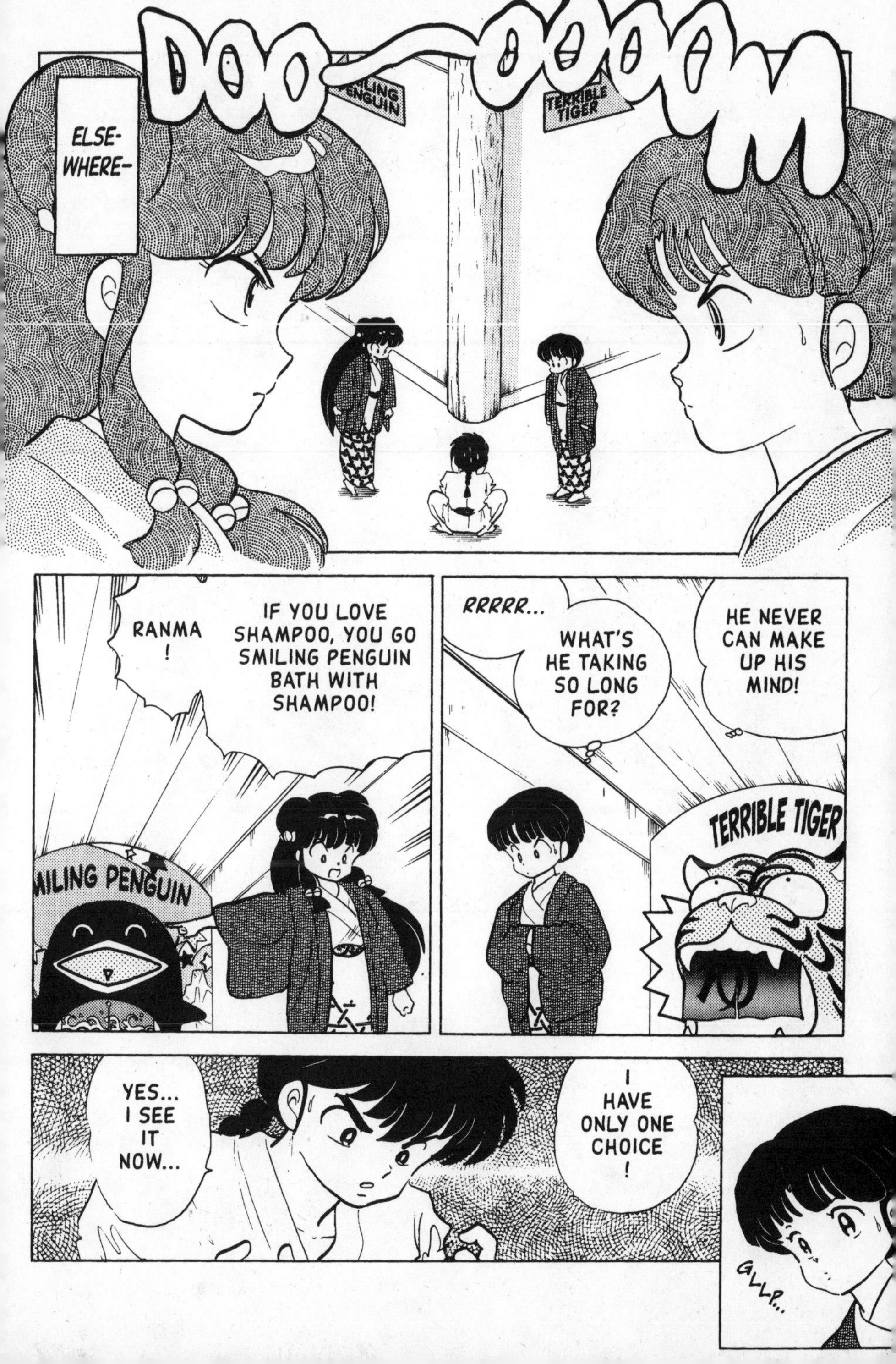
DOO—OOOOM
ELSE-WHERE-
TERRIBLE TIGER
RANMA!
IF YOU LOVE SHAMPOO, YOU GO SMILING PENGUIN BATH WITH SHAMPOO!
RRRRR...
WHAT'S HE TAKING SO LONG FOR?
HE NEVER CAN MAKE UP HIS MIND!
TERRIBLE TIGER
YES... I SEE IT NOW...
I HAVE ONLY ONE CHOICE!
GULP...

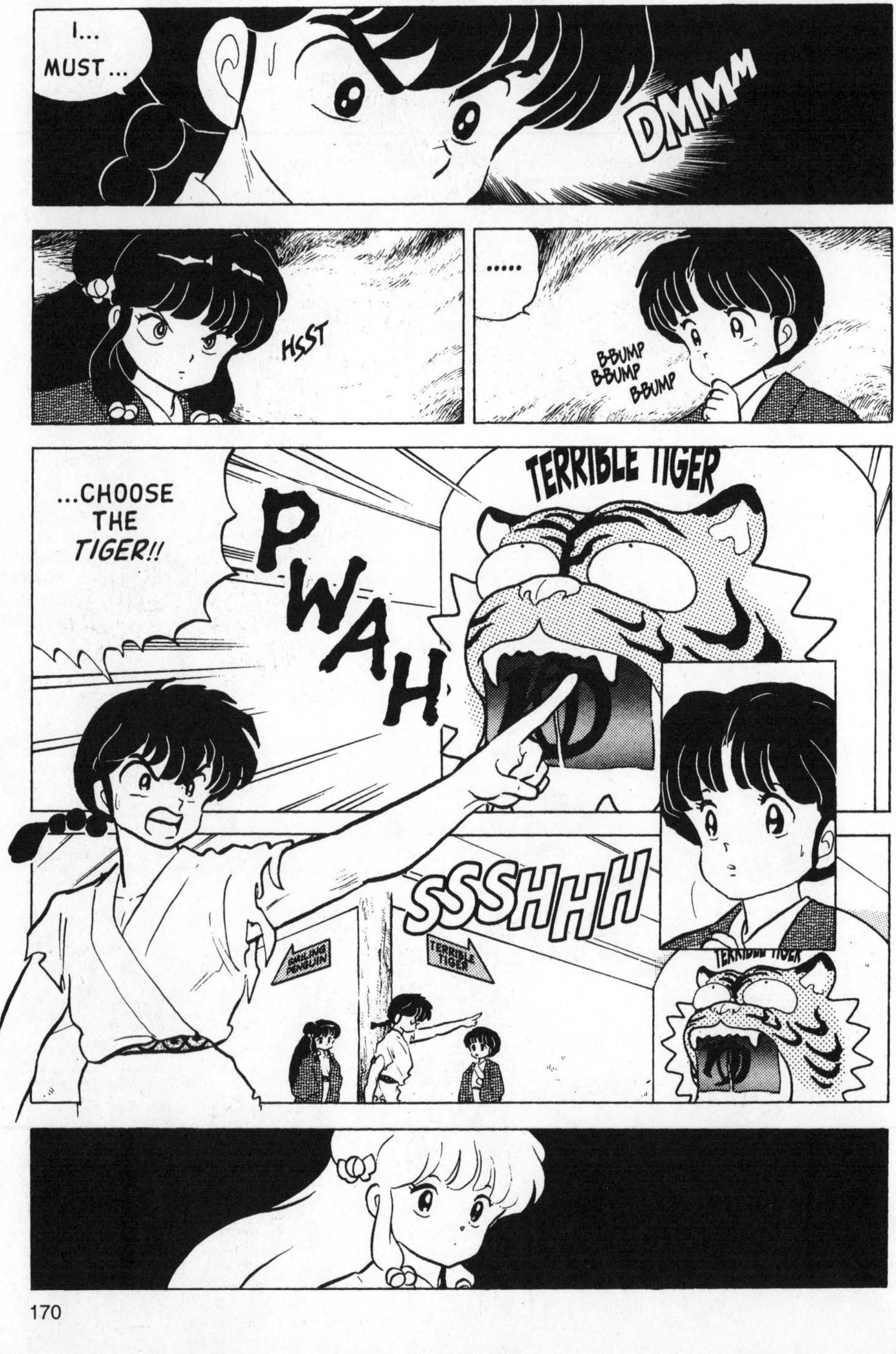
I... MUST...
DMMM
HSST
......
B-BUMP B-BUMP B-BUMP
...CHOOSE THE TIGER!!
PWAH
TERRIBLE TIGER
SMILING PENGUIN
TERRIBLE TIGER
SSSHHH
TERRIBLE TIGER

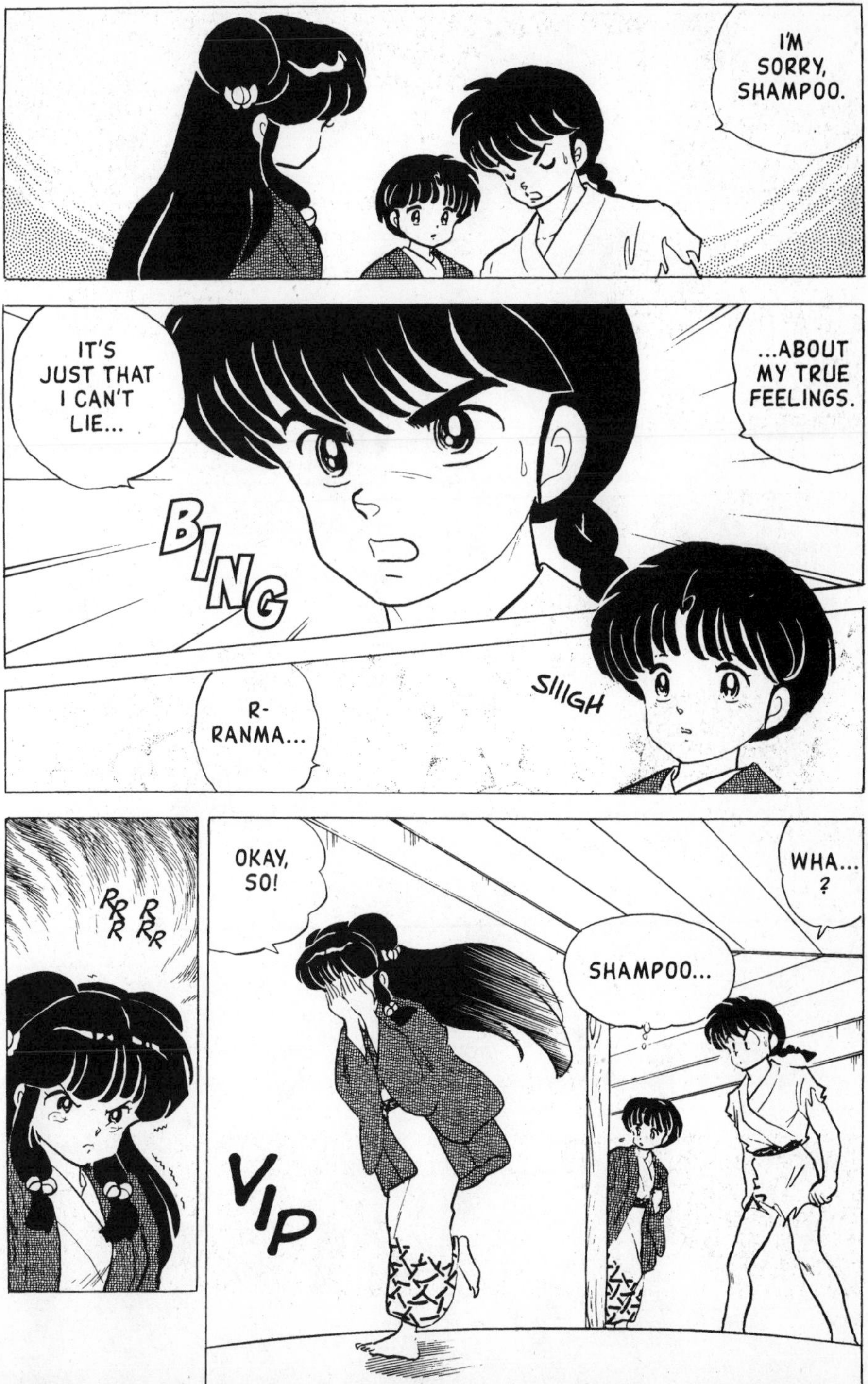
I'M SORRY, SHAMPOO.
IT'S JUST THAT I CAN'T LIE...
BING
...ABOUT MY TRUE FEELINGS.
R-RANMA...
SIIIGH
RRR RRR
OKAY, SO!
WHA...?
SHAMPOO...
VIP

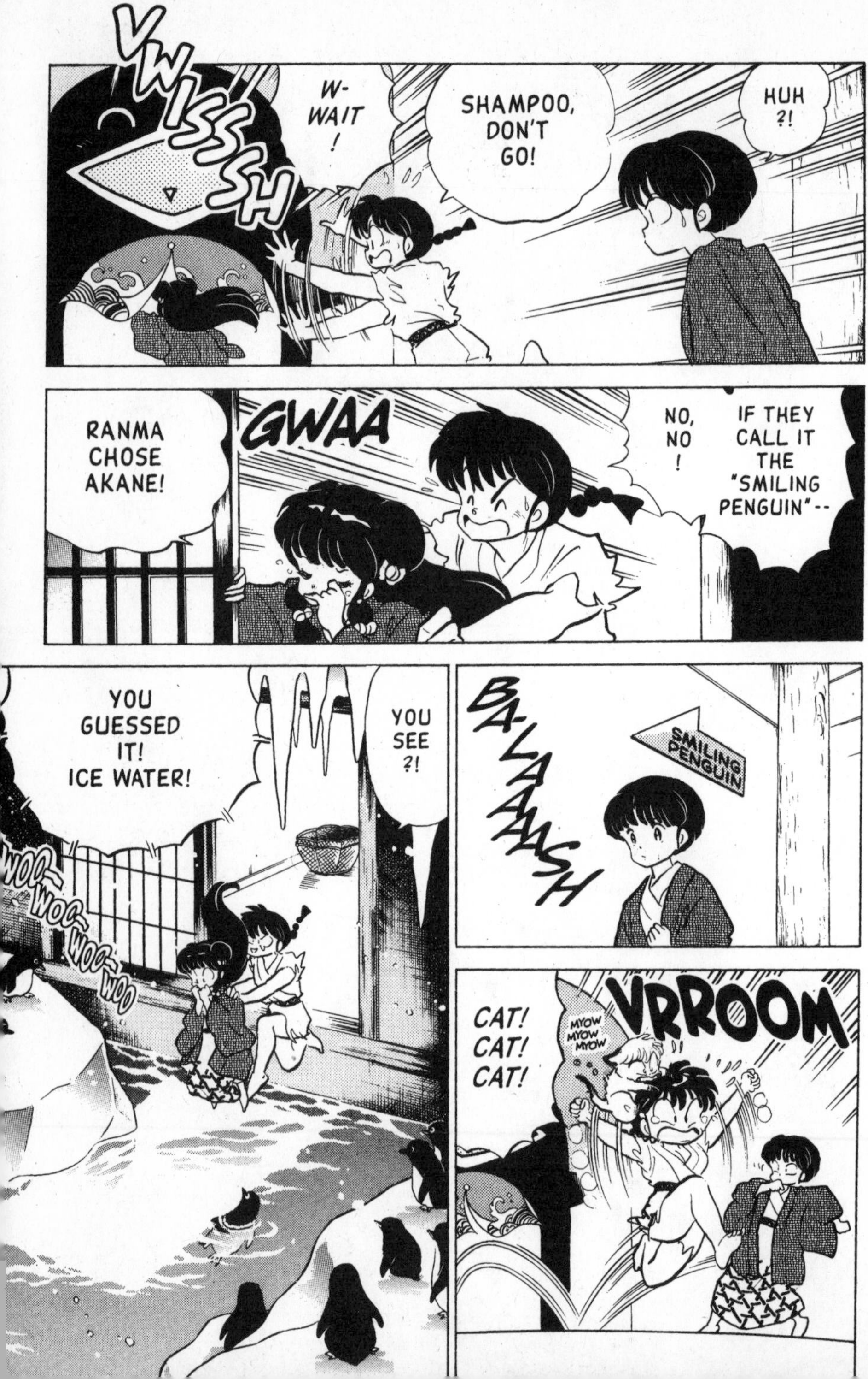
VWISSSH
W-WAIT!
SHAMPOO, DON'T GO!
HUH?!
RANMA CHOSE AKANE!
GWAA
NO, NO!
IF THEY CALL IT THE "SMILING PENGUIN"--
YOU GUESSED IT! ICE WATER!
YOU SEE?!
WOO-WOO-WOO-WOO
BA-LAAAASH
SMILING PENGUIN
CAT! CAT! CAT!
MYOW MYOW MYOW
VRROOM

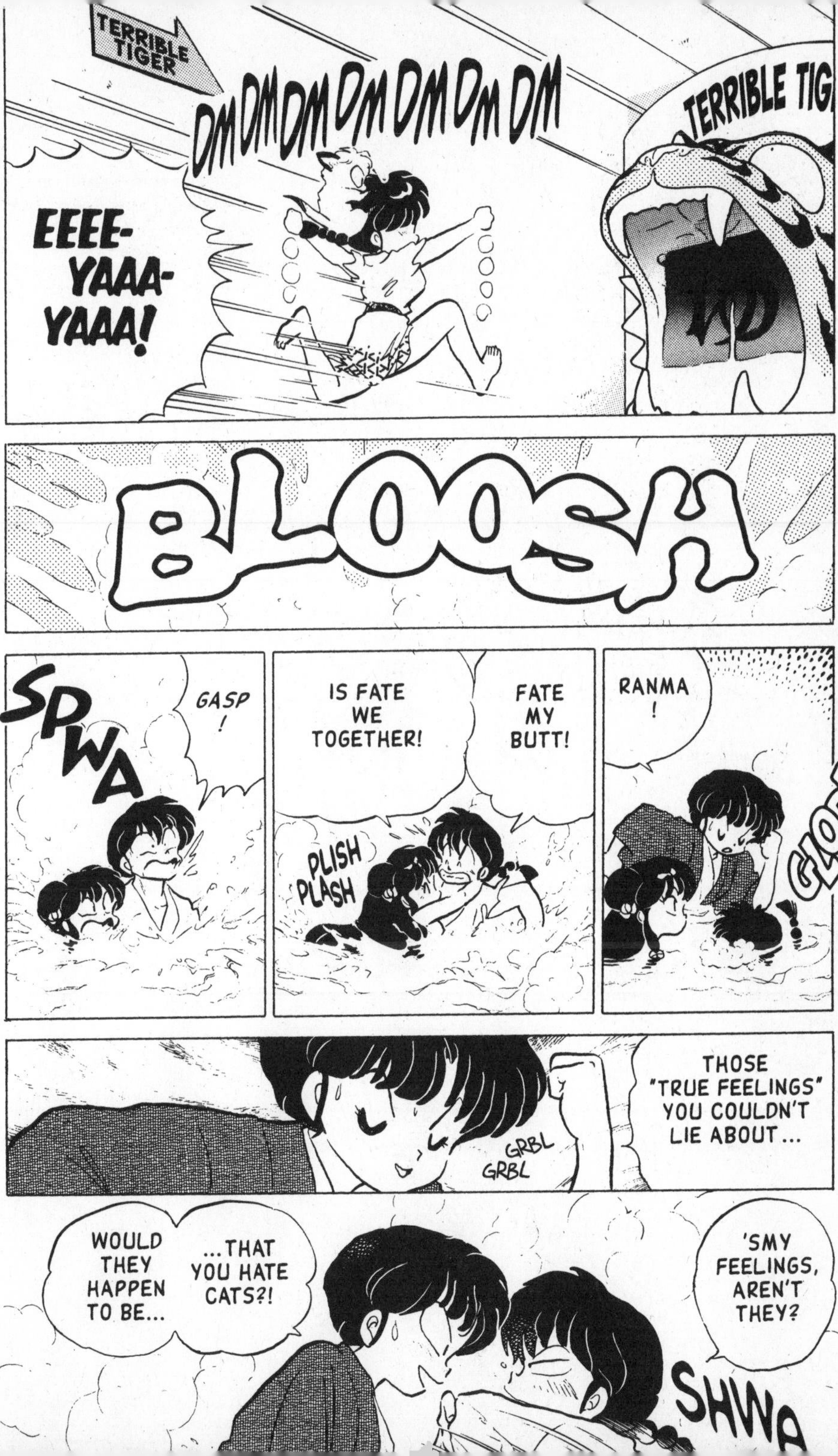
TERRIBLE TIGER
DM DM DM DM DM DM DM
TERRIBLE TIG
EEEE-YAAA-YAAA!
BLOOSH
SPWA
GASP!
IS FATE WE TOGETHER!
FATE MY BUTT!
PLISH PLASH
RANMA!
GLORB
GRBL GRBL
THOSE "TRUE FEELINGS" YOU COULDN'T LIE ABOUT...
WOULD THEY HAPPEN TO BE...
...THAT YOU HATE CATS?!
'SMY FEELINGS, AREN'T THEY?
SHWA

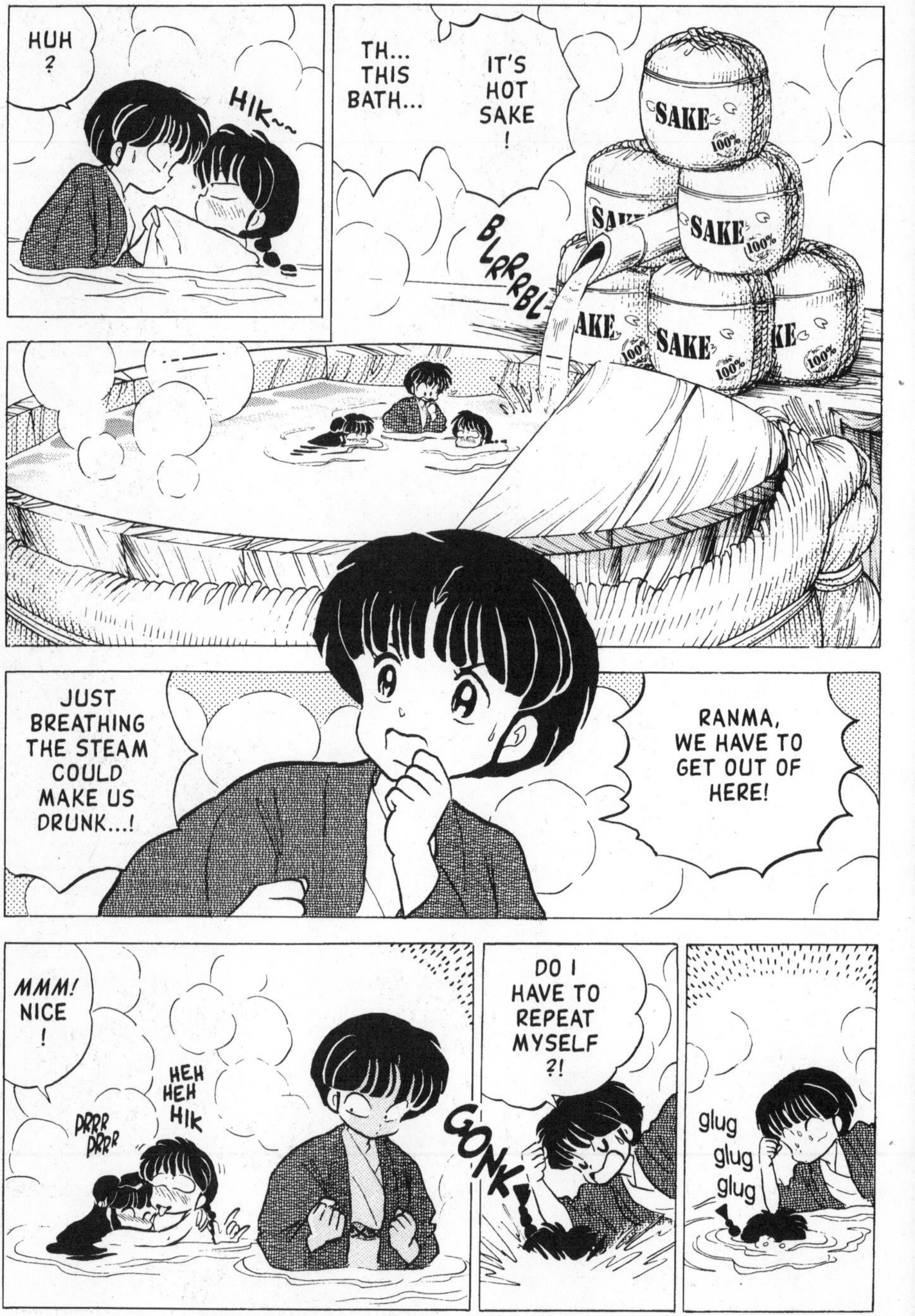
HUH ?
HIK~~
TH... THIS BATH...
IT'S HOT SAKE !
BLRRRBL-
SAKE
SAKE
SAKE
SAKE
100%
100%
100%
JUST BREATHING THE STEAM COULD MAKE US DRUNK...!
RANMA, WE HAVE TO GET OUT OF HERE!
MMM! NICE !
HEH HEH HIK
DRRR DRRR
DO I HAVE TO REPEAT MYSELF ?!
GONK
glug glug glug

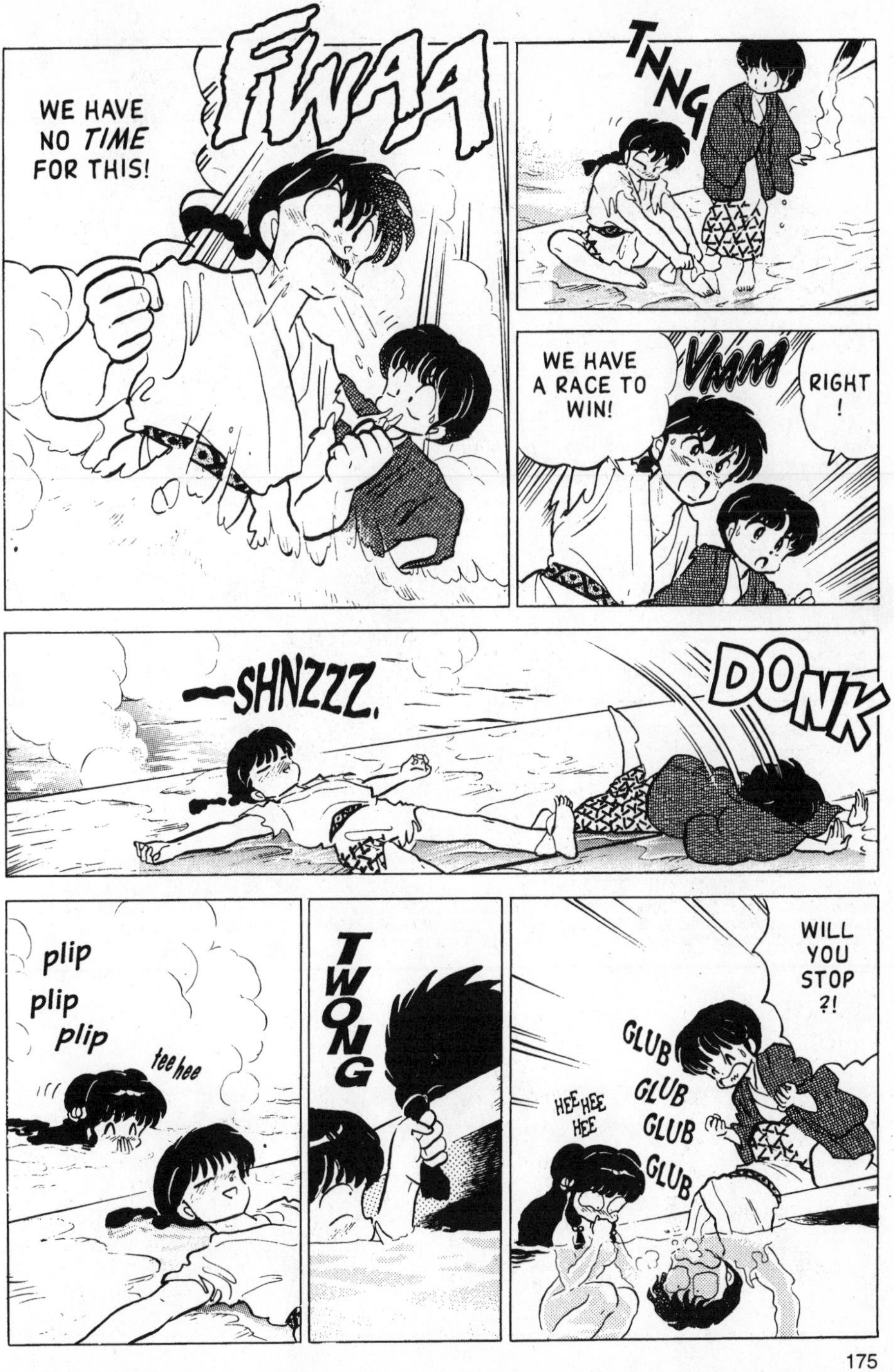
FWAA
WE HAVE NO TIME FOR THIS!
TNNG
WE HAVE A RACE TO WIN!
VMM
RIGHT!
—SHNZZZ.
DONK
plip
plip
plip
tee hee
TWONG
WILL YOU STOP?!
GLUB
GLUB
GLUB
GLUB
HEE HEE HEE

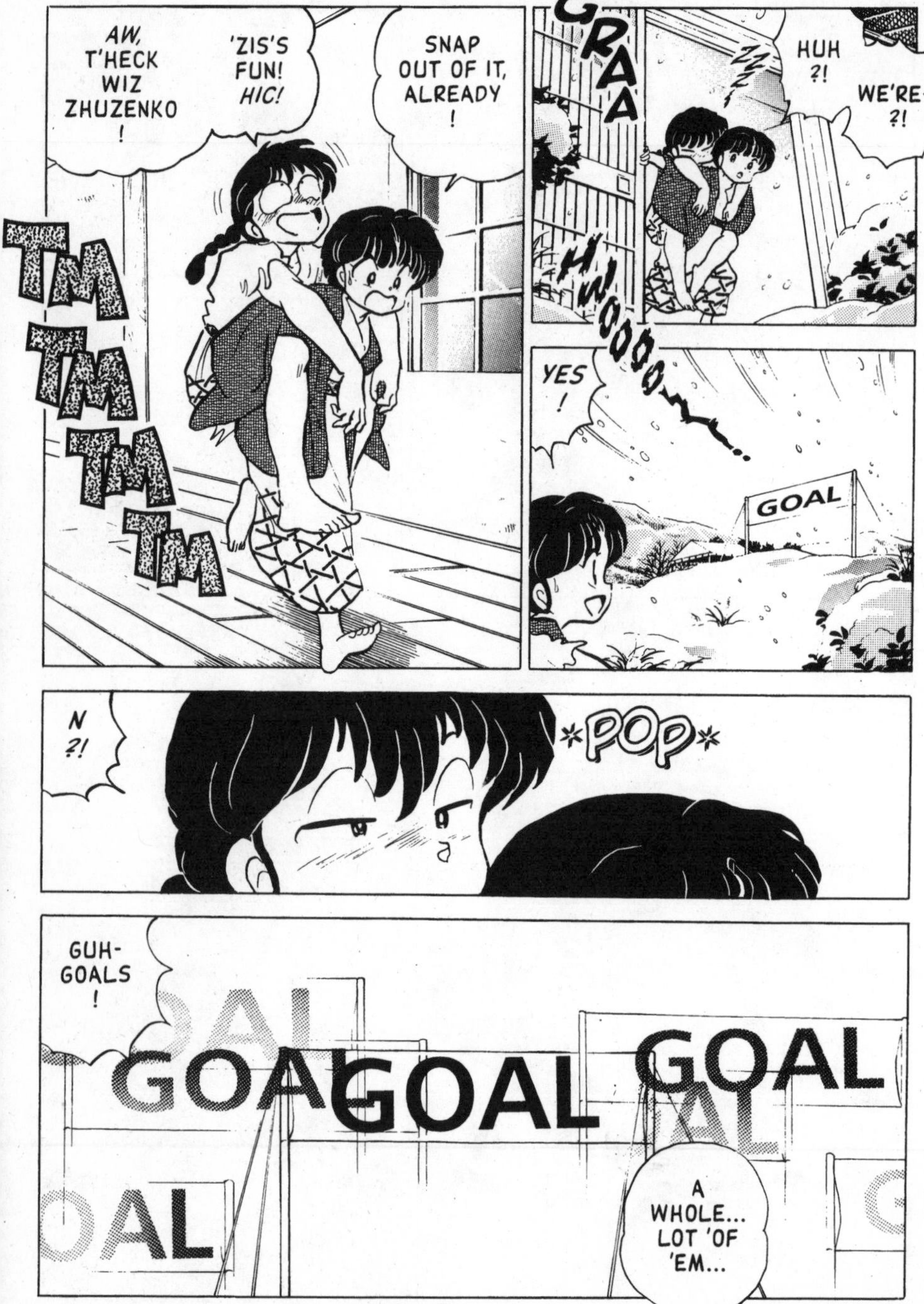
AW, T'HECK WIZ ZHUZENKO!
'ZIS'S FUN! HIC!
SNAP OUT OF IT, ALREADY!
TM TM TM TM TM
GRAA
HUH?!
WE'RE--?!
HWOOOOOM...!!
YES!
GOAL
N?!
POP
GUH-GOALS!
GOAL GOAL GOAL
A WHOLE... LOT 'OF 'EM...

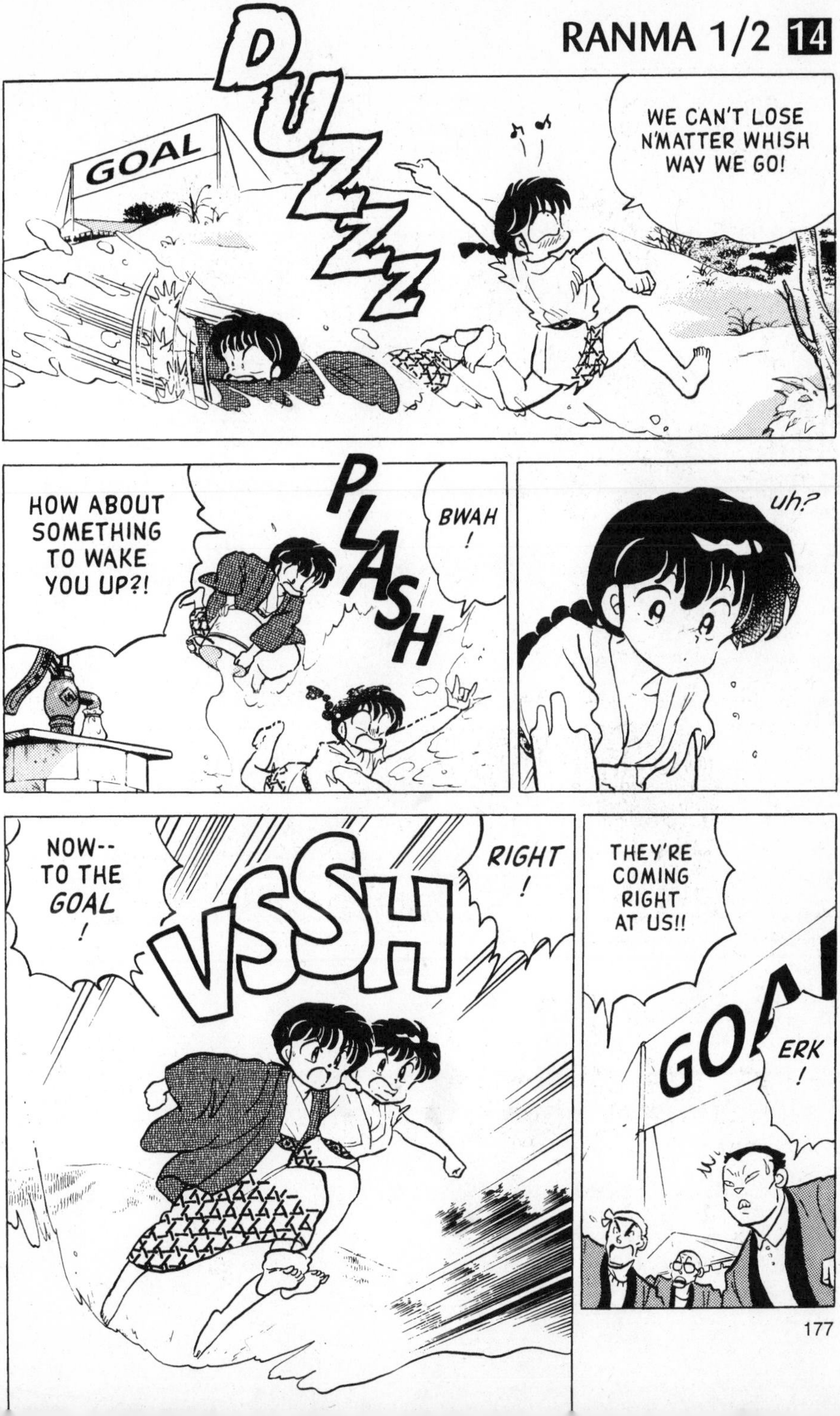
DUZZZ
GOAL
WE CAN'T LOSE N'MATTER WHISH WAY WE GO!
HOW ABOUT SOMETHING TO WAKE YOU UP?!
PLASH
BWAH!
uh?
NOW-- TO THE GOAL!
VSSH
RIGHT!
THEY'RE COMING RIGHT AT US!!
GOA
ERK!

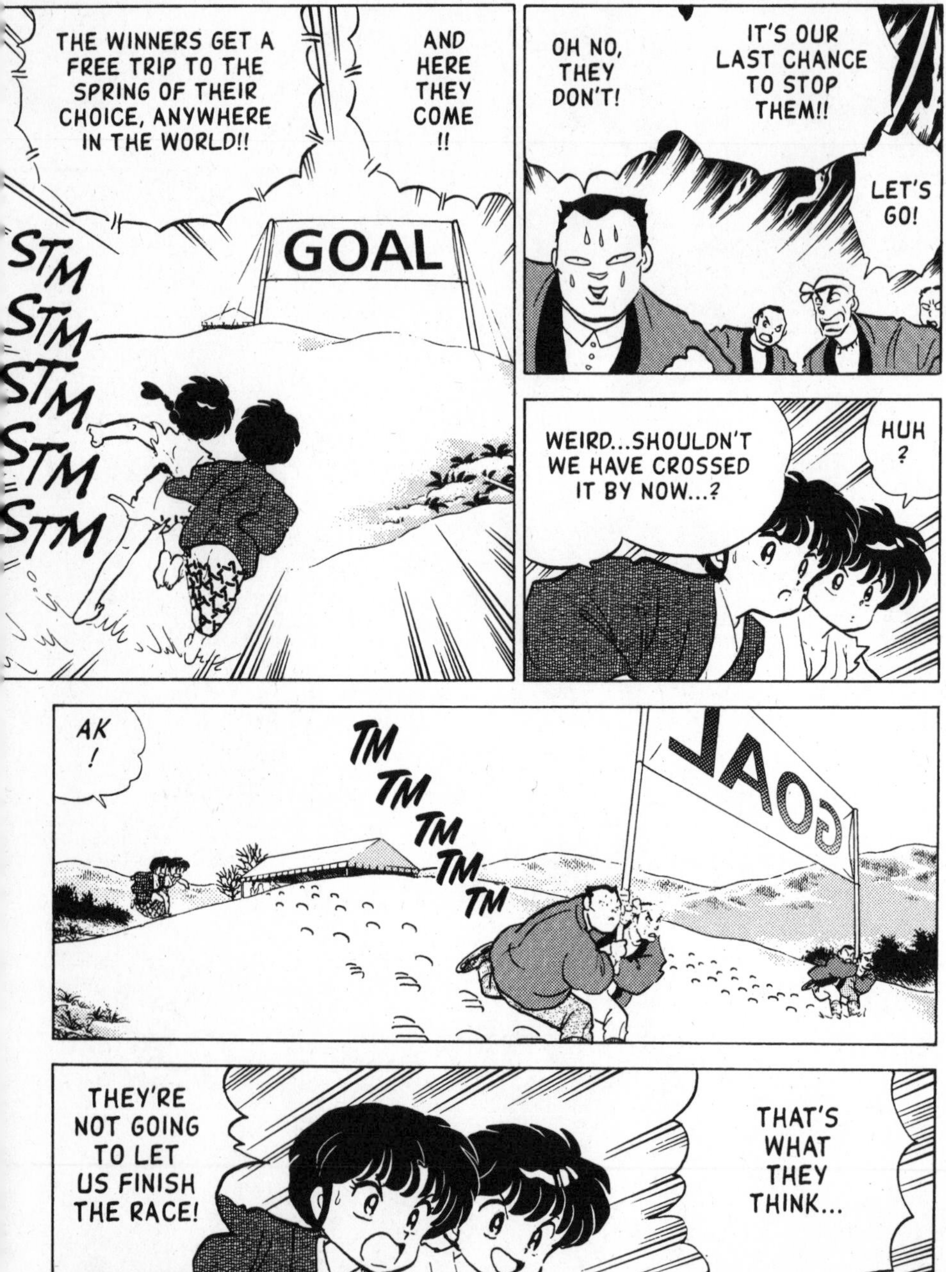
THE WINNERS GET A FREE TRIP TO THE SPRING OF THEIR CHOICE, ANYWHERE IN THE WORLD!!
AND HERE THEY COME !!
GOAL
STM STM STM STM STM
OH NO, THEY DON'T!
IT'S OUR LAST CHANCE TO STOP THEM!!
LET'S GO!
WEIRD...SHOULDN'T WE HAVE CROSSED IT BY NOW...?
HUH ?
AK !
TM TM TM TM TM
GOAL
THEY'RE NOT GOING TO LET US FINISH THE RACE!
THAT'S WHAT THEY THINK...

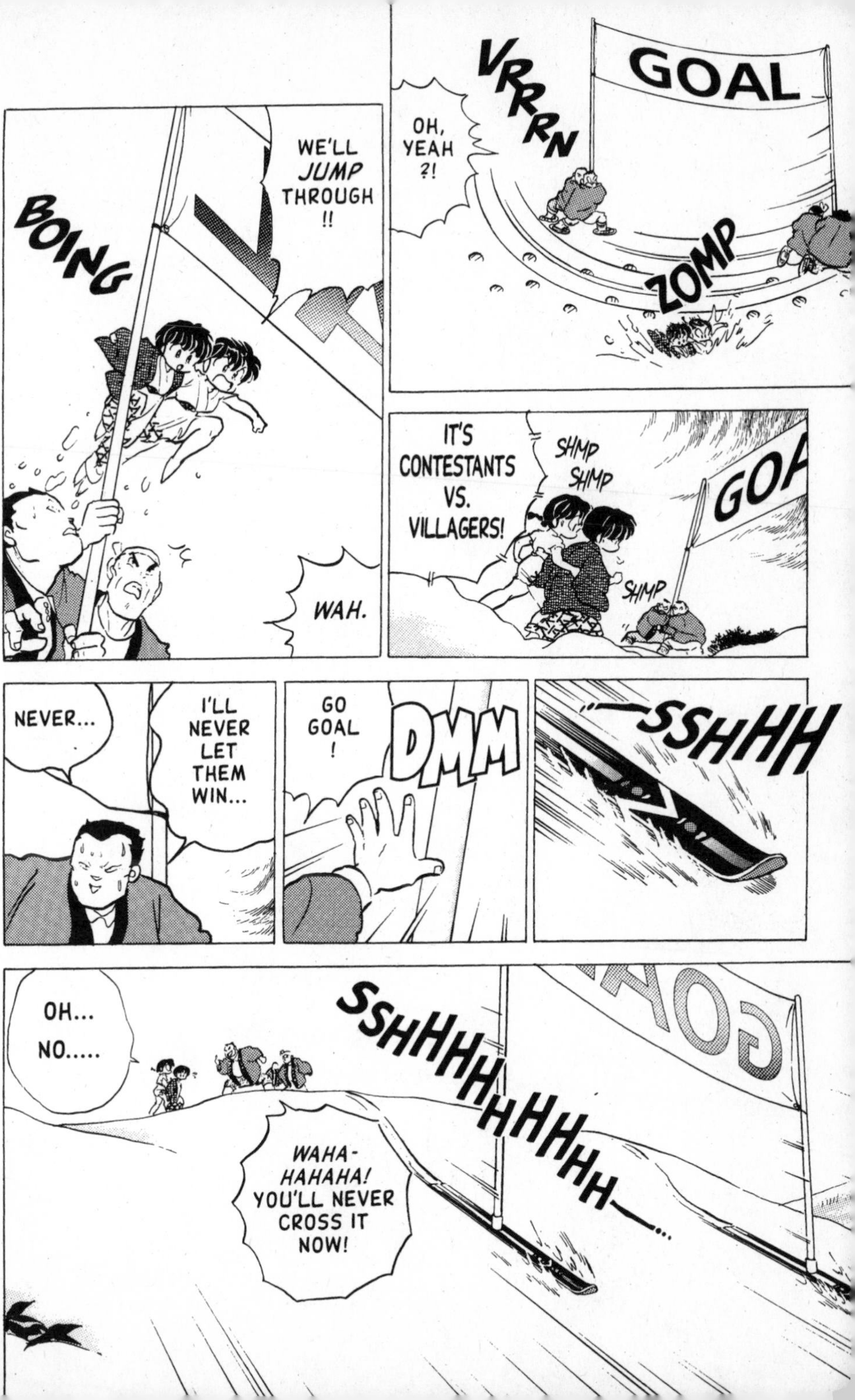
BOING
WE'LL JUMP THROUGH !!
WAH.
VRRRN
GOAL
OH, YEAH ?!
ZOMP
IT'S CONTESTANTS VS. VILLAGERS!
SHMP SHMP
GOA
SHMP
NEVER...
I'LL NEVER LET THEM WIN...
GO GOAL !
DMM
SSHHH
OH... NO.....
SSHHHHHHHHHHH—...
WAHA-HAHAHA! YOU'LL NEVER CROSS IT NOW!

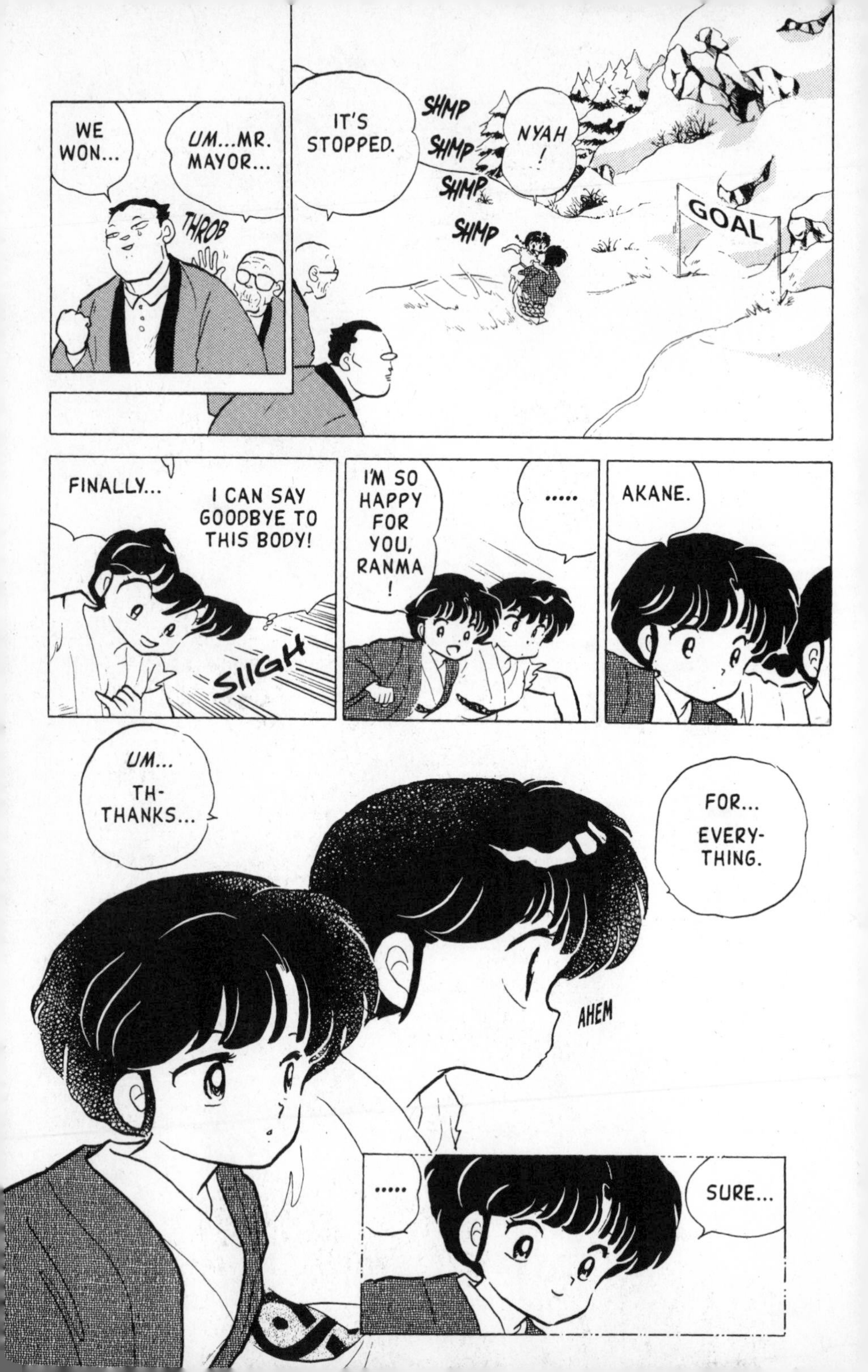
WE WON...
UM...MR. MAYOR...
THROB
IT'S STOPPED.
SHMP
SHMP
SHMP
SHMP
NYAH!
GOAL
FINALLY...
I CAN SAY GOODBYE TO THIS BODY!
SIIGH
I'M SO HAPPY FOR YOU, RANMA!
.....
AKANE.
UM... TH-THANKS...
FOR... EVERY-THING.
AHEM
.....
SURE...

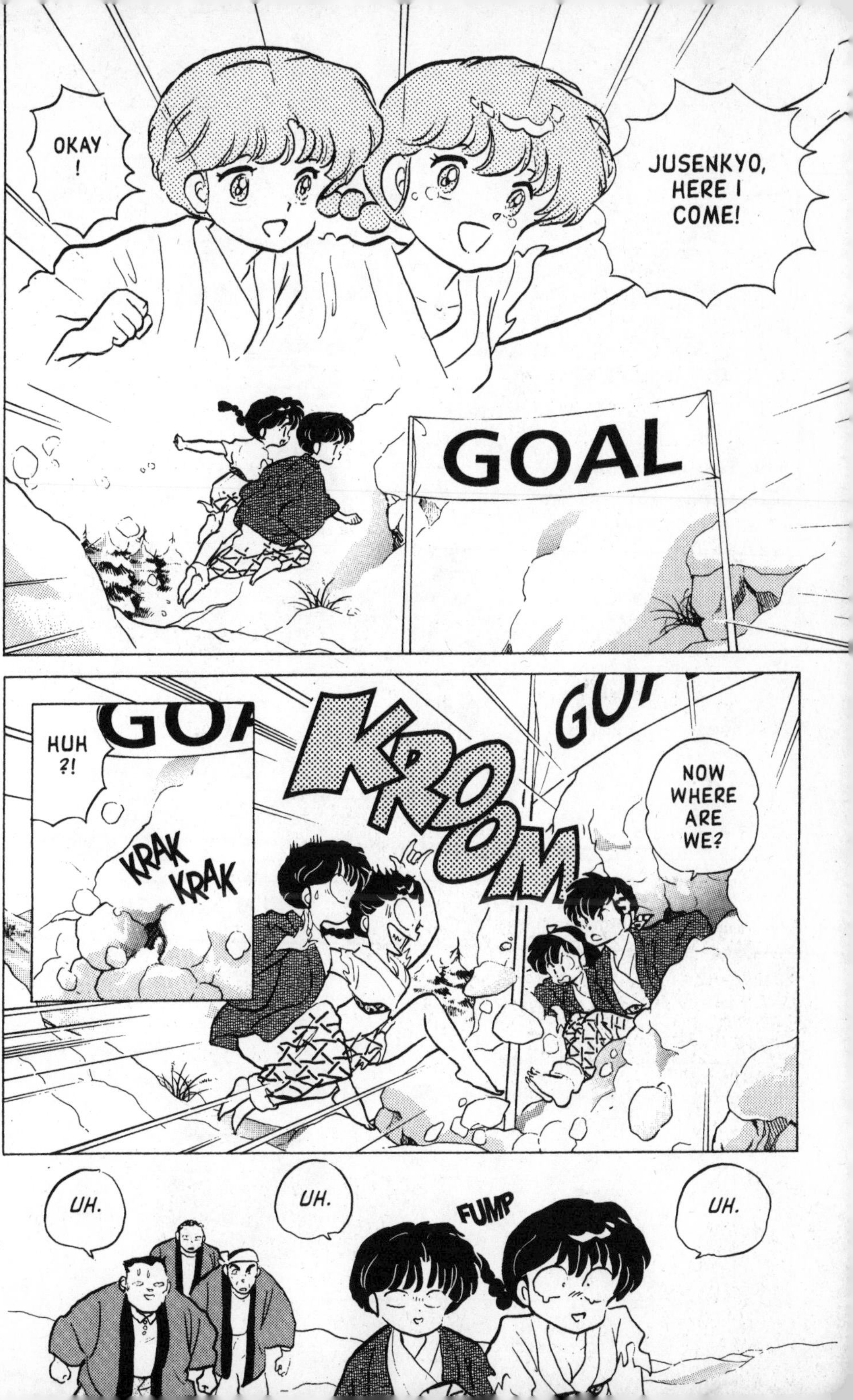
OKAY!
JUSENKYO, HERE I COME!
GOAL
HUH ?!
KRAK KRAK
KROOM
NOW WHERE ARE WE?
UH.
UH.
FUMP
UH.

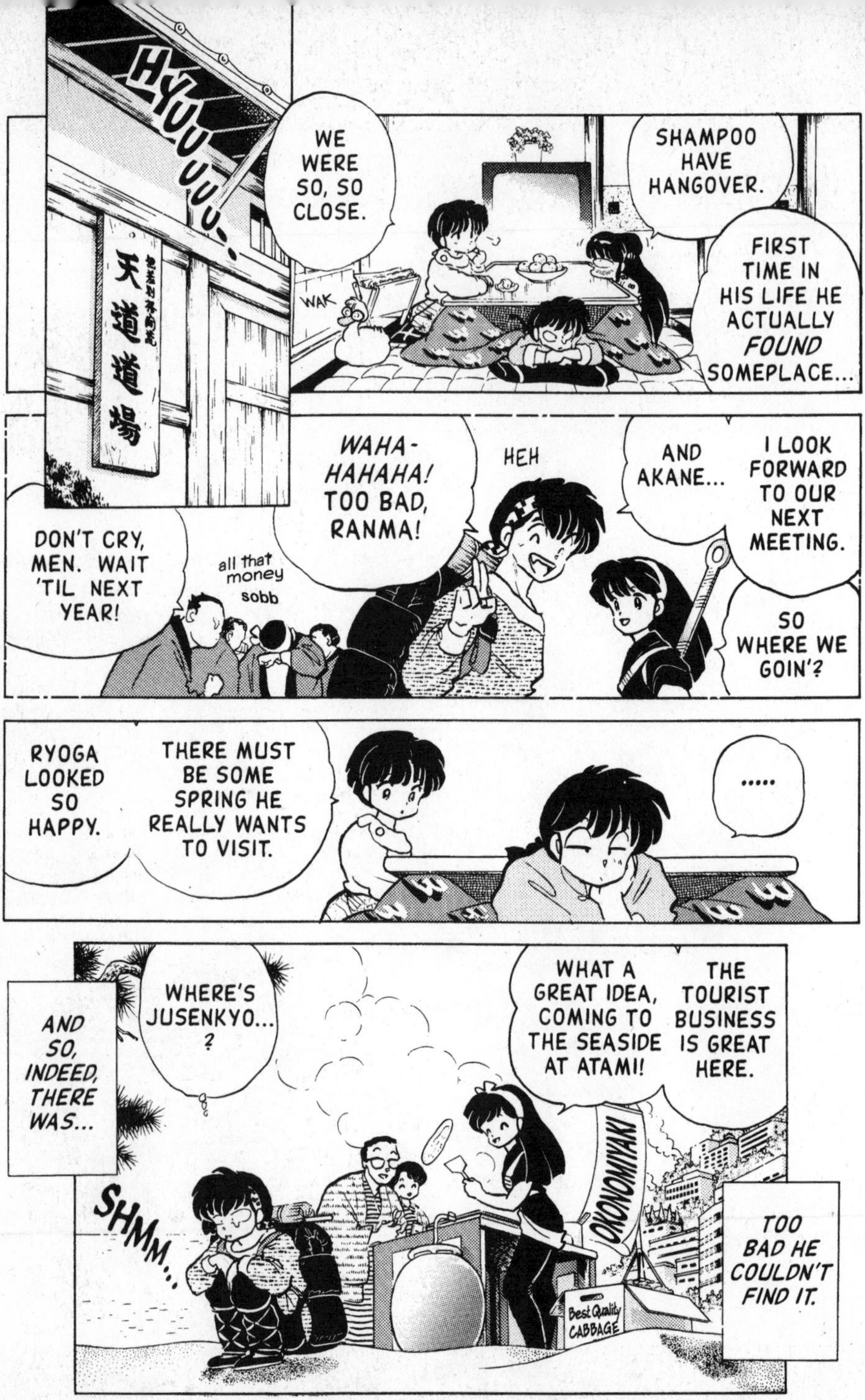
HYUUUUUU...
天道道場
WE WERE SO, SO CLOSE.
WAK
SHAMPOO HAVE HANGOVER.
FIRST TIME IN HIS LIFE HE ACTUALLY *FOUND* SOMEPLACE...
DON'T CRY, MEN. WAIT 'TIL NEXT YEAR!
all that money
sobb
WAHA-HAHAHA! TOO BAD, RANMA!
HEH
AND AKANE...
I LOOK FORWARD TO OUR NEXT MEETING.
SO WHERE WE GOIN'?
RYOGA LOOKED SO HAPPY.
THERE MUST BE SOME SPRING HE REALLY WANTS TO VISIT.
.....
AND SO, INDEED, THERE WAS...
WHERE'S JUSENKYO...?
SHMM...
WHAT A GREAT IDEA, COMING TO THE SEASIDE AT ATAMI!
THE TOURIST BUSINESS IS GREAT HERE.
OKONOMIYAKI
Best Quality CABBAGE
TOO BAD HE COULDN'T FIND IT.

END OF RANMA 1/2 VOLUME 14.

The story of a boy who turns into a girl, a father who turns into a panda, and the weird Chinese curse that did it to 'em!

Rumiko Takahashi's

Ranma ½

Ranma 1/2 ©1999 Rumiko Takahashi/Shogakukan, Inc.

Videos!

Four seasons of the anime TV series, plus movies and original animated videos. Available in English or in Japanese with English subtitles.

TITLE	ENGLISH	SUBTITLED
Original TV Series (Vols. 1-9)	$29.95 ea.	n/a
Collector's Edition TV Series (Vols. 1-6)	n/a	$34.95 ea.
Anything-Goes Martial Arts (Vols. 1-11)	$24.95 ea.	$29.95 ea.
Hard Battle (Vols. 1-12)	$24.95 ea.	$29.95 ea.
Outta Control (Vols. 1-12)	$24.95 ea.	Coming Soon
OAVs Vols. 1-6 (Vols. 1-3 are English-only)	$29.95 ea.	$29.95 ea.
Collector's Editions OAVs (Vols. 1-2)	n/a	$34.95 ea.
Video Jukebox	n/a	$14.95 ea.
Movie: Big Trouble in Nekonron, China	$34.95 ea.	$34.95 ea.
2nd Movie: Nihao My Concubine	$34.95 ea.	$34.95 ea.
Digital Dojo Box Set (9 Vols.)	$199.95 ea.	n/a
Anything-Goes Box Set (11 Vols.)	$199.95 ea.	n/a
OAV Box Set (6 Vols.)	$124.95 ea.	n/a
Hard Battle Box Set (12 Vols.)	$199.95 ea.	n/a

Plus!

Graphic Novels: 13 volumes & counting!
T-Shirts: 7 styles available in different sizes!
Music: 6 soundtracks from the anime TV series and movies.
Monthly Comics: Available by subscription or individual issues!
Merchandise: Baseball caps, Cappuccino mugs, watches, postcards & more!